THE DAMNED

KRISTY BERRIDGE

orn in Perth, Western Australia in 1982, Kristy Berridge was ushered into the world in a decade of bad hair, parachute pants, and blue eye shadow. Fortunately, she managed to avoid all three influences by immersing herself in the business of growing up, and hitched a ride with her  fun-loving, and adventure-filled parents to the sunny state of Queensland. Here she completed most of her education.

Besides learning that boys *don't* have cooties, and that algebra *wouldn't* kill her, she pointedly set the path of her high school career towards success in Art and English-based subjects, and won numerous awards for her efforts.

After high school she went on to study Graphic Design and Illustration at James Cook University, and then furthered her studies at the local TAFE college with an Interior Design course. With this knowledge under her belt, she also decided to undertake a three year Design course at Rhodec International in London, to complete her education and propel her towards the successful career she now enjoys.

She currently resides in Cairns with her husband Navaro, who is her biggest support and a constant source of motivation to finish the next novel.

Shadow Ink Press
P.O Box 352n, Cairns North, Queensland 4870 Australia
Email: shadowinkpress@hotmail.com

First published in Australia 2012
This edition published 2012
Copyright © Kristy Berridge 2012
Cover design, typesetting: Chameleon Print Design

The right of Kristy Berridge to be identified as the Author of the Work has been asserted in accordance with the Copyright, Designs and Patents Act 1988.

This book is a work of fiction. Any similarities to that of people living or dead are purely coincidental.

Berridge, Kristy
The Damned
ISBN-10: 0987524704   ISBN-13: 978-0-9875247-0-6
pp572

For the fans—thank you for your patience.
God knows, you've all been waiting long enough.

I want to say a massive thank you to my editor Rob Deskoski. You have been a fabulous copy-editor and an even greater mentor. Without you, I am certain my writing skills would not have improved and that *The Hunted* and *The Damned* would never have come to fruition. Your input has been valid, appreciated and needed: you're truly a literary champion.

PREFACE

The stranger lifted the warm mug of AB negative to his lips. He took a few swift gulps, felt the sweetness of the warmed fluid caressing his tongue and setting his tastebuds aflame. Like liquid velvet it slid down his throat, strengthening and replenishing his body from within, and filling him with the rich satisfaction that could only come from the taste of blood.

He could feel his arteries dilate, his senses sharpening as life-force began to satiate his awakened thirst. His pulse throbbed under the influx, eventually slowing to a stop again once the blood had dissipated into his system.

It was good to be a vampire.

Body still burning for more, the stranger gestured to the barman for another. This packaged stuff known as Synth Blood could sustain him but was nowhere near as gratifying as fresh blood from a warm human body. He longed to bury his fangs in the neck of an unsuspecting victim, rend at flesh until the warmth of their essence spilled across his tongue, making him whole again. For now he had to suppress his instincts, though, to prevent his detection from the ones still hunting him.

Only one month had passed since the stranger had last killed but his skin already itched with the need to taste a human's fear. As he revelled in his memories of the hunt, an image of his wife came to mind, and with it a sadness that was all consuming. His wife had shared in his bloodlust, his uncontrollable desire to feed. She had hunted beside him, night after night, and eventually murdered because she had rightfully lived as the predator she was created to be. The stranger's blood still boiled thinking about her unrighteous death and the creature that had caused it. But the time for retribution was coming.

He would make sure of it.

The stranger glanced around the bar. It was mostly empty; no real surprise considering it was high noon. The turned vampires would all spend their daylight hours hiding in darkened spaces, waiting for nightfall. Born vampires were able to move around in the daylight but were still forced to avoid direct sunlight. At this point, as the thirst still rode him, the stranger cared little for shelter.

'You travelled far this evening?' the barman asked, setting down a fresh mug of heated blood and jogging the stranger from his reverie.

He accepted it gratefully and took a sip. 'Not especially,' the stranger said, eyeing the barman from head to toe.

The barman was a turned vampire, probably no more than thirty years of age. He had short, sandy blonde hair and unassuming blue eyes. Despite being slightly rotund in the mid-section he was still as beautiful as the rest of his race.

'Are you from Spain or Italy?' the barman asked, an eyebrow rising. 'I'm trying to pick your accent.'

The stranger took another sip. 'I'm Italian.'

'No kidding?' He wiped at a spill on the counter top. 'You must be part of Lucius Valerius's coven.'

The stranger contained his desire to sneer. 'No. I belong to no coven and I especially do not answer to Lucius Valerius. At least, not anymore.'

'Here, here. The last sixteen years under Lucius's rule have been difficult. I really used to enjoy hunting humans before it was outlawed.' The barman absently wiped at another spill. 'Granted, I make money from the sale of Synth Blood and the shelter my neutral bar provides, but it's not the same as the thrill of hunting for fresh blood. The only way I can function now, without being hunted down by Lucius or his thralls, is to stay here where I have all the blood I need. Confrontations with humans are too … tempting.'

'That's pathetic,' the stranger said.

The barman frowned. 'We all do what we can to survive. Sometimes that means swallowing your pride and advocating for the Devil.'

The stranger smiled. The barman didn't realise how on the money he was. Lucius *was* demon spawn.

Taking the stranger's smile as an invitation to talk further, the barman leant forward on his elbows, smiling warmly. 'So what brings you to Paris, anyway?'

The stranger wasn't in the mood for idle chit-chat, but doubted that the barman would leave him alone. 'I'm looking for someone.'

'Perhaps I can help?'

The stranger shook his head, taking a few more gulps of blood. It wasn't his favourite brew, but the liquid was undeniably starting to satisfy his primal cravings. 'I don't think so.'

'If you're looking for a vampire in Paris, I know everyone by name.'

The stranger gritted his teeth. 'I thank you for the drink,' he said, holding up the mug, 'but I wish to finish it in peace.'

The barman scowled. 'I was just making conversation.'

'*Unwanted* conversation. Go find another patron to annoy.'

'There are no other patrons.'

3

The stranger looked around, noting that the few other patrons had left. He'd always had that effect on people.

He glanced at the barman.

Pity.

The stranger drained the remaining contents of his mug and pushed it back towards the barman.

Frowning, the barman turned his back on him.

'Barman, I require another drink.'

'In a minute. I gotta clean,' he said, busying himself with the relatively unimportant task of filling a small sink behind the bar with hot, soapy water.

The stranger drummed his fingers on the counter impatiently. The barman started to wash and stack glasses, now ignoring him completely.

'Barman, I bid you pour me another drink before you make me angry. And before I do something that *you* will regret.'

The barman glanced around and smirked insolently. 'I'll pour you another drink when I'm ready.' He went back to stacking glasses. 'And do not threaten me. I am Vampire, just as you are.'

The stranger sighed. He could have left the bar. He could have sought nourishment from some other venue or even hunted down his own humans. But, now, that wasn't enough.

The stranger, moving with inhuman grace, was behind the bartender moments later, his hands gripping the creature's sides so tightly it could barely move.

The stranger's rage could no longer be contained.

'What the—let go of me!'

'Are you ready now?' the stranger whispered, spinning the barman around to face him. In one swift motion, he sank his fangs deep into the barman's throat, ripping out his jugular in a vicious shower of crimson-slicked gore. As his victim thrashed in his embrace, warm blood poured down the stranger's chin and sprayed across the front of his shirt. As he felt the last of the barman's life leaving his body, the stranger tossed what remained onto the floor with a resounding *thud*.

He wiped the excess blood from his lips, spitting onto the floor.

'Much better,' the stranger murmured, stepping over the body and moving towards the front door without so much as a backward glance. 'Turned vampires—as easy a prey as humans.'

He pushed open the front door and cringed. Where the rays from the midday sun struck him, blistering lines burned across his features. Searching quickly for a shady area through which to walk, he soon spied a darkened alleyway and hurried out towards it.

He considered the next step in his plan carefully. He needed leverage, something that would turn an enemy into a friend, or at the very least, an enemy into an ally.

The Vânǎtors, a fierce race of fanatical werewolves, were not exactly known for their negotiating skills. They were hungry predators, born from the blood of the Vampire and completely uncaring of anyone's needs but their own. They were wild, the very worst variation of a vampire's genetic nature, and were the perfect tool for his vengeance.

The Vânǎtors penchant for vampiric blood would definitely work to the stranger's advantage. Their mating habits produced large packs, enough to cause any vampire trouble. Also, their ability to shapeshift into the form of any human they had previously fed from meant they could move around mostly undetected—a useful trick.

He just needed to figure out what it was the Vânǎtors desired.

The stranger smiled. He saw the future in his mind, laid out in front of him. It was a future he hoped to share with other, likeminded vampires, with any other supernaturals tired of suppressing their natural instincts. The stranger's future would mean no more hiding in the shadows, where vampires reigned supreme and blood was the word on everyone's lips.

A future he could really sink his teeth into.

CHAPTER ONE: GOODBYES

Closing the black leather suitcase in front of me, I slowly pulled the zippers home. The movement seemed symbolic, the closing of one chapter in my life and the start of another. There would undoubtedly be many changes and sacrifices on my part, and probably character and plot adjustments to get used to as well, but it was too late to back out now. This book was only half-written, and I was the one holding the pen.

I sighed. The decision to leave my home in Cairns was entirely my own. I guess I had no right to feel tormented over the choice. Hopefully, my future path would be easier to follow.

I closed the padlock, fastened my suitcase securely shut, and then scanned the relatively empty space of my bedroom. I couldn't help but feel an overwhelming pang of anxiety. Two hours from now this room would merely be a memory in my past. I would be on a plane, bound for Romania and heading into unknown terrain. Life for me was about to change dramatically, and I'd be forced to fend for myself for the first time. That meant no more family and no more friends.

Plus, this was the first time in my life I'd be leaving the country. I was leaving for what I *hoped* was just a temporary arrangement to protect my adopted family from all the trouble I'd inadvertently brought upon them.

As Protectors—the descendants of a Romanian clan well-versed in magical application and theory—they were more than capable of looking after themselves, but I still worried. The Vânători would be coming after me and that spelt a whole lot of trouble. Don't get me wrong: The Protectors were powerful, having spent the last three hundred years perfecting their craft, defending themselves and the human race.

Originally, The Protectors had formed to fight against a small coven of vampires, entering into a war with them over territory lines and the decimation of many villages. It was only when the Vânători were created that an unlikely alliance was formed, Protector and Vampire uniting against a new, common enemy.

Vânători would eat humans like they were lunch box snacks and bred with them faster than mating rabbits, so joining forces to destroy them definitely made the most sense. Though a vampire was still a Protector's biggest threat, the Vânători were crazed blood-drinkers, preying on vamps and humans alike, causing havoc wherever they roamed.

The Vânători were the reason I was leaving town. I wasn't scared of them, and was more than able to handle myself, but they knew my secret—a secret that could cause infinite harm to the people dearest to me.

I'm half-Vânător.

And half-Vampire.

See, mostly I was afraid of the enemy within, of the danger posed by the person my loved ones had called family for the last sixteen years, the person who they had called sister, called daughter.

Me.

I'm not a Protector and I never will be. A Protector's powers are inherent, not learnt, and are honed to perfection by years of training and study. But even without those magical skills I have abilities that can kill, and those abilities catapult me into a league of my own. One day I'll be more dangerous than either vampire or vânător because I'm destined to be both, and therefore, unpredictable.

Only a month had gone by since I had been rescued from the clutches of one of the Vânător's original and *only* twenty pack leaders. Called an 'Alpha', these leaders had been turned some three hundred years ago by a vampiric nutcase with a crooked agenda and too much bloody time on his hands. The Alpha werewolf who had taken me was called John.

John had tortured me for days, probing me for answers about my unusual genetic composition. He'd broken my knee caps, drained my blood, and murdered an innocent girl in front of me, but I had never yielded. I stayed strong, even fighting against his Alpha sway, a fearsome power which elicited physical responses from me beyond my control and was therefore worth fearing.

Thanks to my genetic blending it had become clear that I was susceptible to both the demands of the Alpha's sway and to a vampire's enticement. So, due to my clearly unpredictable nature, I decided that I would be taking a little trip to stay with Protectors in Bucharest, Romania. It was there that the Institute of Magical Intervention (or IMI, as it's more commonly referred to as) housed their main headquarters.

My adoptive parents, Susan and George, agreed that it would be best for everyone if I stayed at headquarters to undergo genetic testing. They also thought that my continued presence in Cairns was a danger but were also curious why I had physical reactions to both vampires and werewolves—especially when I was still *technically* human.

George had promised that the IMI would take care of me and that my decision to leave Cairns would not be in vain.

'You'll be safe there, Elena,' he had said to me. 'Bucharest is filled with Protectors. No Alpha will find you behind their walls.'

'I'm not scared, George. I know how to look after myself.'

'I'm aware. You have proven yourself many times now.'

'It's just—'

'You think leaving is not enough. You're worried the Vânători will attack us, anyway?'

'That does bother me, but no, that's not it.'

'Then why are you worried?'

Our conversation had been short. I hadn't been able to tell George that, even with the threat of Alphas looming, I couldn't shake the feeling that the IMI would somehow betray me. They had numerous factions throughout Australia that could temporarily take me in, but I'd recently realised that sheltering me was not the real issue—no, the IMI had been studying me with zealous interest for years. Now they had an opportunity to keep me close and they were taking it.

I took a deep breath, trying to push away the negative thoughts that always crept forward during times of doubt. I had to focus and remember my main reason for agreeing to go: Lucas.

He was more than just my adoptive brother: he was my friend and the only person on earth that I trusted. A few months in Romania were a small price to pay to ensure his safety.

Lucas was more than a little pissed off that I was leaving. He couldn't understand why the full protection of the local branch of Protectors was not enough to ward off an army of vânători. Even though his powers were growing, and our little faction of ten Protectors had recently befriended three extremely strong vampires, it still wasn't enough. The Werewolves had it in their heads that my blood could fix their genetic deficiencies, would give them the ability to withstand direct sunlight and to self-heal. They'd move both heaven and earth to get their hands on such power.

Self-healing was my first ability, the earliest. The second was the uncanny ability to scent blood from great distances. It was clearly creepy and not yet particularly useful, but since I could also bench press one hundred and fifty pounds like it was a candy bar and think nothing of it, I'd take the good with the bad.

Thanks to years of training with The Protectors in Cairns, I could also kick some serious ass if I had to. But despite the fact that I was super strong, could give Jackie Chan a run for his money and had a nose like a bloodhound, I wasn't sure that my blood was the answer to the Vânător's deficiencies. At least, I hoped not.

I sighed, glancing around me. My bedroom looked ransacked. There wasn't much left inside: just the furniture, some books, and a few items of clothing. My life and everything of importance in it had fit into the small suitcase lying in front of me. So what did that say about me? Was it resounding proof that I'd never allowed myself to value anything enough to hold onto it?

William would've agreed. He knew better than anyone how reluctant I was to invest emotionally in anything, having spent the better part of the last month trying to break through the rough exterior of my heart and reach for the impossible.

As a born vampire, William had walked the earth for over four hundred years, directing his energies towards hunting vânătors. Now his attentions had been redirected elsewhere. His new focus? Me. Despite the fact that I *was* an emotional cripple, I still liked to have fun, and kissing William was definitely the epitome of a good time. I can honestly say that I'm glad we'd met, or rather, that he'd forced his way into my life. William had introduced me to the world of Vampires and taught me much about what I might one day become.

If I was honest with myself, I'd say I do enjoy William's affections but I'm a tough nut to crack. Sure, he's hotter than hell and could kiss like nobody's business but I have eternity stretched out in front of me. I had to be cautious about who I tied my life to. And I felt positive that there was still something missing between the two of us. So maybe leaving the country was a good thing? The journey would at least give me time to think.

I grabbed my trusty knife off the top of the desk, strapping it in its sheathe at the side of my leg the way I always did. It was small comfort considering the multitudes of bloodthirsty creatures out for my blood.

I jumped suddenly as my mobile chirped, a sharp sting from my finger telling me I'd managed to cut myself on my knife's blade. I softly cursed, staring down at the small pool of liquid crimson forming across the cut. Blood ... I remembered the taste, thought about lifting a finger to my lips and sampling the flavour, delighting in its sweetness.

I didn't. Instead, I watched as my abilities kicked in and the liquid slowly reabsorbed back into my system. Eventually, the skin healed over.

I shook it off and reached into my backpack for my phone. The message was from Kayla.

—*I'm really going to miss you.*—

I smiled sadly. I was really going to miss her, too. Kayla was my one human friend. Of course, she had absolutely no idea about what I was and what I was going to become. That conversation had never transpired but, really, how do you tell someone that for now you're human, but when you turn eighteen you're going to become a hairy bloodsucker?

—*I'll miss you too.*—

I sent the message, closing the phone and shoving it back inside the tight confines of the backpack. I didn't really want to think that I might not see her again. Kayla was the only reason I had enjoyed working weekends at Cairns Fine Furniture and Accessories. Without her, it would have been utterly boring. I probably also wouldn't have met William if it hadn't been for her incessant need to drag me to every local rave and party imaginable.

Sighing, I grabbed my suitcase and lifted it onto the floor. I flung my backpack over my shoulder and headed towards the door, dragging my worldly possessions behind me.

I spun around and smiled as the warm scent of sandalwood and spice wrapped around me like a warm blanket. Only one vampire I knew smelt that delicious.

'Were you just going to leave without saying goodbye?'

William dropped down from the window ledge and walked over to me. I was starting to get used to him showing up unannounced. William had spent nearly every day here over the last month: correction—every night. Most of the time we'd just talked, and the rest of the time we'd done very little talking at all.

God, he looks amazing tonight.

He looked amazing all of the time, really, but tonight the black leather pants he was wearing were making me extra hot. I couldn't take my eyes off him. His short dark hair was slightly mussed, yet he still managed to look like he'd just stepped off a photoshoot. His pale skin was positively luminescent, felt soft to the touch and smelt like heaven.

But what I liked most about William was his eyes, those glistening pools of emerald green. I'd never seen anything like them.

Suddenly breathless, his masculine beauty and vampiric charms overpowered me but not for obvious reasons. Even with all of that perfection, sometimes when I looked at William, I saw another—a face that had haunted my dreams for years. This resemblance was what tripped my heart, made me question my unresolved feelings for him.

Was that face merely a figment of my imagination, a memory from my past, or a perverse need to self-sabotage?

William crossed the room, relieving me of my suitcase and backpack, and wrapping me in a passionate embrace that would have choked the life out of an ordinary human being. He pressed his face against my hair and breathed in my scent, our ritual now.

William placed his smooth, cool hands on either side of my face, tilting my head back to look up at him. He brushed his lips gently across mine, pulling away before I could draw any closer. 'Are you going to miss me, Elena?'

I shrugged, suppressing a smile. 'I don't know.'

'You don't know?'

'Well, I'm trying to think of a good reason why I would.'

William grunted. 'Then I shall have to give you one.'

'That's what I was hoping.'

He pressed his lips to mine, our mouths moving with combined desire. Hands sliding down my back, he grasped my backside tenderly, and sending my pulse racing. If I was going to miss anything, it would be this.

William pulled away, his breathing heavy. 'Is that reason enough to miss me?'

I shook my head. 'No way. I need much more convincing than that.' I grabbed at him again, trying to wrap my arms around his neck but could not match him for brute strength. He held me at arm's length, my advances rebuked by my responsible vampire.

William smiled, rubbing his thumb across my red lips. 'You know, for someone who claims to be emotionally stunted, you seem to be well and truly onboard with the physical aspect of our relationship.'

'I've never had a problem with the physical stuff. It's when you go all emotional on me that I freak out.'

'So I've noticed.'

'You won't have to worry about that soon. I'll be gone.'

William wrapped his arms around me, pulling me close. 'I won't be far behind you,' he said quietly. 'I promise that as soon as I have everything in order here, and sort out a couple of things with Marianne and Thomas, I'll be banging on your door.'

Marianne and Thomas were born vampires. They were also twins. Thomas is William's best friend, and Marianne … well, she's clingy. I'd be happy to never see her again.

'You'll make sure that beautiful Audi TT goes back to the dealership where you *borrowed* it from, right?' It wasn't really a question. William had the ability to compel people to do pretty much whatever he wanted, and I needed to know that all the property he'd 'loaned' would be returned to its rightful owners before he cleared out of Cairns.

He nodded.

'And the house? The one whose owners you, Thomas, and Marianne convinced should vacate while you lived it up on their dollar? You'll find them, too, and let them know they can come home again.'

William laughed. 'Of course, and then I'll come for you.'

I sighed. 'You don't have to come to me. Romania isn't exactly the most vampire friendly country, and Bucharest is swarming with Protectors. If you put one foot wrong, William, alliance or not, they won't hesitate to destroy you.'

'I know.'

'So why are you doing this then? Susan and George don't want us to be seen together, and they actually like you. I think.' I shook my head. 'Anyway, Lucas is the only person who knows about 'us'. I mean ... don't you want to be with someone that you don't have to sneak around with?'

George would throw a tantrum if he ever found out that I had been seeing a vampire behind his and Susan's collective backs. George wasn't known for his pleasant temperament, so it was a good thing I was leaving town.

William shook his head and sighed. 'How many times are we going to have this conversation?'

'As many times as it takes for you to realise that I'm not worth all this effort.'

William's nostrils flared at the implication. 'But, Elena, you *are* worth the effort. How can I turn my back on the first love I've felt in over four hundred years? You're asking me to kill a part of myself by walking away.'

I grimaced. 'Don't be so dramatic.'

He growled. 'I'm just being honest with you. I love you, Elena. As much as you try to deny how you feel about me, I will *not* deny my own feelings. I'm too old to be playing games. Besides, I have to come with you: who else is going to keep you out of trouble?'

I shrugged. William was so presumptuous sometimes and that bugged me. I could definitely look after myself.

'Trouble is my middle name. I'll inevitably find some to stir up at headquarters but that doesn't mean I need you to swoop in and rescue me. I'll never be able to thank you enough for helping me escape from John and his pack, but don't stay with me out of some sort of misplaced obligation. We'll always be friends, William, no matter what.'

'Friends?' he said, lifting an eyebrow.

'Yes,' I said, rolling my eyes in response. 'A friend.'

'I rather thought I was a bit more than a friend to you,' he said, squeezing me tightly, his lips nuzzling my ear. 'Perhaps even your boyfriend?'

I pushed him away. 'William, you are *not* my boyfriend.'

He frowned. 'Then what am I?'

'I don't know. Do we have to be something?'

William paused, a petulant curl to his lips. 'You drive me wild, do you know that?'

I smiled, flashing him my most flirtatious look. 'Well, then, I hope you realise that makes two of us.'

William's sullen demeanour quickly brightened, replaced by a smile that split his face from ear to ear. Only a heartbeat passed before he was pressing his mouth to mine again.

I melted.

A knock sounded at the door, putting the stops on my building desire. I pushed William roughly away from me and rushed to answer it, smoothing my hair back into place.

'Relax,' William murmured, 'it's just Lucas.'

I opened the door and found my brother standing on the other side. 'Hi, William,' Lucas quietly said, quickly turning to look at me. 'Mum wants to know if you're ready to go yet.'

I pointed at the suitcase on the floor. 'Yeah, I'm done.'

Silent, Lucas stared pointedly at the suitcase for a long while, frowning. He looked so sad that I started to feel my own misery kicking up a notch.

I put a hand on Lucas's shoulder and pulled him close before he could protest. I was almost surprised when I felt him squeezing me tightly back, the side of his face resting on top of my head.

'I'll miss you, too,' I said.

'Don't go, Elena. I have a really bad feeling about this.'

I pulled back. 'I have to go, you know that. It's not safe for any of you if I stay here.'

'She's right,' William interrupted. 'The Alpha who arrived the day before yesterday already has an eye on this house. We need to keep to the plan if your family has any chance of surviving this.'

Lucas nodded miserably. 'I know that. It's just … I don't know.' He shrugged. 'It seems wrong.'

'Another bad feeling?' I asked sympathetically.

He nodded. 'I just know, deep inside, that going to Bucharest is going to be dangerous.'

I patted his shoulder affectionately. We'd had this conversation more times than I could count, but I'd put most of his ramblings down to separation anxiety. After all, Lucas and I had never been apart before.

I turned back to William, changing the subject. 'So, this new Alpha is watching us right now?'

William nodded. 'He's not too near, but is definitely close enough that I can smell him. I've kept my distance, but it's still clear we have a spectator this evening.'

'Good. We don't want all this to be for nothing.'

'Why can't we just kill him?' Lucas moaned.

'We can't, Lucas. Don't you see that? We need a witness that can run back to Europe to tell the other pack leaders that I'm leaving. If we kill this one, more will come.'

'But it's the perfect opportunity! There are only nineteen left now that John's dead. Each Alpha we destroy puts a dent in their race's reproduction. You know as well as anyone that the sooner we kill the last Alpha, the sooner we'll finally be able to kill the rest of the werewolves without fear of their packs repopulating.'

'I know that seems like a good idea, but its better this way, better for you.'

Lucas frowned. 'How can you being gone be better for me?'

I smiled and looked back at William. 'You know, between the pair of you I have my own personal cheer squad.'

'Don't let it go to your head,' Lucas muttered. 'It's big enough already.'

'Now that's the spirit,' I said, laughing and patting him on the back. 'What kind of send-off would this be if we didn't insult each other at least once?'

'True.'

I laughed, squeezing him tightly again and just narrowly avoiding crushing his rib cage. 'I just need a minute to say goodbye to William and then I'll be right downstairs. Can you please tell Susan and George that I'll be there in a sec? Oh, and please don't tell them he's here.'

Lucas nodded, grabbing my suitcase and yanking hard on it a couple of times. He groaned, only managing to move my possessions a few inches before promptly giving up.

He eyed me suspiciously. 'Did you pour concrete into this suitcase?'

'No, Lucas.'

'Are you sure?' Lucas tugged on it again with little success. 'What about gold bricks? Did you put some of those in there for shits and giggles?'

'*Pfft*. Where would I get gold bricks from?'

Lucas sniffed. 'I hate that your bony ass can lift a fifty-odd kilogram suitcase like it's a jar of peanut butter.' He kicked at it and grunted, rubbing his shoulder. 'I think I just pulled something.'

I hid a smile. Lucas was the only one beside William who knew that I possessed great strength. It irked him to know

I could beat the crap out of him with just my little finger. 'Just leave it. I'll carry it downstairs myself.'

'I'm not weak,' he said, grabbing the door handle. 'Your suitcase is mega-heavy.'

'No doubt.'

'I'm not kidding.'

'I know you're not.'

His eyes narrowed. 'You're mocking me.'

'Maybe just a little?'

William cleared his throat. 'Perhaps you can both finish this later?'

Lucas's face fell. 'That's the problem. There won't be a later.' He slammed the door behind him with a resounding *thud*.

I stared blankly at the back of the timber, focusing on the scent of cheap aftershave that still lingered in the room. I'd never really been a big fan but I'd always associated the smell with Lucas, and now I was going to miss it terribly.

I put on a brave face and turned back to face William. I was holding back the waterworks like my life depended on it. Lucas wasn't just my brother, he was my best friend.

Shit. I am going to cry.

William wrapped me up in his arms, rocking me gently as his fingers curled through the ringlets at the back of my neck. The tenderness of his touch made me want to sob all the harder. And, finally, I did—wailing like a police siren, leaking water like a busted pipe.

When I lifted my face up to meet William's, there were still tears streaming their way down my cheeks. I must have looked like shit, but he didn't seem to mind.

I decided that snot bubbles and puffy cheeks were not going to be how William was going to remember me.

I gripped the hardened planes of William's face, pulling

him to me until our mouths moved as one. He resisted at first, concern for me evident in his eyes, but soon all was forgotten as his breath filled me up, sending my head into a giddy spin.

I moaned gently as William parted my lips and began to explore my mouth with the delicate caress of his tongue. I closed my eyes, letting the feel of his scent wash over me. I wanted to melt into him, disappear amongst the fog of bliss surrounding us, but I was painfully aware that my family was waiting for me downstairs and that there was something outside stalking me.

Reluctantly, I pulled away. William's eyes were muddy and his canines slightly drawn, but otherwise he'd managed to keep himself under control. Practice did make perfect.

William brushed a hand across my wet cheek and gently dusted a kiss across my forehead. He stepped back, heading for the window. 'I'll see you soon,' William said, jumping nimbly up onto the window ledge.

I smiled, wiping my face with my sleeve. I bent down to pick up my backpack and suitcase. 'Yeah, soon would be good.'

He gripped the window frame, looked out over the garden briefly before again resting his gaze upon me. His smile was sad and his eyes spoke volumes.

And then William was gone.

I took a moment to steady myself before slinging the backpack over my shoulder, gripping the handle of the suitcase and taking one last look around my bedroom. For over sixteen years this room had been my sanctuary—now it was time to say goodbye.

I sighed wistfully, spun on my heels and dragged my suitcase out into the hallway. I closed the door behind me, aware that I was probably doing it for the final time.

When I stepped off the last stair and rounded the corner into the living room, there were three very gloomy looking faces staring back at me. My heart wrenched unexpectedly. I wasn't prepared for this, to feel like this.

'What's with all the long faces?' I said, trying to lighten the mood.

Simultaneously, all three shrugged, Lucas clearly the most affected despite Susan wiping at a stray tear rolling down the side of her cheek. For show? Quite probably but who could really tell with my family.

'Hey, look at it this way,' I said, dropping my bags and wrapping them all up in a group hug. 'Lucas, you can have your own bachelor pad on the second story now and no one to call you dumbass every five seconds. George, you can stop taking that blood pressure medication now that I'm leaving. And Susan, well …' I really had no idea what to say to her. Susan acted like my mother and had been relatively nice to me over the years, but I was still sure she was trying to kill us all with her terrible cooking.

I stepped back instead and gathered my bags again. 'Let's just get out of here before that werewolf decides I'm too tasty to resist.'

Lucas snorted. 'Yeah, you wish.'

I shook my head, pretending to struggle with my suitcase as I dragged it across the floor to the front door.

'Here, let me get that,' George said, pulling the handle from my grasp and carrying it out for me.

'Thanks, it's really heavy.'

Lucas rolled his eyes.

Susan locked the house behind us as I watched George attempting to lift my suitcase into the back of their new Toyota Prado. Our old car, the Subaru Forester, had been smashed to pieces by one of the vânātors that had ended up taking me hostage. The windows had been shattered, the front door ripped off its hinges, and the upholstery torn up by glass fragments and my fingernails. I'd made that werewolf pay dearly for what it had done to that car, what it had done to me. After feasting on my blood, dislocating my shoulder, punching me in the face and impaling me on a tree branch, he was lucky death had come so swiftly.

I climbed into the backseat next to Lucas and buckled up. I took my time, glancing back at the house once more, committing every detail to memory.

'Now, when you get to Bucharest,' Susan said, climbing in, 'a man named Chester will meet you at the airport. He'll be waiting for you in the private Arrivals Lounge after you get through immigration and customs.'

'This Chester guy, is he a Protector?' I asked, wondering when I had heard that name before.

Susan nodded as George started the car, pulled down the driveway and out onto the main road. 'Yes. He'll be your liaison at the IMI. He's a very old friend of my family and will do his best to make you feel at home, okay?'

'Okay.'

'You'll like Bucharest,' George added. 'I always have.'

'Yeah, but will I actually get to see any of the city? Or will I be stuck in a laboratory all day, every day, being poked and prodded for the sake of some lab coat's curiosity?'

George grunted, his typical reply to any question I asked that displeased him. 'You always knew that if you went to Romania they would be more than overly curious, Elena. You have to remember that you are a complete anomaly to us. There has never been anyone like you before. Your blood's composition is perfect and there is just so much we don't know about your genetic makeup, and apparently, so much that our enemies could gain. So I'm sorry if you don't get a chance to see the sights.'

'I know I'm not going there to play tourist, but—'

'They'll be protecting you, not holding you prisoner. You chose to do this, remember?'

'So can I come and go as I please then?'

'Not exactly.'

'That's a little vague.'

Lucas winked at me. 'Vague rules are how you prosper, Elena. If you want to get out and about, I'm sure you'll figure it out.'

'Could you not encourage her, please?' Susan hissed. 'The IMI have rules and Elena is no exception. If the Alpha follows her like we're hoping, then planning day trips into the city would not be wise if she wants to avoid being taken hostage again.'

Point taken.

'Like she needs any encouragement from me,' Lucas snorted. 'She's always done exactly what she wants, regardless of the consequences.'

'Hello! I'm sitting right here, you know.'

Lucas shrugged and glanced back out the window. 'Where is headquarters, anyway? We always talk about it, but we never really *talk* about it.'

'In Bucharest,' Susan answered.

Lucas turned and rolled his eyes at her back. 'Well, duh, I know that. Where in Bucharest? Is it in a warehouse, an office building? Or is it underground like our division is?'

She stuttered. 'W-we can't tell you that.'

Lucas and I exchanged puzzled looks. 'Why not?' he said. 'I'm a Protector. Bucharest is the head division for the entire IMI so why would its location need to be kept a secret from me?'

Both Susan and George shook their heads. 'Sorry, Lucas,' Susan replied. 'You're not a full Protector yet and Elena isn't allowed to know because she is technically still considered an outsider. It's not personal, simply precautionary.'

Not personal, my ass.

I scowled, patting Lucas's hand before he launched into a debate. 'It's okay, Lucas, it doesn't really matter. Like you said—if I want to know where I am, I'll figure it out.'

'Elena, please try and remember why you're being sent to Bucharest before you go and do something stupid simply for the sake of satisfying your curiosity,' Susan pleaded.

'Something stupid? You're getting a little too defensive. I know why I'm going, Susan. I'm the one who suggested it, remember?' I backpedalled. 'You don't have to worry. Once this vânător sees me get on the aeroplane, he'll go back to his den and try to figure out another way to get at me, but by then it'll be too late.'

'So then you understand …?'

'Perfectly. And then hopefully after a month or so—'

'You can come home!' Lucas chorused in.

Susan coughed, a quick look passing between her and George that made me more than a little nervous. 'Good. I'm glad you've seen reason.'

'I see plenty.'

What exactly am I signing myself up for?

Frowning, I glanced out of the window, watching the city pass me by for the final time and wondering if I was running from danger or heading straight for it. That was the thing with The Protectors—you never could tell what their true intentions were.

I watched as the lights of the city of Cairns faded into skirting suburbs, various businesses, and restaurants. Driving along Sheridan Street we passed a multitude of backpacker motels and beer gardens that lined the highway, as well as a few government buildings marking the most recent additions to the surrounding architectural landscape. There went the public pool that I had swum in as a child— at least, until Lucas had told me that everyone peed in it and that I'd get hepatitis from swallowing the water. There went the humongous statue of Captain Cook that Lucas had slammed into when backing over the curb while learning how to drive.

He really was a dumbass.

It was ten-thirty, and I could still see people walking the streets, making the most of the sultry night air and enjoying what small nightlife Cairns had to offer. They didn't have to worry about werewolves hunting them down any longer. With me gone, the city of Cairns would once again be safe.

I wondered if right now William was out there, tracking the vânător somewhere in the darkness beyond, or if he was following behind us, keeping a watchful eye on me in case the creature decided to pounce.

I hoped so.

The journey from our house seemed so short in comparison to the distance stretching out ahead of me. Before I knew it, George was pulling into the right-hand lane and turning down the winding, mangrove-lined road leading directly to Cairns International Airport. An escort with a private buggy met us at the car park, loaded my luggage onto its back and then ushered us through the terminal.

'Now, do you have everything you need?' Susan asked, tugging on my hair. I wondered if she knew how much that bugged me.

'It's a bit late now if I don't.'

She sniffed. 'Yes, I suppose it is.'

'There's no room left in her suitcase, anyway,' Lucas pointed out. 'You'd have to unload the anvils first.'

'Can someone make sure he starts to eat some red meat?' I said, jabbing my thumb in his direction.

Lucas scowled darkly at me. 'I'm not a weakling.'

'Protein powder might help, too.'

His scowl deepened.

'And, if all else fails, there's always steroids.'

'Ha-ha, you're freaking *hilarious*.'

I turned my back on him and instead looked at George, who was busy scanning the tarmac. 'Is the vânător here, do you think?'

'I'm not sure,' George answered. 'Our magic doesn't really work that way. But I do know that William will be here tonight to ensure that you get on that plane safely. If the vânător becomes a threat, he will soon sense it.'

My head seemed to spin as Lucas and I gawked at each other.

Do they know about us?

How the hell should I know? Lucas's eyes seemed to say, as he shrugged.

'William will be here?' I asked innocently.

George nodded. 'Seeing how he played quite a fundamental role in rescuing you last time, I figured I would ask him to spare an hour or two to help ensure that you got on the plane safely.' He smiled knowingly, which perturbed me greatly. 'He didn't seem too inconvenienced by my request.'

Of course he didn't. We're swapping spit.

I glanced out across the darkened tarmac, hoping to catch a glimpse of William. I caught sight of something flapping in the nighttime breeze that looked suspiciously like his leather coat. I supposed it might have been the vânător, but instincts told me that William would stay close.

Despite the darkness and the distance between us, I knew I'd be seen with perfect clarity. A vampire's vision was so much more advanced than a human's, better even than a werewolf's. It seemed good to be a vampire.

Minus the whole blood thing.

Oh, yeah, and being dead.

I turned to fully face him now, focusing on that billowing coat and looking for signs of his emerald eyes across the deep shroud of night. 'I think I *will* miss you, William,' I whispered, knowing that only he would hear me. 'It's not every day I meet a hot vampire.' Corny and decidedly unsentimental, I know, but what else was there to say?

I inhaled as I felt his scent lazily descend upon me like a fine mist. It wasn't cloying like his usual enticements but was merely a caress of my soft flesh, like a whisper on the breeze with the promise of future encounters.

I suppressed a smile and turned back around to my family. Lucas was eyeing me speculatively. 'Well, I guess this is it then,' I said, shrugging and taking a step forward to hug each one of them goodbye.

Susan grabbed me first, wrapping her arms around me tightly and pulling my face to her chest. 'Take care of yourself, Elena.'

'I will,' I muffled against her blouse.

She pulled away and wiped at her tear-stained face. I couldn't believe Susan was actually crying. Unless, of course, they were tears of happiness at finally being rid of me.

Yeah. That does make more sense.

I stepped awkwardly into George's embrace, feeling his big hands around me. I inhaled the scent of his aftershave— Old Spice. George patted his hands across my back and then rested one on top of my head. 'Make sure you do what Chester asks you to do. You've already given me heart problems, so do you think you could take it easy on everyone else for a little while?'

I nodded, pulling away. 'I'll give it a try, but I make no promises of saintly behaviour.'

His lips twitched as he moved to pat the side of my cheek. 'I know, but please try. I told Chester that you'd be open to at least moderate cooperation.'

'I promise I'll at least say "please" and "thank you".'

George grimaced. 'I suppose we can't ask for much more than that.'

'Have I really been that impossible to live with?'

He turned away. I supposed most people would have been hurt by George's lack of response. I might have been, even expected a twinge of some emotion to hit me, but strangely I felt nothing. So I focused my attention on Lucas instead.

He was looking down at the ground, toeing at a piece of asphalt under his shoe. His apparent misery was catching.

'Hey, dumbass,' I murmured, pushing him gently on the shoulder.

Lucas looked up, face grim. 'Hey, dickhead.'

Susan and George rolled their eyes and shook their heads. They didn't understand that this was just our way. We weren't really insulting each other, we were saying goodbye.

'I promise I'll call you as often as I can.'

'You better,' he mumbled.

'Maybe you could come and visit, too?'

Susan and George discretely shook their heads.

Okay, maybe not.

Lucas kicked the piece of asphalt clear across the tarmac. 'You know, life is going to be so boring here without you.'

'You've got college to look forward to.'

'What's so great about college?' he said, suddenly angry.

I smiled wickedly, adopting his trademark eyebrow wiggle as I leaned in close. 'You won't have to study at the IMI anymore and there will be girls—lots and lots of pretty girls.'

That cheered him up considerably. 'You're right, E. That *is* something to look forward to. It would be nice to play with the real thing for a while.' Lucas leaned in closer, lowering his voice. 'I'm sick of spending night after night gripping a flashlight and rifling through my Playboy mags.'

'Shit, Lucas, that's way too much information!'

'The pages are all stuck together.'

'Oh, for fuc—'

'From the humidity!' he protested.

I gagged. 'Okay, we are *so* done with this conversation.'

'Seriously. I have rising damp in my room or something. There's mould under my mattress.'

I waved him off, turning around and starting to head for the private jet the IMI had chartered. Lucas grappled with my arm until he caught my wrist, spinning me back around to face him with surprising force. 'I'm really going to miss you, E.'

'The feeling is more than mutual.'

'But I just know that you aren't going to be as safe as Mum and Dad say you'll be.'

'Better the devil you know, Lucas.'

'The devil has a strange way of never appearing as he seems. Just watch your back, okay?'

I nodded, picking my backpack off the ground and swinging it over my shoulder. 'Goodbye,' I said, turning quickly and heading over towards the aeroplane before anyone could see my fresh wave of tears. 'I'll call you when I get there.'

No one answered.

'Good evening, Miss. May I take your bag?' the pilot asked me.

I handed him the shoulder strap. 'Thank you.'

'Just settle yourself inside. We'll be taking off shortly.'

I nodded, turned and headed up the short flight of stairs and into the dimly lit cabin. At the door, I gave Lucas, Susan, and George one hesitant last wave before quickly disappearing inside. Uncertainty slowed my footsteps, as I trudged down the centre aisle and finally settled into one of the plush leather seats at the front of the plane. I watched the pilot enter and stow my bag in a lockable compartment up the front. He then pressed a button, and with a mechanical whirring sound, the stairs pulled up inside the cabin. The pilot gave me a polite nod and headed into the cockpit, closing the door behind him.

I glanced out the little porthole, watching my family as the aeroplane began to reverse up and then slowly turn towards the runway. All three of them now were looking up at the glass windows of the main terminal, and as I followed their gaze, I could see a mysterious figure in a trench coat standing inside. I could just make out the long, dark hair and tanned skin. Defining features were indeterminable because of the distance, but it was clear by his stance that his gaze was fixated on this aircraft.

It had to be the Alpha.

Suddenly, he spun away from the plate glass window and melted into the crowd of people behind. As the plane began to taxi down the runway I tried scanning the darkness for William, but as far as I could tell he was also gone.

Previous encounters had shown that the Alphas were smart. This one probably would have checked the flight log, realised I was heading for Bucharest and no longer staying with this faction of Protectors. Logically, he would see that there was no reason for any of his pack to come back to Cairns.

Now all I had to do was play my designated part. I would go to headquarters, succumb to all the tests that were undoubtedly coming, and then find a way to get the hell out of Dodge before the Devil decided that I was far too dangerous to ever be set free. I'd said 'better the devil you know' to Lucas, but what if you'd never known the Devil at all? Who do you trust then?

CHAPTER TWO: BUCHAREST

'‎'m sorry we have to do this to you, Elena,' Chester said to me, his Romanian accent thick and nasal. 'But we don't let non-Protectors see how we enter or exit headquarters.'

I leant back against the cushioned seat of the car, listening to the sounds of the traffic whirring past outside. From the minute Chester had greeted me at the airport and stowed my luggage in the boot of the black Chrysler 300, I'd been blindfolded.

'It's fine,' I said, even though I was anything *but* fine.

'I know it's probably not what you had in mind, but it really is the only way,' Chester continued. 'Plus, performing the Light of Mellar on you every few minutes would be exhausting.'

The Light of Mellar was a pretty impressive spell. It started out as a thought in the mind of the Protector, manifesting as a large ball of light controlled from within, their hands merely a conduit for the energy. Once large enough, it was then flung at the target, blinding them instantly. The blindness lasted only about five minutes but was very effective at neutralising an attacker.

'It's okay,' I repeated. 'I do understand. I just hope I don't have to wear this thing the whole time.' I grabbed at the cloth around my eyes, only to be stopped by Chester's equally grabby hands.

'No, you only have to wear the blindfold when you are being escorted to and from the building. Once you are inside you are free to move around as you please.' He smacked my hand away again. 'Leave it alone.'

I harrumphed, hands back in my lap. 'So is headquarters above ground or below? Our Cairns faction is below—a kind of *bomb shelter* meets *Hogwarts School of Witchcraft and Wizardry*.'

Chester didn't answer. I assumed he was deciding whether or not giving away such information would crumble the very foundations of secrecy that the IMI was built on. 'It's above ground,' he finally answered. 'Why do you ask?'

'I'm just curious.'

'Why?'

I shrugged. 'I don't know. I guess I was hoping for more information about the place that's supposedly protecting me from being raped and drained by the Alphas.'

'You have nothing to fear.'

'I'm not scared.' Well that wasn't exactly true—I was practically shitting myself over thoughts of being trapped in a foreign country without anyone around batting for 'Team Elena'. Plus, Lucas's reservations had finally crept up on me, making me all twitchy and nervous.

'Aren't you just a little bit concerned? I mean, not just about the Alpha, but I think it would be normal for a girl your age to feel, shall we say, disconnected?'

I wasn't sure I liked his choice of words—'disconnected' implied 'cut off'. 'In answer to your question, no, I'm not concerned or *disconnected*, as you put it. Coming here means keeping everyone safe. Lucas is just a phone call away.'

'Indeed.'

There was a brief pause before Chester spoke again. 'Do you know why the Vânātors are after you?'

I did and no doubt so did he, but I didn't really want to talk about it. The memories were still a little raw. At night, I sometimes still had flashbacks of the dank, dark cell they had imprisoned me in, of Elizabeth's tormented screams, and of John ravenously feasting on my blood. I could vividly remember the feel of his calloused hands on my body, the touch of his lips, and the horrible truth of the situation: he had wanted to rape me. Mostly, I was plagued by my body's reaction to his power, even as every other part of me screamed in denial.

'Elena?' Chester repeated, jogging me out of my reverie. 'Are you going to answer my question?'

I thought about that for a moment. 'No.'

'Why not?'

'I don't want to talk about it.'

Chester grunted. 'Susan warned me you'd be a little … difficult.'

Straining my eyes through the blindfold, I turned my head in the direction of his voice. 'That's not fair. I'm not being difficult; I'm cautious. I don't know you, which means I'm not going to start running my mouth off to you. Besides, I think we both know that Susan and George have given you all the reports regarding my abduction. You don't need to hear it from me, too.'

'Perhaps when you learn to trust me a little more you'll be willing to share some of those details with me. Not all our reports are exact.'

I gave an indignant snort. 'I don't play well with others.'

'Such disdain? You'd think we'd only just met.'

'We have.'

'It's amazing what a child can forget.'

I felt myself frowning. From my quick glimpse of him before being blindfolded, Chester looked like an unassuming man—not exactly memorable, but I doubted I would have forgotten him either. He had short blonde hair, brown eyes and wore a big pair of tortoise shell glasses that perched on the end of his nose. He had a tidy moustache, a plaid shirt with matching pants, and a belt held up by suspenders. Chester had six kinds of pens and pencils shoved into his front shirt pocket and even wore a name tag, yet there was nothing about all that which seemed even vaguely familiar.

'What are you talking about, Chester? Have we met before or not?'

'Trust works both ways, Elena.'

I laughed derisively. 'That's a typical IMI reply if ever I heard one.'

Chester chuckled in response but there was no warmth in it. 'It's a good thing we have *plenty* of time, then.'

'I'm only here for a couple of weeks at the most,' I pointed out.

'Weeks, months, years: it doesn't really matter,' he answered dismissively. 'The IMI want to keep you around until you turn eighteen.'

I calculated the dates. Eighteen was the magic number for a born vampire like me—the date of my full transformation. If today was October seventh, then they were planning on keeping me here for another year and a half.

I gritted my teeth.

Then what? If I turned into a big, hairy beast that drank blood, would I be put down? Or would I be mutilated, reduced to a mere substance for an experiment in one of the IMI's laboratories?

'That's a long time,' I murmured, quickly running through contingency plans.

'Not really. Not when you consider that you have eternity stretched out in front of you.'

'I didn't pack enough clothes then.'

Chester laughed. 'So then you understand?'

I shook my head. 'No, I don't. I thought being here was my decision and if I chose *not* to stay at the IMI any longer then I would be freely able to leave.'

'I'm afraid that is really not your decision to make,' he answered evenly. 'You are still a minor.'

I could feel my temper rising. 'And Susan and George know about this?'

'Why do you think they pushed for you to come to Romania and not some other Australian faction?' Chester touched my shoulder, and though he probably meant it as a gesture of comfort, I slapped his hand away.

He sighed. 'Elena, regardless of the reasons why, you *have* come and it's for a most noble cause. The IMI fully intend to back your decisions, but now that you are finally here and so close to the date of your turning, I'm afraid we cannot risk everyone's safety by letting you leave. There is a much bigger picture to contend with here. Elena, do you realise that you could eventually become more dangerous than either vampire or vânător once you turn?'

'I'm aware of that. Believe me, it's all I think about. But that doesn't mean I should be robbed of all my choices.'

Chester sniffed, but didn't respond.

'Tell me something. Let's say that I decide on my own terms to stay until I'm eighteen. What happens if the IMI decides they don't like what I've become on the night of my turning?'

He remained silent.

'Yeah, that's what I thought.'

Great. I'm toast.

'When we get to the IMI, I want to speak to a manager or something.'

'I'm about as high up in the organisation as one can get, Elena. I run the research department and I'm one of the members that issues directives to the entire IMI.'

'Oh. Well … you're not going to help me then, are you?'

'I have to do what I think is best. For now that is helping you, but later—'

'Later you might change your mind?'

'Possibly.'

We didn't speak to each other for the remainder of the trip. I was too busy thinking through possible strategies for escape. One tactic involved opening the car door, flinging myself out into the busy street and running in the opposite direction as fast as I could; another was winding down the window and screaming my heart out. I also thought about beating Chester to a pulp, screaming my heart out and *then* running away, but none of those options seemed particularly productive. Getting lost in a foreign country was for idiots who had been sold off to a drug-slash-prostitution ring by unsavoury characters. Plus, I still had an Alpha on my trail. The smartest thing for me to do right now was to sit tight until I came up with a decent plan.

In the meantime, I'd learn as much about the IMI's internal operations as possible. It seemed they didn't have any immediate plans to slice and dice me, so I figured that for now I could bum a couple of weeks of free accommodation off them. Afterwards I'd determine the best way to break out and get home again, but obviously only once the Alpha lost interest in me or realised that finding me was a lost cause. I hoped I wouldn't have a meltdown before then.

Fifteen minutes later, the car seemed to dip downwards and then flatten out again. Judging by our slow speed, the random turning, and the constant squealing of tyres on smooth asphalt, I guessed we'd turned into a parking garage of some description.

The Chrysler finally came to a stop and the sound of the partition dividing the front and rear sections rolled down.

'Can I take the blindfold off yet?' I enquired.

'Not yet,' Chester answered, his weight shifting in the seat next to me.

'Which elevator I use?' That was the driver. His accent was as thick as Chester's, but slightly more difficult to understand.

'*Lift de serviciu.*'

'I go to reception?'

Reception?

'Speak Romanian!' Chester bellowed.

'How I practice English?' the driver mumbled. 'I never get oppur, optune … I never get chance?'

'I don't care!' Chester roared, and then partook of yet another heated display in their native tongue. This went on for almost five minutes before, in a considerably calmer voice, he said, 'Take her things to her room. Everything has been arranged.'

The car moved as Chester's weight shifted again. I heard the sound of both the front and rear car doors opening. I started grabbing at the blindfold.

'I said not yet,' Chester chided, flinging open my car door and clamping his hands over my eyes again.

Boy, he's quick. But I'd still seen enough to confirm that I *was* in a parking garage.

'I'm going to take your hand,' Chester said impatiently, reaching down and helping pull me out of the car. 'I'll guide you through the building and take you to your quarters, alright? You must be tired after such a long flight.'

I shrugged. I was cranky now, too, but I didn't think he would want to hear.

Chester began to pull me along, telling me when to take a step or to watch my head. The whole scenario was just ridiculous but at least he hadn't walked me into a wall yet.

We stopped and waited for what must have been an elevator. I'd gleaned that much from the driver—plus, I'd heard Chester push a button and the sound of doors opening, all accompanied by a *ping*. My elevator theory was soon confirmed when he ushered me into the cramped space. The floor seemed to bounce lightly under our feet, and my knees were wobbling the minute the doors closed. The whole thing moved rapidly upwards.

'Steady,' Chester said, catching me. 'We're almost there.'

I listened to the funny sounding elevator music, cringing as a combination of breathy pan pipes and Euro-pop assaulted my ears. Another *ping* and I was rescued from musical murder by the doors opening once again. Chester pushed me forward and out of the elevator, stopping to finally remove my blindfold.

I ran my fingers through my hair, untangling the neglected strands as I took in my surroundings. Monochromatic blandness stretched out before me. I was standing in an extremely long corridor with doors at regular intervals on each side, with each door having what looked to be a security card panel that barred free entry. All forms of adornment were absent.

I glanced behind me and saw that the elevator had its own swipe panel. 'Let me guess,' I said, pointing over my shoulder. 'That's the only way in or out of this place?'

Chester nodded. 'You are not permitted to leave this floor unless you are accompanied by a member of the IMI.'

'As in *you*?'

'Or someone I designate the chore of babysitting you.'

'What about these rooms?' I asked, pointing to the various doors in front of us.

Chester shook his head. 'You'll be given a keycard for access to your room, as well as various other rooms like the gymnasium, if you desire it, and the swimming pool. But all other areas are unauthorised unless one of us comes with you.'

'Right. So I suppose that means I'm kind of a prisoner then.'

'We'd really rather hoped that you wouldn't view it like that.'

'Well, you're not the rat stuck in this cage now, are you?'

He feigned indifference. 'How about I show you the facilities?'

'I'm sure that I'll see it all soon enough.'

Besides, I'd much rather take my own, private tour.

Chester shrugged. 'I'll show you to your room then.' He walked slightly in front of me, leading the way down the white, carpeted hallway, and straight down to one of the doors at the end. After impatiently swiping his access card, there was a flicker of green light on the sensor pad and then a clicking of locks as the door popped open.

Chester held the door to the side, allowing me to enter first. My luggage was already waiting for me in the centre of the floor. The room wasn't exactly huge but was definitely bigger than my old bedroom in Cairns.

To the left of the entry was a small kitchenette with a sink, microwave, dishwasher, and mini-bar fridge. Next to the kitchenette was a dining table for two that I'd probably never use. Past these was a small, white two-seater sofa with a glass coffee table in front, and a stack of Wheels magazines piled high in the centre.

'Wait, *you* know what magazines I like to read?'

Chester smiled, a glint from his gold crown prominent under the bright fluorescents above. 'We know a lot about you, Elena.'

Of course you do.

That became irritatingly clear when I turned around to find a small bookcase with fantasy and horror novels crowding the shelves—all collections from some of my favourite authors. Next to the bookcase was a huge, wall-mounted LCD television replete with an in-built DVD player. In a small glass cabinet underneath there were a large selection of DVDs of the action genre variety. I could see *Commando, Alien vs Predator, The Transporter,* and *Die Hard*—some of the very same kind that I'd usually watch at home.

Off to the side was an opaque glass petition dividing living space from sleeping quarters. In the corner were a small desk, chair, and lamp, as well as a large king-sized bed fitted with stark white linens and two basic foam pillows. It didn't escape my attention that there was no telephone or computer, either. There were also no paintings, plants or features of any kind. Even the tiny bathroom just off the back of the bedroom was utilitarian. My quarters were a very comfortable version of a prison cell.

I wonder if there are any cameras in here? Perverts.

The bedroom and lounge windows were made of fixed glass, dusted in a film that obscured the view of outside but still allowed light to penetrate. The windows didn't open and that made me a little uneasy.

'Well, I might leave you to it then,' Chester said. 'It's late and I'm sure you probably want to get settled. I'll come back for you tomorrow morning and introduce you to our other employees.'

'Whatever,' I said, still staring at the cold room around me.

'All right then. See you in the morning.' He went to leave, paused and turned back. 'Whoops. Elena, there is one other thing. This is the access card you will need to get into the unrestricted areas—including this room.'

I took the card from his outstretched fingers.

'Also, I hate to ask, but you're going to have to give me your blade.'

I clutched the trusty hilt of my knife. Chester must have noticed it in the car or maybe George and Susan had told him that I was carrying.

No way.

I shook my head. 'Sorry, but you can't have my knife. It has sentimental value.'

Chester frowned, his glasses sliding down to the end of his nose. 'Elena, this is policy. No outside weapons are allowed in the building.'

'I don't know anything about your policies, and I don't really care—my knife stays.' I did take a second to see the situation from his perspective, though, and toned the anger down a notch. 'I can assure you, though, that I have no plans to stab anyone here, if that's what you're worried about.'

Smooth.

'Elena, please be reasonable.'

'Reasonable? Explain that concept to a non-magical user, please. As Protectors your hands are your weapons. What protection do I have?'

'Who would you possibly need to defend yourself from here?'

Is he being serious?

I put my hands on my hips. 'Tell you what, Chester, you want me to be reasonable? Then here it is—if you can get my knife off me without using magic then you can have it. After all, don't The Protectors pride themselves on their skills as martial artists'?'

He eyed me speculatively, his gaze resting on my twitching fingers as they caressed the hilt of my blade. He took a step forward, abruptly halting as my blade suddenly appeared in my hand, its reflective surface gleaming in the space between us. I was quick when pressed.

'Ah, we'll wait until tomorrow then,' Chester added hastily, backing up and heading for the door.

I nodded politely and re-sheathed my knife. 'Until tomorrow,' I said, in mocking tones.

Until tomorrow? What was that?

I sound like some uptight character from a Jane Austen novel.

I wandered back into the kitchenette and started riffling through the cupboards and fridge. They were fully-stocked with the essentials, like milk and bread, and in my case, chocolate. I grabbed a Snickers bar and started munching on it, then wandered back over to the sofa and started leafing through some of the magazines. For curiosity's sake, I picked up the remote control and switched on the television. There were plenty of channels to choose from but unless I quickly learnt how to speak Romanian, I hadn't a hope in hell of enjoying the programming.

I switched the TV off again, staring up at the blank screen in defeat. The gibberish was still echoing in my ears and mixed with the confused thoughts in my head. Another bite of my Snickers bar and a dejected sigh did little to ease my apprehension.

I grabbed my backpack where I'd dumped it on the floor and pulled out my mobile phone. I needed to call Lucas. I hadn't expected things to run smoothly when I arrived, but I never thought for a second that they were planning on keeping me here indefinitely. I needed his advice.

I switched on the cell phone: no bars. I wandered around the apartment, holding it up higher, trying in vain to get a good signal. Not even a flicker of network life.

I walked over to one of the covered windows in the bedroom and pressed my phone hard against the glass, again trying to dial home.

Still no signal. Shit!

I snapped the phone shut and blew out a long breath. Maybe it was the stuff they used to cover the windows that was interrupting the signal?

I used my nails to pick at the corners of the glass, searching for an edge to the film that I could catch and rip from the surface. There didn't appear to be one. On closer inspection, I noticed that the film was actually sandwiched between the two pieces of glass.

Double-glazed windows. Damn Europeans and their insulation!

Huffing in frustration, I stalked around the apartment in every direction, jumping up on the sofa, planking on the kitchenette, and even looking for bars by the toilet bowl. Dialling home was starting to look like an exercise in futility. Maybe my room had a cell phone jammer? Just because I'd only seen people using them in the movies did not mean they weren't real, right?

Right?

I moved over to my door, cell phone in hand, and tested the handle. The door opened. At least they didn't have me in lockdown after dark.

I glanced out into the corridor, seeing no one. Pocketing my access card, I closed the door behind me, wandering over to the door directly opposite mine. I pressed my ear to it and listened.

The sound of running water met my ears and I heard a female voice singing a bad rendition of *Splish Splash*. No secret what was going on in that room.

I checked the next door along. From this room I could hear the sounds of a television and muffled laughter. I lifted my head and glanced, slightly puzzled, at the other doors along the long corridor. Some of them had gold-plated numbers like my room and the two rooms I'd just recently eavesdropped on, but there were others that had lettering: 'Lab 1', 'Restricted Access' and 'Swimming Pool'. Others I couldn't read at all given the language barrier.

Regardless, there was definitely something very familiar about the layout of this corridor—evenly interspersed rooms and an elevator at the end? Was I on the upper level of some sort of nondescript hotel? But that didn't make any sense. Why would The Protectors build their headquarters in a hotel, and how could they effectively protect it or hide it from public view?

Still … I did remember the driver mentioning something about heading to 'reception' when I first arrived. If I was in a hotel, or at the very least, a *part* of a hotel, then it was safe to say that I was at least partway through uncovering my location.

Curious.

I walked up to a window at the end of the corridor. It was covered in the same opaque film as my room. I didn't hold out high hopes for a signal, but I flipped the lid on my cell phone, anyway.

No luck.

Cursing under my breath, I headed back to the room where muffled laughter and the sound of the television could still be heard. I rapped on its timber surface and waited. I wasn't sure what I was expecting but it wasn't Chester. 'Elena?' he said, popping his head around the corner of the door. 'What are you doing?'

'You live here, too?'

'Of course. Why wouldn't I?'

'No reason.'

'Did you want something?' There was no masking the irritation in his voice.

I showed Chester my cell phone. 'Why can't I get a signal in here? I'm trying to call a couple of people to tell them I've arrived, but I can't get through.'

He pushed his glasses up his nose. 'No cell phones allowed in here.'

No cell phones, no knives. Did he think I was going to mug him for his phone credit?

'So how am I supposed to call Lucas if cell phones are banned?'

'You can use the IMI telephone in the morning.'

I all but pouted. 'But I would really like to ring him now.'

Chester huffed. 'Look, Elena, it's now half-past twelve. It's also probably very early in the morning back home in Australia. You can use the phone tomorrow.'

I crossed my arms in front of my chest, eyes narrowing. As defiantly as always, I said, 'So what you're telling me is that, not only am I restricted from leaving the building, but all my phone calls are also going to be monitored, too?'

Chester sighed, pinching the bridge of his nose. 'Afraid so.' He started to close the door, but I'd wedged my foot in.

'What about a computer? Do you have one of those that I can use?'

'What for?'

'Does it matter?'

'Everything you do here matters.'

'I want to send through some e-mails.'

'It's all going to have to wait until tomorrow. The computers are in the lab and I'm not going to go and open it up in the middle of the night just so that you can surf the internet. Now, is there anything else?' Chester said, looking down pointedly at the foot I still had wedged in his door.

I removed my foot and thought about shoving it elsewhere instead. 'I guess not.'

'Well, goodnight then.' He slammed the door, the timber quivering briefly in the jamb, my nose now pressed up against the golden lettering.

I huffed furiously, balling my hands into fists at my sides, as I walked back down the corridor and past my bedroom. I scanned the signs on every door I passed, swiping each sensor pad with my access card in the hopes that one of the laboratory doors might magically let me in. Unfortunately, that didn't happen. The only rooms I could gain access to were the swimming pool and the gym, both of which entailed exercise. I wasn't keen on trying that unless I got really, really bored.

I shut the gym door behind me, exhaling in frustration. I fought the urge to punch and kick my way through each and every door, and on into the labs, regardless. After all, I *was* strong and capable. Even sneezing at the door I risked blowing it off its hinges, but I really didn't want to alert Chester that I was much stronger than the average human. The last blood test my local IMI branch had subjected me to was almost two months ago. The results had been negative for changes in my DNA, yet I was still somehow stronger now, almost as strong as a vampire. I had no idea why exchanging blood with John, the Alpha vânător, had caused such a reaction.

Lucas had a theory that the exchange of blood between any supernatural and myself was the catalyst for unlocking my latent abilities. I agreed, unsure of what the werewolf portion of my DNA had in store for me. Would it remain dormant, or would I become a new and completely unpredictable version of a vânător?

A slight whirring sound caught my attention. Mounted up in the corner of the room was a tiny surveillance camera, which was currently swivelling around to get a closer look at something, presumably at me.

Oh, that's just perfect. Now they're watching my every move.

I gave the camera a one finger salute.

Pushing off from the elevator doors, I headed directly back to my room. There was nothing more to be done tonight and jet lag was making me act like a petulant tool.

Given that the corridor was monitored, I figured that my room might also be fitted with devices. Once back inside, I carefully traced my eyes over every surface of the room, looking for signs of surveillance. Not that I actually knew what I was looking for. Paranoia was probably setting in, brought on by a lack of sleep and a six hour stopover in Hong Kong. Still, I checked every crevice and crack I could find.

Sighing with weariness, I finally gave up. A shower and bed was definitely a better idea than rustling around inside air-conditioning vents, checking for surveillance equipment that probably didn't exist.

'Good morning, everyone,' Chester said, as he pushed the door to the laboratory open and ushered me through. My usual response to a statement like that would have been 'Is it?', but since the statement wasn't directed at me, I didn't answer. There were only a few mumbled responses, anyway.

As I entered the room, three people were standing around dressed in white lab coats like Chester. There were also eight people sitting at computers, reading data and studying images on the screens. I didn't have a science degree, let alone a high school diploma, so I had no hope of understanding the information. Plus, all the lab geeks had turned to stare at me now, so I didn't want to look like I was snooping.

'Elena,' Chester said, touching my shoulder and gesturing at the white-coated lab techs, 'this is Stephanie, Anica, and Beryx. You'll learn everyone else's names over time but since there are over twenty-five members of staff on this floor alone, that'll take time.'

'On *this* floor?' I said.

Chester waved me off, pointing to a shorter woman in her late thirties. I really dug her soulful brown eyes and short, blonde pixie-style haircut. 'Stephanie here is American. She's currently staying with us at headquarters because she specialises in haematology. Stephanie not only has a keen interest in your blood but in the composition and beneficial properties of vampire and vânător blood, too.'

Stephanie extended a slender hand. 'I'm so glad to meet you, Elena,' she said in a southern drawl. 'I've been studying the effects of your blood for the last five years. You've certainly kept me on my toes.'

I shook her hand and smiled tentatively. Stephanie's eyes were bright and wide, and stared at me like I was an exciting toy for her to play with. Still, she seemed nice enough.

'This is Anica,' Chester continued. 'I'm afraid Anica doesn't speak much English, but she's an excellent geneticist.'

Anica gave me a fleeting smile, bobbing her head in greeting. She was young, maybe thirty if she was lucky. Anica had straight, black hair that rested in a blunt cut at her shoulders, matched by a severe fringe that almost covered her eyes. Slim, stainless-steel glasses and the over-application of dark eyeliner highlighted her brown eyes. She was extremely skinny, and I noted a few indecipherable tattoos just on the insides of her wrists. I wondered what Anica did when she wasn't wearing a lab coat.

'Hi.'

'Hallo.' Her voice was thickly accented like Chester's.

'And this,' Chester said, pulling me forward to meet the last lab tech in line, 'is Beryx.'

'Cool name,' I said, reaching out to shake as he extended a hand.

'Thank you,' Beryx answered politely. He greeted me gently, surveying my appearance rigorously enough to make me uncomfortable. His eyes were plunging towards territory that William would have kicked his ass over and we'd barely just met.

Beryx appeared to be around the same age that I was. He had auburn coloured hair: long, wavy, and tucked neatly behind his ears. His eyes, strangely enough for a human, were nearly as black as night. If I hadn't been currently seeing an exquisite, remarkable-looking vampire I might have been interested.

'What do you do?' I asked, trying to stop all the staring.

He looked up and scratched at his chin, finally releasing my hand.

'Beryx is my assistant,' Chester said, answering for him and frowning. 'You'll have to forgive his bad manners. As you can imagine we are here quite a lot and don't get out much. I imagine that he hasn't seen a girl of your beauty. Ever.'

Beryx flushed a deep shade of red and looked away. 'That's not true,' he mumbled under his breath, blushing a shade deeper. 'Not that you're not beautiful. It's just that I go to school and there are girls there. Some are pretty, some are not so much, but I do see pretty girls.'

'I'm real happy for you, Beryx,' I said, smiling awkwardly and praying hard for a subject change. 'What is it that you both do, anyway?'

'I'm a molecular biologist, specialising in gene mutations and cell development,' Chester continued. 'Beryx is studying human movement and development, as well as taking genetics as a secondary course at the university.' He smiled like a proud father. 'But if we are being very specific, I myself also have a degree in psychology and business management, with a minor study in languages and foreign correspondence *and* chemistry.'

'So you're a major smart ass then?' I said, my gaze zeroing in on an e-mail programme sitting open on one of the lab techs' computer screens. Sniggers erupted from around the room, including from a few people I hadn't met yet. Eavesdropping was such a bad habit.

Chester frowned, tugging at his suspenders and letting them snap back loudly against his chest. His hands quickly found solace in the pockets of his pants, perhaps to hide his tightly clenched fists. 'I wouldn't say that I was a *smart ass*, as you so rudely put it.'

I focused my full attention on him now, a half-smile forming on my lips. 'It wasn't a question, Chester.'

Beryx had a smile fixed awkwardly on his face, features still flushed from embarrassment. Stephanie covered her head with her hands to hide a smirk, and Anica looked so confused that I wanted to buy her a translator.

I walked over to the computer I'd spied before, ignoring the people that were still laughing. 'Can I use this for a minute?'

Chester shook his head. 'No.'

I probably shouldn't have insulted him.

'I won't be long and I promise I won't read any private data. I just want to tell Lucas I'm okay.'

The room fell quiet.

'I said, no.'

I put my hands on my hips and tried not to glare at him. 'What about a phone then?'

'Not right now.'

I changed tactics. 'Chester. May I *please* use the telephone?'

Ten points to me. That actually sounded so sincere that even George would be proud.

Beryx chuckled, turning back to look at the screen behind him. Anica had already darted off to study some documentation that was pinned up against the back wall. Stephanie was now loading small vials of blood into a centrifuge and cataloguing the details.

'We don't really have the time right now,' Chester said, turning away and heading over to a small desk that was littered with papers.

'But last night you promised that I could use a phone in the morning. Well, it's morning now. At least, I think it is. You really can't tell with that stupid film all over the windows. Do you know it's bad for you not to have at least some daily exposure to the sun? It creates a vitamin D deficiency, which I'm sure you know given your pasty pallor. No offence.'

'Are you finished?'

'I just want to use the phone.'

'Later.'

I frowned, following him. 'Chester, you do realise that even in prison the inmates are allowed to make one phone call.' I narrowed my eyes at him. 'Don't make me ask for a lawyer.'

Chester laughed in spite of himself.

Who said I was joking?

'Tell you what, Elena. Let's get these initial tests out of the way first and then we can go and use the phone.'

I patted the knife that was still strapped defiantly to the side of my leg. 'You better mean that.'

Or I'll gut you like a fish …

Kidding! As if. I'm defiant, not a psychopath.

Chester swallowed, jaw clenched, perhaps taking a moment to choke back a nasty rebuttal I would have unleashed if our situation had been reversed. 'Straight after your tests, I promise you can call your family.'

'Fine.' It wasn't like I hadn't expected the IMI to run tests on me when I arrived.

Chester rubbed his hands together eagerly, motioning for Beryx to come and join him. 'I think we'll start with the basics: height, weight, body fat composition, resting heart rate—all that kind of thing.'

'Whatever,' I said, rolling my eyes.

Beryx trotted over to us, tape measure in hand. He also held a clipboard, a pen and a smile as wide as an elephant's ass.

'Where do you want me?' I asked him, lips pouting.

He flushed crimson. 'U-um,' he stuttered, 'y-you can stay where you are, but if you could just s-spread your arms and legs that would be g-good.'

I cocked an eyebrow at him questioningly. Spread your

legs? Okay, I hadn't heard that one for a while. Well, not since Kayla and I had headed to those last few raves together.

Beryx closed his eyes, biting his bottom lip as he attempted to shake off my last comment. He re-opened his eyes a few seconds later and stared at the floor.

'Easy there, Beryx,' I murmured, smiling up at him. 'That won't be the last time you say that to a girl.'

His dark eyes snapped up to mine in horror. Chester shook his head, his expression showing he felt like he was dealing with two very trying children. 'Beryx, if you could just get it together long enough to head up the initial tests that would be great.' Chester walked back to his desk and sat down. 'Perhaps you could take Elena into the gymnasium where there is a little bit more room and privacy. I would like you to complete the heart rate tests and physical fitness levels as well.'

'Oh, that just sounds like too much fun,' I muttered sarcastically. With everything they apparently knew about me, didn't anyone here know I hated to exercise?

Chester smacked his lips together, eyeing his blood-red assistant, a small smile on his lips. 'It seems that you and Elena are going to get along just fine.'

I rolled my eyes at his attempt at innuendo. 'Oh, we're going to be just like this,' I said, crossing my fingers. Chester shooed me off with one hand, digging through the pile of papers on his desk with the other. I took note of the phone seated on the desk beside him.

'Elena, would you mind following me, please?' Beryx said, his accent thick but easily understandable now that his stuttering had subsided.

I followed him out of the room, glancing back at the phone on the way. It just didn't make any sense that I'd be forbidden to call my family.

'This way,' Beryx murmured, ushering me along with a gesture.

'So, Beryx, how long have you been working for the IMI?'

He scratched his head while I fell into step beside him. 'Like any other Protector, I started my training here once I turned twelve. Then, after I met Chester, I became interested in some of the research they were doing here and decided to study a similar field at the university. After my first two years obtaining good results, Chester offered me an internship. He said I had *potential*.'

'You speak English really well, too.'

Beryx nodded. 'My mother has always spoken to me in English since I was young. She migrated here from England when she was a teenager and has been living here ever since. My father is Romanian, so I speak both languages fluently.'

'How old are you?'

'I'm twenty.'

Thought so.

Beryx opened the door to the gym and ushered me inside. The lights flickered on the moment the lock re-engaged. A lone treadmill, a few dusty weight machines, and the rather unpleasant odour of stale sweat greeted me as we wound our way to the back of the room.

Beryx placed his clipboard on a small bench in the corner. The bench was covered with moth-eaten towels, and the movement sent plumes of dust billowing in all directions. He sneezed and then quickly gathered up the tape measure, holding it with a fair amount of trepidation.

I grinned. His nervousness was a novelty after hanging around a cocky vampire and a filthy-minded brother for so long. 'You want me to spread it, right?' I didn't wait for him to start blushing again so I changed positions, standing

with my legs apart, arms raised on either side, and waiting
for him to progress past awkward.

Beryx licked his lips as he knelt down beside me. He
measured my arms—their length and breadth—as well as
my head, legs, torso, instep, thighs, and every other part
he could think of. By the time Beryx was done, his hands
were shaking uncontrollably, but he was smiling like he'd
just won the lottery.

And then a thought occurred to me.

Beryx would undoubtedly have an access card to both the
laboratory and elevator.

'Okay, I'm done,' he said, climbing off the floor, almost
bumping my nose with his rapidly ascending head.

'What do you want me to do now?' I said, in the most
flirtatious voice I could muster. I even batted my eyelids
for good measure.

Beryx licked his lips again, staring hungrily at my mouth.
I suddenly imagined him unhinging his jaw and swallowing
me whole like a python.

I stifled a laugh. 'Beryx?'

He shook his head and grabbed the blood pressure
machine tucked inconspicuously under the bench, wrapping
it around my arm. While he pumped, he continued to stare.
The guy had a one-track mind.

'So, do you live here, too?' I asked. 'In the building, I
mean.'

'No, I still live at home with my parents. It's just easier
while I'm studying.'

'Are you here every day?'

Beryx shook his head again. 'No, I'm only here on
Mondays, Wednesdays, and Fridays, or unless lectures are
cancelled or I'm bored.'

'Do you get bored often?'

He nodded. 'Sometimes I *do* feel like I live here.'

I dived right in. 'But, when you are here, don't you feel like you're trapped in a bubble?'

'What do you mean?'

'It's so closed off from everything. My room is like a little white box with only one way in or out, and that only leads to more white boxes. I don't even have a window to look out of and I bet there's a great view of the city from the outside.'

'There is. I mean, there was, but now that the windows are covered up it's hard to tell.'

'The IMI covered up the windows recently?'

He nodded. 'About a month ago.'

Right after my decision to come here, I bet.

'It would have been nice to see the city,' I said, gently pressing the issue.

'You know, from this floor alone there used to be an excellent view of University Square,' Beryx mused.

'University Square?'

'It's quite famous, kind of a local landmark. It's five minutes' walk from here—across the road from school, so I don't have to worry about catching public transport.'

Well, that was so much easier than I'd thought.

'Wow, that's amazing,' I gushed, delighted. 'What about this building? Is it just another crummy high-rise?'

Beryx pulled a face. 'This *hotel* is one of the most popular places to stay in all of Bucharest. It is certainly not a 'crummy high-rise', as you put it. The top three levels are used as the IMI's headquarters and the remaining nineteen are for accommodation. That's how we bankroll the entire project.'

'It's not a very good hotel though, is it?' I said, playing along but trying not to push too far. 'I mean, they don't even give you a telephone in your room, and frankly, the cell phone reception up here is crap.'

He smiled. 'Is that why you and Chester are at odds?'

'Yes. I just wanted to call my family to let them know I'd arrived safely.'

Among other things ...

'Well, good luck with that. This floor is restricted. Incoming and outgoing calls are all monitored. And as for your cell phone, you won't be able to use it.'

'Why not?'

'There are jamming devices installed for security reasons.' Beryx paused, unwinding a stethoscope from around his neck. He placed the chest piece under the blood pressure cuff on my arm and listened, writing the results down on his clipboard.

'Why do they go to so much effort? What are you guys working on in the labs to warrant such extreme measures?'

'Now, if I told you that I'd have to kill you.' Beryx smiled but there was a truth behind that smile. I returned the gesture, wanting to keep the information flowing. He released the air from the cuff, unwrapping it and tossing it onto the bench behind him.

I moved closer to him, wanting to keep him focused on me and my line of questioning. 'So, back to my cell phone ...'

He shook his head. 'No good. You'll either have to wait patiently for Chester to let you use the phone or you'll have to take the elevator down to the tourist accommodation levels to find a signal.'

'I noticed that they do video surveillance here, too?'

'Only in the labs and the corridor. The private quarters are always left unmonitored for privacy reasons.'

'Even mine?'

Beryx licked his lips again and glanced down at my mouth. 'As far as I know.'

Bam! Just ten minutes later and all of my major questions were answered.

I took a step back, and his eyes flicked upwards as he shook his head again. 'Would you mind running on the treadmill now?'

I placed more space between us. 'Why?'

'I need to check your resting and accelerated heart rate.' Beryx moved forward again, tentatively reaching for my arm.

'Running won't make a difference.'

He stared at me blankly, his fingers circling my wrist to take my pulse. 'Why not?'

This is Vampire 101 stuff—how could he not know this?

'I was born a vampire, Beryx, I self-heal. I could run for three days straight and never get tired or puffed out.' Okay, not entirely true. I would eventually fall asleep on my feet but technically I still wouldn't be physically exhausted.

'I'd like to see that.' Beryx's eyes dropped down to my chest.

What you really mean is that you'd like to watch my boobs bouncing up and down, right?

'Is it really necessary that I do this?'

Beryx scratched at his head again and glanced at his clipboard. 'Chester said—'

'Okay, okay, but I did warn you.' Sometimes it was just quicker to do what was relatively painless and save the complaints for something a little more worthwhile.

Sighing, I jumped up onto the treadmill. Removing my sweater, I used the sleeve to wipe away a layer of dust on the controls and started jogging. I was careful to adjust my speed to suit my usual running stride. Truthfully, I was surprised the mechanical mat moved at all without any groans of protest, given the serious lack of underuse this room seemed to have undergone lately. 'How long do you want me to do this for?'

'About ten minutes, I suppose.'

'Ten minutes, ten hours—it's all the same.'

'Why did you take your sweater off?'

'Because I'm still mostly human and I perspire. I'm not a full vampire yet and can't regulate my temperature.'

'You mean because you're not dead yet?'

I shrugged. 'Well if you want to put it *that* way.'

Beryx looked confused as he pointed at my legs. 'Don't you get tired at all? Don't you have muscle spasms or cramps or anything like that?'

'I feel momentary muscle burn or strain in my joints, but my self-healing kicks in so quickly that I really don't register the more uncomfortable moments.'

'What about your breathing?'

'I told you, I don't get puffed.' I paused. 'What exactly *do* you know about me, Beryx?'

He hesitated, looking back down at his clipboard and twirling the pen around in his fingers. 'Not much.'

I kept running. 'What exactly is "not much?"'

A guilty look danced across his features. 'I'm not allowed to discuss that kind of information with you.'

Hmph. So now he decides to clam up.

'You're probably right,' I said, changing tactics. 'You and I don't know each other very well yet, do we?' I flashed him another sweet smile.

'I don't think that really makes—'

Then the door to the gym beeped as it unlocked and opened, and Beryx quickly went quiet.

Stephanie rounded the opening and smiled. 'I just thought I'd come and get you, Elena. I need to do some blood work on you.'

Of course you do.

I slowed down and stepped off the treadmill. Beryx came rushing over to take my pulse, pressing his fingers against the side of my wrist and counting out the beats. When he was done he looked back at me, amazed. 'You were right.'

I smiled. 'I usually am. It's just a shame that no one else realises that until after.'

Beryx grinned as he wrote down the results, simultaneously scooping down to pick up my sweater off the floor. 'Thanks,' I said, grabbing it off him and throwing it back on as I followed Stephanie out.

As I left, I turned and flashed Beryx a final, teasing smile. *I'm so bad.*

'Where to now?' I asked Stephanie.

'I'm taking you to my private lab. There's a small cot in there that you can lie down on if you feel nauseated by the sight of blood.'

Ha—freaking—ha.

Stephanie led me down the white corridor to a room marked 'Lab 2'. Beryx had been hot on our heels but walked past us as we slowed, heading back to the original lab. He turned and waved eagerly to me, waiting for my return gesture before disappearing inside. I could tell that I was going to have my hands full later with that one.

I followed Stephanie into the second lab, closing the door behind me. As the lights clicked on, I found myself in yet another room decked out in white laboratory equipment. Stephanie moved away to a bench in the corner and gestured for me to take a seat on the small, white cot behind her. I obliged, having no interest in perusing the data charts and chemical beakers strewn about.

Stephanie pulled out a piece of rubber from the top desk drawer and wrapped it around the top of my arm, just above the elbow. She flicked my skin a couple of times, trying to find a good vein. Turning back to the bench top behind her, Stephanie grabbed a freshly packaged syringe, a few vials, and some alcoholic swabs that I'd smelt the second she'd opened the packets.

She swabbed my skin and then ripped the plastic packaging open to assemble the syringe. 'Are you ready? Would you prefer to lie down?'

I shook my head. 'It's fine.'

Stephanie gently placed my arm on the raised trolley by the side of the cot for ease of access. I felt a sharp prick as the needle slid into my arm, and a slight dizziness overcame me.

'Your blood is absolutely amazing, you know,' she enthused, exchanging one of the now full vials for an empty one. 'I have been studying it for a few years now, and believe it or not, I still can't seem to figure out the logistics of your twenty-fourth chromosome. We have no idea how it ties in to the composition of your blood or the properties behind your consistently regenerative qualities. I mean, I have theories about your DNA, but …' Stephanie paused. 'You know, it's funny. Now that I'm seeing you in the flesh, it's quite clear to me that it's not just your blood that is affected by this genetic anomaly.'

'What do you mean?' I said warily.

'Well, of course I've seen photos of you. I practically watched you grow up but that's nothing compared to seeing you in the flesh.'

'Stephanie, I'm still not sure I'm following.'

She emptied my blood into the last vial, extracting the syringe and taking off the rubber band on my upper arm. As she turned around to grab a gauze pad, a small globule of red, hot blood poked its way out of the newly formed hole in my arm. I sucked in the heavenly scent of its aroma, but while I considered whether to lick my arm clean, the hole closed up again and took what little blood there was with it.

Stephanie swivelled in her seat, staring down at my newly-healed arm. 'Well, I guess I should have expected that.' She smiled. 'Guess you won't need a Band-Aid then?' She stood up and started writing on the side of each of the blood vials.

'Stephanie?'

'Hmm?'

'What did you mean about my blood not being the only thing affected by my breeding?'

She didn't look up. 'Well, from what Anica's studies have shown so far—as well as that of countless other scientists over the years at the IMI—your vampiric genes seem to predispose you to self-healing and, consequently, contribute to your natural good looks.' Stephanie laughed. 'But you probably knew all that already.'

I waved her on.

'Well, given that you have werewolf DNA mixed into your extra chromosome, we expected some sort of outward, observable changes. It doesn't seem to have had any effect on your growth as a regular human, though. Past tests have indicated that your internals, reproductive capabilities, and physical appearance are all like that of any other human or born vampire of your age. It's only been since that first incident where you drank blood that we've been wondering if our earlier theories about the Vânător gene remaining dormant were true. Although there appears to be no indicators of any changes within your blood, your instincts and physicality seem to have slightly altered, possibly dragging that more dormant side of your nature to the surface—and particularly since you started drinking blood again.'

'What do you mean *again*? The first time I'd drank blood was when I'd encountered John, that Alpha.'

Stephanie's eyes widened slightly but quickly returned to neutral. 'Of course, how silly of me. It was a bad choice of words.'

'Wait. Are you saying I've drunk blood before?'

Stephanie turned away and shook her head, her eyes focusing back on the vials of blood before her. Her hands began to shake. 'No, like I said, just a bad choice of words.'

She's definitely lying to me.

'I don't think it was. Chester hinted at the fact that I'd met him before when I was younger. Had I drank blood then?'

'Not as far as I know,' Stephanie said, smiling brightly.

I wanted to discuss it further, but she'd closed off from me for now. 'What about the changes you were talking about? What did you mean?'

'It's nothing. You probably already sense the changes within you. What difference do my perceptions make?'

'I'm curious, I guess. No one at the IMI back home was scientifically minded. There wasn't anyone I could ask about my genes there. You said you've been studying my blood for years, so I guess I just wanted to know what you've figured out.'

Stephanie finally looked back at me, though her eyes appeared slightly unfocused as if stuck somewhere in the fog of her own thoughts. 'Tell me something, Elena. Did you enjoy drinking the Alpha's blood?'

Was there much point lying about it? 'Yes, I enjoyed it.'

'Would you do it again?'

'I honestly don't know.'

'Do you need it?'

I shook my head and laughed nervously. 'No, of course not. I'm still human, albeit with a few weird modifications—but I'm still human.'

'Does the taste of the blood seem familiar to you?'

'Are we digressing here or talking about my childhood again, perhaps?'

Stephanie looked away again. 'How far back can you remember?'

My eyes narrowed to slits. 'Is there a particular memory of mine you're hoping will surface?'

'Do you remember having bitten anyone before?'

This was starting to annoy me. 'Well, are you talking about the day I chewed my way out of my dead mother's womb? Or are you talking about the day I took a chunk out of Lucas's shoulder?'

Stephanie stiffened.

'Either way, I don't remember either incident. The first one happened the day I was born, and biting Lucas happened when I was three or four. Even Lucas doesn't remember the incident all that clearly.' I stood up from the cot slowly. 'Do you want to tell me where you're going with these questions?'

She sighed, flexing her fingers on the edge of the counter. 'Chester wanted to know if you remembered much of your past.'

'Why?'

Stephanie shrugged, the dim expression on her face suddenly replaced with another bright smile. I could see she was forcing it, her cheeks pushed out beyond straining point.

Okay, I wanted her to stop now because she was really starting to freak me out.

'It's a standard question.'

I could feel my brow pucker into a deeper frown. 'Then why don't I believe you?'

A haughty look crossed her features. 'Do they not seem like important questions to ask of a *supposed* human who enjoys drinking blood?'

'I guess so but—'

'No buts,' Stephanie interrupted. 'Some of these questions might lead to answers that will help me piece together some much needed information!'

'Such as?'

'Do you know how unlikely it is for you to have been born with your blood, blood that is genetically untainted and without type?'

I shrugged.

'It's impossible,' she continued. 'There has never been one historically documented case like yours before. All humans are born with a blood type. There are markers in the blood reflecting as much but not for you. You have a type all of your own now.'

'Okay.'

'I call it type 'X'.'

'That's original.'

'What would you call blood of a type you've never seen before?'

I felt myself shrugging again.

Stephanie slammed her fist down on the counter top, her teeth grinding together in agitation. 'Damn it! I really need to figure this all out. I need to understand you, Elena!'

'Okay, okay, calm down.'

'I can't calm down. So much is at stake and yet you baulk at answering a few, simple questions!'

'Well, what exactly is at stake?'

Stephanie's agitation seemed to ebb again, and she took a quick, deep breath that seemed to calm her considerably. She waved a quick hand in dismissal. 'It's nothing. I get a little too excited sometimes when I talk about blood.'

I was still frowning. 'Have you considered other hobbies?'

Stephanie forced a laugh. 'Perhaps I should.'

We were both quiet for a minute, the two of us standing there awkwardly. 'Do you know why I have funky blood?' I finally asked, breaking the silence between us.

'It's all just speculation. I have no real proof.'

'What have you got?'

That excited look slowly crossed Stephanie's features again. 'I have blood comparisons from other born vampires of your age. Those comparisons are technically tied to their human lives so they still have blood types and distinguishable markers. I'm starting to think that your uniqueness and rare blood quality may have less to do with you and more to do with *who* you might have inherited it from.'

'Hey?'

She sat down again on the stool in front of me. I resumed my earlier position on the cot. 'Your blood had to come from somewhere.'

'My parents?'

Stephanie shook her head and scooted her chair closer to me. 'I'm not talking about your mother.'

I swallowed. 'Then, my father?'

She nodded slowly, glancing over her shoulder as if afraid someone might be listening in.

'Do you know who he is?' I whispered, a strange sense of curiosity washing over me.

Stephanie turned to face me again, drawing nearer. 'No. No one here actually knows who he is, and that has always been the great mystery.'

'So what makes you think all my specialness comes from my father?'

'He *is* a vampire. That much is obvious, so he must be the carrier. Plus, your mother passed all the tests as a regular human.'

'But I also have Vânător in me.'

'Which is something that should have hindered your cell development, yet here you are, compositionally perfect. No, it has to be from your father. There has to be something that sets him apart from others of his kind because I've tested numerous vampires before, both turned and born— as well as vânătors—but have never come across blood like yours until now. It's almost as if you were manufactured, not born.'

I tried not to think of myself as whitegoods. 'But I *was* born.'

'Yes, you were.' Stephanie smiled, getting up from her stool. She walked back to her lab bench and arranged the vials of my blood onto a stand, placing them in the small fridge at the end of the counter. 'I should probably get you back to Chester now. He has some other tests that he wants to perform and doesn't like it when I hold him up.' She paused, thumbing the pen in front of her. 'Can I ask you something?'

'Okay.'

'If for some reason there was a way to use your blood to help people—sick people—would you donate it willingly?'

What a strange question.

'I guess it depends. If you figured out a cure for cancer or something and my blood was the answer ... then, yes, of course I would. It would be selfish of me not to. Why? Is that what you're hoping to achieve, why there's so much at stake?'

Stephanie shook her head, her mask of neutrality closing back over. 'No. Forget I asked. I guess I just wanted to know what you would do if someone actually asked you.'

'As opposed to forcing me?'

'Yes. No. Elena, are you planning on breaking out of here?'

Okay, subject change.

'Why? Are you about to hand out directions?'

She didn't find that amusing. 'The IMI will not willingly let you leave.'

'So I figured.'

'I mean it, Elena. Leaving here is not an option.'

'Did Chester tell you to say that?'

Stephanie fidgeted, looking at the camera mounted up near the top of the door. 'I just don't want to see any unnecessary pain befall you. You seem like a nice girl.'

'I'm really not. Ask Chester—he'll tell you.'

'He doesn't know you.'

'None of you do.'

Stephanie frowned. 'Please, Elena. I wouldn't have said anything if it wasn't important.'

'Point duly taken.'

'So you won't try to leave?'

I smiled for the first time since our conversation had started. 'Not today.'

CHAPTER THREE: MESSAGES

waited as the phone rang, anxiously lacing my fingers around the curls of the telephone cord as each dial went by unanswered. Granted, it was one o'clock in the morning back home in Cairns, but Lucas would answer soon enough. Who else would be rude enough to call at this hour of the morning?

Come on, Lucas, please pick up.

I'd finally been permitted to use the IMI's telephone. Of course, Chester allowing me its usage was based solely on my agreeing to comply with all initial testing. He'd just neglected to say that the initial testing was going to carry on for five days. I probably should have asked for more detail when I'd agreed, but I guess you never could predict when someone was going to screw you over for simple telephone privileges.

I'd thought about stabbing Chester.

Yes. I really had. Especially on day three, when my cell phone battery died and my charger's plug wouldn't fit into their European outlets. Dialling out might have been a bum option according to Beryx but it still really pissed me off.

Okay, so—honestly—I wasn't really going to stab anybody. As much as Chester seemed to be morphing into an irritating prick, he wasn't the Devil and he didn't deserve to be stabbed, at least, not fatally.

Besides, grievous bodily harm had been struck from the

schedule two days ago. Someone who shall remain nameless had snuck into my room while all of these 'tests' were being performed and had taken all of the weaponry out of my suitcase. Not to mention that the trusty knife I'd been hiding underneath my pillow was also gone, stolen while I was sleeping.

That part freaked me out the most. So, I guess that he who shall remain nameless deserved a round of applause for being able to get one past me. They also deserved genital crabs.

So, the stabbing idea was well and truly out. Unfortunately, that also left me at the mercy of the IMI. I was still ace at hand to hand combat and strong enough to literally poke someone's eyes out but was using those skills warranted? What real harm had befallen me besides rigid phone privileges and stolen property?

Oh yeah, that's right.

They'd also infringed on my personal space; had put me through endless questioning and tests, including the monitoring of both my physical and emotional state; and there was also this really weird obsession Chester had with poking around inside my mouth, looking for fangs.

Ring-ring. Ring-ring. Ring-ring.

Just because the smell of blood was enticing, and I was partial to its taste, did not mean I was going to be able to whip out a set of sharp teeth every time a crazy scientist stuck a popsicle stick in my mouth or waved a packet of Synth Blood in front of me.

'Hello?'

'Lucas!' I all but squealed down the phone.

'E?'

'Yeah, it's me! What took you so long to pick up?'

'I was asleep,' he answered groggily. Then Lucas cleared

his throat and yawned. 'Why haven't you called? You left almost a week ago.'

'I've been trying to, Lucas, believe me,' I groaned.

'So what was the hold-up? Did you forget how to use a phone?'

'No. I wanted to call you but I haven't been allowed near a phone until now.'

'What do you mean allowed?' he said, suddenly sounding infinitely more awake now than before.

I paused and took a deep breath. 'You know, you were right about me not coming here.'

'What's happened?'

'Nothing really. They've been fairly accommodating considering. It's just ...'

'It's just what?'

'I know their amicable behaviour is only temporary. Chester told me that the IMI has no intentions of releasing me. They have cell phone blockers so I can't contact you guys, they won't let me use the telephone unless they say so, I can't use the computers ... I have no other contact with the outside world. They even stole my weapons; I feel like I'm living in a prison, and they're running tests on me nonstop. I just want to come home, but I know that I can't do that either.'

'Elena, how—'

The phone went dead.

'Hello? Lucas?' I shook the receiver and then held it back up against my ear. 'Hello?'

The door behind me flew open, shuddering violently against the rubber door stopper. A man I'd never seen before entered, yanked the phone out of my hand and slammed it back onto the cradle. Looking cranky, he started yelling at me in Romanian. He was spitting quite a bit, too, narrowly missing me with each foul-smelling projectile.

I couldn't understand anything he was saying but it was obvious he'd been listening into my phone call. He kept pointing angrily at the phone and saying 'No! No! No!', all the while accompanying his babbling with other, questionable hand gestures requiring limited translation. It was quite rude, actually.

'I can't understand you,' I shouted. 'You need to speak English if you expect an answer.'

The man paused to listen for only a second before continuing to rant at me like a lunatic. Was he deaf? He kept shaking his head, pointing at the phone and repeating that 'No! No! No!' mantra, like I'd suddenly understand him just because his voice raised another octave.

I shook my head in frustration. 'Thank you,' I shouted above him, voice dripping with sarcasm. I gave him the snidest version of a thumbs-up that I could manage. 'I understood that crap so much better the second time around. Maybe you should yell louder.'

The man blinked at me and stopped. My thumbs-up must have thoroughly confused him.

As Chester walked in a moment later the man turned, launching into another incomprehensible discussion in Romanian. He used a lot more hand gestures this time, mostly involving fingers pointed either at me or at the phone. I decided that if the stranger didn't stop waving his digits in my face, I was going to shove them up his nose, all the way in and past the knuckles.

Chester listened carefully, occasionally looking at me as the story built into a crescendo of guttural noise. He nodded patiently, promptly ending the conversation a few minutes later when I let out a loud sigh of boredom. With a few short words, Chester ushered the disgruntled man from the room, closing the door as he left. It was suddenly very quiet in the small space.

It was Chester's turn to sigh, pinching at the bridge of his nose. Perhaps George could've shipped over his stockpile of blood pressure medication.

'Elena, you disappoint me.'

I frowned. 'I wasn't aware that my private conversation was under such scrutiny.' I should have realised, though.

Chester waved a hand to shut me up. 'I know that you are not exactly happy about being here, but kindly do not tell anyone, even Lucas, what we do at this facility. And I'd appreciate it if you did not talk about the IMI in such a defamatory fashion.'

'Come again?'

'I do not want you badmouthing this facility or anyone in it.'

I wasn't really sure what to say to that.

'Elena, you may talk about the weather, your interests, Romanian television shows or anything else of unimportance. But, and I warn you now, if personnel overhear anything in your conversations that translates as sensitive they will cut you off immediately, and you will be banned from all phone privileges in the future.'

'You are joking, right?' I felt like I'd landed smack-bang in the middle of a straight-to-DVD thriller. So their plan was: isolate me, experiment on me, and then kill me? Sure, that would have been totally cool if I hadn't been the main character.

'I don't joke,' Chester answered.

I shook my head slowly, my disbelief evident. 'You know this isn't the CIA, right? You're not in the FBI or the NSA or any other government acronym you can name.'

'Your sarcasm does not amuse me.'

'But it's just a phone call. My brother's a Protector like one of you, and all I was doing was whingeing to him, not divulging world-ending secrets. I'm allowed to whinge—it's in the teenage handbook. Look it up, it's not illegal.'

Chester shook his head at me. 'You have no rights here, Elena. You are an outsider.'

'But Lucas isn't. He's a Protector.'

'For now.'

'What the hell does that mean?'

'Do not raise your voice at me.'

I snorted. 'That was not raised, Chester. I can yell louder if you like. My point is that this argument shouldn't be happening at all. Outsider or not, I've been more than compliant with all of your absurd and ridiculously drawn out demands.'

'You're here for as long as I say you are here.'

'So we're back to that again?' I frowned deeply. 'I seem to remember us having this conversation five days ago, Chester. I said then that I was only going to stay here as long as it was necessary. You can't hold me here against my will.'

Chester gave me a thin smile. 'As the head of the research department, I can do whatever I want and I don't owe an orphan child like you any explanations.'

'But I just want to use the phone.'

'Then comply.'

I took one deep, calming breath. 'This is total bullshit. The problem isn't even really the phone call, is it? It's just a way for you to mark your territory. Why all the pretence, why let me think I'd be free to call home, anyway? It's clear now more than ever that you have zero intentions of letting me out of here, so why pretend I have any choices?'

'You do have choices.'

'Then organise me a flight back home. I'll sort out the Alpha situation some other way.'

Chester's contrived smile turned somewhat devious, his

annoying gold tooth shimmering under the fluorescents above. 'That ship has sailed. Living in Cairns was only a temporary arrangement, one that kept you distanced from the vampires and vânătors. Now that the situation has changed and both species are aware of your existence, it's imperative that we keep you to ourselves.'

'To what end? And don't tell me it's for the greater good or for the safety of those around me. I can't believe that you would keep me here if there wasn't something else you wanted from me, something that you'd considered worth hiding all these years.'

'That is true.'

'Then, what is it?'

Chester shook his head. 'That's privileged information.'

I gaped at him. 'I want out of here, Chester—now.'

'That won't be possible, I'm afraid.'

I took another deep, deep breath and then another. The situation had escalated so quickly I now felt myself quivering with rage. 'If I want to leave, I can. You and the IMI should probably know that before this goes too much further.' I hadn't felt this cornered or angry since John had abducted me. The ironic thing was that Chester had called vânătors 'monsters'. Then what the hell did that make him?

Chester actually had the nerve to laugh. 'I'd almost forgotten what it's like to witness a teenage outburst. It makes me thankful that I never had children. Now, would you like to try that phone call again? Or do you need another couple of days to think about your behaviour before I let you near another telephone?'

I started muttering to myself and fought back the sudden urge to choke Chester to death with his own suspenders. He ignored me. 'I said, do you want to try that phone call again? Or do you want to go back to testing?'

I'd like to test my foot in your face. Does that count?

'All I want is to get out of here, but since I haven't figured out when and how to do that just yet, I'll take the damn phone call.'

Chester looked positively smug. 'Just remember that we are always listening.'

'It's good that there are a lot of things I know how to say without speaking, isn't it?' I gave him the finger, just to prove my point. Childish, I know, but I couldn't help myself. I should've screamed instead.

'And so the teenage theatrics roll on,' Chester said, his tone droll and nose turned up at my extended digit. He gestured to the phone sitting on the side of the table and settled himself comfortably into the chair behind his desk. He started, drumming his fingers on the worktop and waiting for my next move.

Putting my fingers to better use, I ignored him and began to dial Lucas's mobile number again. How was I going to get out of here? I couldn't exactly talk to Lucas about it in front of Chester. I couldn't make a run for it, either, with the building filled with magic users. What I really needed was one of those access cards … or William. If he'd have shown up right now that would've been perfect.

Lucas picked up on the fourth ring. 'Elena?'

'Yeah, it's me again.'

'What just happened?'

Chester leaned forward on his chair, flashing me a warning look.

I turned my back on him, mostly because if I looked at his face right now I'd probably shove my fist right through it. 'We must have got cut off.'

'Are you okay? You sound like you hate it there, you said it was like a—'

'I was just kidding,' I said quickly, cutting him off mid-sentence. 'Sometimes I look around this place and catch myself thinking that I'll never leave.'

'O-kay,' Lucas said, enunciating the word slowly. 'Elena? What's really going on?'

'I can't say.'

'You can't say because you're not sure? Or you can't say because you really can't say?'

'I really can't say.'

'Is someone listening to you?'

I laughed nervously. 'You could say that.'

'So what can you say?'

'Very little, apparently.'

'I see,' Lucas said quietly.

'How are things with you?' I probed. 'Have the Vânători made contact again?'

'Nah, it's been really quiet here. A few did pass through town after the Alpha left, presumably to make sure you hadn't returned to Cairns, but nothing since. This place is totally boring without you. I mean everything is exactly the same as before: school, work, training, Mum's shitty cooking. I hate that you're gone.'

'I meant what I said, Lucas. When I can, I'll come home.'

'You better.' He sighed. 'I mean, I love Mum and Dad—you know that—but I don't have the same relationship with them that I have with you. Sometimes it doesn't even make sense that we're not related. Do you know what I mean?'

'I do. That's why I'm here, remember?'

I wouldn't put up with this shit for anyone else.

'I remember.' Lucas was silent for a moment. 'This might sound crazy, but the second that your plane was up in the air, something in me started to, I don't know ... change.'

'What do you mean?'

'It's hard to say. And I'm not sure what I mean. I just feel kinda strange all over now that you're gone.'

'Maybe you're coming down with the flu?'

'Maybe,' he concurred. 'Hey, can you tell me anything about headquarters? Mum and Dad won't give me squat.'

'I'll bet,' I answered bitterly.

Lucas was quiet again, no doubt sensing my discontent. 'What's the view like from your window?'

'What?'

'I said, what's the view—'

'I heard you, Lucas, I'm just not sure I—' A slow smile spread across my face when I realised what he was getting at. 'There isn't one.'

'What a bummer to be in Bucharest and not able to see any of it. It's probably because you're underground, isn't it?'

'No. Actually, it's so nice here I feel like I'm staying in a hotel.'

'That must be nice. I'm glad they're looking after you. Mum said as much when she spoke to Chester a couple of days ago. She also said that there were a lot of Protectors to watch over you. At least … one hundred?'

'Double that figure.'

'That's a lot of firepower.'

I blew out a frustrated breath that stirred the loose hair of my fringe. 'Tell me about it.'

'I wonder if they'll show you any of the local sights while you're there.'

'I hope I get to see University Square. Apparently it's pretty much central to everything and within walking distance of anything worth visiting.' I looked over my shoulder. Chester had started to get up from his chair. He did not look particularly happy with me, and when Lucas didn't answer me immediately, I started to worry I'd pushed my luck again.

Then Lucas coughed, and I sagged with relief. 'Any other defining landmarks you're interested in?'

'No, but hopefully that won't matter.'

'Why?'

'I want to see them for myself.'

'Planning a field trip?'

I looked back at Chester, who was gripping his desk tightly, his eyes narrowing and lips set in a thin line of disapproval. 'Yeah. The sooner the better.'

'I understand,' Lucas answered. 'I'm sorry.'

'Don't apologise. You did warn me.'

I looked away from Chester again, twisting the phone cord around my fingers. 'Are you still in contact with—' I racked my brains, thinking of another name for William.

'Yes, I am,' he said, catching on immediately. I didn't know why I called Lucas a dumbass all the time. He was actually smarter than I gave him credit for.

'And?'

'He called yesterday. He's tying up some loose ends but did say that he was going on an extended vacation soon.'

'Any idea when he's planning on leaving?'

Lucas groaned. 'I didn't think things would be this bad, Elena,' he whispered. 'You shouldn't have to rely on him, so I'm so sorry.'

'When is he leaving, Lucas?' I said, more forcibly than before.

'Any day now,' he said miserably, frustration evident in his voice. 'But he said something about making a few stops along the way. He didn't give me any information, of course, but you know how he is. He is worried, though.'

'Did he say as much?'

'Yes. He's wondering why his travelling companion hasn't been returning his phone calls.'

'Maybe there isn't any cell phone reception where she is?'
'Sounds like a good reason.'
'Maybe you could help him find her, Lucas?'
'I'll try, but I haven't got much to work with.'

The door to the room flew open again and the same disgruntled man from earlier charged over to Chester's desk, talking in hushed Romanian. The man was relentless. 'I have to go, Lucas. I miss you, but make sure that you don't make a fuss over me. I wouldn't want anyone to worry, and it might cause problems here.' I paused. 'You know what I mean, right? When people worry, word generally gets around.'

'Got it,' Lucas said. 'Will we be talking anytime soon?'

I glanced over my shoulder; both men were glaring at me, expressions irritated. 'It doesn't look like it but hopefully the field trip might work out.'

'Be careful, E.'

'In or out, Lucas, apparently it doesn't matter.'

'I'll fix this.'

'You can't. Just tell our friend that I wish him well on his vacation, and that I can't wait to see him again.'

'I will.'

'Don't forget to remind him that travelling can be very dangerous.'

'I'll let him know.'

'Love you, dumbass.'

'You too, dickhead.'

The phone went dead. I placed the receiver back on the cradle, spinning around slowly and ready to face the backlash from the double-layered conversation.

'Who were you talking about?' Chester demanded angrily.

I wrinkled my nose in confusion. 'What are you talking about? Wasn't our conversation menial enough for you?'

'Don't play with me, Elena. I wasn't born yesterday.'

'And?'

'What's his name?' Chester pressed.

I looked at him, my eyes crinkling at the corners and lips curling into a mischievous smile. 'Search me.'

Chester's nostrils flared, his face turning a mottled red. That only made me smile all the wider. 'Answer me, Elena.'

'I just did.'

'You really are trying my patience. If you don't tell me, then I'll have to ask Lucas myself.'

I shrugged. 'You do what you think you have to.'

Chester looked at me for a long time, staring with those huge, magnified brown eyes behind tortoise shell frames, waiting for an answer more to his liking. Such a shame that he wasn't going to get one. Angry red face and gnashing teeth were not going to circumvent my stubbornness.

Eventually, Chester huffed impatiently and turned away from me, talking once again to the podgy man with squalid breath.

'Well, I'll leave you both to it then,' I said, getting up off the chair and calculating the best way to slide out the door without having to touch either one of them. I attempted to shimmy past the stinky Romanian but he wasn't budging.

'Wait,' Chester answered, holding up a hand, 'I'll be escorting you to dinner this evening.' He sneered. 'Apparently Beryx can no longer be trusted around you.'

Busted.

The personnel officer left the room first, sneering at me as he fingered his walkie-talkie like some trigger-happy mall cop. He disappeared behind an unmarked door next to the elevator which I assumed was their surveillance room, judging by my brief glimpse of monitors and assorted computer equipment. I was rewarded with one last angry glare before the door slammed in my face.

Chester placed a warm hand on the small of my back, propelling me down the corridor as he shut the door to his office firmly behind us. I looked up as the small, wall-mounted camera in the corridor whirred around to watch us waiting for the elevator to arrive. I resisted the urge to poke my tongue out.

My stomach suddenly rumbled, embarrassingly loud. With all of the drama in Chester's office, I'd forgotten how hungry I was. The kitchen area, or 'mess hall' as Beryx liked to refer to it as, was where we were headed and was located on the level directly below this one.

Chester called the elevator, his other hand still nestled in the small of my back, trying to hold me in place. His touch sickened me in more ways than I could count, but I had to play this smart, so stayed perfectly still.

We waited.

When the elevator arrived—ping!—I went in first, hugging the corner so that I could keep my eye on Chester at all times. When the doors closed, he wasted no time in re-launching into his tirade. 'I'm watching you, Elena,' he said, stepping closer to me, 'so don't try anything.'

'I don't know what you're talking about. I'm just standing here.'

Chester snorted. 'Don't be smart, girl, because you know exactly what I'm referring to. So don't think for a second that I won't make your life here impossible if you don't start to comply. I will cut all your telephone privileges.' He paused. 'Amongst other things.'

Oh, this I gotta hear.

'Such as?'

'I can take away your privacy, too'

I wondered if Chester even realised what a total asshole he was. I was about to tell him because, I mean, it never hurts to be honest with people. Then I thought about breaking his jaw instead—that'd be fun.

I really need to get out of here.

I started to think through my options. William couldn't be counted on for help. According to Lucas, William was still in Cairns wrapping up loose ends, so it was up to me to get myself out of here. I'd been studying all the possible exit points for the last week and the only way in or out was via the elevator or through the glass windows. There were over two hundred Protectors in this building at any given time, so I'd have to plan my escape logically and carefully. I'd probably only have one chance.

In the meantime?

I stared at Chester, choosing the expression I allowed to cross my features carefully. 'Look, we need to talk,' I said, crossing my arms over my chest.

'I've said all I can say on this matter.'

'Well, just listen then because I'm not done, and I'm only going to say this once.'

'Is that—'

'Stop threatening me,' I interrupted. 'I've killed vânători with my bare hands, consumed blood and have seen things that you can only imagine. You have no idea what I am truly capable of, and as long as I am living and breathing, you never will.' I paused for dramatic effect, leaning in close so I could whisper in his ear. 'And, Chester? Ask yourself this: do you really want to know what I could do to you if you keep threatening me? Because keep pushing me, asshole, and I won't hesitate.'

Chester blanched, taking a quick step back but managing to keep his cool despite the unveiled threat. After several seconds of just staring at me, composure ebbed and ire set in; his face suddenly washed over with red. Chester's hands clenched into fists, and blue, crackling light danced across the knuckles. Despite the display, though, he wisely kept his mouth shut.

When the elevator stopped, I stepped off first, showing Chester I was not afraid to turn my back on him. Plus, with so many people milling about on this floor and heading to dinner, it was unlikely that he would pick now to punish me with so many witnesses around.

I surveyed the familiar area of the mess hall and breathed in the welcoming scent of lasagne, noting the diners' ever-watchful gazes. Half-breed spotting seemed to be a hobby around here.

I tried my best to ignore the scrutiny as I spotted Stephanie on the far side of the large, open dining area, sitting next to Anica.

I grabbed a large plate of meaty lasagne from the counter top and headed over, walking by a group of seated employees who whispered to each other as I passed. There were roughly one hundred people packed into the mess hall tonight, dinner usually being a quiet affair. Most of the staff would head home to their families at night—only the singles, the diehard technicians, and lab workers seemed to hang around after six. Given that it was a Friday night, I wondered what they were all still doing here. The food wasn't that good.

Due to Beryx's loose lips, I'd gained some insight into the IMI's activities. This level alone was full of labs where they conducted weaponry experiments, staged technical training for new Protectors, and carried out many other restricted projects I'd never be permitted to see. Perhaps Friday nights were 'let's test the nuclear warhead' night or 'induction of the new trainees' night. Either way, I didn't care enough to ask because, hopefully, I was getting out of this place tonight.

'Hi, Stephanie,' I said, settling down in the plastic chair beside her. I bobbed my head at Anica.

Stephanie hadn't shown any signs of her split personality since my first day and smiled warmly at me. 'Hi, Elena. How's your day been?'

'Well, today I strolled up and down the corridor a couple of hundred times, you know, just for a change. Then I went for a swim, Anica took some skin samples from my backside, which was then shortly followed by a round of questioning from Chester.' I flashed her a bored look. 'That had to be the highlight of my day because Chester's so much fun. I really have no clue why that guy doesn't have more friends.' I rolled my eyes.

Stephanie chuckled, motioning for me to go on.

'After all of that, I finally got to talk to my brother, followed by some enlightening verbal abuse from that dickhead in suspenders across the room.'

Stephanie's smile dimmed, her gaze flicking across to look at Chester who was settling into a table across the mess hall. 'I'm sorry it's difficult for you here.'

I shook my head. 'Don't worry about it. I've been in worse situations, believe me.'

'I bet you miss your family and friends,' she said, pushing around the lasagne on her plate. I'd already started scarfing mine down. Anica glanced from my face to Stephanie's and then back, probably trying to quickly translate what we were saying but still looking lost. I could have tried talking to her but who could be bothered?

I nodded. 'I know. I've only been here for five days, but I miss my brother like crazy.'

'He's lucky to have a sister that loves him so much.'

'Lucas is my whole life. I would do anything for him.'

'I suspect the feeling is mutual,' Stephanie said, patting my hand. 'It's amazing what you find yourself doing to help the ones that you love, even if what you are doing feels wrong or goes against everything you'd normally believe in.' From the sudden, faraway look in her eyes I realised we were no longer just talking about my relationship with Lucas. I glanced down at the half-eaten lasagne on my plate rather than pushing further.

'So what happens here on the weekends?' I asked, changing the subject.

Stephanie shrugged. 'Not much, Elena. There's no work, which is great. I think most people who live here—like me and Chester—leave the building to clear our heads and try to have a semi-normal life.'

'So no one stays here?'

'Well,' she began, and then hesitated. 'Now that you're here, I suppose Chester or someone else from the lab will stay to keep you company.'

'But not you?'

Stephanie shook her head and buried her fork into the pile of lasagne in front of her. 'No, not me, but since the rest of your Year Eleven requirements have been shipped over from Australia there'll definitely be something to keep you busy.'

I sighed loudly. I'd really hoped those algebra questions were not going to follow me here. How wrong was I? 'Tell me you're kidding? Chester would rather see me bubbling away in a test tube over a Bunsen burner than studying. Why the hell would he bother to make sure I completed Year Eleven?'

Stephanie shrugged, glancing around uncomfortably. 'I don't know, Elena.'

'The guy is whacked. If I were you, I'd go work for someone less crazy.'

She didn't comment, probably because previous experience showed she was a little messed up in the head, too.

Stephanie hadn't even blinked when I'd hinted at Chester's future plans for me—that couldn't be a good sign. I finished off the rest of my meal in silence, dropping my fork in frustration. 'Well, I'll leave you to it then. I hope you have a great weekend, Stephanie. I guess I'll see you Monday. Bye, Anica.'

I walked off without delay. I had no allies in this place and doubted even Beryx, with his weird infatuation for me, would turn his back on the IMI to help bust me out of here.

I searched the crowd for Chester as I crossed the hall, wanting to avoid him so I could get back up to my room and start officially plotting my escape. As usual, he was sitting by himself at one of the tables in the corner. He ate his meal slowly, stopping after every mouthful to daintily wipe at his moustache with a napkin.

Chester looked up as I approached, his expression growing dark. 'Do you want something, Elena?' he asked bitterly.

'When you're ready, I'd like to go back upstairs.'

'I'm not ready; I'm still eating.'

I smirked. 'If you don't want me to loiter, give me your access card and I'll head back up on my own.'

Chester didn't seem amused by my proposition. He pondered the rest of his meal in silence, scraping the last few mouthfuls together, chewing them slowly. After hunting with a napkin for crumbs in his moustache, he'd still made no move to hand me his access card.

When he was finally finished, Chester pushed the plate to

the side and lazily stood, turned and sauntered off towards the elevator.

When the doors slid open, we both walked inside, riding the elevator back up to the top floor without speaking. The tension in the air didn't shift as the doors opened, didn't change as Chester abruptly pushed past me like I was as insignificant as a pebble in his shoe.

As he brushed past, I tripped, falling back against the wall of the elevator so that I had to quickly thrust out my hand and grab the handrail to steady myself. Ironically, Chester's need to be rid of me as he headed straight to his room at the far end of the corridor meant that he was facing away from me and the open elevator doors.

It quickly dawned on me that I was in the 'secure' elevator alone and could go anywhere. No access card required.

Jackpot.

I poked my head around the elevator doors and looked up as the surveillance camera whirred around to watch Chester pacing quickly off down the corridor. Personnel were obviously unaware that I was with him.

This was my best chance, my only chance. I rapidly pressed the button for the ground floor, which I imagined would contain the reception area and lobby. The elevator doors began to close just as Chester turned around, finally realising that I was not keeping pace with him. I gave him a cheeky wave as he stared at me in horror, the shiny metal doors of the elevator rapidly sliding shut.

The elevator began its descent, and I relaxed. The panel in front of me lit up as, one by one, the car passed down through each floor. That strange, rhythmic music kept pace with the elevator's speed as it descended towards the bottom floor.

Soon afterwards, the doors opened, revealing a lavishly

decorated reception area and lobby. There were white marble tiles covering the floors and thick, round pillars of marble that rose to spectacular heights up into the roof, spreading so high that I had to crane my neck in order to see. From the ceiling hung two golden chandeliers covered in hundreds of tiny crystal baubles glittering brightly. Directly under this crowning glory of sparkling lights was a large reception counter, panelled in rich, burnished mahogany. People pressed forward for attention, crowding around the staff. In front was a thick gold plaque spelling out the name of the hotel: The Grand.

I smiled.

Jackpot.

Before the elevator doors closed shut behind me, I reached back inside and quickly pressed the button for every floor from top to bottom. That'd at least slow the IMI's security down. To the right, I quickly spotted a massive, gold-plated revolving door that appeared to lead out onto the street beyond. It was in constant motion, people hurrying in and out: rushing out towards the waiting taxis in the valet area or heading inside to greet waiting friends. I spotted a few people that I recognised from one of the lower level labs lounging together on a couple of leather sofas in the lobby bar. I ducked quickly to the right, keeping out of their line of sight and hurrying towards the exit.

I scanned reception as I walked, aware of the insistent buzz from a telephone at the concierge desk that was practically begging to be answered. A tall, elegantly dressed man with dark hair daintily lifted the receiver. As he talked, the concierge looked around and searched for something in the crowds of people that surged past—searching for me.

I didn't hesitate as I pushed through the spinning glass doors and exited out onto the street.

The smell of exhaust fumes hit me first. Taxis queued in the valet area sat with engines idling, waiting for their fares. There were other scents, too, both strange and unfamiliar, air that was laden with spices and the smells of home-cooked meals and city smog.

I didn't linger, jogging past the taxis and heading out into the nighttime street. I had no clue where to go but decided to head left.

I prayed that my spectacular, off-the-cuff escape didn't draw more unwanted attention. It would be all too easy for a vânător to locate my scent, even amongst the heady aromas of the city. William had once described my smell as completely unique and entirely too appetising, and I didn't want anyone else with a supernatural sense of smell around me when I was without a weapon.

Bucharest was an incredibly noisy city, the air filled with incessant car honking and the lively sounds of people everywhere—talking, laughing, shouting. After my week in captivity, the hubbub surrounding me was overwhelming. I kept jogging, watching vast amounts of traffic stream past and out onto three-lane roads already bursting at the seams.

I smiled at a group of young people as I passed, eliciting two completely different, but not entirely unexpected, reactions: the girls gave me looks of disdain, and the men gave me long, lingering looks of appreciation. I was used to both. I kept smiling, though, happy that I hadn't managed to wander off into some seedy back alley where it was likely I'd get roughed up a little.

I'd found University Square.

To the right, and across yet another busy intersection, was Bucharest University. I would head over there first and see if I could find some nice frat boy to lend me a telephone, maybe offer me a place to stay until I made my next move. I knew I'd be relatively safe there with my scent lost amongst the overly-pungent aroma of young males. At least, that was what I was hoping.

As I made my way towards the intersection, I watched the streaming headlights and the seemingly unending mass of oncoming traffic. My eyes followed the activity, trying to judge when it would be safe to—

Shit!

I froze in mid-stride, my entire body—even my eyes—unable to move. My limbs were locked rigid, feet planted solidly on the ground as if glued there. Someone had just hit me with the Hevannatara spell. How had they found me so quickly?

'Elena,' Chester said firmly, sidling up beside me and placing a hand on my shoulder. 'What did you think you were doing?'

Getting as far away from you as possible.

'You had to have known that you wouldn't get far.'

All I could do was keep watching the traffic passing in front of me. I was going to be as stiff as those four statues in that park behind me for at least five minutes, and judging by the security team that now encircled me, I wasn't going anywhere after that.

'You know, it didn't have to be like this, Elena,' Chester continued. 'I was trying to make sure you were comfortable with us, that you wouldn't feel like you had to run.'

Yeah, well you should have thought about that before you admitted you might kill me in two years.

'I don't think that'll be possible now,' he continued. 'It's now apparent that you have no intention of following our guidelines, so we're going have to take tougher measures with you.'

My fingers began to twitch, and my eyes slowly started to shift. 'I'll leave again,' I slurred through numb lips.

Chester nodded. 'I have no doubt of that. It's why I'm going to move you to a more secure location, somewhere you can't break out of.'

I sniffed. The action started out as an indignant response but it soon turned into something else, something instinctual. I flared my nostrils and sniffed, drawing in the tangle of scents on the wind deep inside in an effort to pinpoint what had drawn my attention. I could smell something ... wrong.

Uh-oh.

My skin began to prickle. Chester was still carrying on about taking me someplace with no phones or chance of escape, but I was too preoccupied to really care.

I could smell an Alpha.

I concentrated as hard as I could on wiggling my fingers, slow at first, but more vigorously as time quickly passed. I tried to get my hands involved, followed by my wrists, arms and, finally, shoulders. This sense of muscles loosening soon spread and quickly the all-over stiffness began to ease.

When I finally managed to stumble into Chester, the Alpha's scent was practically on top of me. Thankfully, Chester had stopped talking long enough to gesture to the security team, who created a tight circle around me. Ironically, they were the least of my problems. Even Chester, with all of his threats, was a piss-ant on my current scale of what constituted an immediate problem. I'd just proven that I could get away from the IMI if I really wanted, but I couldn't say the same for an Alpha.

I felt my skin tingling from head-to-toe. A lump formed in my throat, and my knees started trembling. The heady aroma of raw earth and sweat beat against my skin, igniting fires of recognition deep within. I remembered that smell as if it were yesterday—John's scent had been exactly the same. I knew that he was dead, but I couldn't mistake that smell. 'We need to leave right now,' I said to Chester, attempting to move forward again on sluggish legs.

The security team blocked my efforts.

'I'm not letting you out of my sight, Elena,'

I shuffled from foot to foot, trying to hurry full feeling back. I wasn't sure if I could run yet. Damn Chester and his stupid magic! 'I'm serious. We need to get the hell out of here right now, and if you don't get out of my way, I'm going to mow you all over.'

He laughed—the idiot actually thought I was joking. 'You can follow me back to the hotel now.'

'Fine. Whatever. Just get going!'

Chester's eyes narrowed on me. 'You're being far too agreeable. What's wrong?'

I glanced around as we walked. Amongst the stream of people flowing past I could see no one that stood out, but for me to scent the creature so strongly he had to be close by. And with its ability to take the human form of those it'd fed from, the creature could look like anyone.

I started pushing through the security team to hurry back to the hotel. I didn't want to go back but knew it was the only place nearby that would be safe. The Alpha would never be stupid enough to launch an all-out assault against an entire building full of Protectors just to get at me.

'Elena!' Chester yelled, tugging on my arm as I tried to start hurrying for the hotel. 'Stop running or I will have to use the magic again.'

'Don't do that!' I cried, trying to shake off the six pairs of hands holding me back. 'Chester, we need to get out of here now. The Alpha is coming!'

'Where?' he said, glancing over his shoulder.

'I can't see him, but I can feel him, and if we don't get back inside the hotel soon he'll make his move.'

'How interesting,' Chester murmured, glancing around the square.

I shook my head. 'It won't be so interesting when you're dead, will it?'

'That won't happen. There are seven of us, plus you, to help fight him off.'

I was shaking my head again, struggling to break free. 'You don't understand. He has the power to make me do whatever he says.'

Chester scoffed. 'Should I be worried?'

I nodded. 'I would be, and in all honesty, if he asks me to hurt you I'm not sure that I'd be that cut up about it.'

'Maybe we should stop and see how this plays out, though. You know, as an experiment,' Chester said, signalling for the security team to hold me in place.

'Are you freaking crazy!' I shouted.

He scratched his chin thoughtfully. 'Beryx would be quite useful right now. His studies in human movement might provide us with some interesting data—in particular, your reactions to the Alpha's scent.'

Jesus Christ, this idiot's serious.

'You are one crazy bastard,' I said, kicking down hard on the instep of the security guard behind me. He howled, jumping backwards and accidentally head-butting the security guard standing behind him. I broke the nose of the hulking brute next to him with one swift elbow, punched two more in the solar plexus, and kneed the first meathead who had tried to restrain me in the groin. I just shoved Chester out of the way, even though I deeply wanted to strangle him.

'Elena!'

'I'm going back inside, you idiot,' I yelled over my shoulder as I took off.

I could already hear the sounds of the guard's pursuit, their feet slapping against the pavement, breathing coming in quick, uneven gasps. Chester called out to me but I wasn't slowing down for anyone. I rounded the corner, past the hotel's neatly pruned hedges, and sped through the valet area. I dodged a taxi that had just started to speed off, ignoring the angry blast of the horn that followed, and headed towards the hotel's revolving door. I didn't look back, just in case I spied the Alpha lurking in my peripherals.

Pushing through the doors, I ignored Chester as he fell into step with me a few seconds later, followed closely by a slower paced, more wary security team. They were huffing and puffing, rivulets of sweat already running down the sides of their pockmarked and square-jawed faces, staining the underarms of their uniforms. I quickly crossed the lobby and spammed the elevator's call button.

The overpowering scent had followed me here, though, and began to insinuate its way across the surface of my skin. It probed the soft points of my body, searching for a way inside, a way to make me succumb to its master's will. It stoked my slow-building, inner fire.

I held my breath.

Chester coughed meaningfully.

'Look, if we can just set up some sort of controlled experiment where you can interact freely with the Alpha and I can observe your behaviour, I think it could be beneficial. Oh, I should probably do some tests when we get back inside—check your hormone levels and what not. And Beryx? I should see if he wants to come back in and—'

He kept on like that for a while as we waited. Chester's love of science seemed to be making him oblivious to any imminent danger; even the bruised and beaten security team remained alert enough to keep looking around reception warily.

I all but fell inside the elevator when the doors finally opened, pulling Chester inside with me while he continued to babble on and on about how exciting it was to be in the same vicinity as an Alpha. After a week at headquarters I had thought the creature might have given up pursuit, so I was in a lot more trouble than I thought.

As the elevator doors began to close, the scent sharpened to a point. I found myself stumbling forward, reaching out to press the red button labelled 'Open Doors'. Chester was lost in his own little world, but thankfully one of the security guys recognised the severity of the situation and hauled my ass away from the control panel.

That was when I finally caught sight of the Alpha. It had the same face I'd seen watching me at the Cairns airport only a few days ago, now no more than fifty meters away from me, directly across the lobby and just inside the revolving door. I had to employ every ounce of mental strength I had left to avoid pummelling more security guards, jump through those closing doors and run directly into the Alpha's waiting arms.

I could feel him beckoning to me.

Long, dark hair glistened underneath the soft light of the lobby chandeliers. His skin was smooth and tanned, highlighting the thick muscle of his masculine jaw line. Deep amber eyes stared at me with a hungry intensity I wished I'd soon forget. His trench coat billowed around him as a rush of wind poured forth from the revolving door. Underneath, he wore nothing more than black leather pants. His bare chest throbbed with taut muscles and was covered in soft curls of hair.

The Alpha was purpose-built, all strength and speed. He had obviously molded his current form out of the best human physique he could find. And he was beautiful to behold, even more so than John had been.

I lunged forward, my hands pressing up against the shiny, metal surface of the elevator doors, feeling the chilled exterior sliding beneath my fingers. The doors closed more slowly than I had ever thought possible.

Finally, as the doors came together with a gentle clink and the lift began to ascend, I exhaled in relief. I could feel the Alpha's hold on me dissolving as its commanding scent dissipated, and found myself at last able to step back from the doors.

Chester was still blabbering on beside me; I heard little. He appeared to be talking more to himself than anyone else, anyway, making notes on a little notepad he'd had stored in his pen-filled lab coat pocket, muttering something about setting up an exciting, new experiment.

I ignored him, mostly because I'd probably cry if I'd kept listening. So what was I supposed to do now? If the Alpha had waited a week in Bucharest on the off-chance that I'd escape the IMI's facility, what's to say that he wouldn't wait another week or even a month? Was I supposed to just stay here with Dr. Jekyll and hope that his planned experiments weren't dredged up from some sort of creepy horror film?

Well, this seriously blows.

I could either stay with Chester and his research team or risk another escape attempt that would undoubtedly lead me directly to the dark-haired danger down in the lobby. Both options were distressing. I guess I could try waiting for William, but that really pissed me off. I didn't want to seem dependent; I hated that more than anything.

Then again, charging my way out of this joint with a

badass vampire on my arm raised the chances of a successful escape considerably. So I was just going to have to swallow my pride and wait.

Supposing, that is, if he still came for me.

CHAPTER FOUR: FINALS

tapped my pen against the notepad impatiently, trying to conjure up the final answers for the exam from the dark recesses of my non-algebraic mind. It was a close to impossible feat for someone like me, lacking the mental ability to mathematically equate numerals, letters, and symbols together. Oh, and then come up with a correct answer. For all of my physical capabilities, I still lacked academic excellence. And who the hell gives a shit about factorising quadratic equations, anyway?

I glanced at Beryx, who was sitting directly across from me. He was holding a small, brass pocket watch in his hand, bouncing his knee up and down frantically as he glanced between me and its tiny clock face. He flashed me five fingers.

Shit. Five minutes left.

I looked down at the test paper again. All the words and symbols seemed to blur together into an inky mess. What were those last few questions about again?

I raked a hand through my hair, brushing it away from my face. Five minutes to go, six questions unanswered, several of them algebra-based. The first two were multiple choice. Something about 'how many kilometres' and 'what bearing would I be heading'—blah, blah, blah.

I circled 'C' on both questions, two non-educated guesses. The last four mathematics questions required written calculations. I had about as much chance of getting them right as I did of shitting a brick. I gave the first question a quick glance over, anyway, hoping I'd get lucky. Didn't I read something about this last night? Hadn't Beryx even tried explaining this concept by using the salt and pepper shakers as props, as well as various other condiments from the refrigerator?

I shook my head. I'd spent that whole time laughing at him and wondering how my muesli bar had become the 'X' on a graph. I don't think he realised he'd just confused me more.

Beryx flashed me two fingers.

Well, crap—there was no way I was going to work this out now. I'd spent the last month pent up inside my room and studying hard for these exams, but even with Beryx's help, I felt no smarter now than I had before. Being surrounded by scientists with multiple University degrees, who constantly flung around large, complicated words, had put a few chinks in my armour.

I dropped the pen down on the page and threw my hands up in the air. 'I'm done.'

Beryx ceased twitching and came over to look at the paper lying in front of me. 'You didn't answer the last four questions.'

'I know.'

'You still have a minute left.'

'Beryx, I can't even take a bathroom break in under a minute and you expect me to whip out answers for these?' I snorted. 'You're dreaming.'

He frowned. 'You should at least know the answer to the last one. We talked about that last night.'

'I remember,' I said, smirking as I pictured him pushing bits of food around my tiny dining table. 'I just don't remember the important parts.'

'Well, times up now anyway.' He picked up the test paper and placed it inside a large yellow envelope. 'I have to send this back to Australia for grading, but you should know in about a week or so whether you've passed Year Eleven.'

I rolled my eyes. I didn't really care if I passed Year Eleven or not. Chester was planning on chaining me up permanently after I graduated. I'd retaliate by going all primal and hairy, and he'd make a floor rug out of me.

'You don't seem pleased.'

'Should I be?' I said, pushing off from my chair and heading over to the fridge to grab a Mars Bar. 'I still have my senior year to go.'

'And college,' Beryx tacked on.

I shook my head. 'What's the point?'

'Are you serious?' he said, staring at me incredulously. 'You're going to be immortal and you aren't at least going to go to college?'

'Don't look at me like that, Beryx. I'm not going to college because I'm not interested. Plus, I probably won't get a chance to attend if Chester has his way.' I tore back the packaging on my chocolate bar, biting off an unladylike portion and settling down onto the couch. I started leafing my way through the latest copy of *Wheels* magazine.

'Well, what *are* you interested in?'

I held up the magazine, showing him the article about the BMW M6 that I was currently reading.

'Cars?' Beryx said in disbelief. 'You're interested in cars?'

I shook my head. 'Not just cars. I like motorbikes as well. Basically any vehicle that goes fast.'

'You know, Elena,' Beryx said, as he came and sat down beside me, 'you're not like any other girl I've ever met before. Spending the last month with you has really opened my eyes.'

Not wide enough. You're still blind, Beryx, and your boss still intends to kill me.

I looked at him, still chewing the giant wad of chocolate. I tried to speak but only managed: 'Ish tha a goo fing?'

Beryx cringed. He must have glimpsed the half-masticated piece of chocolate rolling around in my gob. 'I think so.'

I finally swallowed. 'Does that mean you're gonna help me break out of this place?'

'Elena, please stop asking me that.'

'Why? It's not like I can leave on my own. That Alpha hasn't given up on getting to me, and if I do get out, he'll find me just like he found the security detail Chester sent out to hunt him down.'

'Is it really all that bad here?'

I rolled my eyes again. 'Now how many times do I have to answer that question? Every time I see you I tell you that Chester is out to get me, but you keep ignoring me.' I gave him a level look. 'I need to get out of this place, Beryx. Bad things are going to happen to me if I stay. If you like me as much as you keep telling me you do, please don't let that happen.'

Beryx sighed. 'That's not my decision to make, Elena. I already got into trouble for supplying you with that information about this hotel. I don't want to be permanently expelled from the clan because I helped you get away.'

'So you're happy to let Chester keep abusing my basic human rights?'

'He is not as bad as you say.'

'Oh yeah? What little evil experiment has Chester got lined up for me this afternoon?'

'As far as I know, he's given you the rest of the day off to recuperate from your exam.'

'How magnanimous of him.'

Beryx looked at me and frowned, his fingers twitching slightly in his lap. 'Please don't be so hard on him, Elena.'

I snorted, swallowing another bite of chocolate. 'Take it easy on him? Have you been paying attention to all of the crazy things that jerkoff's been asking me to do over the last month? Don't ask me to go easy on *him*.'

'Elena, I told you that he was joking about cutting your arm off.'

'That's bullshit and you know it! Was he joking when he asked if I could jump off the fourth floor balcony so he could test the extent of my healing abilities?'

'Okay,' Beryx said, holding his hands up in surrender. '*That* remark was serious. But, Elena, you have to understand that you have us collectively completely stumped. We have some of the best scientists and lab technicians in their fields working at this facility and none of them are getting any closer to decoding your genetic secrets. You are perfect inside and out, and that is an anomaly. Even vampiric blood has its defects and impurities; yours does not. Can't you understand that we are all just so curious?'

I got up from the sofa and headed over to the window, laying my head against the cool glass. I couldn't see out, but I needed to move around, needed to put some space between me and these overzealous science people.

What's taking you so long, William? I'm going crazy in here.

'Elena?'

'I heard you, Beryx. It would just be nice if you could acknowledge that I'm a person, not just a pin cushion.'

'But you're not a per—' Beryx stopped short, though I pretty much gathered how that statement ended. 'I'd better go,' he rushed on. 'There's a tonne of work in the lab for me and Stephanie and Anica will be waiting for my return.'

I didn't answer. What would be the point? My thoughts and feelings were falling on deaf ears.

Beryx quickly scrambled up from the sofa, grabbing the yellow envelope containing my exam answers off the coffee table and heading for the door. He paused, his fingers brushing the handle as he turned back to look at me.

I tilted my head against the cool glass and glanced at him through blurry eyes. 'Yes, Beryx?'

He stared at me in silence for several seconds, his eyes pleading for forgiveness; I had none to offer. For a brief moment I thought that he might say something—his lips opened with purpose but then clammed shut. Instead, Beryx shook his head in dismissal and left the room without looking back.

So much for my apology.

I blew out a weary breath and pushed away from the glass. From the way the window creaked softly under the pressure of my fingertips, I knew it would take only one light punch to blow a hole right through the centre of the unpliable surface.

I'd thought about it, believe me. Then I'd tie all of my linen together and throw the makeshift rope out the window, climbing down the side of the building to freedom. The only problem? I was staying on the nineteenth floor. Not exactly a solid plan if I wanted to avoid going *splat*.

There was also the Alpha's lingering presence to consider. Chester was still trying to figure out a way that The Protectors could locate and capture it. He'd already sent out three separate groups of the best security personnel that the IMI had to offer, scouting for a wolf-like creature that was likely to tear them to shreds and feed off their remains.

His was a fool's errand.

I'd told Chester about the Alpha's above-average

intelligence, that it wouldn't be as easy a trap as he'd assumed. With the aid of magic, Chester had responded, The Protectors were virtually unstoppable. That was despite the men and women who'd gone on the hunt still being missing. They'd left one month ago today, the same night of my attempted escape, and it wasn't hard to surmise what had happened to them.

His next plan was to lure the creature back to the hotel, using me as the bait. The only reason those plans hadn't been carried out was because Chester was fearful that I'd run away again if given the opportunity.

And he was dead-set right.

With all my thoughts of escape, I was starting to doubt whether William would ever come to Bucharest. I wouldn't blame him if he didn't. I wouldn't want to get mixed up in my troubles either.

I shook my head and chewed on my lower lip. This was exactly the reason why I avoided relationships. People let you down, even without knowing it.

I sat back down on the couch and went back to reading. Packing a 5.0 litre V10 engine, I knew this new BMW M6 would move like the wind. I especially liked the lightweight aluminium body, which imparted the car with an excellent power to weight ratio. What I didn't like? The bloody price tag.

Reading about cars always made me happier. I could close my eyes and picture the feel of the engine thrumming underneath me, the soft leather steering wheel under my fingertips, and the cushioned bucket seats holding me steady as I drove my current fantasy vehicle to its absolute extremes. Today, though, the magazine held no comfort. Reading the specifications still made my heart race, exciting me in a way that nothing else could, yet I found myself re-reading the same lines over and over again. Eventually I gave up, throwing the magazine back down onto the coffee table in frustration. What I really needed was someone to talk to—someone I could trust. A phone call to Lucas would have been ideal, but Chester listened so closely to all our conversations now that he was practically inside of them and it made me feel uncomfortable.

Something was wrong. I'd heard it in Lucas's voice the last time we'd spoken. He was agitated, and I just wished I knew about what so I could help him through it.

I decided to go for a swim, thinking the water might be soothing. I wanted to take my mind off Lucas and I didn't fancy watching the bizarre Romanian game shows on television. If I stayed in my room any longer I was going to pull my hair out worrying.

I scrambled up from the sofa and headed over to the wardrobe, sorting through the drawers until I found my bathing suit—well, my bikini. Kayla had picked this one out for me, so it was a little more daring than I'd usually have chosen. She'd insisted, though, saying that it was a crime to cover up a figure like mine. I wasn't so sure that I agreed with her. I thought my legs were too long, my skin too pale, and my boobs too small.

Despite myself, though, I smiled as I thought about Kayla. I wondered what she was up to these days and if she was keeping happy.

I held the little red pieces of fabric in front of me, my smile slowly turning to a speculative grimace. Beryx was hopefully going back to the lab like he'd said. The last time I'd run into him while dressed in my bathing suit, he'd all but writhed around my legs like a cat, vying for affection. I didn't fancy a repeat episode.

Tossing that horrible thought aside before I changed my

mind, I stripped off my clothes, tossed them into the corner of the room and slipped into the skimpy bikini.

As I stepped into the corridor, I saw no spectators and relief flooded through me.

Closing the door behind me, I padded quickly over to let myself inside the pool room. Glossy white tiles covered the walls, as bland as the rest of the building and just as I'd expected. Smaller, non-slip mosaics covered the pool's interior surface. The only source of colour in the room came from an ambient glow emitted by a pale blue spotlight beneath the water's crystal depths.

I put my towel and access card down on one of the white canvas deckchairs surrounding the pool and then walked around to the steps at the shallow end. The water was a little warmer than I thought it would be, but I preferred that to flat-out cold.

Bending down, I cupped the warm water with my hands, splashing it down the sides of my arms and neck.

I shivered as I stepped into the pool but not from the temperature of the air or the tepid water around my ankles. It was something else, a tangible feeling like the caress of flesh or a warm breeze blowing through my hair. Goosebumps erupted across my skin as I quickly realised I was no longer alone.

I frantically searched the confines of the pool room, the hairs on my skin prickling with intense awareness. I saw no one but I supposed that didn't really mean anything. If there was one truth about vampires and werewolves that would forever go uncontested, it was that if they didn't want you to see them, then you probably wouldn't.

I tilted my head back, sniffing the air and vaguely terrified that the Alpha may have finally found a way inside. One month had passed since I had seen it, since I'd felt it beckoning to me. This weird sensation was not unlike the scent of his persuasion, but was less intense—it was more like a gentle touch or a warm breath across the back of my neck.

Breathing it in more deeply, it suddenly hit me—that scent of sandalwood and exotic spices that always made my knees buckle.

Shit!

I slipped, falling awkwardly backwards with a loud *splash*. I felt the sensation of drowning, a mix of anxiety, recognition, and excitement confusing my limbs and muddling my thoughts. The warm waters lapped at my face and I struggled to gain my footing at the bottom of the pool. I probed its depths with my feet, trying to reach for the surface so I could see.

A second later I regained my footing and burst through the surface of the water, gasping for air and spinning around on the spot. I brushed long strands of dark, wet hair away from my face.

'William?' I called tentatively, a little unsure. 'William, are you here?'

There was no answer.

Frowning, I inhaled again, trying to breathe through the smell of chlorine lingering on my skin. I could still hear nothing and that familiar, enticing scent had abated. 'William? If you're here, answer me.'

After several heartbeats and the room continuing to sing its silence, I slammed my hands down on top of the water in frustration, cursing loudly. Was I so damn desperate to get out of here that I'd started imagining things?

I swore again—profoundly unladylike but it sure as hell made me feel better.

Soft chuckling erupted from directly behind me. I spun

around in surprise, water splashing over the edges of the pool. My breath caught in my throat and my heart lurched painfully as I saw William standing there by the edge of the pool.

'I haven't seen you in over a month,' he said, still chuckling as he walked slowly into the pool dressed in nothing but leather pants, 'and the first thing I hear out of your mouth is—'

I was about to admonish him for climbing into the water partly dressed—leather was a bitch to dry—but all that came out was, 'William!' I splashed my way across the length of the pool, throwing myself into his waiting arms. 'You're here!'

'Of course I'm here,' William said, wrapping his cool arms around me as I nestled my face against his hard, naked chest. 'Where else would I be?'

That was a good question. I had no idea what William had been doing for the last month—and *now* I was a priority? Just where the hell had he been?

I buried my face harder against him, not wanting him to see the hint of resentment etched on my face. I guessed a month was more like a couple of days for a vampire with eternity stretched out in front of him. I guess I really couldn't be too annoyed with him. Technically, William didn't owe me anything, but an explanation about where he had been or who he had been doing it with would have been welcome.

When I was certain that I'd rearranged my features into a smile again, I pulled back and looked up into his eyes. William hadn't changed a bit. Then again, I supposed he never would.

William smiled warmly at me, planting a kiss on my forehead as I studied every inch of him, realising I'd remembered every plane of his face flawlessly. Unchanging though he was, his green eyes—despite being as vibrant as ever—were wider than necessary, his smile slightly pinched at the edges. He was happy to see me, no doubt, and yet something wasn't quite right.

I ran my fingers across his bare chest, checking that he was real, that I wasn't imagining some sort of delusional afternoon delight. I'd been so bored and frustrated lately that I'd frequently day-dreamed scenarios like this one. 'You really *are* here,' I murmured.

William shivered and pulled me closer. 'I'm really here.'

My fingers dipped below the surface of the water, running down his stomach until they found the waistband of his leather pants. 'Why jump in fully-clothed?'

'I took my t-shirt off,' William said, his voice husky. He jabbed a thumb at the small pile of cotton, sunglasses, and shoes sitting on the rim of the pool. Too bad that my earlier splashing had gotten them as wet as the rest of him.

'How did you get into the IMI without alerting security?'

William pointed a finger at the roof this time, his eyes never leaving mine as my fingers inched slowly over his hips and around to the back of his pants. 'The air conditioning ducts.'

I glanced up. 'With all their high tech surveillance equipment, you just slipped in via the air-conditioning system?'

'They have motion sensors next to the vent openings, but I don't think they're working at the moment. Either that or they only turn them on at night.'

'I wish I'd thought of that,' I said, looking up wistfully and sighing.

He pulled me back into his arms and started to smooth his hands up and down my back. 'I really missed you, Elena.'

'You did?' I said, looking back to William. 'I was beginning to think that you weren't coming.'

That's right, E. Try not to sound too needy or desperate.

'I'm sorry. I tried to get here as quickly as I could, especially after Lucas told me how miserable you were here.'

I waved him off. 'What have you been doing, anyway? Lucas said you had some loose ends to tie up.' I honestly wasn't digging for details. It was a perfectly legitimate question to ask a friend that hadn't been seen in a while.

Yeah, pffft, okay.

William squeezed me tightly. 'It's nothing you need to worry about.' He paused and then kissed the top of my head. 'I'm here now, and that's all that matters. Everything will be just fine.'

I didn't scoff, which was a miracle, and I didn't roll my eyes either. I deserved some kind of medal for that remarkable feat of restraint. I hated that he'd just assumed everything would be perfectly fine now the muscle had arrived. But what I hated even more is him blowing my questions off completely. 'Why don't you want to talk about it?'

'There's nothing to tell, Elena. I'm here with you, we're together again and, honestly, that's all I really care about right now.' William's tone was dismissive, and he seemed to have no desire to pursue this avenue of conversation any further. I might have kept on asking questions, anyway, but I had my own set of problems to deal with right now, like getting the hell out of this place.

'Well, I'm glad that you're here, too,' I said, pushing the conversation forward. 'But, now that you are, we have to talk.'

William's arms stiffened around me, and he quickly pulled away. Regardless, I needed to tell him about my encounter with the Alpha.

I smirked. 'It's not what you think. It won't be one of *those* conversations.'

He shook his head and pressed his fingers to my mouth, looking towards the door. 'No. Someone is coming.'

I heard the swipe of an access card from outside and a *beep* as locks disengaged. The pool room door opened a few inches. Auburn hair was the first thing I saw, followed by pale skin and dark eyes.

It was Beryx.

Crap.

I spun back around but William was already gone. His t-shirt and shoes remained, giving me the brief hope that his appearance wasn't a figment of my imagination. Hopefully, Beryx wouldn't pay too much attention to William's clothes because there was no way those size twelve's were mine.

I swam over to the side of the pool, gripping the edge as far away from William's belongings as possible. 'Beryx? What do you want?' I tried not to sound impatient, but it was difficult as I was still annoyed at him for calling me a 'non-person' earlier.

I discreetly looked up at the air conditioning vent. I couldn't see any sign of William, not even a wet stain or trace that he was back in the roof.

'I forgot to ask you if you wanted me to hang around until after six tonight so I can escort you down to the mess hall for dinner?' Beryx asked, shifting my focus back to him.

I shook my head. 'No need. I won't be having dinner this evening. I'm not—' I squealed in fright as, under the water, I felt cool fingers brush against my thighs.

Beryx reeled backwards as if I'd slapped him in the face. 'What? What is it?' he asked, manically looking around the room.

I bit my tongue and kicked out at where William must

have been standing. 'Nothing, sorry,' I stammered. 'I thought I saw a bug on the wall behind you.'

Lame.

He glanced behind himself, an expression of scepticism on his face. 'A bug?'

I nodded. 'Yeah, a bug.'

Underneath the water, I could feel William begin to kiss my ankles.

'It was a big black-haired, green-eyed bug.'

'Right.'

I lashed out again, but William caught my foot and began sucking on my toes instead. I began to giggle uncontrollably, trying to kick him hard in the face, but he had a tight hold on my ankle.

Beryx stared at me incredulously. I didn't blame him. 'Are you okay?'

I slapped my hand against the edge of the pool, howling with laughter. 'I'm great! I'm just so happy that my exams are finally finished for the year.' This time I managed to kick William right in his perfect face. The toe sucking immediately ceased.

Beryx frowned heavily, tucking his hands into the pockets of his lab coat. 'Are you sure? You're acting very strangely.'

I pulled my serious face back on. 'Sorry, I had too much sugar at lunch. It makes me kind of loopy. I start hallucinating sometimes, seeing bugs and—look, was there something else that you needed?'

He studied my expression for a moment—lips tight, eyes scrutinising. 'I just came in to see if you wanted to have dinner with me tonight, but now I'm thinking that you might need some time alone. You seem ...' Beryx didn't finish, though, probably because he was watching himself after his earlier comment. 'Unless there's a chance that you and I can …'

I shook my head. 'No, Beryx, I'll be fine. I'm bound to start crashing from that sugar high soon or fall in a heap from brain strain. Your study sessions have run me into the ground, you know.'

'I hope they helped you pass.'

I put my knuckles in my mouth and bit down hard enough to draw blood as William's lips found me again, kissing a wet path from my knees all the way up to the top of my legs and across my stomach. It didn't tickle, but it was definitely making me squirm. Any second now his head was going to break the surface of the water and Beryx would definitely see him.

Not good.

I closed my eyes, momentarily ignoring Beryx's presence and the sweet droplets of blood that had pooled around the indentations my teeth had made on my knuckles. I could only concentrate on the sensations that ripped through me as William nipped at the flesh of my hips, stroking my thighs in a way that stirred heat deep within.

I opened my eyes again; I was embarrassed that Beryx was still there, still standing near the pool room door, still watching me with bewilderment. I could only imagine what he was thinking.

I looked down at my knuckles. There were bite marks all over them and trails of blood running down to my wrist, the wetness of my essence glossing my lips like red paint.

Beryx took a step towards me, eyeing my hands. I licked my lips, tasting a sweetness that made my mouth water. My eyes rolled backwards in pleasure.

Self-healing kicked in. The blood on my hands reversed course and the angry bite marks began to clear. Beryx looked no less interested. 'Elena—'

'I'm really grateful for all of your help, Beryx, and I want to thank you for the dinner invitation, but I won't be coming tonight.' I let my hands slide under the water, the last remnants of my blood like little clouds of red mixing with the chlorinated water around me.

'Elena, what's going on?'

'I hope that you have a great weekend and I'll see you on Monday.'

'Are you sure you're okay?'

'I'm fine.'

'But you're hands ... the blood ...'

I held my hands up for his perusal. 'No blood, see? Everything's fine. I just want to be left alone for a little while.'

'Okay,' Beryx answered tentatively, taking another step towards the door. 'I guess I'll just see you later then.'

'Great. Bye, Beryx.' I almost breathed a sigh of relief as his fingers gripped the handle of the door, but he paused and turned around again.

Would he never leave?

'Elena?'

'Mmmm, yes?' I groaned, briefly closing my eyes again and trying not to scream for two entirely different reasons.

'What I almost said before in your room. I just wanted you to know that I don't really feel that way. You *are* a person to me.' Beryx hesitated when my eyes found him again. 'In case you missed my hints, I like you ... a lot.'

'I like you too, Beryx.' The truth of that statement actually shocked me—I did like him. Not romantically, but if we were in any other situation I could honestly see us becoming friends.

Beryx took another step back towards the pool. 'I've wanted to tell you that for a while now. I know it doesn't mean much to someone like you who probably gets lots of offers but I had to get it off my chest. I also know that I'm a Protector, and well, you're going to be immortal and the two of us can't really be together unless—' He shook his head, eyes thoughtful. 'I'm sorry, Elena, I shouldn't have said anything. Not with everything that's going to happen.'

I cleared my throat. Words were lodged somewhere halfway down there. I was beginning to think that I shouldn't have encouraged his initial infatuation. 'Beryx, what are you talking about?'

'I like you.'

I smiled half-heartedly. 'That's not what I meant. What's going to happen? What did you mean by that?'

Beryx scooted closer again. 'There are things that I think you should know,' he continued, 'things that might make you start considering me as, well, more.' He looked thoughtful, his eyes clouding over and fingers flexing nervously at his side.

William chose that moment for his head to break the surface of the water. I quickly pushed him back down again and shuffled closer to the edge, effectively sandwiching him between my legs and the wall of the pool. 'What sort of things are you talking about, Beryx?'

Beryx blanched, looking back at the door. 'Things that I shouldn't tell you.'

Now I was really interested. William's tender underwater caresses were all but forgotten in the face of the mystery unravelling in front of me. 'Tell me, Beryx. You have my undivided attention.'

William pinched my knee.

'Now's not a good time. They're expecting me back in the labs, which is why I wanted to have dinner with you.'

'So, we'll have dinner.'

'Really? I thought you just said you weren't hungry?'

William pinched my knee harder than before. I tried not to whimper—message received. 'Maybe we could have breakfast tomorrow instead? I know you don't usually come in on the weekends, but I'm up for it if you are?'

'You'll have breakfast with me?'

'Of course.'

'Like a date?'

I tried not to grimace as Beryx's whole face came alive, a vibrant smile beaming its way across his features. 'Sure, like a date.'

William pinched me twice as hard. I kneed him hard in the ribs to make him stop.

'Until tomorrow then,' Beryx sighed, before spinning on his heels and heading for the door.

I rolled my eyes. What was with the people in this place using such archaic speech? I was already straddling the undead with my legs; I didn't need to hear dead language as well.

William emerged from under the water, a huge grin plastered on his dripping wet face. 'I thought he'd never leave.'

I smacked him on the shoulder as he pulled me against him again, nuzzling the side of my neck. 'You could have gotten us both busted,' I said, scolding him.

'Possibly,' William murmured, 'but I had other things on my mind.'

'Now so do I. Did you hear what he said?'

'More or less.'

'Aren't you curious?'

'Not at all.'

I slapped his shoulder again as he started nibbling on my ear. 'Stop it. Whatever it is, it's obviously troubling Beryx.'

I shuddered as William's tongue darted out, tracing the delicate lobe of my ear.

'Should I care?'

'William!'

'Yes?'

I pushed him away. 'I said, stop.'

He pulled back, looking at me in confusion. 'Why are you angry?'

'I'm not. You're just being ... I don't know. Look, you don't understand what it's been like for me. I've been stuck here with these crazies, trying to figure out why I'm so important to their research. It's obvious I'm here out of more than just mere curiosity. They've said it was for the protection of others, on account of not knowing what I could become, but I'm not so sure, William. If Beryx knows the real reason, I'd like to hear it. The Protectors aren't the people I thought they were.'

'Well, can I kiss you *now*?'

I screwed my face up, at the same time sweeping my palms across the water and splashing him with a small tidal wave of manifested irritation. 'What the hell is wrong with you? Are you even listening to me?'

'I'm going to get you out of this place, Elena. What does it matter what the IMI's future plans for you are?' William didn't wait for my answer. He pulled me against him, grabbing my thighs and tugging me close—I could either wrap my legs around his hips or fall over backwards. Despite wanting to struggle on general principal alone, I relented; as our bodies entwined, his hand twisted through the curls of my hair, tugging me gently forward so that he could plant a delicate kiss across my lips.

'William, this isn't—'

'Hush.'

William's lips brushed slowly across mine, savouring their touch and flavour like a fine wine or the ripest fruit plucked straight from the vine. I was about to protest again, but in all honesty, what was the point? He wasn't listening, and Beryx's promise of a mystery revelation was fading fast. Soon all I could think about were William's lips.

He looked at me then, his eyes dark and dangerous, all traces of emerald green consumed by the darkness of the Vampire within.

'I'm making you thirsty,' I stated, trying to pull away.

William held me tightly to him. 'Always, but I *will* fight it.'

'You don't have to.'

'I've done it before.'

I blinked at him in surprise. 'You could smell my blood? Even under the water?'

He shook his head. 'I tasted it when you washed your hand in the pool.'

'Oh my God, I'm so sorry! I didn't think.'

'Sharks can sense a drop of blood in the ocean from miles away, Elena.'

What a lovely image.

I grimaced, attempting to untangle myself from a vampire determined to maintain a death grip on my thighs. 'Well, now I feel bad. It's hard enough for you to be around me without me waving my bloodied knuckles around in your face.'

He smiled. 'It's fine.'

I gave up trying to escape his hold and let out an exasperated sigh. 'It's not.'

'Yes, it is. I just have to learn to control myself again. The blood was a test, though admittedly the water did dilute its full potency. I still passed.'

I wrapped my hands around his neck and rested my

head against his shoulder. 'This thing we have, William, it shouldn't be this hard for you. You should be with your own kind so you don't have to repress your natural instincts so much.'

He growled in rebuttal, fingers digging painfully into the flesh of my thighs. 'Everything worthwhile is hard, Elena.'

I lifted my head from William's shoulder, looking fully into his still, dark eyes. 'Would it really be so bad if you did bite me?'

'I can't even begin to tell you how bad.'

'I'll heal. I always do.' Without waiting for William's response, I kissed him. Not the soft, careful kisses that were a part of William's usual repertoire but a full-on assault of his lips—the kind that leaves you breathless.

William's hold on me stiffened. His fingers went from gripping my thighs to digging into the skin of my lower back. As our kiss deepened, his erect posture and ebony eyes showed tell-tale signs of his waning restraint. 'William,' I breathed, frustrated, 'kiss me properly.'

'I am.'

'You said yourself that you needed to learn control again. Consider this good practice.'

'Practice?' he muttered through clenched teeth. 'Your scent is everywhere—in my breath, on my tongue, and crawling across my skin.' William shook his head. 'I thought I was fine but now I can barely think straight.'

'You were all over me when Beryx was here,' I pointed out.

He sighed, staring down at me like I was a frustrating child. 'The water diffused your scent and the sound of your blood pulsing through your body. I wasn't as tempted then as I am now that you're forcing yourself on me.'

I snorted indignantly.

Forcing myself. As if.

William grasped my chin in his hands, angling my face towards his. 'We can try again later.'

'What's the point?'

I knew that I sounded petulant, but I didn't care. All our encounters ended this way. Until I turned, we would never fully be able to enjoy each other's company and that fact always left me bitter and wanting.

'Elena—'

I jerked my head away from his hand. 'Don't worry about it.' I untangled my legs from his, this time encountering zero resistance. I pushed away, wading into shallower water, needing to put that little bit of space between us.

'Now you're angry,' William called out behind me.

'No,' I lied.

I reached the shallow end but William was already there, head breaking the surface of the water. His eyes were muddied now, not dark like before, but he still wasn't fully himself. William grabbed my hand under the water and pulled me to him, faster than I could protest, crushing me against his chest in a way that made me wheeze.

'Don't be mad at me, Elena,' he said, stroking a single, possessive hand down my back. 'I'm still a young vampire. I *will* learn control.'

'I'm not mad at you,' I said, catching my breath as I wiggled, trying to break free.

'You are.'

'I'm not.

William laughed, droplets of water rolling down the pale skin of his wet cheeks, perhaps on a mission to greet his parted lips with the eagerness I'd possessed not minutes before. 'You're flushed, Elena. So you're either embarrassed or angry.'

'Okay. I'm angry now, but mostly because you're baiting me.'

His chest rumbled with derisive laughter but he managed to curb it as my glare turned piercing. 'Would you rather be with … what was his name?'

'Beryx,' I snapped, knowing that there was no way William could have forgotten. He just wanted to make Beryx sound insignificant. Four hundred and forty-four years old and William was still playing mind-games like a teenager.

'Ah, yes … *him*,' William acknowledged, ever-darkening eyes taking in my vexed expression and the arms now folded tightly across my chest. 'He seemed …' William stopped, taking a breath and gritting his teeth. 'He seemed quite interested in you.'

I dropped my arms, palms slapping against the surface of the water in frustration. 'So, what if he is, William? The information he inadvertently let slip helped direct you here. And, tomorrow, he just might tell me what Chester has planned—aside from killing me.'

'If he makes a move on you, I'm going to—' He stopped abruptly and looked away, the muscles of his jaw tightening.

'Hold the phone,' I uttered in disbelief. 'Are you jealous?'

'Of course I'm jealous,' William growled. 'You're mine and I have no intention of sharing you with anyone else, no matter who they think they are.' William turned his back on me, slamming his hands against the edge of the pool as another snarl tore loose from his throat. I prayed no one could hear him, or that no one would notice the several dislodged mosaics and bits of crumbling mortar now adrift in the water. William might as well have left a sign saying 'stupid, bad-tempered vampire waz here'.

'Okay—let's get one thing straight,' I said, when no security team came bursting in through the pool room door. 'Although I think it's kind of cute that you're jealous right now, I'm definitely not *yours*. I don't belong to anyone. And, secondly, why do I get the feeling that there's more to that comment than you're telling me?'

He remained facing away from me, hands now splayed against the slick surface of the tiles, the muscles of his back bunching then releasing with barely restrained tension.

'William, does this sudden possessiveness have something to do with you being missing for the past month?' I was fishing in the hopes that I might snag something decent out of him. 'What *have* you been doing?' I said, pressing him when he failed to respond.

'Piecing a couple of things together.'

'Like what?'

He looked back at me then, his hardened eyes barely visible under the wet caress of his fringe. 'It doesn't matter.'

'Obviously it does. The mere topic's making you grumpy.'

He turned and leaned back against the pool's damaged edge, resting on his elbows. I thought I saw a small smile pull at the corner of his lips but it was fleeting, if indeed it happened at all. 'Let's just say that I needed to work a few things out. Plus, I needed to ensure that your existence remains unknown to a few people that I know would be dying to get their hands on you.'

'Like who? Other vampires?'

'It doesn't matter. I'm here now and you're relatively safe at the IMI. It appears that the others I speak of are still unaware of your existence.'

I snorted. 'William, who is it that doesn't know that I exist?'

And then the gap between us was closed in a rush of swirling water and his mouth moved over mine. So much for concerns regarding my welfare. This was the sort of kiss

I'd been waiting for, our mouths moving as one, breath intermingling.

Afterwards, my head became hazy, the fog of his sweet essence slowly claiming my sense of control. I had enough resistance left in me to know that he was enticing me, overpowering my mind, avoiding my questions. Not quite enough resistance to push him away, though. No, he felt too good.

I knew that I would soon forget all my concerns. William had secrets, there was no denying that. We all have them but at what cost? Was I supposed to trust that William was looking out for my best interests? Or would he be like the Protectors, using me to serve some selfish purpose of his own?

One thing was for sure, one truth could no longer be denied—I couldn't really trust anyone, not even my William.

CHAPTER FIVE: EXCHANGE

I threw one of the fluffy white towels from my bathroom at William. He caught it gracefully and began towelling down his wet hair, surveying the space. 'Nice room.'

'You're kidding me, right?' I said, admonishing him for his poor taste. 'This is bland central. The most colourful thing in this room is the food in the refrigerator.'

William shrugged. 'I like white: it's clean, tidy and simple.'

I snorted. 'Boring is more like it.' I muttered it under my breath, though I had no doubt that he'd heard me.

William smirked as he wandered over to the coffee table, towelling off his body and leather pants as he looked over my reading material and DVD collection. I was still standing in the doorway of the bathroom, dripping wet, caught up in the haze of our earlier make-out session. I couldn't help but stare.

William raked his fingers through his short, dark hair, turning around to look at me with curious eyes. It was only then that I realised that I was still gazing at him like an idiot. With an abrupt turn of my head, I looked away and began drying myself off. 'So, where are Marianne and Thomas?'

'Back in London,' he said, sitting down on the sofa and picking up one of my magazines to flick through.

'Is that where you've been?'

'Not exactly.'

'So you went back to London for a little while after I left Cairns and then you went somewhere else?'

William shrugged. 'Something like that.'

'Where?' I was determined not to let the matter drop.

He looked up at me then, eyes hooded. 'I travelled all the way through Europe.'

I continued rubbing my body down, mostly to give my hands something to do that wasn't strangling him in frustration. 'Was your trip to see friends or family?'

'Neither.'

Obtuse. 'So, where did you go, specifically?'

William looked back down at the magazine and pointed at the page. 'Have you read this article on the new Ducati Streetfighter? I went for a test drive in one last week when I was passing through Bologna. They're an absolutely beautiful piece of machinery. It took me a while to find its groove, but after a few miles, the bike and I formed quite a bond.'

I rushed over and glanced down at the page, my face breaking into a huge grin. 'You got to ride one of those? Oh my God, I'm so jealous of you right now. What was it like?'

He smirked again, turning the page. 'It was good.'

'Don't tease me, William. Tell me everything.'

He flicked through the pages, a smug look now riding that slow spreading smile. I caught on pretty quick. 'Hang on a second,' I said, trying to snatch the magazine away from him and failing, 'stop trying to change the subject.' I backed away after another attempt of the snatch and grab in case he reverted to tactic number one—kissing.

William's smugness quickly faded into a frown. 'No, I'm not.'

'Now you're just being a dick.'

William threw the magazine down onto the coffee table,

his features souring in an instant. 'Elena, I really do not want to discuss this with you.'

'Well then you shouldn't have brought it up in the first place! I respect your right to privacy, but by the pool you said that I was yours and that you were protecting me. I have a right to know what you think you're protecting me from, William.'

He sat staring into space, not answering for a long while. 'Do you believe people can change?' William finally said, his voice barely above a whisper.

I blinked, unsure where he was going with this, but relieved that he was at least talking now. 'I think that depends.'

'On what?' he said, turning to look at me again.

I wrapped the towel around myself and sat down next to him. 'Well, I think people can change for a number of reasons. Some people change because they want to: change their physical appearance, their personality, their job ... you know, superficial stuff. But they can also change for stronger reasons, for something more personal than surface issues.'

'How so?' William said, eyeing me curiously.

'You're seriously asking me?'

He nodded.

I shrugged. 'Well, okay, let me think. Events or circumstances that can really shatter a person, like personal tragedy, death, sickness ... I guess they could have a profound effect on someone and cause them to alter the path of their lives.' I cringed, as I thought of that one other reason a person could change. 'And love. I guess that love could change someone, too, if they let it.'

William's nostrils flared. 'Some are too old and set in their ways to change, Elena.'

I shook my head. 'No one is above change. Most of the

time it just happens without you even realising it and if you're motivated to protect the ones you love, well, you'll do whatever it takes.' I let my voice trail off as I thought about Lucas, over on the other side of the world, caught up in the tangled mess I'd help weave.

'Look at me,' I said, coming back to myself. 'I hate being here. It was the stupidest decision I ever made, but I made it because the life of my brother is infinitely more precious to me than my own.' I reluctantly smiled, hating what I was about to admit to William, yet I carried on anyway. 'I think that might be how *love* changes people. It makes you push your own desires and needs to the side to focus on what would be best for the person you care about the most.'

'It's a lovely sentiment,' William added bitterly.

I sniffed. 'The same sentiment that supposedly makes you want to protect me.'

William scoffed. 'It would be nice to think that change was possible even in the blackest of vam—beings,' he quickly amended. 'But love, mercy, and appreciation of others are not qualities these people can easily adopt.'

'Regardless, change is the one thing that no one can stop, William. Even when you are standing still, the world and the people who are in it move on by. You, better than anyone, should know that time changes everything: what you know today could change tomorrow and set you on a new journey that you never thought possible.' I gently pulled William's face towards me. 'I'm starting to learn that change is a good thing—good or bad, it means that people grow. Don't you think that the kind of people you're talking about might have been swept up by the power of change at some point over the years?'

'No.'

'William ...'

He took my hand in his and squeezed tightly. 'Thank you.'

'Huh?' The sudden deviation in conversation had me confused now, as a steely look of resolve now firmly entrenched itself on his features.

'Elena, your words have wavered doubts that were weighing heavily on my conscience. But I realise now, as you were explaining your unselfish love for Lucas, that what I have done to protect you was right, even if others disagree.'

So we were back here again. 'Protect me how? From who?'

He shook his head in dismissal.

'William, was it *you* that you meant when you were asking if it was possible to change?'

'No.'

'Was it me?'

'No.'

'Then who?'

William shook his head again and smiled ruefully, touching a finger to my cheek, sweeping it gently across my skin. 'I may have done wrongs in my past but there are some people out there, Elena, which you just don't need to be acquainted with.'

Sinking back into the sofa, I threw my hands up into the air in defeat. 'I don't know why I bother.'

'Don't worry. Whatever happens, I will always try to make sure that you are safe.'

'Can you please stop talking in riddles! Just say who you're talking about and let me make up my own mind.'

He shrugged, making a play for hands that were now balled into fists in my lap.

'I mean it, William,' I said sternly, slapping away his advances. 'Stop playing games with me.'

'I don't play games, Elena, and I'm sorry if you are

not satisfied but I have no intention of giving you any information that may put you in harm's way.'

'So I don't get a say?'

'Not in this case.'

'Don't patronise me. I don't like people making decisions for me and if you aren't going to tell me, then you might as well leave. There are already so few people in my life that I can trust. If I have to add you to that list then there's no reason for us to continue whatever this thing is between us. I'd be better off on my own.'

William slowly stood, regret a fleeting sentiment that flashed in his emerald eyes. 'Then, so be it. I'd rather have you angry at me than in danger. And to hell with Araqiel's orders.'

'Who the hell is Araqiel?'

William stood up on the arm of the sofa and grabbed at the underside of air-conditioning vent up in the ceiling, ignoring me and cursing softly under his breath.

'William?'

'Don't worry. I'll leave now.'

God, he was being so infuriating! Could this situation he was keeping me away from really be so horrible that he was willing to just leave me indefinitely? Did I really want this information so badly that I'd just let William walk away, completely stuffing up my chances of getting out of the IMI and away from that Alpha?

I reached out and grabbed William's hand. 'Wait.'

He looked down at me, eyes filled with a sadness that made my heart wrench painfully.

'Don't go.'

He replaced the vent covering and jumped down from the arm of the sofa, pulling me close. 'Thank you for understanding.'

'Yeah, well,' I said, shrugging free of his hold, 'I guess I just decided there are other, more important things right now.'

He forced a smile, tucking a lock of my wet hair behind an ear. 'You won't regret it.'

But why do I have this terrible feeling that I will?

I sighed. 'Look, I'm going to go and get changed,' I said and headed towards the bathroom. 'When I come back out, we need to talk.'

On the way, I grabbed the first thing I could find from the wardrobe—a white, strapless sundress with embroidered purple flowers around the top of the bodice and hemming at the bottom. I closed the bathroom door behind me, praying that William would still be there when I came out.

I threw the now damp towel over the edge of the bathtub, stripped off my bikini, and stepped into a fresh pair of underwear. I quickly slipped into the dress and zipped up. I adjusted my boobs for good measure so they sat nicely in the bodice, pulling them up slightly to make them seem a little bigger. God only knew why, but I thought it a good idea at the time.

As I washed and moisturised my face, I could hear sounds coming from the tiny kitchenette outside. William was still here. I smiled to myself with relief.

Oddly enough, though, I thought I could smell cooked cheese. Was that the *ding!* of the microwave—was he making something to eat?

Cracking the door open slightly, I found William dishing pasta out onto a plate. The aroma was tantalising and I realised immediately that I actually *was* hungry. If William hadn't have turned up, I probably would have accepted Beryx's dinner date down in the mess hall. There were rumours they'd be dishing out ravioli this evening—one of my favourites.

I walked out of the bathroom and headed over to the kitchenette. William turned at the sound of my approach, smiling as he placed a plate of macaroni on the small dining table in front of me. He handed me a fork, and a can of Coke, too. William was a long way off being back in my good books, but the cooking certainly helped.

I sat down and sniffed at the food. It certainly smelled edible. 'So, who's Araqiel?' I threw that out for good measure, testing where our conversation might go.

William flashed me a wry smile. 'Eat.'

Okay, so he still isn't going to talk.

I stabbed at the pasta, chewing slowly and savouring the delicious flavour before swallowing. 'It's good, William,' I said in surprise, shovelling a larger forkful into my mouth. 'Where'd you learn to cook like that?'

He grinned and spun around, picking up a cardboard box off the counter. 'According to the little man in the chef hat on the back of this box, all I had to do was pierce the plastic film with a fork, put the frozen meal in the microwave for six minutes, let sit for two, uncover it and then stir.'

I started to laugh. 'That's not cooking, William—that's reheating.'

He shrugged. 'Semantics.'

'What about you? Have you fed recently?'

'About three days ago.'

'Must be nice not having to worry about eating more than once a week.'

'I try not to think about being thirsty when I'm around you.'

I took another mouthful, chewing slowly, and decided that a change of subject was in order. 'Have you spoken to Lucas lately?'

William shook his head. 'Not for about two weeks.' He paused. 'I gather the IMI don't let you call him regularly?'

'No. I've only spoken to him twice since I first arrived. The first time I gave him as much info as I could on the hotel's location, and the second—well, I was being heavily monitored so we couldn't really talk openly and honestly like usual.'

'You miss him,' William surmised.

'Like crazy.' I looked up then, smiling radiantly at him. 'But now that you're here, I'm hoping that will change.'

He smiled back at me, brushing his fingers down the side of my cheek. 'How so?'

'You're going to help me escape.'

'When?'

'Tomorrow, after I've had breakfast with Beryx. I want to find out everything he knows. Plus, Chester seems to be the only technician that hangs around to keep an eye on me on weekends. Well, the personnel and security team are always standing by, too, but they don't really count. I've evaded them before.'

'Chester?' William asked, raising an eyebrow.

'Yeah. Trust me, you don't want to meet him. Some of the crazy stuff he's asked me to do in the name of science is just bloody ridiculous.'

'Such as?'

I laughed nervously, suddenly uncomfortable. 'Well,' I began, unsure how William would react. 'Chester asked if he could cut off my arm to see if it would grow back. Then he asked me to jump off the fourth floor balcony to see if I could self-heal after I went *splat*.' I worried my bottom lip as I saw William's features tighten. 'He stabbed me with his letter opener, but he said that was an accident and—'

The growl that suddenly erupted out of William's throat was menacing and pulled me up short. 'William, it's okay,' I said, touching his arm and staring as his eyes darkened and his canines rapidly grew long. 'I told you that I can look after myself. It's the Alpha following me that I'm really worried about. Chester I can handle, but the Alpha has already devoured three of his security teams whole. It's one of the reasons I'm glad you're here. I may be able to get out of this place, but once I'm outside, I'm at risk. I can't outrun that creature like you can.'

This time when William hissed it was so loud I thought the windows were going to shatter. I put hands over my ears, looking at him in horror as he rapidly transformed into full vampiric form. At the tips of his fingers talons lengthened into sharp knives, the normally milky pallor of his skin vanishing under a new transparency that highlighted the toughened muscles and blood-filled veins within.

William sprang up from his chair, immediately headed for the door. I caught his arm, trying to force him to halt, but he spun around and growled right in my face. The sound that tore out of the back of his throat was as vicious as a rabid dog tearing shreds off an unwanted intruder.

I dropped his hand, and took a few cautious steps backwards. I hadn't seen William this worked up for months, not since he'd rescued me from John's maniacal clutches. Even then, he'd been more in control than now.

For the first time since I'd met William, I was truly afraid of what he might be capable of.

William cocked his head to the side, seemingly aware that he might have frightened me, appearing to regain some measure of control. He watched my feet carefully as I kept backing up. I only halted because there was nowhere else to go with a wall digging into the small of my back.

William's long, clawed fingers left the handle of the door. He turned around to fully face me, straightening up from that deadly crouch that I knew signalled he was about to kill. He stretched his powerful neck from side to side, letting loose a procession of thunderous cracks. The fine, blue trails of veins I could see running beneath the surface of his skin began to fade, and his canines quickly pulled back. William's black eyes slowly morphed back into those familiar emerald depths that I recognised. 'Elena,' he said, taking a hesitant step forward.

I met him halfway, pushing myself away from the wall behind me and taking a few tentative steps.

'Elena, I'm so sorry. I didn't mean to scare you. I merely heard your words and all I could think about was killing them all, killing them and then going out and ripping that Alpha apart.'

I frowned. 'That's the stupidest plan I've ever heard.'

William shook his head. 'You have to understand, Elena, that I would rather die than let anyone hurt you.'

I slowly stepped forward until I was standing directly in front of him. 'I understand exactly what you are saying, but that doesn't mean killing everyone in sight is a brilliant idea—otherwise, I would have done it myself. I've put up with their tests and the crazy experiments because I knew that the only way I'd ever actually get out of here was with your help. So, after my last encounter with the Alpha, I made an agreement with Chester that I'd be on my best behaviour. Just so he wouldn't lock me in a cell somewhere and throw away the key, like he'd threatened to.'

William looked as if he wanted to say something, possibly argue against my logic, but quickly closed his mouth and bit back his retort. His hands were curled fists at his sides.

I sighed. 'I love that you're trying to defend me, but I don't need you to kill everyone for me. Some of the people here aren't all that bad. I just need your speed—like I said, I can't outrun that Alpha. But you can.'

He nodded. 'I'm sorry, I just didn't think. I love you and that sometimes means I can't see reason.'

'Yeah, well,' I said, mumbling uncomfortably and shifting from foot to foot. 'I like you a lot, too.'

William chuckled lightly, leaning lazily back against the bedroom door. 'You haven't changed at all, have you?'

'It's only been five weeks.'

'And that's a lifetime to be apart from you.'

I snorted in disgust. 'And I think you've gotten even soppier in my absence. We need to man you up a little bit.'

That final spell of anger melted away as he laughed, reaching for me. 'And I think you've enjoyed every minute of my blatant affection for you.' As if to prove a point, he scooped me up into his arms and carried me over to the bed, setting me down in its centre with care.

What had just happened? We'd just been fighting and now this? Half an hour ago the guy had been lecturing me on pushing his vampiric limits—now he was whisking me off to bed? Even back in Cairns, things had never gone this far.

'You're so beautiful,' William murmured as he lay down beside me, shifting my body easily so that I lay draped in the crook of his arm. He stroked my thigh gently, the surface of my skin goosepimpling.

'And you? Well, what can I say?' I said, shivering and laughing nervously. 'You're hideous.'

Oh my God, Elena. Think first and then speak, you freaking idiot.

He clicked his tongue in response to my attempt at sarcasm. 'Am I making you nervous, Elena?' William said, kissing the tip of my nose, pausing, and then dipping down to my mouth.

'Truthfully?' I said as his lips gently caressed my own,

fingers still working on the flesh of my thighs. 'You're freaking me out.'

William propped himself up on one elbow and looked down at me. 'You never have to be afraid of me, Elena.'

'I'm not afraid of you. I said you're freaking me out—there's a difference.'

His eyes narrowed. 'How so?'

'You keep running hot and cold, for one. It's a little confusing and ...' I trailed off, not quite sure how to finish the sentence.

'What is it?'

I shook my head and looked away. I could feel my face beginning to turn red. 'It doesn't matter.' William could have never understood that as a virgin the thought of progressing anywhere past kissing really had my knickers in a proverbial twist. He was nearly five hundred years old: he'd probably been with hundreds of other vampire women, all of them ten times more accomplished at these matters than I was. I knew how to kiss him—that seemed to come naturally—but all the other stuff that Kayla used to talk about, like Karma Sutra inspired leg flips, glowing thunder beads, and flavoured condoms? Well, I had zero idea how to perform any sexual activity with proficiency or finesse. The last thing that I wanted now was to embarrass myself, especially if that's where things were heading.

'Elena?'

'Do you want to watch a movie or something?' I said, trying to change the subject.

William frowned at me. 'I'd much rather stay *here*, on the bed, with *you*.'

I cringed. What he was suggesting appealed immensely, but I just didn't have the guts to follow through. Plus, there was the whole pregnancy thing which pretty much poured icy water over the heat flaring up inside of me.

William touched his fingers gently to my chin, turning my face back around to look at him. 'You're frightened of me now because of how I reacted before, aren't you?'

I shook my head. 'You did scare me, but no, that's not it.'

'Well, what then? I thought I was the one usually putting on the brakes.'

I chewed on my lower lip and debated the answer, deciding that directness was the best course of action.

'Do you want to sleep with me?' I slowly asked.

William swallowed deeply. 'More than anything,' he breathed, his eyes suddenly smouldering with barely contained desire. 'But you and I both know that I can't touch you like that until after you turn.'

I nodded, feeling a little more nervous than before. 'What about the other stuff?'

The corners of his lips twitched. He was going to make me say it just because he could see it was giving me 'the ickies'. 'Other stuff?'

Mongrel.

'Please don't make me say it out loud,' I whispered.

William's eyes were filled with longing as they raked up the length of my body. 'I gather you are referring to other sexual activities executed below the waist?'

I rolled away from him, my face flushing a whole new shade of crimson.

God, how old am I?

He chuckled, pulling me back despite my profuse protests. I didn't want him to see my face. 'Why do you ask, Elena?'

I hesitated, looking at William through my fingers, unwilling to reveal my face just yet. 'Umm, I just thought, well, you know … the bed.' I pointed down at the mattress and then quickly re-covered my heated flesh.

He smiled, pulling my hands away from my face and touching a finger to my lips. 'Nothing can ever go that far, Elena. I still cannot fully control myself and I don't want to risk your life that way—bed or no bed. So for now, for both of our sakes, I think we should stick to kissing. What do you think?'

I breathed a sigh of relief. 'Okay, cool.'

'Don't sound so relieved.'

'I'm not, it's just—'

'Wait,' William said, his smile broadening as far as his lips would stretch. 'Did *you* want to sleep with *me*?'

I sniffed and looked away. 'I'm *so* not answering that question.'

William was laughing that deep laugh of his now, but soon his breathing hitched and his voice lightened, a modicum of his former control slipping. 'I could make you.' He rolled over on top of me, nose touching mine, his breath caressing my lips.

I tensed, feeling the hard length of him stretched out over my body. I had a feeling some boundaries were about to be crossed. 'You can't make me do anything I—'

He cut me off with a kiss—soft, gentle and so restrained that it made me restless for something more.

As our lips moved in unison, I wrapped my arms around his neck, nestling my hands at the base of his scalp. I twisted my fingers through the damp, silken strands of his hair and suddenly hoped for a taste of that carelessness. His lips, although working their magic, were still too gentle against mine—too careful, too restrained.

I stroked the length of William's spine, feeling the coolness of his skin beneath my fingertips and smiling.

He shuddered beneath my touch, and as I closed my eyes I felt the intensity of our kiss deepen. His hands soon began searching out their own path of pleasurable torment upon my body.

William's fingertips gently grazed my neck, my arm, and the sides of my thighs, tracing circular patterns on my skin. A fire erupted across my flesh that I could no longer contain; I could feel myself burning from the inside-out, with no idea how to douse the flames or even if I wanted to. I'd never allowed myself to get this close to a man before and certainly never expected that the first would be a vampire that lusted after my blood.

I blamed everything on the bed.

I found myself wrapping my legs around William's waist, pulling him closer to me. I was no longer nervous, but instead suddenly felt empowered and capable, like my body knew exactly what to do and all I had to do was follow its lead.

William parted my lips and tenderly began to explore the inside of my mouth with his tongue. I moaned, the small sound echoing across the silent room. William gave a satisfied growl as he delved deeper, much further than a kiss between us should ever have gone.

I was gasping for breath as he pulled away a moment later.

'Elena,' William whispered, resting his forehead against my own. This abrupt surrendering to common sense was torturous; my body's only desire was to consume him entirely, to be consumed by him.

'We must stop now, Elena,' William said with rasping breath, a hint of forcefulness in his voice. He looked down at me, his hard, lean body quivering against mine, hands balled into fists as he balanced above me. I could almost see William's internal debate raging within.

Keeping my legs locked around his back, I reached up to touch William's cheeks, my fingers caressing the rigid planes of his face. His eyes darted back and forth, bouncing between the veins in my wrist and the ones on my neck.

You would think I was smart enough to heed the warning signs, to listen to William's protests, but obviously not. I was suddenly pulling him to me once more, ignoring the screams of common sense from inside my head, and thinking only of the pleasure of tasting him again and again.

I searched out the sweetness of William's lips and he succumbed without protest, once again fanning the flames of our desire. I could feel him straining against me, reluctant and cautious, his eyes squeezing tightly shut.

I tried pulling him closer but he was much stronger than I, despite the obvious reluctance of his body to disobey.

'Elena, you need to stop this now. I don't have the strength,' he rasped.

I changed tactics. I let my tongue glide in a seductive trail across his lips, feeling a small flicker of satisfaction as he shuddered in response above me. 'Neither do I.' The full power of his compulsion had overcome me, whether he liked it or not.

'Elena, you must try.'

'I don't want to.'

'Neither do I.'

I should have chosen my next words carefully—I didn't.

'Then don't.'

'You shouldn't offer this,' William breathed against my ear, his words barely audible between clenched teeth.

'You shouldn't compel me,' I said, yanking his head back by a fistful of hair and kissing him.

'I'm not.'

It was the last thing William said before his body suddenly

went slack, the full weight of him pressing into me. The gentle brush of lips soon turned into a savage possession of each other's bodies. His hands cupped my thighs, pushing me down hard into the mattress, the intimate pressure of his body against mine overpowering. I never wanted it to end, but I could slowly feel him slipping away.

William yanked his head out of my grasp and gasped aloud. I opened my eyes. His teeth were fully drawn, his eyes blacker than the darkest night. 'Elena, I have to stop!' he gasped, grabbing my legs with lengthening talons that dug painfully into my flesh.

'No, not yet,' I said, raising my upper body in attempt to meet with his lips once more.

William growled, his black eyes glaring back at me, chest sharply heaving in and out as he fought to regain his strength of will. I was going to win—when had I turned into such a hussy?

Shit.

His self-control finally snapped and I found William shoving me, almost violently, back onto the mattress. His hands wrapped around the back of my neck, yanking my head back. I slid my hands underneath us, letting my fingers glide over the rock-hard muscles of his abdomen and down the soft trail of hair that started just at the top of his leather pants.

William shivered at my touch.

The unexpected taste of blood jolted me back to my senses, my eyes flying open as William's fangs sliced through my lower lip. My sweet essence drained as we kissed, blood mingling in our mouths, a delectable torment that I could only think of as dangerous.

William lifted his face from mine; his eyes were shimmering obsidian depths containing a new kind of hunger.

'William?' I said tentatively.

He looked down at me and licked his lips, body stiffening slightly at the sound of my voice. He made no further move, just kept staring at me with those eyes as empty as the night. Blue veins pulsed expectantly beneath the surface of his skin.

I reached up and touched William's face. His lips pulled back into a snarl, eyes following the line of veins that throbbed at my wrist. I couldn't believe that I'd been selfish enough to push him this far. William had vowed never to let things get to this point, to never let his thirst get the better of him and now here I was, encouraging him to break his resolve.

'It's okay,' I said quietly, stroking his face with one shaking hand. 'If it's too much, if you can't control yourself, don't hold back.'

William snarled again, his fingers tightening around the base of my neck, his talons digging deep enough to puncture flesh.

'I'll heal,' I added, pulling his head back down. 'It's okay, William. You don't have to fight what you are.'

William's lips slowly drew back from his teeth. I turned my head to the side, feeling him straining against the urge as his entire body quivered. He still fought for control, but we both knew he'd gone far too long denying his true nature.

I knew his resistance came solely from the fact that he'd killed his own mother in a feeding frenzy after he had first turned; however, that had been centuries past. William could no longer deny what he was; he had to forgive himself. He needed to know that it was okay to take what he needed in order to survive as long as it didn't hurt those around him. I knew that he would never really hurt me, that he'd know when to stop.

Stroking his face again, I pulled his mouth down towards my neck. A feral snarl erupted from his throat, and I smiled. Even though he was burning up with thirst, he still resisted its call to spare me from pain. 'It's okay,' I repeated. 'Just stop before I black out.'

William's teeth were suddenly piercing the flesh of my neck. Warm rivulets of blood poured down my skin. I bucked underneath him, crying out as a thankfully momentary pain faded into pleasure, as he buried his face deep in my neck, taking his fill.

My eyes began to feel heavy. My limbs grew weary and muscles weak, as my life's essence rushed out of me. I felt William's hand leaving my thigh to reach up and stroke the side of my face with a tenderness I had not expected from him while feeding.

I kissed his fingers and caught the scent of something highly appealing. The smell was strangely like that of blood, so close to my own but different.

As William's finger dipped into my mouth, I was vaguely aware that it was the blood that swum through *his* veins that smelt good—too good to simply ignore.

I closed my eyes, focusing on his scent, something I'd never been able to do before that moment. As I pictured the warmth of his blood touching my lips, something began to happen to me, something unexpected. I licked William's finger and, surprised, found my own teeth beginning to extend. My tongue licked the oversharp points of my canines, canines that could so easily break through William's skin.

Whoops.

But I did it anyway, shuddering as the overwhelming sweetness of his blood dribbled down into my mouth. The taste of it danced across my tongue and ignited my senses, filling me and heating my body from my toes all the way up to the tips of my fingers. William tasted even better than I could have ever imagined.

He quickly tore his finger out of my mouth, leaving a trail of blood smeared across my lips and chin, before bounding off the bed so swiftly it left me breathless. As William looked in horror down at the punctured flesh of his finger and then back at me, I greedily began to lick his blood from my lips. I then wiped at my chin with a finger and started sucking on that, too.

'Elena,' William breathed, voice filled with pain, 'what have we done?'

My head suddenly felt heavy, my eyelids like concrete. William stared at his bloodied finger, still wearing that horrified expression like what we'd done was criminal. I couldn't agree; I was blissfully happy in that moment.

William rushed back over to the bed, pulling back my top lip to reveal my newly-erupted fangs. As his fingers brushed the pointed edges, he swore. He swore so long and hard that I would have blushed if I wasn't still riding so high.

'William?' I said, reaching out dreamily to cup his face. 'You taste good.'

He began to shake his head. 'How could I have let this happen?'

As he talked, I could feel the strange sensation of my fangs receding.

'Maybe it's not too late. You didn't have enough of my blood.' William sprang up and started to pace beside the bed. 'You can't have turned yet because I didn't feed you nearly enough for that. That has to count for something.' He paused. 'Elena, I'm so sorry. I can't believe I did this to you—it's unforgiveable.'

My eyes shuttered. 'S' okay,' I murmured. 'I wanted it, too.'

'Not like this,' he whispered. 'How will you ever forgive me?'

I sighed, not bothering to fight a yawn. 'There's nothing to forgive.'

William bent down and kissed my forehead. 'I'll never let myself do this to you again, Elena, I promise you that. I know what I must do to keep you safe.' He left my side and started to pace again, head down and arms folded across his chest. 'I should have done what Araqiel said. I should have taken you to them—if I had maybe this wouldn't have happened.' William paused. 'Maybe none of the hardships you've gone through would have happened if it wasn't for my interference.'

'Okay,' I answered, barely coherent. The need for sleep was beginning to overwhelm my senses entirely.

I felt William's cool body press against me, his weight sinking into the mattress. He kept whispering over and over again how sorry he was. All I wanted was to hold him tight and tell him to stop being so ridiculous, but my words were slurred, just like my thoughts. After sleep, when I woke up again, we could talk this through rationally.

I felt something cool brush against my lips. There was something unsettling about that caress but I had no strength left in me to open my eyes. I couldn't fight what I felt was coming and that scared me.

As I fell into oblivion I lost the fight to hold on, the darkness welcoming me like the arms of an old friend. Words were lost whispers in the back of my mind and the strength I needed to keep William here had passed. There was nothing now, no fight to win, but only shadows and the promise of tomorrow—a certainty neither of us could run from.

CHAPTER SIX: DISCOVERIES

Lucas looked down at his watch: it was almost midnight.

Frustrated and slightly anxious, he rose from his mattress and started pacing across the floor of his bedroom. Elena was supposed to have called tonight. She'd promised him the last time they'd spoken and no recent disjointed or strained conversations should have prevented that. They may not have been able to have had a decent conversation since she'd left, but hearing her voice was a comfort. He missed her.

Lucas kicked at the leg of his desk chair and cursed.

I never should have let her go. Something's wrong.

He almost laughed at this admission—as if he could control her. Elena always did exactly what she wanted, whenever she wanted, regardless of the consequences. She dove into bad situations headfirst and then checked the depths afterwards.

She'd been so determined to put distance between them and for what? So she could prevent a Vânător invasion? Elena hadn't realised what she'd walked into, had misjudged the IMI's intentions and put herself at risk yet again.

Lucas shook his head, running his fingers through long, blonde hair. No, life just hadn't been the same since Elena had left. Granted, everyone at the IMI had been deliriously happy that Elena was gone, her presence being likened to the plague by other, more vindictive Protectors. Not even his parents had been upset by her absence but that wasn't really a surprise to Lucas now, since discovering the finer details of Elena's transfer.

Bastards. How could they be involved?

His latest little discovery was a doozy: the IMI's long term plans now superseded the preservation of the human race and instead centred on species' annihilation. Lucas had briefly skimmed the documents for himself; he would never be the same again. He couldn't quite wrap his head around everything he'd read just yet but in time he would.

He glanced down at his watch for the umpteenth time—midnight. Lucas had so much to tell Elena that he was practically bursting at the seams. The only problem was that he probably couldn't without headquarters growing suspicious. Lucas didn't doubt for a second that the moment he mentioned Chester's research the phone would go dead between them. So how could he alert Elena to the danger she was in and to escape as soon as possible? And why the hell wasn't William returning his calls? He was the only one who could help get Elena out of Bucharest safely!

He sighed and raked a hand through his hair again, perspiration turning the strands greasy. 'What the hell, Elena! Why aren't you freaking calling me?'

Had something happened to her? Was he too late?

Lucas felt his hands ball into fists at his sides; magic like an electric current crackled and fizzled across the taut skin of his knuckles. He could feel the power rising within him, his anger feeding its energy, filling the palms of his hands with a bright heat. But, for all his ability, Lucas felt useless. How could he help Elena across the other side of the world?

Cursing and kicking at a chair, he flopped back down onto his mattress.

If I don't hear from her by next Friday, I'm going to Bucharest myself. Damn you, Mum and Dad, you traitors.

How could they have raised Elena, pretended to love and protect her, knowing ahead of time that on her seventeenth birthday Elena was going to be shipped off to the IMI for dissection?

It made Lucas sick to think of it.

In some ways he wished he'd never found the dossier. Okay, 'found' was the wrong word. He'd *purposefully* picked the lock on George's desk to search for secrets, but he'd never expected his own parents to be involved.

Inside the file were numerous photos of Elena at different stages of her childhood and adolescence. Beneath those were reports of various incidents she'd been involved in: mostly accidents or instances of self-healing that George and Susan had themselves incited. But there were also detailed documents about when she'd first encountered the Vânători, her reactions to them, as well as her relationship with William.

Finally, at the bottom of the pile he'd found the signed documentation relinquishing Elena to the IMI's Bucharest headquarters on her seventeenth birthday, one year before turning. The document reported that she was going to be under surveillance for six months, during which time she'd be tested and experimented on until they fully understood the logistics of her half-breed nature. On her eighteenth birthday, the document matter-of-factly stated, they would kill Elena and then harvest her blood to manufacture some sort of serum. This serum could be affected into a weapon and be able to be used against both the Vampires and Vânători, collectively.

Lucas had not been able to read any further than that. George had walked in soon after, catching him in the act;

he had *not* been happy. His father hadn't answered any of his questions either, had just shoved Lucas out of his office and slammed the door shut.

They hadn't talked since.

Lucas had tried approaching his mother about it, but she'd shut him out, too, had kept shaking her head and telling him that he was mistaken.

Yet, there was no mistake this time. That feeling of dread he'd had when Elena had left burned ever hotter through his veins now.

The phone rang. Lucas was so surprised he nearly dropped his mobile. But he could see from the name that flashed up that the caller wasn't Elena but Marianne, William's hot vampire friend. Normally, he would have smiled; tonight, Lucas was disappointed.

Sighing, he accepted the call, anyway.

'Lucas,' Marianne said quickly, 'what do you want?' She was abrupt, just like always.

'Hey, Blondie, thanks for calling me back.'

'Do not call me that,' she hissed.

Probably not wise to bait a vampire, but Lucas had an inkling this one liked him, despite the hostility. 'It's about Elena.'

'Isn't it always?' Marianne groaned. 'What has happened to Princess now?' Marianne was no fan of Elena. Jealousy definitely had something to do with it; Lucas and Elena both knew she had a major jones for William.

'I'm not sure. That's why I rang you. Do you know where William is?'

'Probably with *her*.'

'He's in Bucharest? Already?'

'Last I heard,' she muttered. 'Stupid if you ask me. That place is crawling with Protectors. She's definitely not worth it.'

Lucas bit back an ill-tempered retort by momentarily tapping the mobile against his forehead, desperately trying to manufacture a little calm. If Marianne hadn't been so damn hot he might have told her to shut the hell up. After all, it was *his* sister she was bitching about.

'Why do you ask?' Marianne said, her previous irritation melting to suspicion.

Lucas hesitated. Would telling Marianne help or hinder his cause? 'Do you have another number for William? The one I keep ringing says his phone's switched off.'

'I keep getting the same message, too. Don't worry, though,' she breathed, taking a little time to control the distaste in her voice, 'his intent was clear when he left. He was making his way to spring Elena from the IMI's headquarters in Bucharest.'

Lucas breathed a long sigh of relief. So she was going to get away from that place after all.

Good.

'Is something going on?' Marianne asked.

'Nothing I can't handle.' He paused, thinking through his options. 'I don't suppose that you and Thomas would put me up for a while?'

She snorted. 'We're back in London and we don't shelter blood bags. Why?'

'Things are a little weird at home.'

'You want me to kill someone?'

Lucas laughed in spite of himself. 'I appreciate the offer, but I guess I'll just wait for Elena to contact me. If William is busting her out of headquarters, then she should contact me soon.'

'Was there something else? This conversation is starting to bore me,' Marianne murmured, voice drifting.

'No, we're done.'

'Good.'

'See ya later, Blondie.'

'Bite me.'

She hung up.

At least Lucas felt better now: Elena was safe.

CHAPTER SEVEN: REVELATIONS

I found myself standing in the middle of a room that was dimly lit by crude torches. Each burning bundle was a long arm of wood, tightly wrapped in cheesecloth at one end. Flames licked appreciatively at the fabric, each flicker dancing with the shadows and causing an eerie glow. From an iron grate in the roof line above, the soft glow of the moon shone into the stone-clad room, helping to illuminate a table in the centre of the room.

The table's surface was worn with age and stressed from years of exposure to the elements. The timber had silvered and cracked in many places, stained with a dark ink in some areas that resembled blood. There was a well-used candle at the table's centre. Its once tapered body was now contorted into a melted mess of dribbling wax that splayed out around it like a puddle of water. The flame flickered in and out, struggling with what little life it had before the wind would inevitably blow it out for the final time.

Around the table were five chairs, each bearing individual carvings. The most elaborate carved and largest of these chairs had an inscription: *Lucius*. The other four chairs, although embellished, were not as grand as the first, and bore their own names: *Decimus*, *Maximus*, *Marcus* and *Tiberius*.

What kind of crazy-ass dream is this?

I turned as the battered timber door behind me swung inwards, extinguishing the candle in the centre of the table, casting shadow across its surface. The flaming torches on the wall danced, then finally guttering out as if commanded.

I blinked, trying to adjust to the sudden lack of illumination. The grate above allowed only the moonlight to penetrate; its ghostly luminescence settled over the large table, only visible now that my eyes began to adjust.

I moved to the now open door. In the dark passageway beyond there was no one, only a steel door and a set of stairs to my left. I was about to venture into the darkened space and find what lay beyond, when something made me halt.

I turned around, touched by an invisible force that twisted my shoulders and moved my feet. Now, on one of the engraved chairs, a man sat, head bowed in front of him. I would swear that chair had been empty moments before.

His hair was thick and dark. His arms lay on the table in front of him, their skin pale and streaked with fine lines of pale blue. His nails were long, black and sharp, and dug easily into the table's surface, creating small indentations under his fingertips. He wore no shirt, and hasty glimpses at his turned back revealed scarring, showed long sinewy lines of toughened flesh that were raised and marred with a slight pinkish hue.

Curious, I stepped forward to get a closer look at the man; I felt somehow drawn as I reached fearlessly into this supposed dream, trying to assert control. It seemed like the man was silently calling to me, an unspoken message in the calm of the night, with a familiarity that seemed to span the depth of my imagination and my very soul.

I reached for him, feeling the power between us grow stronger.

He moved, a sudden whip of his head levelling narrowing eyes at mine. Those eyes were as black as night and oozing aggression; below them, his lips formed a vicious snarl, the sharpest of teeth slow to reveal.

He was a vampire.

The creature leapt up from the chair in one swift movement, limbs a blur in the darkness. Behind him, the chair dropped to the floor with a soundless crash.

I took a step back as he dropped into a defensive crouch, one I had seen many times before. I could sense he was going to attack me, taste the anticipation across my tongue. Sparks of tension filled the air between us as his muscles twitched, expectant.

The creature launched himself through the air with lightning speed and deadly force. He was a blur of limbs, his body landing on my ethereal, dreamlike form as if I were truly there. I was pushed to the ground, my palms scraping against the cold stone beneath and drawing blood, but, it didn't hurt. I seemed to feel no pain here.

As we both grappled for dominant position, his hands seized my face, holding me tightly while every inch of his dark eyes washed over me in a way I'd never felt before: not sexual, and not part of a vampire's thirst. No, he was judging me, seeing down into my very soul and reading the person that I was—gazing at the very essence of my being.

I made an effort to speak, the words catching in my throat as he yanked my face to the side, exposing my neck. His teeth grazed skin seconds before biting down, as he pierced through flesh and tore down to the bone. Again, there was no pain, no pleasure; only a fear that begun to blossom as my mind started to unravel, my head filling with pictures of people and places I had only ever dreamed about.

I screamed.

I woke with a fright, sitting rigidly upright in bed and reaching for the lamp on my nightstand with shaking fingers. I switched on the light, willing the cold, white room around me to fill up with its warming glow, a light that would illuminate my surroundings and flush away the lingering darkness of the dream. This was the first nightmare I'd had since I was a little girl, and the first one I could ever remember that had felt completely real.

Sweat trickled down the sides of my temples. My hair was damp and hung limply around my face, slick against the back of my neck.

I took a deep breath—first in, then out—and counted to ten, hoping it would calm my racing heart and settle my nerves. My dream had been so much more vivid than anything I could ever recall. I could still taste the fear on my tongue, feel those teeth piercing my neck. Strange images and voices still flitted through my mind.

Crazy.

The man himself, rather than the dream, had been what had honestly frightened me the most. He seemed so familiar to me, in ways that I could not fathom, more familiar than William and Lucas put together. That in and of itself seemed strange as there was nothing about his appearance that resonated within me; I had never seen him before, and did not know his name.

I swallowed deeply, wiping the sweat away from my forehead and neck, brushing my hair from eyes and glancing down at the empty space on the mattress beside me. As I stood, I pushed my blankets off me, climbing slowly out of bed.

'William?' I muttered into the dimly lit room.

No answer.

A feeling of dread washed over me, as memories of the previous night flooded back.

I darted out into the living area but found nothing but empty space. Then I checked out the bathroom, for good measure, even though I knew he wouldn't be there. William hadn't used a bathroom in centuries.

He was nowhere to be found.

'William, this isn't funny,' I called out shakily, running back into the living area again and glancing up at the air-conditioning duct with hope. 'Please, come back down from there.'

There was still no movement or sound.

I climbed up onto the arm of the sofa so I could get closer to the air-conditioning vent. I tilted my head back and sniffed well-ventilated air, trying to catch wind of his scent, hoping against all hope that he was just reconnoitring the IMI to get a better idea of our escape route.

But still there was nothing, only the faint smell of mould and rat's droppings.

I glanced around, feeling my heart wrench painfully. Although I didn't want to believe that William would leave me hanging like this, it was quickly becoming obvious that he was gone. I wanted to believe that he wouldn't have just left without saying goodbye but I couldn't be sure.

I turned around, surveying the room more carefully, trying to digest the inevitable. It was then that I spied the handwritten note sitting on top of the dining table. I cringed. I knew in that moment that if I crossed the room and picked up that piece of paper, reading it would shatter my faith in William into a million pieces.

I shook my head. I couldn't deal with this right now.

I went back into the bedroom, curled up on the bed, switched the light off and just stared at the walls until my eyes dried out. Eventually, I rolled over, closing them in defeat. If William really was gone then there wasn't a damn thing I could do about it.

I groaned and pulled the blanket up over my head. It was probably my own fault, anyway. I should never have allowed my feelings for him to have pushed things so far. I should have known that eventually William would leave me or let me down.

Why now, William? Why now when I need you most?

Drinking my blood had obviously scared him away and now I was royally, goddamn screwed.

Jesus, you just had to open a vein for him, didn't you? You idiot, E.

And the finger? Why the hell did you snack on his digits!

I cursed, promising myself that I wouldn't cry. I was probably going to scream a little bit, but I was *not* going to cry. Tears were for the weak and being weak was not going to get me out of Bucharest.

As I had once said to William, 'ignorance is bliss' and I still believed that to be true. It was the mantra I was going to keep repeating to myself until daylight dared to erupt through the windows and introduced me to the reality of a new day dawning. Maybe then I could accept the truth: William was gone.

I stared down at the piece of paper on the dining room table. William's message was carefully drafted in a tidy scrawl, his first two words resonating in my mind like a symphony of well-strung bullshit.

I'm sorry.

What kind of lame apology is that?

So far, I'd spent three hours ignoring the letter, trying to slip back to sleep. But those unread words were practically screaming up at me and I could now no longer ignore them. I was going to have to read it, whether his words cut me like a knife or not.

I held his stupid letter tightly between my fingers and those two infuriating words kept repeating in my mind—two words I wanted to ram up William's perfectly formed ass.

I'm sorry.

If William thought that he was doing me any favours by leaving me here, then he was sorely mistaken. Nothing he could say would aptly justify him leaving in the middle of the night without explanation.

I sighed, rubbing my fingers across weary eyes, forcing those two hated words to come into focus once again.

I'm sorry.

I forced myself to read on, chewing on my bottom lip, and wishing there was something in my room that I could punch—preferably my stupid vampire.

Elena, I know that you will probably never forgive me for leaving you like this, but I love you too much to keep putting you in harm's way. What I have done is unforgiveable, not just to you but to my own sense of morality.

I can no longer be trusted around you.

I am going to put some distance between us. It's the only way I can think of to get over your scent, your

*essence, something I can now no longer ignore. As soon
as I have a grip on my thirst again, I will come back for
you.*

    If you will still have me ...

    Forever yours,
    W.G.

I screwed up the note and slammed it into the rubbish bin
by the sink. What a frigging copout. What about me? Did he
even think about how his leaving might make me feel? Did it
occur to him that I had enjoyed the whole experience—the
kissing, the touching, even the biting? Did he realise that
he'd totally stuffed up my plans for escape and left me in
the hands of these mad scientists?

    Of course not.

    I threw my head back and screamed at the top of my
lungs, screamed until every last breath was expelled from
my body. My fist connected with the dining room table,
melamine and timber shards spraying around me in a halo
of simmering anger. I kicked one of the chairs clear across
the room but was still not satisfied, as I watched its metal
legs buckle and wall plaster rain down like snow.

    This was exactly the reason why I never wanted to pursue
a relationship or fall in love. Someone always gets hurt,
someone inevitably gets let down, and there's always a lot
of screaming when the situation goes pear-shaped. That was
precisely why I usually tried to shield myself from all of this
bullshit. And now no amount of self-healing was going to
mend my shattered trust.

    I screamed again, a deep, primal roar that emptied out of
my lungs until my chest ached and my throat burned. What
was left of the mangled dining table soon joined the chair

on the other side of the room, hurtling through the wall between the living room and bedroom and leaving nothing more than a pile of kindling and damaged wall plaster.

Moments later, I was jumping back in fright as the door to my room unexpectedly flew open. Chester came rushing in, fingers dancing with blue flecks of light and flanked by three members of his personnel team. They too shimmered with power and were edging towards me warily.

'What happened?' Chester roared, bounding across the room and looking for the source of my outbursts. 'Who was here? What did you do? Are you okay? Is it the Alpha?'

I dropped down onto the remaining dining chair, too tired and frustrated to even look at him. His words seemed to blur together into a string of unintelligible garble. What could I say, anyway? My boyfriend dumped me because my blood's liquid chocolate and he's suddenly gone on a sugar-free diet?

The personnel team fanned out around the room, checking my bathroom, under the bed, and examining every nook and cranny in the tiny apartment. They weren't going to find anything—William would have made sure of that. The only evidence that he was even here was the note in the garbage bin and my ever-expanding foul mood.

Chester came to my side and rested his hands on my shoulders. I shrugged him away. He was the last person I wanted to be touching me right now. I just wanted to be able to scream and yell in peace without Dr. Crazy around.

He persisted, grabbing at my upper arms and shaking me as if I was in some sort of trance. Maybe I was—who knows? 'Elena, speak to me. What happened here?' Chester said, slapping me hard on each cheek.

Bad call.

I turned and hissed at him, the sound reverberating

across the room and shaking the opaque glass panes in their frames. It was the sound of a pissed off vampire, a sound I was intimately familiar with, and a sound that *shouldn't* have come from me yet.

Chester pointed at me with one, trembling finger and took a few cautious steps backwards. The personnel team mirrored his response, though still appeared ready to strike at me if necessary. 'Get her to the lab immediately,' Chester said to the others. 'Something ... something has happened to her. Elena has ... are those fangs?'

Surprised, I reached up and felt the pointed tips of two super-erupted canines protruding past my top lip. Applying a little pressure, I easily pierced my fingertip. Several tiny droplets of blood inched their way down my fingers in a barely notable caress. I explored their length, tracing the slightly irritated, surrounding gum line and overall penetrative length.

Holy shit, this is really happening!

Chester and his team started moving towards me with carefully measured steps, hands held out in front of them as if trying to decide if I was as dangerous as I appeared. I supposed I might have been.

I immediately dropped from the chair and fell into a crouch, something primal inside of me shifting to the surface. It was a part of me that didn't appreciate being touched, cornered or caged—a part that was wild and could never be tamed. And that unknown part scared the absolute crap out of me.

'Chester,' I said slowly, trying not to lisp with my protruding fangs, 'please tell your men to back away. I'm not exactly sure what's happening to me right now and I don't want to hurt anybody.'

'I can't do that, Elena,' Chester said, taking a step forward, magic dancing across his fingertips as a crackling reminder of his power.

'Please try.'

'Now? When things are just getting interesting?' he answered, taking another step.

I drew in a deep breath and drove my fists into the debris lying around on the floor, smashing it into shards. This was vastly better than losing control on soft, irreparable flesh. A fight was on the way and my body knew it. Something inside me was now focused on the approaching men, weighing them up, and gauging which was the biggest threat.

'Please,' I repeated. 'I'll come with you to the lab right now—just back off. I'm not sure if you'll win once I get started. I feel different now, I feel … better.'

Chester smirked, seemingly confident in his own abilities. 'Well then, I'll make this easier on everyone.'

He stepped forward, pointing his fingers directly at me and yelled, '*Hevannatara!*'

Blue light surged from his fingertips, stabbing me square in the centre of my chest. I froze, instantly, down in that crouching position—legs slightly askew, head tilted back, and my body leaning forward on tightly held fists for support. It made me wish I'd had the foresight not to have worn a dress.

'She's secure,' Chester remarked, dropping his hands back to his sides. 'Take her to the lab.'

I was secure all right: the spell had ensured ultimate discomfort as my muscles contracted, limbs stiffened, and my tongue swelled; it brimmed with obscenities that wished to be spoken.

Two members of his personnel team hesitantly stepped to my side. One of them poked me in the arm to make sure I was still stiff, while the other one began to hoist me off the ground, gripping me under my armpits. They carried me to the door where Chester now stood, a pleased look on his face.

Needless to say, getting me out of the room was awkward. They had to turn me sideways in order to make me fit through the opening and banged my elbows three times. Oh, and did I mention they smashed one of my knees against the security sensor pad? I would have sworn at them, but my lips couldn't move.

They carried me down the corridor, eyes forward, legs splayed, and shoulders hunched. Chester was fronting the pack. In the distance, the elevator opened with its usual *ping*. I caught a whiff of Beryx's aftershave and the hairspray that Anica used to keep her perfect hairdo in order; there was also the subtle smell of Stephanie's talcum powder. Their aromas were no more pungent than usual, so whatever was happening to me had not affected my sense of smell.

What the hell had William and I done last night to give me a shiny, new set of canines? I was fairly certain that a significant amount of blood needed to be exchanged in order for a vampiric turning to occur. I'd only had maybe a few drops of William's blood, surely not enough to begin the change from human to vampire?

'Good grief,' Stephanie said, rushing down the corridor to my side.

Chester slid his access card into the lab door and ushered his men inside. A third one had grabbed my feet, politely averting his gaze so as not to look up my dress. I really appreciated that.

'Personnel just called us, Chester,' Stephanie said, looking down at my crouched and stiffened figure. 'What happened?'

Chester shook his head. 'I don't know. One minute I was reading the Saturday paper and then she was screaming her lungs out.' He pointed to my fangs. 'Now look at her.'

Stephanie drew back when she finally noticed what Chester's finger was rudely pointing out. 'She's already turning?! How can that be?'

Beryx edged through the door and around her, crouching down low in front of me. He looked nice today—his hair was silky and clean, his shirt pressed and he wore a tie. Beryx must have gotten himself ready for our breakfast date (which had completely slipped my mind until now). 'She was acting kind of strange when I saw her yesterday afternoon by the swimming pool,' he added. 'She kept laughing for no reason, and screaming at imaginary bugs that weren't there. Perhaps she was hallucinating?'

'Be careful, Beryx,' Chester chided, his arm darting out to restrain him, 'she's not herself. This spell will wear off soon and even she admitted to not understanding what's happening to her. I don't wish to see you hurt.'

'Well it's obvious she was going to attack,' Stephanie muttered. 'Her offensive stance is typical of a vampire.'

Anica said something in Romanian, and Chester nodded.

'She wouldn't hurt anyone,' Beryx said, swiftly coming to my defence. 'Not if she could help it.'

'For God's sake,' Chester said, pulling him away by the scruff of his neck, 'you keep forgetting what she is. All of you are. Not only is she vampiric, but she's a mixed up vânător, too. Do none of you remember that they are our enemies?'

I can hear you.

Beryx frowned. 'It's not her fault that she was born this way. She doesn't act like other vampires or vânătors.'

My fingers twitched.

'She's coming around,' Chester muttered. 'Put her up on

the gurney and strap her down. You should be able to move her limbs by now without breaking them.'

You better be right about that, you jackass.

The personnel team lifted me carefully onto the gurney and tugged at my legs. My limbs were still stiff and quite unresponsive, but after much manoeuvring they finally managed to lay me flat and tie my extremities down.

I licked my lips and blinked. Feeling was definitely starting to come back now.

'Elena?' Stephanie said as she stroked my hair tentatively. 'I'm just going to take a blood sample, okay?'

Like I have a choice.

'Beryx. Can you do a check on the canines, please, before she totally reanimates?' Chester began a physical sweep of my body. 'Make sure you use instruments instead of your fingers.'

Beryx came back to the gurney with a dental probe in one hand and a pair of rubber gloves in the other. He quickly slipped them on.

'I won't bite him,' I slurred at Chester.

Beryx gave me an appreciative smile before gently pulling back my lips. 'Umm, Chester,' he said, looking up from my mouth and over at his mentor.

'Yes?'

'Her canines are gone.'

'What?'

'I said, her canines are gone.'

'Yes, yes I heard you,' Chester said impatiently, walking around the gurney and prying my mouth open himself to get a closer look. If only he knew how tempted I was to chew off his fingers, as I smelt the blood pumping beneath the surface of his skin like I did.

Hang about—that was something new. I'd always been

able to scent blood but never while it was still in someone else's body.

'Where have they gone?' Chester said, prodding around my mouth with his fingers. He was so rough that I bit him, just for shits and giggles. Yep, Chester should have followed his own advice.

'Ow!' he said, extracting his finger and shaking his stinging hands. 'You said you wouldn't bite.'

'I said I wouldn't bite Beryx.'

'Maybe the canines only appear when she's thirsty or irritated,' Stephanie supplied in her Southern drawl, ignoring the exchange between Chester and myself.

'That's an interesting idea,' Chester murmured, turning to whisper something to Anica in Romanian. She promptly disappeared, reappearing a few minutes later with a bar of chocolate and a tetra pack of Synth Blood.

Synth Blood was supplied by a company known as Synth Corp—a product that we used back home to lure the vânători into our traps. From what little I know, Synth Corp was based in Europe and the company produces substitutes for every type of human and animal blood available. Rumour had it that the company was originally built to help supply the constant demands of the European hospital system, but it had become clear to me that the Vampiric population were major purchasers of their goods. I had seen William and his friends drinking the product on a number of occasions in the past.

Chester took the chocolate bar out of Anica's hands, ripping open the plastic packaging. He held it up in front of my nose like I was some kind of ravenous dog and then touched it against my mouth.

I took the bait, biting off a huge chunk and chewing it hungrily. I knew he was testing me, but I was also testing myself. I ate some of the human food and still liked it.

Good.

I finished chewing what was left in my mouth and then swallowed. I went in for a second bite now that my hunger had stirred, but by then Chester was placing the chocolate bar onto the bench behind him. 'Hey!' I cried out, 'who said I was done with that?'

Chester rubbed a finger through his blonde moustache, looking thoughtful. 'When I get to the bottom of this you can stuff yourself stupid, Elena. But for now I just want to test out a couple of theories.' He punctured a hole in the top of the blood pack and pushed a bendy straw into the hole. The sweet smell of blood filled the air, and I found a new kind of longing filling the pit of my stomach.

'You know,' I said, staring at the straw with anticipation, recounting the flavour from the night before, 'I'm probably going to like this blood as much as the chocolate.'

Chester nodded and placed the straw against my lips. Beryx, Anica, and Stephanie all crowded in eagerly to watch the little experiment. Who would have thought it was *this* exciting to watch someone drinking fake blood?

My lips closed around the straw, and I began to suck. It was a little cooler than I would have liked but apart from that it was pretty delicious. Not as good as fresh blood but near enough not to complain.

'That's just gross,' Beryx said in his heavy Romanian accent, cringing in disgust yet still overtly curious enough to not look away.

I flipped my hand over in the metal restraints and gave Beryx the finger.

Chester pulled the straw from my mouth just as the blood was starting to satisfy the ache from within. He placed the Synth Blood next to the leftover chocolate bar on the bench behind him and then turned back to start digging around inside my mouth, again looking for pointy canines.

'It's not food or thirst that causes their appearance,' Chester said, scratching at his moustache again. 'Perhaps she needs to be starving for the canines to extend naturally.' An evil sort of gleam crossed his features and settled deep in the depths of his overly-magnified brown eyes.

I glared at him. 'Don't even think about it,' I said, angry. 'If you take away my food for the sake of a stupid experiment, guess who I'm going to come after for my next midnight snack?'

Beryx stifled a laugh, helping Stephanie tie off the belt around my arm. I winced as the needle punctured my flesh and blood started to drain from my system. I could feel it trickling out of my veins, backtracking for the singular purpose of filling up vials for more superfluous tests.

'There,' she said a few moments later, releasing the arm band and gently tapping my skin where the needle had just been.

I glanced down. Well, I still healed just fine. And quickly, too.

Stephanie and Beryx promptly disappeared over to the other side of the lab, Vacutainers in hand. They began placing drops of my blood onto slides and studying them under their microscope, making notes on the computer beside them and mumbling under their breath. I couldn't hear exactly what they were saying, but judging by the looks on their faces there was nothing new to report.

'Maybe Stephanie is right,' Chester muttered to himself. 'Maybe you just need to get aggravated in order for your, shall we say, 'inner nature' to come to the fore?'

I rolled my eyes.

'What can I do to irritate you, Elena?'

I started to laugh. 'Just keep talking because that usually does it for me.'

He frowned, and I laughed harder. 'This isn't a joke, Elena. Tell me what has happened in the last twenty-four hours that has caused this change within you?'

My face fell flat, and I quickly fell silent as I thought about the night that had just passed. Between my nightmare, William's sudden departure, and the fact that I was now strapped to a gurney, I was rapidly becoming pissed off again.

'Nothing has changed. Every crappy aspect of my inescapable life is exactly the same,' I muttered in sour tones. It was all I could think about: that stupid note in my rubbish bin and the growing animosity I was starting to feel towards William.

I'm sorry I'm stupid, Elena. I'm a stupid, dumb vampire.

Gah!

'Elena, it can't be nothing.'

Nostrils flaring, I fought to control my temper. 'If I said nothing happened, then nothing happened. So would you give it a rest and stop putting your goddamn fingers in my mouth!' I turned my head, cursing creatively and muttering under my breath. 'I get a few minutes where I think everything's going to be okay and then what happens? Someone shits on me, that's what. Jesus, if I didn't have these erratic teenage hormones, I'd be out of here by now.'

'I'm sorry?' Chester asked, looking at me in confusion.

I groaned. 'Oh God, not you too! I swear, if I have to see or hear those two pitiful, bullshit words one more time I'm going to punch a hole through someone.'

'Elena, do we need to have one of our little talks?'

I rattled my restraints. 'What I need is to be left alone for a little while. You've taken my blood and you've poked around inside my mouth—what more do you need?'

'Eye tests, hearing tests, sensitivity tests, allergy tests, speed tests, stamina tests … the list goes on and on.'

'Yeah, well, not today. I'm too damn cranky to be your pincushion.'

Chester cleared his throat as a whistling sound came from out of his nose: the sound of Chester trying to control his small eruptions of laughter. He quickly tightened the straps around my wrists and ankles. 'When have I ever given you a choice? You forget your place in the world, Elena. Protectors are at the top, humans underneath. At the very bottom of the scale are the Vampires and Vânători. You rate lower than that because you do not belong anywhere.'

'Chester!' Stephanie admonished. 'Was that necessary?'

'No, it's fine, Stephanie,' I said, feeling my temper rising and my teeth grind together. 'I've always known that Chester was an asshole.'

'Well, then,' he said, laughing again and shaking his head. 'It won't be a surprise to you to know that I'm not letting you off this gurney until I'm quite finished with you.'

I sneered. 'That's what you think.'

Okay, enough was enough.

I yanked hard with both my wrists and ankles, and the metal shackles that forcefully held me down began to creak wildly. They contorted under the strain and finally ruptured, each snapping at the locking mechanism and falling, in pieces, to the floor.

Chester stumbled, reaching behind himself and knocking a desk lamp to the floor. He froze in surprise, his mouth gaping from shock, as bits of broken bulb crunched underfoot. Beryx, Anica, and Stephanie remained exactly where they were, eyeing me anxiously as I got up from the gurney and jumped down onto the floor.

Behind me I felt the crackle of magic and spun to catch Chester building the Light of Mellar between his hands. Blinding me with that spell would usually have been an effective way to disable me, but today I doubted anything would keep me down for long. Magic or not, I was determined to not put up with the IMI's crap any longer.

Canines rapidly extending, I could feel my senses thrown into overdrive at the prospect of imminent attack. I could smell Chester's sour breath, taste it on my tongue, could hear his uneven breathing like gale-force wind in my ears. I rose to my full height, ignoring that primal urge to crouch and pounce. I would not be intimidated by Chester; his magic would prove useless against my sheer willpower and determination.

His top lip curled into an evil little smile. He snapped his suspenders, straightened his lab coat, and then slapped his palms together, the friction of movement creating a glowing light that he held tightly in his grasp. He glanced briefly back at Beryx and the others. 'It appears that not only do her canines grow when she is angry, but she also develops superior strength.' Chester kicked at the broken chain by his feet and it rattled against the floor, coming to a stop by a nearby cabinet.

I threw my head back and laughed derisively, loving every minute as his cocky facade crumbled before my lack of fear. 'I've always been strong, Chester. I just never let you see it until now.'

Chester's eyes dimmed. 'Why would you hide such a gift?'

I shrugged, flashing my canines, revelling as he flinched. Something very primal inside of me hungered for his insides—for blood. 'I did mention that you had no idea what

I was capable of. Perhaps you should have listened to me when I told you not to piss me off.'

'It seems to me that you need to be reminded of who is in charge around this place, Elena.'

'Just try it, asshole, and we'll see who comes out on top.' I stepped forward, my movements mirroring Chester's.

'Elena!' Beryx called, rushing forward from behind me to protect his mentor. I bared my teeth again, saliva dripping from the pointy ends.

'Stay back, Beryx,' Chester warned.

But he kept on coming anyway.

I held my hand out behind me to keep Beryx back, sensing his approach rather than seeing it. I didn't want him getting caught in the path of my ire, particularly not now that I had the taste for revenge on my tongue.

A tingle of power surged all the way down my outstretched arm, pulsing through my veins and slipping across the surface of my skin like liquid, before exiting through my fingertips. The force was electric, burning my skin on its way through, and as I turned I saw a visible wall of shimmery liquid appear that distorted the image of the laboratory behind me.

Beryx ran straight into that shimmery barrier, rebounding with a thwack and falling backwards onto the floor. Screaming, he clutched at his nose in pain.

Anica bobbed down behind a laboratory bench, only one arm visible as she shouted, pointing at the shimmering wall. Beryx was moaning and scrambling away from me, his shoes skidding against the floor as I looked down at my hands in shock.

'Elena, what did you do?' Stephanie screeched, sliding onto the ground next to Beryx and cupping a hand around his broken nose. Blood was pouring like liquid chocolate down his face.

The smell hit the air around me with an intensity that made my stomach groan and my throat burn with thirst. 'I don't know,' I said, shaking my head, still staring at my hands in astonishment. 'I just wanted him to keep away, safe from the fight.' I looked up then, pressing my hands against the barrier and trying to peer through the distortion so I could see him better. 'Beryx, I'm so sorry. You know I would never hurt you intentionally.'

'Enough of this!' Chester yelled.

I hissed and spun around, watching as his magical ball of light shot directly at me.

I dropped into a crouch, lunging to the side and throwing my arms out in front to protect myself. Power surged down my arm just as it had before, exploding out of my body with invisible force.

That force hit the ball of light dead on and sent it hurtling back towards Chester like a spike from a professional volleyball player. It caught him right in the middle of his chest. He staggered backwards, clutching at the gurney for support and sending pieces of equipment crashing to the ground as he stumbled around blindly.

'What have you done to me?' Chester screamed.

I studied my hands again, completely at a loss. I should have been the one stumbling around, but I had somehow reversed the Light of Mellar's course and sent it charging back at Chester. Since when could I interfere with Protector magic? And since when did my hands get all supercharged?

Seriously, what the hell is going on?

I dropped to my knees, suddenly overwhelmed, feeling drained. The air felt like it had been sucked out of my lungs and my skeleton had suddenly turned to jelly. The only other time I'd felt this way was when John had nearly drained me of blood. So why was my head suddenly feeling like it was being pounded with a baseball bat?

'Something's happening to me,' I whispered, falling forward onto the floor, my face penetrating the now fading barrier. The sound of Chester crashing blindly around the lab only faintly reached my ears.

'Don't touch her,' I heard Stephanie say to the others in awe. 'She's like nothing we've ever seen before.'

I tried to reach out to them but they were too far away, scrambling to distance themselves from potential harm. I could feel everything slipping, unconsciousness beckoning, sleep the only surrender. I wanted to fight that urge. I needed to keep my eyes focused on Chester but it was no use.

My eyes slid shut, knowing that the moment I surrendered Chester would make his move. His blindness would only be temporary, and when he recovered he'd never let me set foot outside the doors of the IMI again. I would truly become a prisoner, and this time, he'd make sure I could never escape.

CHAPTER EIGHT: CALCULATING

C hester clambered to his feet, as his vision slowly began to clear. Objects invisible to him only moments before now swam into focus, still blurred around the edges but slowly sharpening.

How did Elena deflect my magic? Since when can a vampire, let alone a half-breed, use our own magics against us? Impossible!

To Chester this just proved more than ever that his research was of the utmost importance.

'Are you okay?' Anica said in Romanian, rushing to his side.

'I'm fine,' he answered, gripping the gurney next to him as he wiped at his eyes.

'Chester, Beryx is hurt,' Stephanie said, standing behind him. 'It looks like whatever Elena just did has broken his nose. I think we need to either get him to the hospital or re-set it as soon as possible.'

'Do it here,' Chester muttered. 'The public system will slow us down.' He paused, looking at his injured protégé. 'Are you alright?'

Beryx was shaking. Probably shock. 'It hurts.'

'Of course—your nose is broken,' Chester replied rather unsympathetically.

Beryx frowned, perplexed by the lack of care from his mentor. But, then again, distraction came easily to a man like Chester. He'd be salivating with the possibilities of Elena's latest revelations and Beryx could already see the wheels turning inside Chester's head. What would happen now?

'You all realise that our schedule will have to be moved forward.'

Beryx and Stephanie exchanged solemn glances. Anica seemed confused. Chester repeated himself in Romanian for her benefit, and her face lit up. Beryx thought she enjoyed the idea of carving Elena up almost as much as Chester did.

'Chester, you can't,' Beryx pleaded, oozing blood. 'She's not like what we expected her to be, but I don't think she's out of control.'

'She broke your nose!'

'I believe her when she said she would never intentionally hurt me. It was an accident.'

'All the more reason to move forward,' Chester persisted. He released the edge of the gurney and knelt down beside Elena's crumpled body. 'She's more powerful than we expected and that essentially makes her more beneficial to our long term plans.' He touched his fingers to her wrist, feeling a steady pulse. 'You have to put aside your childish infatuation for her, Beryx. She isn't human like us; she's a perfect hybrid of two powerful species that we've never been able to replicate. We must take advantage of that.'

'Maybe there's a reason we can't replicate her qualities,' Stephanie said, as she stuffed a wad of paper towel onto Beryx's nose. 'After all, we've been attempting to re-create Vampire pregnancies for what? The last five years? And none of those experiments have ended in another version of Elena. The closest we've come to any sort of blended success is her adoptive brother, Lucas, and we still have no idea how, when, or even if Lucas will mutate.'

'Lucas is our backup,' Chester chided, 'and he will develop. We know Elena's blood has special qualities, and it's just a matter of when her DNA will surface within Lucas.'

'But the serum is unperfected,' Stephanie pushed. 'If you want to keep Lucas as a backup, that's fine, but our primary focus should be on keeping Elena alive. That's better than draining and killing her.'

'I am aware of that,' Chester snapped.

'She'll try to escape now for sure,' Beryx mumbled. 'I told you to be nicer to her.'

'She will be contained,' Chester replied, dropping Elena's wrist and standing again. He started pacing the room, his eyes never leaving his subject. 'Keeping her alive means fresh supplies of blood. We'll need that to get the formulations for the serum right. We've only been able to make real progress since she arrived.' He started to smile as a thought occurred to him. 'What if we use fresh Vânător blood instead of the vials we collected from her birth?'

Stephanie shook her head. 'I see where you're going with this, Chester, but Elena said that the Alphas are dangerous. Trying to catch one is ludicrous. Maybe we need to let the idea go before more of us are seriously hurt.'

Chester snorted. 'We are Protectors!'

'And yet look what one little girl did to you, did to Beryx? She managed to use our own magic against us.' Stephanie sighed. 'We've had her here for over a month and this is the first time we have gotten an inkling of what she could truly be capable of. The last thing we want to do is create another unstable species like the Vân�tors. The Vampires take ownership of that disaster but who's to say we won't be worse off if we continue to develop this serum?'

'But that is my point exactly!' Chester exclaimed, pointing at Elena. 'The Vampires have the power to grant immortality and they shared that gift with animals. Animals! Why shouldn't we, the protectors of humanity, be able to heal ourselves, run fast, see in the dark, hear everything from miles around, and live forever? Why are our enemies the only ones who should be bestowed with such gifts? Think of what we could do if we could harness those qualities. We could pick and choose, weed out undesirable traits ... the opportunities are limitless.'

He kicked at Elena's immobile legs. 'What makes her so special? She's the snottiest damn teenager I've ever met in my life and yet she has been given gifts of which she is completely undeserving. Don't you think it is our right to be on an equal footing with our enemies?'

'They aren't supposed to be our enemies,' Beryx said quietly. 'Remember that the alliance is supposed to make them our allies.'

Chester waved his hand around impatiently. 'That alliance was made by our ancestors. Times have changed, people have changed since then.'

'What if we can never harvest a serum from her blood? Isn't it enough that we have been given the gift of magic, a gift that even vampires and vânători do not possess?' Stephanie said.

'What good are our five or six spells in comparison to speed, strength, and immortality?'

'But why her?' Beryx demanded. 'Why do you have to use Elena? If the IMI has instructed you to harvest those qualities then just use our other vampire test subjects instead, or wait for Lucas to mature. He's a Protector—he'll volunteer to help when he realises his role in all of this.'

Chester shook his head impatiently. 'None of you see it, do you? Elena's blood is perfect. Our vampire test subjects are all inferior by comparison. We don't need to strip away defective genes and pluck out the best sections of her DNA to produce an untainted source, because we already have that. We just need to figure out a way to formulate the serum so that it will harness all those qualities and blend them with our human systems, without disrupting our own genetic code. Surely you want that most of all, Stephanie?'

He fixed her with a pointed stare.

Stephanie looked away, almost guiltily.

'But she is still half-Vânător. Do we really want that section of her DNA mingling with our own?' Beryx said.

Chester smiled, his gold tooth gleaming evilly. 'Imagine how much simpler it would be to wipe out the Vampires as a whole if we turned the species they created against them?'

'I'm not sure I follow you,' Stephanie said, interrupting him. 'The Vampires and the Vânători are already enemies.'

'Yes, but the Vânători still hunt and kill us. What if we could make it so their only goal was to kill vampires?'

'How?' Stephanie and Beryx said in unison. Anica pulled the blood-soaked paper towel from Beryx's nose as they talked, focusing her attention on that instead. Chester would give her a rundown in Romanian later, anyway. Whatever it was, Beryx thought, she would be on board, as she was nothing if not a loyal follower of the IMI.

'We will work out why Elena is vulnerable to the Alpha's call, turn that around, and use it so that we can command them all.'

Stephanie grimaced. 'I think you're reaching, Chester. It might not be that simple.'

Chester frowned heavily. 'Come on, we are already half-way there. The last six weeks with Elena have been very helpful. We just need to figure out how to bond the serum to our own DNA, which is the reason you and Anica are here. You're supposed to be the best in your fields. I suggest you shelve that negative attitude and start coming up with ways to make this serum happen, otherwise it won't just be Lila who suffers.'

Stephanie paled, visibly cowed at the sound of her daughter's name.

'Worst case scenario, we could always figure out another way to get the Vânătors to side with us,' Chester mused.

Beryx screamed as Anica quickly re-set his broken nose. She hadn't even warned him; blood quickly started running anew.

'What about Elena?' Stephanie asked, looking back at her crumpled body.

Chester gave her another little kick, but she didn't seem to move. 'Strap her back down on the gurney. According to George she was drained over and over again by that Alpha back in Australia. I say we take as much blood as we can without killing her, wait for her to regenerate, and do it all over again until we have enough of a stockpile to get this serum right. After that, while she's still out cold, we take her to the coal factory and dump her in a secure room from which she can't escape.' He paused. 'I want to monitor these new abilities she seems to have randomly developed. And I want to see just exactly what would happen if we put her face-to-face with an Alpha.'

Stephanie flinched. 'You're really going to put her in with that Alpha, the same one that killed all our security teams?'

Chester helped Anica lift Elena back onto the gurney and strapped her down. Beryx looked like he was going to be sick.

'Do you have a problem with that?' Chester said, glancing at Stephanie.

Stephanie shook her head grudgingly. 'I want this serum to work just as much as you. My daughter has only a few years left on this earth.' She paused, wiping gently at the corner of her eye. 'I'll do whatever it takes to extend her life.'

'That's what I thought,' Chester answered, reaching out to pat her arm. 'We do this for all Protectors, not just the ones that we hold dear to our hearts.'

Stephanie nodded again, forcing herself to grab her equipment so she could begin the exsanguination. Beryx could see her interior struggle, hands shaking but persistent. Who would not do anything and everything they could to save their child?

Anica checked the new restraints and made sure Elena was strapped down extra tightly. She looked mummified, bandages firmly wrapped around her torso and the gurney. Breaking free would be difficult no matter how strong her new abilities made her, with her caught like a fly in a spider web.

Chester began another full oral cavity search, making notes on Elena's changed physicality and enhanced abilities. Beryx stood to the side, fingering his sore nose, and wondering if he shouldn't still go to the hospital.

Stephanie inserted a needle into Elena's arm and began the withdrawal. She'd never felt so sick in her whole life. She wasn't just a haematologist now—this made her something else, something horrible that Stephanie would no longer be able to stand when she looked in the mirror. She wanted to turn away from her part in this madness but couldn't. Defiance paid no dividend, and despite her guilt, Stephanie would kill Elena a thousand times over it meant that she could have Lila just for one more day. It was a distressing thought, but true nevertheless.

The door to the lab burst open. One of the men from personnel came running over to Chester, a panicked expression on his face. 'Pick up the phone,' the man said, rumbling Romanian at Chester.

Chester looked confused but slipped off his rubber gloves and trekked over to his desk, noting the flashing light on the telephone. Pressing the red button below it, Chester lifted the receiver to his ear. 'Yes?'

'Chester? It's George Manory.'

Chester smiled, looking over at Elena lying unconscious on the gurney. 'George, nice to hear from you. How is the family?'

'This isn't a social call,' he said gruffly. 'I'm calling because we've had a major security breach.'

Chester frowned, gripping the phone tightly. 'What are you talking about?'

'Lucas saw the file.'

Chester closed his eyes, took a deep breath and tried to contain his anger. 'How much does he know?'

'Bits and pieces. I think he might have seen references to the serum.'

'What about his part in all of this?'

George grunted. 'I don't think he knows. I stopped him before he read too much.'

Chester cursed loudly and shoved the stack of papers from his desk onto the floor. Beryx, Anica, and Stephanie all looked up in surprise. 'Can he be silenced?'

'I am not killing my own son if that's what you're asking me. I already agreed to this experiment, but I won't take that next step, Chester. Don't ask me to.'

'Of course not,' Chester huffed impatiently. 'You know we have greater plans for Lucas. I was merely asking if there was any way to keep him quiet.'

There was silence for a moment. 'Do you want me to include him? Refresh his memory about Elena and the scar?'

'Is there a chance the information could be leaked?'

'His loyalty to his sister is extremely strong. If they speak again soon, he will try to tell her. I'm most certain of that.'

Chester almost groaned aloud at that, looking back at Elena. 'I told you to keep them apart when they were younger,' he said, hissing the words under his breath. 'Now, George, because of your incompetence our whole of headquarters has been compromised. And when Lucas completes his training and transition it may not just be for the benefit of the IMI.'

'You and I both know that keeping them apart after the accident was impossible. They were bound together by blood.'

Chester studied the pile of papers on the floor and pondered. 'Are there others he could tell?'

George laughed, though there was no humour in it. 'Ironically, even though he hasn't told anyone at the IMI, Susan and I have noticed that lately he has become friendly with some vampires.'

'The ones that helped you save Elena from that Alpha?'

'The very same.'

'Does he know that you know?'

'He suspects. He's distant and untrusting since Elena left.'

'Then we have no choice.'

'What do you want Susan and me to do?' George said quietly, almost apologetically.

Chester sneered, irritated that his long-time friend could let him down so badly. 'Oh, I think you've done quite enough.' He slammed the phone down onto the receiver.

'What's happened?' the others asked.

Chester took a deep breath. 'The whole operation has been compromised. We have to move to Plan B immediately.'

'Plan B?'

Chester nodded. 'You all know what you have to do.'

CHAPTER NINE: PRISONER

B right lights flashed in front of my tired eyes, momentarily blinding me before disappearing and again leaving me down in the dark. I waited. The blackness enveloped me, a comfort after the sting of such sudden brightness.

I moved forward. There was no path, nothing to follow and no instincts to guide the way. There was nothing but the underside of a raven's wing, nothing but that usual, comfortable place behind closed eyes. This time, however, instead of reassured I felt only suffocated and oddly disorientated.

I could tell that I was dreaming again. This place was not like unconsciousness, where there are no thoughts or images flitting through the mind. Here, I was ethereal; here I was the only thing I could see moving against the void.

I spotted the lights again. Were they near or far? I couldn't tell. My hands reached out but my fingers found nothing but empty space. I tried running, hoping I was heading in the right direction. The glow seemed to grow bigger and brighter in the distance, and I knew I was gaining ground. Suddenly, the lights approached me faster than I thought possible, flashing again in that strange procession of colours and contrast, forming an image—an image I had hoped never to see again, yet somehow craved.

The stone clad room of the previous night's dream drifted

into focus, torches on the walls burning brightly under night's cover, flames once again casting their eerie light across every wall. There was a new candle in the centre of the table now. It had been pushed down into the melted wax of the old one, and its tiny flame flickered luminance over the papers littered across its wooden surface.

Why was I back here again? Hadn't I just been in the lab with Chester? Or had *that* been the dream? Was I right now still sleeping soundly in my room, William tucked in beside me, strong arms wrapped around me while he plotted our escape?

The old timber door beside me opened and I waited for a repetition of my previous dream, for the flames to die and for the scarred vampire to appear at his place at the head of the table. I wasn't looking forward to it.

Instead, I watched as five men passed me by on their way to the table. Predatory in their movements, tall, and somehow imposing within that small space, they were led by the man from my previous dream. Now, however, his was not the form of the fearsome creature I'd seen before. His skin was still pale and evocative of the Vampiric ideal, but he was now dressed in long, black slacks and a deep purple button-up shirt; over the top, he wore a beautifully crisp, black dinner jacket. The first two buttons of his shirt were undone, revealing the scarred flesh of his neck. A delicate gold chain and plain ring dangled there, shining under the pale candlelight of the room. The man thumbed it absently and walked right past me without so much as a backward glance.

He stopped at the head of the table, gaze sweeping the room. I noted that the true colour of his eyes was a strange mingling of green and topaz, not unlike my own—a flat white canvas, forest green base coat, with peppered topaz over the surface. 'Organised chaos' was how Susan used to describe them.

His chocolate brown hair was still neatly combed like I'd seen previously, the base of his hairline twisting and rolling in unusual curls. His lips were thin and slightly pink, and he wore a mask of two day old stubble. His eyes crinkled at the corners, reflecting smile lines, although right now his features were neutral.

The man took a seat in the chair marked *Lucius* at the head of the table. He was obviously their leader, the power of his command seemingly rolling off him in waves. The other four men took the opposing seats around him, similar in appearance and age and holding themselves in an upright manner that also demanded a degree of authority and respect.

They sat forward in their chairs, pointing eagerly at the papers in front of them and talking to one another so quickly their lips blurred. I wished that I could hear them. I could see, feel, smell, and touch in this dream, but was deprived of sound.

I took a tentative step forward, wanting to see what it was they were all looking at. Maps of Europe, with a particular focus on the area around Austria, Poland, Hungary and the Czech Republic were sprawled across the table-top. The one called Lucius kept circling a finger around Hungary and Romania, while the other four listened, watching him intently with a strange kind of adoration pasted on their bright faces.

Why can't I hear them?

I took another step forward, vying for a closer look, but abruptly stopped when a sudden hum of energy crackled across my skin, not dissimilar to that which I'd felt just before breaking Beryx's nose. But this sensation felt real, almost apart from the dream. My whole body was crackling and buzzing as if I'd just jammed a butter knife in a toaster and would not let go.

In my periphery, I could see the old timber door swinging open again as another four men strode into the room. The crackle of energy caressing my skin quickly dissipated at their intrusion, my distraction perhaps the cause.

My breath suddenly caught in my throat as I turned, running directly into the last man to enter. Our bodies briefly touched, and I felt an absolute assault of my already confused senses. Then he was walking right through me, tearing through my body and temporarily binding my form to his. His flesh swam through my ethereal projection, filling me completely with a scent that was beyond amazing—a scent that made my toes curl and my eyes roll backwards. His heart collided with mine, his mind swum through my thoughts, and his breath tangled with the heat of my lips.

We were as one.

As our bodies finally separated, the man stopped, briefly peering over his shoulder before turning. A slight furrowing of his brow mirrored my own growing confusion. Had he felt my touch? Or was his reaction the bittersweet fiction of my mind's own creation?

The unusual mix of his grey-green eyes caught me off guard, swallowing my whole being with a single look that made my entire body ache with awareness.

It's him.

This man I had met before in my dreams—dreams that I had never told anyone about, dreams where he had had swirling silver eyes. The only difference was that, though his face was exactly the same, right now his eyes were different.

I reached out to touch him but he'd moved, perhaps to

distance himself from my intangible spirit form before spinning on his heels to join the others.

I glanced back and forth between him and Lucius, trying to draw a connection between the two. Lucius had previously never appeared in my dreams before last night, and neither had any of the other men crowding the stone-clad room. The silver-eyed man's role in my visions had always been as my lover, my protector, my comforter ... so what or who the hell was Lucius?

The men talked without interruption. Lucius had sensed my presence in the last dream but in this one he did not.

Why is that?

I quickly studied the newest arrivals. These four men were all incredibly handsome but in completely different ways. I was assuming they were vampires and there was no reason not to when everyone else appeared to be—even Silvereyes was a vampire, though, in previous dreams I was sure he'd been something else.

The first man to enter had short, spiky blonde hair, dyed pink at the tips. His youthful appearance indicated he was in his late teens, so I suspected that he was probably a born vampire. Two of the others were around the same age. Silvereyes was a little older, as far as I could tell.

The guy with the pink hair seemed to wear a lot of eye make-up, needlessly accentuating the brilliance of his blue-hued eyes. With fingernails that were painted black and arms covered in black, rubber bracelets, he wore a ratty t-shirt with the logo *Satan Rules* scrawled across the front in red. The entire outfit was finished off with black denim jeans, black biker boots heavily buckled down at the sides and wore several gold ear cuffs in his left ear. He might have looked threatening if he hadn't been so pretty.

The second man, standing beside Goth Boy, was also

blonde but minus the artificial colouring. He, too, had piercing blue eyes but his hair was as straight as a tack, resting just below his ears, and with a fringe that curved down stylishly in front of his left eye. The other side of his fringe was tucked neatly behind his right ear. Poking up from the pocket of his jeans was the hilt of a knife, the edges of the blade clearly visible as it strained against his thigh. This man brushed his fingers back and forth across the handle absently, an automatic response to a habit I suspected he had always had. It made me miss my own knife terribly.

The third man looked the most unusual. He was of Asian descent, his skin smooth and tanned—a strange look on a supposed vampire when they were usually so pale. His eyes were chocolate brown, his hair long, black and straight. It hung down to the middle of his back like a curtain, secured only by a small hair tie that still allowed strands to escape and frame either side of his face.

He wore a clean, white shirt that concealed bulging biceps, and stood with his hands tucked into the pockets of his long, black suit pants. He was very tall, maybe over six and a half feet and towered easily over everyone else in the room; but, even so, he could not overshadow the beautiful being standing right behind him.

My gaze was drawn to Silvereyes ... again. I think it had something to do with his scent: an aroma that was so familiar and comforting that my feet automatically shuffled forward, the smell of well-worn leather and pine forests after the fall of spring rain stirring up memories from a distant past.

He was leaning up against the stone wall behind him, one foot crossed in front of the other. In his hands was a long blade that he spun in-between deft fingers. The blade's edge caught my reflection, which was strange given that it was dirty and stained with dried blood. He wore no shirt, leaving little to the imagination.

Black leather pants hung low on his hips, emphasising the definition of his toned abdominals and stomach, and showing off his taut, slim thighs. His hair was chocolate brown, the same as mine, and it rested loosely against his shoulders in a wavy caress, highlighting the strong, angular planes of his cheek bones.

Silvereyes looked like a dark, angelic warrior from some backwards fairy tale. He wasn't the sweet prince or the daring knight, but was also no nemesis either. Yet he seemed somehow lost—a victim of circumstance stuck in a world in which he really didn't belong. I wanted to help him; I had no idea why.

I laughed.

This is just a stupid dream.

This is not a dream. A voice whispered in my mind. *Remember, trust.*

Who the hell said that?!

Embrace. Remember.

The words echoed through my mind, the voice somehow familiar, reminding me of a time not so long ago when I'd thought I was going crazy and hearing voices that warned me away from William.

Thank God this is just a dream. I would ignore the voices and not let them get the better of me. I'd done it once, I could do it again.

I was brought back to myself as all four men suddenly stepped forward, as if beckoned. My dark warrior also moved away from his place by the wall, coming to stand near the front of the pack. His knife had been re-sheathed in a leather harness set across his back, and he was now engrossed in the silent conversation.

I turned away, looking back at Lucius. He was standing again, pointing at the maps in front of him and talking hurriedly, lips a blur. He was telling them something, possibly a directive, but nevertheless I still couldn't hear.

The newest arrivals soon stepped away from the table, nodding politely at the seated older men before heading for the door. The tall Asian led the way and was followed by the two blondes. My dark-haired warrior hung back.

I took a curious step forward and everything dimmed. The timber table and the four men sitting around it melted into a blur. My dark warrior's face was soon shrouded in black, only the flecks of grey and silver in his eyes piercing through the fog in front of me. Lucius disappeared completely, taking more of the light with him. The clarity of my dream began to dissolve and it was then that I realised I was back in the dark again, surrounded by nothing but the cover of a blank mind and empty thoughts.

And then there was nothing but darkness and the unending night.

I groaned and rolled over. An ache in the back of my head thumped incessantly. My arm was partially numb, probably from lying on it for what must have been hours. I was shivering, too, my teeth rapidly chattering together.

I struggled to lift my eyelids, opening them only partially to reveal a bright light from above wending its uncomfortable way across my face. I really felt like shit. Was this still part of the dream?

Cold metal pressed against my shoulder and all the way down my left side, feeling like ice against my skin. I tried hauling myself into a sitting position. That took some real effort on my part, what with the pounding headache and sore arm. Neither would usually be a problem due to my self-healing trick but I felt deflated, drained. There was enough sleep caking the corners of my eyes to suggest I had been resting for quite a while—another mystery.

I groaned again as unwanted memories flooded back, forcing me to remember what had transpired before I'd slipped into a coma. So, I'd confronted Chester and caused a scene, revealing the multiple facets of my special abilities, both new and old.

I shook my head and rubbed at my eyes, wishing the headache would ease so my vision could clear. I didn't like feeling so much pain or discomfort, which showed just how much I took my self-healing for granted. Maybe I had somehow meddled with my ability's effectiveness after exchanging blood with William?

Crazy.

I blinked a couple of times, the harsh fluorescent lighting from above finally breaking through my blurred vision and exposing the details of the space around me.

Well, shit. This can't be good.

I looked up. Solid steel walls surrounded me, stretching to dizzying heights and funnelling upward towards a hole covered by a metal grate in the ceiling. On top of that metal grate sat a heavy steel cover that was firmly closed, blocking out any light from beyond. It seemed like I was in a chimney stack or some sort of a giant outlet valve, conjuring up images of a sugar mill or coal factory like from some of the old movies I'd seen. The only semblance of hope for my escape was the small, steel door I could see set into the wall behind me. Either way, I knew what this place was—it was my prison.

'Chester!' I roared, my voice echoing off the metal cage surrounding me.

There was no answer.

I was right. Chester had done exactly what I thought he would: make sure that I could never escape again, especially now I was more of a curiosity to him than ever before. I should have kicked my own ass for not being able to control my temper. If I hadn't started that fight, I'd still be strapped to that gurney in the lab, with viable escape options still open to me.

I screamed Chester's name, again and again, but there was still no response. I figured he was either ignoring me after what had happened in the lab or was somehow watching me, perhaps by camera. There was no way Chester would stray too far away from such an exciting, new development. He'd stay close, carefully picking his moment to confront me. I was hoping he'd come soon; I was itching to test out my new fangs.

I hauled myself up off the floor and walked over to the door, pulling on the handle in the hopes that some idiot might have forgotten to lock it.

They hadn't.

I rammed the door with my shoulder, over and over again, with all of the brute strength I could muster. I knew there would be no budging it, though, but even so my not trying felt more ludicrous than pounding away at this impossible task. I knew from my time as John's captive that steel was the one thing that could seriously impede a vampire's strength.

Ten minutes, several sore limbs and a fist full of bleeding knuckles later, I found myself sliding down the back of the door and to the ground. I pulled my knees up towards my chest and wrapped my arms around them, the bitter chill of solitude claiming my body whole. What would I do now, trapped in the bitingly cold, in this inescapable prison with walls that seemed to close in by the minute?

I closed my eyes and cursed William loudly. Again, what crappy timing—couldn't he have had his moral breakdown after he'd helped bust me out of the IMI? No, instead, the shithead had left me to fend for myself so he could go off and battle the inner demons of his conscience.

Asshole.

I buried my face against my knees. Seconds, minutes, even hours might have passed. I had no real grip on time, as the unending disappointment of William's actions pressed heavily on my mind.

Really, though, I could scream and curse his name all day but it wasn't going to change the fact that he was gone and I was going to have to figure this out on my own.

I peeked over my knees and looked around the room again, feeling nothing but hopelessness flood through me. Okay, so maybe there wasn't a way to escape on my own, but someone had to eventually open that door to feed me.

Didn't they?

William, you giant shithead!

If William wanted to be all by himself then that was fine by me. I was a self-healer, both physically and mentally. I had a freaking chimney I had to figure out how to escape from. Running through all of *his* bullshit issues should be the very least of my problems.

So, then, how the hell do I get out of here?

I surveyed the room, this time with more considering eyes and came up with only two plausible options. Option One was climbing out through the grill above, but I was about fifty feet too short, and as far as I knew, my new abilities didn't extend to suction caps growing from my fingers so I could climb the walls like Spiderman. Option Two was the steel door behind me, but that was going to involve waiting for my handler.

I'm not getting out of here anytime soon.

There wasn't much to work with in the room, either; just an old bucket which I presumed was my bathroom. It was amazing that I kept winding up in situations that involved a steel cell, crazy people, and one lonesome pee bucket. Anyone would think that I actually liked being a captive.

My head slumped against my knees again, as I stared at the bucket on the other side of the room, an idea blooming in my head.

Okay, so how did I do that thing?

I was alone, so I may as well try and figure out what had happened to me in the lab. The protective barrier that I'd spontaneously made appear couldn't be magic. Years of living with Protectors would not mean their abilities had suddenly rubbed off on me, and this *thing* didn't seem typical of a vampire or vânător's powers either.

I stared at the bucket across the room, thinking concentration could be the key to repeating my 'trick'. I crossed my fingers and hoped for some serious David Copperfield action. Learning how to harness this new ability could very well give me the edge to get out of here.

So I kept staring at the bucket, wondering if I actually *could* manipulate objects with my mind. After all, I'd deflected a spell, created a shiny barrier. That didn't mean I was telekinetic, it just meant … well, I had no idea what it meant but I had to start somewhere.

Sweat began to trickle down my brow as I concentrated on the bucket. More time passed, my body shaking and face beginning to contort into a myriad of crazed wrinkles and narrow-eyed movements. I probably just looked constipated.

Okay, so staring isn't working.

I tried to talking to it instead. 'Come, Bucket,' I said,

commanding authority. Nothing happened; I shouldn't have been surprised.

Should I be polite?

'Please, Bucket, come here.'

Again, nothing.

I held my hand out in front of me this time, wondering instead if my body was the conductor for this newfound power. The barrier had appeared shortly after I'd thrown an arm out to ward off Beryx, so my theory seemed sound. Some Protectors also used hand gestures to direct their own magic, providing an outlet or guide for the forces that followed.

I tried wiggling my fingers in the bucket's direction and then combined that with a command when the first attempt remained unsuccessful. 'Come, Bucket.'

Nothing.

I clicked my fingers at it as if it were a dog and I its master, and then started beckoning to it with my hand. Finally, when my patience wore thin, I tried waving at it. 'Come, Bucket, come!' I shouted, repeating every hand gesture I'd even seen the Protector's make, as well as a few of the ruder ones I'd perfected over the years. I must have looked like a total idiot to anyone who might have been watching.

'Bucket, you better get your tin-can ass over here before I come over there and kick the shit out of you!'

I'm yelling at a bucket.

Again, there was no reaction, other than my rising blood pressure; not exactly a surprise. What had happened in the lab was probably a fluke or some sort of by-product unknowingly created by the Protectors' own magic. I was no Harry Potter, and I should never have believed that I could've been.

Huffing in frustration, I channelled calm and folded my

arms over my chest, wondering if I was a total idiot for expecting the bucket to rush towards my embrace.

My head flicked up in astonishment as, with a clatter, the stubborn bucket immediately rose up from the ground and floated through the air towards me. I tried to catch it but instead recoiled in shock, dropping the bucket like a hot potato and scooting as far away from it as possible. The bucket clattered noisily to the floor.

'Bloody hell,' I screeched at the now still and silent bucket. 'You moved!'

I scrambled back to my feet, edging slowly towards where it lay. The bucket was just sitting there on its side, unmoving, so I touched it with my toe. There was no response. I toed it again and took a tentative step back.

Move, I whispered to it inside my head.

At my mental command, the bucket bounced onto its side, rolling over a couple of times with a *clang* and chasing me across the room.

'Shit, shit, shit!' I squealed, jumping back and running up to and against the other wall. 'This is really working!'

Sit still, Bucket!

The bucket immediately froze, leaving the chase.

Thank God. I was really freaking myself out here. 'You stay still now, you hear?' I exclaimed, pointing a finger at it.

The bucket didn't answer. I wondered if I could make it talk, too?

I shook my head, closing my eyes and then whipping them open a second later; I felt the urge to not let my guard down around this now clearly advanced bucket. Crazy, I know, but despite only being in solitary for what felt like a few hours, I was already starting to think like a psycho. I wondered how long it would take being cooped up here to actually send me crazy?

I'd seen that movie *Castaway*, starring Tom Hanks. Tom had made friends with a soccer ball—Wilson—for lack of company. A couple of weeks in this place without proper human contact, and that bucket and I just might patch up our differences.

I rolled my eyes. I should have been making the best of a bad situation and figuring out a way to get out of there before I started naming my bucket, naming it something like 'Bob'.

I picked the bucket up with shaky fingers. There was no point being scared of Bob. He was just a bucket, just a bucket, and he seemed to do exactly what I said. I just had to focus on making him *not* chase me. I could do that.

Mentally, I told Bob to levitate up to eye level and directly in front of me. I thought it best to keep my commands simple at this stage. I mean, we were just getting to know each other.

He complied.

'Well that's pretty cool,' I murmured, as my confidence grew and I watched Bob begin to spin around and around in mid-air. I made him lap the room a couple of times, eventually coming back to rest back in front of me. He was super-obedient now, and I felt a little bad about flipping him off earlier.

My smile faded as a sudden wave of nausea gripped me. I stumbled, falling backwards into the wall, my hands grappling for purchase on the smooth, steel walls. My eyes shuttered and blurred and I struggled to keep them open wide. Finally, overcome with fatigue, I slumped the rest of the way to the ground. I fell right by the door, my elbow banging painfully against Bob's steel handle on the way down.

Ugh. What now?

I rested my head gently against the door, my eyes closed, and waiting for the sickness to subside. My stomach felt a tumultuous mess; the pounding in my head was as painful as it had been earlier when I'd first woken up.

Five minutes passed and I still felt like shit. The pain wasn't nearly as bad as it had been, but I dared not move until the worst of it had abated. Recovery was a seemingly slow process but eventually, after what seemed like a lifetime but was about half an hour, my body began to heal.

I rose slowly, staggering slightly as I did but managing to keep myself propped up with one hand against the wall. Curious as to whether my new ability was what was draining my strength, I mentally asked the bucket to smack itself against the wall a couple more times. As it heeded my commands—*clang!, clang!*—I started to feel those dizzying waves of lethargy once more.

Bugger.

So it looked like this new ability had its drawbacks after all. How useful could this telekinesis be if I passed out each time I used it? Perhaps, with practice and a little time, I might be able to control it without rendering myself comatose.

The bucket crashed to the floor: partially because I was about to pass out and partially because a tiny hatch in the door behind had suddenly flown open, startling me.

I spun around as fast as I could, stars still dancing in front of my eyes as I swayed and tried to collect my bearings.

'Hello, Elena,' Chester said calmly. 'Are you comfortable?'

What a stupid bloody question.

'What do you think?'

He laughed and tinkered with his glasses. 'I'm sorry about your new quarters but there was really no other choice.'

'There's always a choice,' I said through gritted teeth, my mind wandering back to William and his latest blunder.

Jeesh.

'Yes, well, in this case, there isn't. Now that you seem to have begun turning at a rapid rate, and I finally have an explanation as to why, I had no choice but to move you to a more secure location. Plus, you broke Beryx's nose and may have put the rest of my staff in danger.'

My eyes narrowed at him through the gap. I was going to let the second half of his statement slide because it was true—I obviously did have a temper—but I couldn't discount the first half. 'What do you mean you know the reason why I'm turning?'

Chester dived into his pocket, uncrumpling a screwed up piece of paper. He was holding William's letter of apology. So … they must have ransacked my room looking for the answers.

I sighed, thinking that my stupidity knew no bounds. I should have eaten or burned the letter like the secret agents did in those really good spy movies. Now, because of my neglect, Chester was a little bit closer to figuring out how vampires were turned rather than born—formerly a major mystery to The Protectors.

Bravo, Elena, you dumb shit.

'How did a vampire get into the IMI, Elena?' Chester's voice held a note of urgency, though he did well to disguise it behind the anger.

I quickly read the note again as he held it up for me. There was nothing in it to indicate that William had been with me last night. 'I don't know what you're talking about.'

'Don't play games with me.'

'I'm not. I've had that note for ages.'

'Who is W.G.?'

'No one.'

'Elena, you really are trying my patience.'

I scowled. 'Do I look like I give a shit?'

Chester sniffed, adjusting his glasses again. 'Well, how you act is your choice.' He paused, an evil sort of smile touching his lips. 'I just hope you're not hungry.'

'So, that's your latest plan? Starving me until you get what you want?'

'More or less. You've been here for already just over a day so I bet your stomach is growling quite loudly right now. You were passed out for quite some time.'

As if on cue, my stomach made an odd sort of gurgling noise. 'What day is it?'

'It's Sunday, the eleventh of November, but if I were you I'd stop counting the days.'

'Chester, when I get out of here, I swear I'll make sure one way or another that you'll pay for this.'

'Yes, yes,' he said, shaking his head, 'I suppose that you *would* think that you're smart enough to get out of here.' Chester slammed the small opening closed with a *bang* that echoed loudly in my ears. 'Teenagers,' I heard him mutter, as he walked away from the door, 'they think they're invincible.'

I listened until Chester's footsteps had disappeared completely and then slumped down against the door again, exhaling heavily in frustration. I was in all kinds of trouble and didn't have the first clue how to fix things.

I beckoned for Bob to join me. He flew across the room in an instant and landed in my arms. I had nothing better to do except starve, apparently, so with my fingernails, I carefully started scratching on a set of eyes for my new friend. It took me hours, but when I was done I'd managed to give him a mouth, too. I left out the nose, though, as he didn't need to be smelling my business.

'Looks like it's just you and me now, Bob,' I said sadly, staring down at the empty bucket and admiring my handiwork. 'But I gotta tell you, if I catch you watching me while I pee, we'll be having words.'

Bob didn't answer me.

For that, I was grateful.

CHAPTER TEN: VISITORS

I looked up at my toes and wriggled them around; they still moved, although I half-expected them not to. I was surprised that any part of my body was moving given the lack of sustenance I'd been surviving on. I was feeling so lethargic and malnourished that I'd actually begun to wonder how much longer I could live like this.

I wiggled my fingers, holding them high above my head and shielding my eyes to cut out the glare of the fluorescent on the wall up above. It had burned nonstop since I'd arrived, blurring the lines between day and night until I'd forgotten how much time had actually passed.

I turned my legs from side to side, looking at them objectively as they rested up against the wall before me. They looked thin—not quite broomstick thin, but definitely thin enough to make my skinny jeans seem baggy, and enough to make my knees look like smooth bone.

My arms weren't much better. If I lost any more weight I'd start to look like a spider, or worse still, a gangly runway model with an eating disorder.

Screw that. How long have *I been here?*

It had to have been at least six days since I'd first woken, maybe even a little bit longer judging by my lanky-looking frame. The only sustenance I'd received was a small cup of milky porridge, delivered once a day. At least, I thought it was once a day since I'd only received my cup-o-slop six times so far. I supposed it could have been less given how hungry I was.

And I was beyond starving. My stomach ached with a need for food that was so intense I could almost ignore the sudden cramping that had started to twist my insides. At this point I would have eaten anything—even my own appendages were vaguely starting to resemble shish kebabs.

I tapped my feet against the wall and cupped my hands behind my head, looking through the brightness of the fluorescent and up at the metal grate. I was still contemplating how to get up there. Problem was, even if I did get up there, I was probably too damn weak to open the grate at the moment. Knowing my luck, the grate would be automated instead of manually operated, making the task impossible.

I swore. I'd been doing it a lot lately, and it was slowly becoming my answer to not having an answer. On the upside, though, I'd had plenty of time on my hands to practice my new telekinetic ability thingy. The bucket still seemed to chase after me occasionally, but I was definitely getting better at controlling it. I also found that the more I focused on using that section of my brain, the longer I was able to sustain the activity. This was just like doing Sudoku, except fun.

Still, Bob the bucket was hardly a decent companion. The only people who came to my prison were Chester and the person who delivered my daily cup of slop. There was also the person who routinely blinded and restrained me with magic while they cleaned out Bob, but I'd prefer not to talk about that.

Chester visited regularly. At least, it felt like he did because every session was exactly the same as the one before—pointless and time consuming. He'd sit in front of the door on a wooden folding chair with the small hatch open, clipboard and pen in hand, and would start slinging questions at me. Chester would always make sure to sit just out of my reach and would never lose his temper or open the door, no matter how hard I tried to bait him.

And the flood of questions just kept on coming. Chester seemed convinced that if I'd hidden my superior strength from him for almost two months, then it was guaranteed I was hiding other things, too.

He was right, of course—a girl's always got secrets—but I had no intention of ever telling that jackass anything that could be useful. So far the only things Chester had learned were: my favourite colour is yellow; I can burp the entire score from *The Sound of Music* after downing a can of cola; I hate country and western music; and, cucumbers are the devil. If Chester could build a dossier of useful information out of that bunch of crap then he was doing really well.

But one thing was certain—information or no, if I ever got out of this place I was going to kill him. I wasn't speaking figuratively; I really was going to kill Chester. I didn't care anymore about the past training I'd had with Vincent, Malcolm, and Peter back in Cairns, training that had urged me to never hurt humans. Chester didn't count, because he wasn't human: he was an ass. And since asses are donkeys, and definitely not human, he'd soon be one dead Eeyore.

I tilted my head back as the tiny hatch in the door flipped open yet again and my porridge cup was placed through the opening.

I rolled stiffly into a sitting position, attempting to push myself to my feet and stumble over to the hatch before its bearer could disappear, and with them their insignificant offering of food. The opening was already closing, but I was quick enough to get my hand through the slot. 'Wait,' I croaked coarsely, through the dryness of my throat, 'please talk to me.'

There was no answer.

'Please, can you just tell me what day it is today? How long have I been here?'

A hand lashed out, slapping hard against mine and forcing it back inside.

Angry, I lashed out again more powerfully this time. I was weak from the lack of sustenance but still remained much stronger than the average human, grabbing whoever it was by the hand and roughly dragged them down to their knees so I could see their face.

'B-Beryx?' I stuttered, choking in surprise as his solemn face appeared through the gap.

His bottom lip trembled. 'I'm so sorry, Elena.'

'How could you let him do this to me?'

Beryx touched the plaster set across his broken nose. 'Chester is right. You're dangerous.'

I loosened my grip and sat forward so he could see my face more clearly. 'I never meant for you to get hurt, Beryx. I was trying to protect you from the fight and I didn't want you to get in the way when I had no idea how I would react. I was out of control.'

He nodded numbly, cautiously looking up at a small, wall-mounted camera behind him. 'I'd better go.'

'Because someone's watching?'

'Yes. I'll already be in trouble for talking to you.'

I looked up at the camera, focusing my mind on its hard, metal casing being crushed; hoping my most recent practice would pay off. Cracks started to slowly appear, the metal groaning under my mental assault, until finally the camera shattered. Its pieces fell to the floor with a clatter. What was left dangled from wires, lenses pointing away from Beryx and me, and at the metal walkways.

A small ache had already flared up behind my eyes, but I didn't care. I was happy to finally be able to fight back, no matter how small the gesture, buying me more time with Beryx.

'Did you do that?' he asked, looking at the pieces of the crumbled camera by his feet. He didn't look at all surprised so there must be cameras in my chimney. They'd probably been watching me practise all along.

I nodded, no point pretending otherwise.

Beryx was quiet for a moment. 'What happened to you?'

I sighed. 'I can't explain it to you, Beryx, and you'd never understand anyway. I just need for you to know that I would never intentionally hurt you or anyone else that means me no harm. Keeping me here is cruel.'

He pondered my answer. 'Chester isn't one of those people, though. You would hurt him given the opportunity.'

He had me there. 'I'll be honest, Beryx. I'm going to crush him like a bug if we ever come face to face again.'

'That's why *I* can't let you out of here,' Beryx said quietly. 'Chester is like a father to me, and I don't want to see him come to harm.' He glanced over his shoulder and then back at me again. 'They'll be coming soon. They'll want to know what is taking me so long and why the surveillance camera is down.'

I grasped his hand again, almost dropping it out of fear when my awareness of the sweet essence of his blood became something I could no longer deny. Beryx's racing pulse was a gentle, drumming reminder under my fingertips; his aroma was cloying, teasing, and so damn irresistible that his meagre protests were lost to my ears. All around me was the steady rhythm of his pulse, the beat of his heart, and the rush of blood through his veins.

I felt my canines slide out despite myself, stomach painfully cramping. My mouth hungered for the sweet taste of copper, and my grip on Beryx tightened. 'Beryx, how long have I been here now?' I said, looking away and trying to ignore the call, needing to taste his lifeblood on my tongue.

Beryx tried pulling free of my grip, but my mind was elsewhere now and I held tight. Temptation still rode me, common sense far from my thoughts. Now, teamed with his whimpers of discomfort and persistent struggling, Beryx was unconsciously feeding the predator within.

'A week, I think.'

'What day is it?'

'Monday, the nineteenth.'

Yep, I've been here over a week.

I quickly released him and let that fact sink in, before I did something I might regret. I turned away from him before Beryx could notice how close to the edge I really was, slumping back down onto the floor, with my stomach painfully heaving.

It would be so easy to spin back around and take what I needed … so very easy.

Instead, I snatched the little cup of sloppy porridge, chugging down the contents quickly and praying that was enough to sate my thirst. After a few moments, I realised the ache inside of me had not eased. I needed so much more than they were offering. 'Can I get a little more food in here?'

'I'm sorry, Elena. Chester checks what I bring to you. He's trying to break you down.'

'So I gathered.'

'He's a scientist. Sometimes Chester's humanitarian

tendencies get left behind when he's caught up in his experiments.'

'It's no excuse, Beryx. He's trying to kill me and you know it.'

He didn't answer.

'You should probably get going,' I said bitterly.

Beryx shuffled forward, lowering his face close down by the hatch. It was something I could feel rather than see, his breath warm on my neck, the smell of his blood thick in the air. I didn't dare turn around. 'Before I go, I just thought you might like to know … you passed Year Eleven with a B-minus average. Your results arrived this morning.'

'Great,' I muttered sarcastically. 'Will that B-minus get me out of here?'

'It's doubtful.' Beryx paused, and then his hand was touching my shoulder. 'I like you, Elena, I really do, but I like my job more. So I'll see you again on Wednesday, okay?' He didn't wait for my answer, shutting the hatch behind me. It was just as well, because I was about two seconds away from turning my head and sinking my fangs into flesh.

Close call.

I gasped and clutched at my stomach as another painful spasm wracked my body. This time was much worse than before, a pain beyond feeling, beyond hunger or thirst. My throat was starting to burn, my flesh feverish and lips desiccated. The recent offering of food had been meagre, but I had still just eaten—I should be feeling better, not worse. What was Chester trying to prove by doing this to me?

I fingered the sharp points still protruding past my lips, worried about why they hadn't yet receded. How could I possibly learn to control that which I didn't fully understand?

I closed my eyes, trying to focus on anything but the

pain. What I really needed, besides some food, was Lucas. He could always make me laugh, or say something stupid enough to make me feel better. It had been far too long since we'd spoken, and I missed him so much it hurt.

I tried focusing on the darkness behind my lids instead, blocking out the physical world and ignoring the fire in my throat. I welcomed sleep; but the face I saw in the darkness wasn't William's. It was the face that had occasionally haunted my dreams in the past, a face so familiar yet unknown.

My dark warrior.

Calm drifted over me as I pictured his face with a clarity beyond reason. Over time I had memorised every detail, finding no flaws in his features, just a perfection that bordered on the impossible.

His features began to fade as the darkness closed in and I began drifting. Weightlessness soon lifted me into oblivion.

I spiralled down into that conscious state of sleep, back to the place where renderings from my own imagination had previously come to life. Behind my closed lids, colours began blurring past my eyes, images slowly appearing with the returning of the light. I was not standing in the torch-lit, stone-clad room I had expected to see.

I found myself in a darkened field in the middle of nowhere.

I peered around. Night had fallen here, but I could still see the breeze ruffling the grass underfoot. In the distance, I could make out the movement of something or someone approaching.

People, maybe?

As the shadows drew closer, their outlines became more distinguishable—definitely people. They were running towards me at impossible speeds, so fast I could have confused them with the wind. Yet, with every fervent step, my awareness of each figure grew, and they began to slow down, much like the frame-by-frame feature on a DVD recorder.

How is this possible?

I shook my head, feeling stupid. This was my dream, and I could obviously do whatever I wanted here, see whomever I chose, and touch whatever I wished to feel. I was imagining that cold grass beneath my feet, tickling my toes; the stems of the wild flowers brushing at my ankles, wilting slowly from the coming onset of the winter; the leaves on the tree beside me, steadily falling to the ground due to the whispering wind; and the hooting of that owl sitting opposite me in that tree. All were a part of my fantasy.

I watched as the figures continued to approach, my vision sharpening and my senses heightening as I relaxed into my dream state, each pounding footfall bringing them that much closer to me.

I blinked. I could now see that these were the four young men I'd encountered in the stone room of my previous dream. My dark warrior headed up the group, striding with the grace of a gazelle and the speed of a cheetah. His hair tangled in the wind, moonlight highlighting the angular planes of his cheekbones and reflecting off the glossy depths of his shining eyes.

The others kept pace behind, their gait just as graceful. The vampires' usual blurred movements were somehow easily perceptible to me. I could see the rise and fall of their chests now, muscles tensing in mid stride, and the determined set of their obsidian eyes.

They finally caught up with me, moved past, and kept going.

As I watched them speed past, I wondered if I could skirt

the boundaries of my previous dreams; I was aching to chase these creatures, keep pace with them, and be one of them.

I started laughing as I ran, beginning to move faster than I ever thought possible. The wind whipped through my hair, and my feet barely touched the ground as each stride took me further than the last. The sensation was incredible, and I was already gaining ground on the group up ahead.

They started to slow, my dark warrior holding up a hand and signalling for his companions to halt. I laughed as I glided by, feeling slightly foolish for getting carried away, running so far past that I needed to circle back around. I slowed when the group came into view again, my feet thudding against the dew-covered grass as I attempted to draw to a stop, leaning back with all my weight. I faltered and skidded, sliding like a kid covered in grease over the slippery surface of the dewy grass.

I squealed like an idiot as I headed on a direct collision course with my dark warrior, but having far too much fun to really care.

He looked up. Whether Silvereyes actually saw me or not I didn't know, but the second before we collided, he closed his eyes. I did, too, mostly because imagining swimming through his insides again set my teeth on edge. But this time, oddly enough, that didn't happen.

I ploughed into him, my partially physical being head-butting his shoulder so hard that I was quickly rebounding sideways and back towards the ground. My hands braced for the worst of the impact, my arms taking the brunt of the pain but the aftershock still jarring my joints. Behind my eyes I was seeing stars, and the flesh of my feet was quite chaffed after such quick deceleration, despite the damp grass.

'Bloody hell,' I muttered, hauling myself back to my feet.

'That was unexpected.' I dusted my hands off on the back of my dirty dress.

My dark warrior spun around, eyes searching the night, but never quite settling upon me. The others around him seemed to be talking, too, but I still couldn't hear their words. He brushed a hand over his shoulder, touching the skin where my face had smacked into him, eyes narrowing.

The others suddenly moved forward, forming a tight circle around him and restricting my view. As one huddled mass, they watched as my dark warrior dropped his hand from his shoulder, dipped into the back pocket of his leather pants and retrieved a cell phone. He flipped it open, bringing it to his ear and no doubt listening to someone on the other end of the line.

He looked off to the right and into the distance, lips moving soundlessly. Abruptly, Silvereyes snapped the phone shut and dropped it back inside his pocket. The others looked to him expectantly, their black eyes wide as they watched him pointing a sure hand back in the direction he had been studying only moments before. They conferred briefly.

The Asian vamp and the two blondes didn't seem to need more direction than that. They took off again, all purpose, leaving my dark warrior behind. He watched them go, his back taut, and muscles bunching as he slowly scanned the darkness. And stopped as his eyes seemingly spied mine. At first I thought it was coincidence, his soulless eyes settling upon my flesh; but as he reached out and touched my cheek, I knew we were suddenly both right there together.

Silvereyes dropped his fingers from my cheek and to my lips, slowly running them down my face and neck until they curled through my hair. My dark warrior pulled me closer, his eyes locked on mine—emotionless and empty.

In the next instant, he was gone. The pressure of his caress vanished and again all that was left was the void, a taunting darkness that once more consumed me. Except that, this time, the darkness was not as peaceful as before: it was irritating, noisy even. God, a loud banging sound seemed to be coming from directly behind me and was getting progressively louder until—

'Elena, wake up!'

I cursed and slowly opened my eyes, finally back in the land of the living. A hollow aching stabbed me directly in the stomach, my pain worse than ever before. I could feel the burning in my throat again, and my hands were trembling. Why did that asshole have to wake me up?

I sat up slowly, spinning around. 'What do you want, Chester?'

'I thought you might want to talk.'

'To you?' I snorted loudly. 'Not likely.'

He *tsk-tsk*ed at me. 'That's not very friendly now, is it? Aren't you hungry yet?'

'Why don't you step inside and let me show you.'

Chester was quiet for a moment. 'So it's blood that you want?'

I frowned. My earlier encounter with Beryx had stirred certain urges but I hadn't even thought of that. I mean, I was hungry, and the constant groaning in my stomach reminded me of that, but I'd never considered that I'd need regular supplies of blood.

'It seems that you have something of a dilemma on your hands then,' Chester said with a crooked smile. 'It would appear that you're in need of some nourishment other than ordinary food.'

'Are you offering?' I said, licking my lips and studying the veins in his neck.

His grin broadened as he lowered himself further to better see me through the little hatch. Smart—he was still keeping his distance from me. 'No, but I do have another offer for you.'

'And that would be?'

'A meeting, in exchange for a tetra pack of blood and some food.'

My eyes narrowed. 'Explain.'

Chester pulled his tortoise shell glasses off his nose, cleaned the lenses slowly and returned them to his face. 'We have located the Alpha that has been tracking you. He's been watching this facility almost nightly, presumably waiting for a glimpse of you.' He paused, waiting for a reaction. I gave him nothing. 'I'm very curious about what will happen when I put the two of you together.'

I snorted. 'You're crazy. You do know that, don't you? You can't put me in the same room as an Alpha. That's a very dangerous idea, not to mention stupid.'

His expression turned serious. 'Not under controlled circumstances, it's not. And, besides, he won't attack when there are so many of us around and he is so clearly outnumbered. I'm assuming that's why he watches and searches for ways to get to you rather than attacking.'

I cursed. 'Chester, in case you forgot, I *am* half-Vânător. I'm susceptible to the commands of the Alpha, even if I don't want to do whatever he asks me. I'll be completely helpless at resisting him. Do you understand what will happen if you let him in here?'

Chester didn't answer, but I carried on regardless. 'If he finds a way to break me out of here and tells me to kill everybody in the local vicinity, then I'll have to do it, without hesitation.' I paused and stared back at him, all seriousness. 'There are just some aspects of myself that I haven't learnt how to control just yet. Who knows how far I could go? Doing this would be a grave mistake, Chester.'

'It will be fine,' he said, dismissing my worries with a wave of his hand. 'The experiment will be controlled.'

I wanted to scream at him. 'You've seen what I can do, Chester. Do you really want to put those abilities in the wrong hands? And what if he decides he wants to mate with me? Are you just going to stand there and let that happen, too?'

Chester scratched thoughtfully at his chin. 'Well, it would be interesting to see what you birth and how your body reacts to the pregnancy.'

I sneered. 'You're a poor excuse for a human being, Chester. Just go away now. No deal.'

He stepped back from the door. 'Suit yourself.' Chester reached for something on the other side of the door. A mechanical whirring sound could be heard and then the metal grill at the top of the chimney started to retract. The large metal plate rose up and sunlight streamed down into my holding cell. I shrunk back, squinting under the sudden brightness.

Realisation dawned. 'You're going to just let him in here!' I screamed. 'What the hell is wrong with you?' I smashed my fists against the hatch in frustration, the metal denting only slightly beneath my blows.

'You're strong, Elena. You can hold him off.' Chester said this smugly, malevolence fully evident in his voice as he closed the small hatch.

'The Alpha takes a hold of my physical being, you moron. I can't hold him off if he commands me to go to him!'

Laughter echoed from under the door as the sound of Chester's footsteps dwindled down the metal passage outside.

Stunned, I spun back around and glared up through the opening. At least the Vânător wasn't coming until the sun went down, which meant I still had a couple of hours to figure out what I was going to do when he arrived. My options were few, practically non-existent, and my body was still too damned weak. Fighting John, another Alpha, had been beyond my skill set. And now? The sad truth was that I was still lacking.

I shook my head, raising my face to the sunlight and screaming at the top of my lungs. It didn't sound as impressive as I'd hoped, but it released a fair amount of pent-up aggression.

Why was this happening to me? Wasn't there one other person on the entire planet that could share some of my unrelenting bad luck? Did I really deserve to keep getting shit on by the heavens above? Couldn't someone or something give me a freaking break?

I slumped to the floor, pulling my dirty, white dress underneath me to keep warm. I looked back up at the opening and stared at the sunlight until it hurt my eyes. Its warmth caressed my skin, and I sat there feeling very sorry for myself.

'Why?' I said absently, looking up to the overhead clouds and above. 'Why the hell are you picking on me?'

As the last remaining piece of afternoon sunlight disappeared into the shadows, it gave way to the dawn of another night. I waited. The vânător would soon rise from his daytime slumber and start searching the night, looking for something he had spent almost two and a half months waiting to get his claws into—me. Now, thanks to Chester and his stupidity, the Alpha was going to get his chance.

I carefully watched the opening at the top of the chimney. My eyes never strayed from that small hole, a hole that represented both potential freedom and a way for death to find me. Every second that ticked by felt like an hour, and every moment that the shadows grew heavier, so did my heart.

Behind my head, the small hatch groaned and slowly opened. It was Chester, the pungent scent of his musky aftershave wafting through the opening; the clinking of assorted pens in his lab coat pocket was loud enough to wake the dead. He was pulling up a chair just outside the door, and a quick glance in that direction proved me correct. Now Chester had brought out a small notebook in preparation and was holding one of those pens up in front of him. He'd already begun taking notes.

I sneered. 'You really are a sick bastard,' I said as I slowly got up, eyes still watching overhead. 'I really hope that Alpha finds a way to get to you first so I can watch him tear you to shreds. Better yet, I hope he asks me to do it for him.'

Chester ignored me completely and continued scribbling notes down on the pad in front of him. The scratching sounds of fine-tipped ballpoint on paper grated at my nerves, feeding my already growing anxiety.

An ominous howl suddenly echoed down through the night air above me. The Alpha was close—too close.

I tilted my head back and sniffed at the air, hoping my recent enhancements had also strengthened my sense of smell. A cold breeze tickled my nostrils as I sorted through the various scents filtering through the room, some more recognisable than others. I could smell the tang of oiled machinery, and the heavy stench of coal and smoke. Over that was the smell of fresh blood—human blood—but I couldn't be sure if it had been spilt by the Alpha or if my senses were just more finely tuned then they had been before.

As another howl broke through the night, I finally caught wind of a scent—raw earth and man sweat. It was the same smell that John had exuded, a smell I would never forget.

I closed my eyes, steeling myself as the sound of talons scraping against metal started tearing chunks out of my confidence. The Alpha was quick, a *click, click, click* the only sound of its scrambling progress over the factory rooftop. There was silence for a moment, and then a heavy *thud* in the room before me. I could smell its scent swirling all around me, teasing and terrifying.

My lips parted as his essence slithered across my tongue. I heard an interior calling that left my heart pounding with anticipation. Slowly, I opened my eyes and looked into the vibrant depths of his amber orbs. I was shivering, both at his sudden nearness and the heat in his gaze.

The Alpha took a step forward, his taut, naked body drawing my eyes downwards. I would never get used to looking at these creatures naked. Heat was already blanketing my face as my eyes lingered on his, *ahem*, growing state of arousal. Vânǎtors were innately sexual creatures so it didn't surprise me, but watching the Alpha's reaction to my presence made me nervous.

The werewolf in front of me could shapeshift into any human form it had previously fed from, tempting and teasing its intended victims, and finally taking them against their will. Just like John before him, this Alpha's body was ripped, both powerfully muscled and awash with sexual charisma. But that didn't change the fact that they were disgusting creatures that enjoyed preying upon the weak and innocent, something of which I wanted no part.

'Elena,' he said in a deep, throaty voice, his hand reaching out to touch me.

I took a step back. 'How do you know my name?' I already knew the answer but I was stalling. Talking was better than the alternative, especially now that he seemed more than ready for me.

'John told me all about you … and your blood.' He sniffed at the air, savouring my scent, and as his eyes darkened he reached for me again.

I ducked beneath one outstretched arm and scuttled away from him. 'Stay away from me, vânător. I didn't help John and I won't help you either. And if you don't want to end up dead like your friend, then you'll keep your distance.' My words lacked any real conviction, and as I spoke them I could feel my mouth go dry. I'd never felt so intimidated, so helpless.

The Alpha eyed me for a moment, no doubt weighing up the intent behind my words. He must have smelt my desperation because in-between one breath and the next he was smiling again, scent washing over me and beckoning to me with a finger to come to him.

I resisted, pushing my back up against the wall and praying it would stick to me like glue.

'Come to me, Elena.'

'No.'

The tang of his scent grew sharp, turning into that familiar pull that John had used to whip me to do his bidding. 'John told me you were powerless to resist us, to resist our power, so stop trying to fight it.'

Taking a frustrated breath, I found my body pushing itself away from the wall, turning its back on any control I still had. Internally, I was yelling at my legs to stay exactly where they were, but they ignored me, stubbornly marching my traitorous body to him without hesitation.

He wrapped me in his embrace and pressed himself roughly against me. My hands flattened out against the smooth, hard surface of his warm chest, feeling his heart beat beneath my fingertips. The Alpha ran his fingers through my hair, gripping my neck tightly and yanking my head back, a movement that exposed the smooth flesh of my neck. His nose dipped down, brushing almost hesitantly against my skin, soaking in my essence.

An unpleasant memory reared its head: John, doing exactly this, right before his fangs pierced into my flesh with eager glee.

The Alpha breathed deep, his hot breath blowing against my skin and lips grazing one of my throbbing veins. 'You're thirsty,' he said quietly, looking back up at me with hooded, black eyes. 'They have not been looking after you here.'

This isn't making sense. Why the hell should he care about me?

I chose not to answer, mostly because I needed to focus all of my concentration on breaking free of his influence. I was so weak compared to him—Chester had certainly seen to that, whether deliberately or not.

'Be still, Elena,' he said, speaking gently as he brushed his cheek against mine. The smooth feel of his tawny skin sent shivers down my spine.

'Let me go, you overgrown pound puppy,' I whispered, pushing my hands against his chest.

'My name is Roshan.' He gripped me tighter to him. 'And now that I've finally got you in my arms, Elena, there is no way that I will ever let you go.' Roshan grasped my head tightly, entwining the locks of my hair in his fingers as he lowered his lips to mine.

Knowing what was coming, I turned my face, only to feel another wave of his essence glide heavily across my skin.

It reached down into my lungs and begged me to claim a part of myself I had always denied; and, I succumbed. As his soft, warm lips pressed against my own, I stiffened, unprepared for the tender, almost tentative nature of that kiss. His lips were searching, not demanding, as his fingers caressed my hair.

Confusion set in, and then I felt heat, and then something else that was building up inside me. His lips continued to tease my own, and as Roshan pressed himself harder against me, I groaned; his building arousal mirrored my own. I tried to stop, screaming at myself to pull away, but my lips were eager, delighting in that taste .The feel of him was sending me wild. I hated myself, hated that I had no control, but I couldn't stop.

Roshan's hands left my hair, gliding down my back and cupping my buttocks. He ground intimately against me until I could feel every inch of him with absolute clarity.

E, you have to stop! Pull away from him, use your abilities—anything!

'Elena,' Roshan breathed against my lips, 'I need to taste you.'

I grimaced, despising the way I enjoyed his fingers burning against my flesh. His digits caressed their way down my thighs, slowly gathering the hem of my dress and sliding it upwards.

'Fascinating,' I heard Chester whisper from behind the door. I'd completely forgotten the old pervert was even there.

Roshan's head whipped to the side, and he growled loudly. Instantly releasing me, he bounded across the room and over to the door. Chester looked unperturbed, though, and continued to scribble down notes.

Roshan barrelled into the door with an impressive *boom*, pounding his fists against the steel and peppering it with large dents. *Clang-clang, clang-clang.* He was no more successful at breaking through than I'd been, and I wasn't sure if I should be upset or feel relieved.

He roared in anger, all while Chester, sitting comfortably on the other side of my prison, laughed to himself.

Roshan spun back around to glare at me, his nostrils flaring as he glanced up at the opening above us. 'Come, Elena,' he said, the full authority of his animalistic nature pouring into his voice. 'It's time to leave.'

I shook my head, terrified at the prospect of staying yet just as unwilling to leave with him. Not that I really had a choice, as my feet started moving forward anyway, and I found myself standing next to Roshan's lithe form.

He wrapped his arm around my waist, hoisting me off the floor and into his burly arms. Looking up, Roshan bent his knees and with a powerful flexing of muscle, leapt upward towards freedom.

Our escape plans were short-lived.

The metal grill was already closing, and Roshan's head smashed painfully into the toughened steel, sending us plummeting to the ground. We crashed with thunderous force back to the floor in a tumble of arms and legs. Roshan was out cold, his form automatically shifting from human to wolf as he slid into unconsciousness.

I was already screaming. My left arm had somehow got bent around behind me, snapping as we'd landed, and my right leg crushed under the weight of Roshan's body. Werewolves were heavy beasts.

Tears stung my eyes as I rolled onto my side, waiting for my healing abilities to kick in and make me whole once more. It was taking a little longer than usual, and that was something I blamed on Chester for depriving me of food, water, and basic sanitation.

'Elena, are you okay?' Chester asked, voice dripping with indifference. A quick glance in his direction revealed an uncontained smirk. His eyes were still trained on the notepad in front of him.

I hissed at his blatant coldness, fangs lengthening, my whole body quivering in anger.

This is his fault, and will make him pay!

A burst of telekinetic energy exploded out of my body, speeding through the metal door and sending Chester's chair flying. I heard him slam against the metal wall behind the stack with a sickening *thud*, chair disintegrating into splinters. I heard him groan as he slid to the floor, and hoped the bastard was either passed out, or better yet, dead.

I moaned loudly and attempted to push Roshan's heavy form off of me. His unconscious body was a dead weight, and several strained minutes passed before I managed to slide my leg out from under him. I cursed and punched him in the head, the pain from my leg flaring up again. I cradled my arm to my chest and slumped back to the floor. I studied the rusted-tinge on the grate above, the distraction of thought the key to waiting out the pain.

I closed my eyes as old pains resurfaced—the burning in my throat, and the cramping of my stomach so bad that I wondered if I was suffering from organ failure. The hurt was worse than the broken limbs from the fall, even more so than being impaled on a tree, a near fatal incident from my last tangle with an Alpha. This was different, almost intolerable—this was pain-on-pain.

From outside there was a stir of movement and a groan from Chester. 'Who-who *are* you?' I heard Chester say blearily. 'How did you—' His words were cut short as the sounds of fists pounding flesh punctured the silence of the stack.

I swallowed my pain with a moan, crawling towards the door with one arm, my other arm cradled against my chest. My leg was beginning to feel better, sinew reknitting and twisting together, yet I still probably shouldn't move it.

What's going on out there?

I glanced up again at the mechanical whirring of the grill as it once again opened up in the chimney above. What was Chester playing at?

'Those buttons don't open the door, Sebastian,' I heard an unfamiliar voice say. 'What do you want me to do?'

'Search that Protector. He may have a key in his coat; otherwise, we'll circle back around and see if there's another way inside.' This voice was accented, sounding almost Italian and vaguely familiar.

'Wow, can you guys smell that?' said another voice.

'Smell what? The vânător or the human?' the first voice answered.

'It has to be human.'

'Keep away, Caleb,' the familiar voice murmured. 'You knew this was going to be difficult.'

I slowly pulled myself to my feet, my leg almost fully healed and my arm not too far behind. Flexing my elbow gently, I turned and looked down at Roshan's still form piled on the floor in a heap. His diaphragm rose and fell as I watched—damn, he was still alive!

I kicked him, but Roshan didn't respond, the movement making his tongue loll out of the side of his snout. He was definitely unconscious but I dared not underestimate him.

'I found them,' the first voice said, drawing my attention back to the door.

I pressed myself against the wall, so I could keep eyes on both the door and Roshan, and hastily looked around for a weapon. As far as I could see, Roshan had nothing of use—his brute strength meant he needed no weapon—and I doubted if Bob the bucket would be any use.

I braced myself, assuming a fighting crouch. As the key rustled in its lock, I finally felt my arm snapping back with a *click* into place. The internal mechanisms of the door engaged, and there was momentary silence before the handle turned. The door clunked and then groaned noisily as it slowly swung open, revealing the impossible.

I staggered, cupping one hand to my mouth and falling over Roshan in the process. I landed on the floor with a *thump*.

He's here! How can that be possible?

My dark warrior stared back at me in equal surprise, the other members of his party fanning out as they stepped inside the confined space of the stack. 'You,' he breathed, taking a tentative step forward, his eyes softening as he took in my dishevelled appearance. He said nothing more, merely staring with the same look of astonishment that twisted my own features.

I closed my eyes and shook my head, suddenly laughing at the absurdity of it all. I pinched the skin on my arm, trying to wake myself up again. 'This is just a dream,' I whispered, 'just a stupid dream that I'm going to wake up from any moment now.'

I opened my eyes, expecting to find myself once again alone in the chimney stack. I wasn't—all four vampires were still there. So was Roshan, who was quickly gaining consciousness, his wolf form morphing slowly to the human once more.

My dark warrior's three vampiric companions looked quizzically at each other, turning their bemused expressions on their leader and then finally back on me.

Roshan lashed out, grabbing my ankle and pulling me

towards him. I squealed as I slid across the floor, finding myself once again imprisoned in his arms. 'Elena,' he breathed groggily as he kissed my forehead, kissed my lips.

'E-Elena?' the dark warrior said, stuttering slightly. 'Your name is Elena?' He paused, staring at me opened-mouthed. 'So, you're human then. I thought you were an apparition sent by Lucifer himself to test me. But how can you be real? Your chance died out long ago.'

What?

Roshan growled, finally realising that we were no longer alone. He shuffled around on both hands and feet, dragging me roughly across the floor until I was lying behind him. Roshan furiously flicked his head around, from one vampire to another and slowly rising up into a crouch. His tawny skin began to grey, as his fangs and talons lengthened.

The other three vampires mirrored his exact actions, skin hazing to transparency, veins shifting to the fore and pulsing with untapped energy. One cracked his knuckles; another vamp slowly licked the pointed tip of his fangs. One with pink-tipped hair puckered his lips at Roshan, stepping forward, taunting him.

Sebastian only had eyes for me, though, eyes that were wide and filled with disbelief.

I scrambled to my feet, edging around the perimeter of the room and as far away from all of them as possible. This new reality was cloying, stealing my breath from me. Arrayed in front of me were the vampires of my dreams and a nightmare Alpha engaged in the hunt, but were they real or imagined? Both worlds seemed to blur together, instilling me with a sense of deep fear.

Roshan must have sensed my retreat, because he turned and growled, watching angrily as I skirted away from him and around to the other end of the stack. Underneath the surface, the vampiric part of me was clawing its way towards release, challenged by the werewolf's domineering demeanour. My fear subsided, and a feral rage rose up in its place, a bubbling resentment that fed directly into my darker nature.

Human logic faded, and I found myself dropping into a defensive crouch. My fangs quickly grew, the urge to rend and tear flesh made my mouth water with anticipation. I leaned forward on steady fingers in preparation for the fight.

'Um, is she supposed to be able to do that?' the one called Caleb said, his confusion obvious as he pointed at me with one taloned finger. At least he'd scented me as human.

My dark warrior shook his head, disbelief still marring his expression. 'She isn't even supposed to exist, Caleb, so I don't know what the hell she is.'

'Elena is mine!' Roshan snapped, as he scrambled towards me.

I hissed at him and rocked forward, my eyes watching his every move, and calculating how best to incapacitate him quickly. 'I belong to no one.'

'She's not what I expected,' the blonde vampire said under his breath.

'I thought *she* would be a *he*,' the Asian one answered, voice a whisper.

'She's perfect,' Sebastian said, rising to full height and holding out his hand to me. He took a step forward, fingers outstretched. 'Come to me, Elena. I will keep you safe.'

I searched his eyes for truth, looking for lies or the promise of more suffering—there was none. In the recent past I had put my faith in all the wrong people, and I wasn't about to walk blindly into another trap. However, as I looked more deeply into his swirling grey-green eyes, seeing the glint of recognition as he stared back at me and felt the unwavering connection that surpassed dreams, I knew I'd be safe.

Roshan roared with anger, and the spell was broken. I flinched back, blinking as a fresh wave of his Alpha scent descended upon me. It consumed me whole, suffocating and clawing at my skin. 'Elena,' he said, 'come to your Alpha.'

I screamed in frustration, the sound once again hoarse and weak as it gurgled up out of my throat, expelled in a wheeze. My body ignored all mental protests and pulled itself upright to cross the room towards him.

'What's going on?' the Asian said.

'I don't know,' Caleb answered, 'but I think we should attack now and ask questions later. She's making me hungry.'

My dark warrior growled. 'You will *not* put her life in danger. I forbid it, Caleb.'

Caleb rolled his eyes as the other two vampires slinked back. 'Sebastian, one bite isn't going to hurt.'

'I've already warned you, Caleb,' Sebastian stated with relative calm, but the violence in his expression belied his soft words. 'Don't make me repeat myself or you will be sorry.'

Caleb sniffed but remained silent. He focused his attention back on me, licking his lips absently.

I stepped reluctantly into Roshan's arms, my body and mind at cross-purposes. I was so near to him now that the smell of his body filled my senses, making my stomach ache fiercely with need.

Roshan pressed my face against his chest, my nose rubbing against the heated flesh of his skin. His heart thumped wildly in his chest. Roshan may have been an 'immortal' like these vampires, but he had a pulse and could still be killed. That filled a part of me with hope.

I pressed my lips against the hard muscle of his pecs.

The salty taste of his sweat touched my tongue, my hunger rising. Roshan shuddered at my touch, his arms wrapping tightly around me. His arousal was growing once more. My mind was elsewhere, my body instinctively reacting to what was coming.

My fangs grew in length until they nicked the surface of his skin, drawing a single droplet of blood. And that was all it took.

I plunged my teeth into his flesh, feeling the warm liquid of his essence spilling down my throat in a cascade of sweetness, immediately easing the burn in my throat as it flowed into my bloodstream. Caramel and chocolate danced across my tongue, that delicious taste always taking me by surprise.

I moaned, hearing Roshan's groans of delight turn quickly into displeasure as he yanked at my hair, pulling me away from him. My teeth gouged at his flesh as they came out. I found myself rushing forward again, my tongue catching the spilt essence before I could be shoved away.

'Stop!' Roshan growled, pulling even harder at my hair.

I whimpered, licking what blood remained off my lips. The pain inside me was intolerable and I roared with the need to be properly sated.

Something in Roshan's expression softened as he pulled me closer again, his hands tenderly cupping my face. 'Not now. When we return to my den, you can feed.'

And that was something I could not allow.

I sprung back at him, grabbing his arms and holding him down as my teeth sought out the surface of his flesh still freely flowing with blood. He struggled, still much stronger than I was, but I was determined, and very, very hungry.

'Elena, stop!' he ordered, using the commanding timbre of his Alpha voice. 'No more biting me.'

I complied.

'What the hell is going on here?' Caleb mouthed, looking to the others for explanation. They returned blank stares, shrugging.

My body and Roshan's intertwined, the blood from his chest spilling down onto my dress and ruining it indefinitely. I longed to press my lips against that flowing redness, his express order all that was preventing me from touching him.

'Enough,' Sebastian said, stepping forward with purpose. 'There are four of us, Vânător. You have no hope of winning against us all, so stop playing games and let the girl go.'

'She's mine,' Roshan repeated, looking up. He bent low at the knees and again sprung powerfully up towards the open shaft.

Events after that happened too quickly to follow. One minute I was being held firmly by Roshan, flying back up towards the top of the chimney, and in the very next, I was pulled free of his grip and was tumbling back towards the ground again, cringing.

I didn't hit it.

Hands lifted me, hands that were surprisingly warm and that cradled and comforted me. Sebastian held me close, resting my head against his shoulder as he quickly scooped me up. 'Don't worry, Elena,' he cooed gently as we headed through the door, 'I have you now. And everything is going to be fine.'

I looked up at him, wondering if I should pinch myself again. 'Who are you?'

He smiled, glancing down at me with weird intensity. 'I'm Sebastian,' he murmured. 'Apparently, I'm the man of your dreams.'

CHAPTER ELEVEN: REALITY

Sebastian's statement was presumptuous but also completely true. In one way or another, this man had been starring in my dreams for years now, riding my thoughts and somehow become my yardstick for perfection that I unwittingly searched for in others. I still couldn't believe that he was real and was here. Right now. Talking to me! The whole situation seemed absurd, possibly even staged, but I'd never told anyone about my dreams. How could Sebastian have known that I'd dreamt of him?

Am I dreaming now?

I touched a finger to his cheek, watching the smooth skin beneath my fingertip gently give way. It was warm, alive under my touch, which was something that was not exactly a vampiric trait.

'Elena, what are you doing?'

'Making sure you're real.'

'Oh, I am very real, I assure you. It's you who shouldn't be.'

I poked him again, and then shrieked as Sebastian whipped his head to the side and playfully nipped at my fingers. 'Okay, you can put me down now,' I said shakily, balling my hands against my chest.

He shook his head. 'Until I get you away from this place and somewhere safe, you're staying in my arms.'

'I don't need for you to carry me.'

'I'm sure you don't,' Sebastian said, tightening his grip around my legs and pressing me ever closer. 'But that's where you're going to stay until I say so.'

'How do I know you're not dangerous?'

'You should feel it.'

I sniffed. Dream guy or not, I didn't know him and had to be careful. Any escape would involve having two legs on solid ground, running hard and, possibly, fighting. 'I want to walk.'

'No.'

I frowned, my agitation growing. I'd never expected my fantasy man to be annoying. 'Put me down now, Sebastian. I won't ask again.'

'Can you just stop talking and trust me?'

'Trust you? I don't even know you.'

'At least stop talking then.'

I looked at him, horrified. 'Don't tell me to stop talking.'

Sebastian cringed, flashing me an apologetic look. 'I only ask because, right now, your breath is a little on the rancid side.'

I folded my hands across my chest and looked away, desperately trying not to reveal how mortified I felt. 'You try getting locked in a freakin' steel chimney for a week and tell me how you look and smell at the end of it,' I mumbled under my breath. 'No food, no toothbrush, no shower. You do the math.'

'You're still talking.'

I turned back and glared at Sebastian with impressive force, my tears drying up almost as quickly as they'd begun. He actually laughed, fuelling my desire to stamp all over this fantasy, return it, and ask for a refund. He'd never been so brutally honest in my dreams.

'That's better.' Sebastian paused, his eyes softening. 'You know, if you're one of those women who need to talk every five seconds there are other ways to communicate. Do you know sign language?'

I'll give you sign language.

I gave him the finger, pretty sure that it still meant 'up yours' in any language.

Sebastian chewed on his lower lip, presumably biting back another smile. 'Okay, fair call.' He still didn't put me down, holding me tightly despite my struggles. As he ducked through the doorway and entered the walkway beyond, I settled down, distracted as I saw Chester lying spreadeagle on the ground before us. He had a massive welt on the side of his face, his tongue lolling out the side of his mouth. Chester may have been dead.

'Relax,' Sebastian said, pulling my face towards him. 'He's going to be unconscious for a while, but you don't need to worry about him.'

I wasn't worried about him; I was seriously upset that I had missed my opportunity to knock him out myself.

I struggled forward again, trying to wriggle out of Sebastian's embrace, and wanting to land a kick or two on the moron's lifeless body. Or better yet, drink Chester's blood and satisfy all my aches and pains.

'Elena, please stay still.'

'Let go of me,' I hissed. 'I'm not finished with him.'

Sebastian pulled me roughly to him, pinning my arms to my sides. 'Elena, stop it! You have to remember that this man is a Protector. No matter what he has done to you, if you kill him or drain his blood it will be the end of the treaty between both our races. He has seen us and knows that vampires were here. If the treaty falters, then who will be responsible for defeating the Vânătors?'

'I don't care.'

'Sure you do.'

I shook my head. 'Right now I'm hungry, smelly, and tired, and all I want to do is make myself feel a little bit better. Kicking the crap out of Chester is an excellent place to start.'

Sebastian sighed but kept on walking. 'And once you kill him, then what? Are you happy for the Vampire race to suffer the consequences of your selfish actions, simply because this one pissed you off? Is war what you desire?'

'You have no idea what Chester put me through.'

'Regardless, you must rise above it.'

I sniffed. He was right, but I didn't like it. 'You know, I liked you much better before you started talking.'

Sebastian wrinkled his nose as if weeding out a bad smell. 'At this point in time, the feeling is entirely mutual.'

I slumped against him again, feeling defeated, I eyed Chester's limp body. I vowed that one day, one day really soon, he'd be the one to writhe around in pain. It didn't seem fair that, when he woke, all Chester would suffer was a headache and a black eye. After everything he'd put me through, he deserved so much worse.

Sebastian moved quickly down a metal staircase, glancing left and right before leaping over the main walkway, and then bounding up onto an overhead riser. This path didn't seem to actually lead anywhere, but Sebastian didn't linger. He bent low and then leapt forward again, landing up on another steel platform high in the roof; and then jumped quickly through a massive exhaust vent, which was already mangled from their earlier entry.

Sebastian carried me through and then climbed a short steel ladder at the end, leading up to the rooftop above.

I breathed in the night air, my nose burning from the

slight chill. I was revelling in the sweet scent of freedom, despite still being locked in the vampiric arms around me. Traversing the whole escape route took less than two minutes, which made a mockery out of the IMI's security; I found myself sniggering internally. It got me wondering why Roshan had not come for me sooner. Did he, like me, have a deeply held fear of The Protectors?

Once we were up on the roof, I carefully surveyed the landscape around me. I was being held in an area littered with warehouses, junk yards, and industrial storage facilities. Smoke billowed up into the night sky, belched indiscriminately into the atmosphere by dirty stacks like an old drunk smoking his pipe. Only a short distance away I could see the lights of the surrounding suburbs and more industry, glowing against the horizon like a false sun promising an early dawn.

'Sebastian,' a voice called from behind us.

We turned. 'Eric,' he said, answering the tall Asian vampire as he approached. 'Where are Caleb and Nicholas?'

Eric shrugged. 'Probably still hunting down the Vânător.' He looked down at me then, as if suddenly remembering I was there. 'Where are you taking her?'

'Somewhere safe.'

'Excuse me,' I said, struggling again in Sebastian's embrace, 'but do I get a say in this at all?'

'No,' they both answered.

'I wasn't really asking,' I muttered under my breath. Sebastian clamped a hand over my mouth, wrinkling his nose in disgust.

'I'm going to run her across the border into Hungary. Nicholas has a place in Budapest where she can get cleaned up. After that, I'll take her home.'

Home?

'What about the Alpha?' Eric asked, looking back down at me again. 'It's a rare opportunity for us to encounter one such as he. We should pursue him, destroy him.'

'He's not a part of our duties, so if they end up killing him, fine. The most important thing tonight is to keep Elena safe and get her out of the country as fast as we can.'

'What does Lucius want with her, anyway? Her blood?'

Sebastian glared at Eric as I gasped. 'That's none of your business.' He didn't wait for an answer, just stepped forward and sprung from the rooftop down to the ground below, his feet only lightly disturbing the soil underfoot as we landed.

'Put me down!' I screamed, his hand leaving my lips. 'I don't want to go with you!' My hands flailed wildly and I clipped his chin, the shock of the blow causing my knuckles to ache.

'I'm trying to protect you.'

'You're taking me somewhere to be eaten, I know it!'

'That is not my intention.'

'Then let me go.'

'I let you go and then the Alpha hunts you down, rapes you, feeds itself and then kills you. Is that what you want?'

I grew still. 'No.'

'Then shut up and let me protect you.'

Sebastian took off at a fast run, my angry retort lost to the wind. As the force of inertia pressed heavily against me, my head snapped back against Sebastian's shoulder. My skin sagging against my bones, punishing muscle and sinew; my breath became stuck in my throat, clogged by a multitude of bugs; and, my eyeballs strained in their sockets, and I was fairly certain I'd find them poking out my rear end when we finally stopped. I probably would have thrown up but after being starved for so long there was barely anything inside me to bring up.

I closed my eyes and prayed that some higher power had heard my earlier pleas, that Sebastian rescuing me from the IMI was a blessing and not a curse, and that I wasn't crazy and imagining this whole thing. I'd recently befriended a bucket, so anything was possible.

I felt myself frowning. I was pretty sure there was something wrong with my fantasy man. Sebastian wasn't being very nice to me—he should have been swooning all over me, caressing me and whispering words of comfort in my ear, not pushing me around. Normally, I would never have let someone tell me what to do and I didn't usually let strange men touch me like this. I'd certainly never played the part of damsel in distress before; it just wasn't my style.

I squeezed my eyes closed ever tighter, trying to sort out what was reality through my haze of indecision and mounting complications. The dreams that I'd been having were obviously not dreams at all, and could possibly be attributed to be another side effect of the blood exchange. Dreams of Sebastian before the exchange had only come in snippets; in contrast, my recent dreams had been like full motion pictures.

So, what did it all mean? Could I now see into the future? Or, at the very least, was I now able to view the present elsewhere? And if either of those theories held true, why had Sebastian and Lucius both been included? What power or circumstance had drawn me to them?

I opened my eyes slowly, peeking out through one cracked lid and glancing up at Sebastian. His eyes were completely black now and were focused purposefully on the horizon. The rush of wind around us blew his hair back from his face. His teeth were tightly clenched, jaw muscles bunched and straining as we surged forward.

I whimpered, suddenly feeling overwhelmed as

everything the last few months had thrown at me finally hit home. I was so weary and wondered if I'd ever feel safe again. Sebastian must have heard me because he brushed a hand gently across my forehead, tucking my hair behind my ears—a comforting yet pointless gesture in the endless wind.

'Be patient, Elena. We'll be there soon,' he said, leaning in close to my ear.

I buried my face against his chest, not wanting Sebastian to see the weakness in me. I didn't want to be anywhere soon except for home—I wanted to go home and see Lucas.

'Soon' turned out to be a totally bullshit estimation, at any rate.

It was roughly four hours later that I felt the pelting wind on my face begin to ease and the silhouettes of passing buildings becoming distinguishable once more. I hadn't spoken a word in that entire time and neither had Sebastian. We'd both undoubtedly been lost in our own thoughts.

Sebastian slowed to a more reasonable pace, people glancing warily at us as we passed the outskirts of what I had to assume was the city of Budapest. After the event of the previous evening, it was small wonder why people were staring—Sebastian was pelting along, carrying a dirty woman in a formerly white and now blood-stained dress.

We were quite the spectacle.

He ducked down an alleyway, disappearing around a corner that was clear of passersby and then leaping high into the air, shooting upwards towards the apartment building towering above us. Sebastian landed on the edge of a metal balcony rail with the grace of a circus performer, poised perfectly five floors above the ground. Barefoot, and with curled over toes to steady his grip, he dropped onto the terrazzo balcony with a soft thud.

Slowly, Sebastian lowered me to the ground. My feet were numb, having fallen asleep a few hours before. I grimaced, my knees buckling as feeling slowly returned in the form of stabbing pins and needles. Sebastian caught me before I fell, holding me up and carefully unwrapping my arms from around him. When he seemed certain I could again support myself, Sebastian reached under the mat by our feet and pulled a small key from underneath it. He quickly unlocked the double balcony doors leading into the bedroom.

A wave of dizziness spilled over me. My stomach was growling loudly, and I felt my insides contort, as if some vicious beast was trying to claw its way out from the inside. I had the overwhelming urge to throw up.

'What's wrong?' Sebastian said, lightly touching my back.

'It hurts.'

'What hurts?'

I looked up at him, eyes scrunched up. 'Everything.'

'What can I do?'

'I think I need blood. It's the only thing that's made me feel marginally better before.'

Sebastian took me by the hand and led me inside the darkened apartment, the stale smell of neglect filling my nostrils. I slumped against the closest wall for support, wishing I could disappear into those shadows. 'Stay here.'

'Where else am I going to go?' I looked out over the balcony, highlighting my point. But Sebastian was already gone.

He returned a fraction of a second later. 'There isn't any blood in the house. I'm going to have to go to a neutral bar and buy you some, but I'll be back as soon as I can.'

'A neutral bar?' The confusion was clear in my eyes.

Sebastian frowned. 'Have you been living under a rock for the last sixteen years?'

I grimaced. 'More or less.'

He stepped over to the doors and closed them behind us, locking the latch and switching on the overhead lights. A nondescript bedroom was revealed as illumination bloomed around me. 'The neutral bars are a place where vampires can go to feed. There's generally one, possibly more, in every major city. It helps us curb the need to hunt humans for blood when it is so readily purchased.'

'Like pubs for the undead?'

'Exactly.' Sebastian took a few steps towards me. 'There's a bed behind you. I think you should sit down before you fall down; you look quite pale, Elena.'

'How couldn't I know about neutral bars?' I groaned sarcastically, as I slowly lowered myself down onto the bed. The mattress was so soft that I almost moaned. Sleeping on that steel floor for a week had proved quite a hardship. 'The Protectors never mentioned anything.'

Sebastian sneered. 'Well, they wouldn't, would they? That would mean acknowledging that vampires were becoming more civilised, more self-controlled. It's easier for The Protectors to think of us as monsters, biding their time until the Vânători are dead and they can finally turn on us. Our alliance is only going to hold for so much longer. Now they have the answer to killing off the Vânători completely within their grasp, the Protectors are going to take full advantage of this opportunity.'

I buckled over as another cramp hit me hard, gripping the crisp linen sheets tightly in my hands. 'I hate to point out the obvious,' I gasped, 'but you Vampires started it.'

Sebastian's eyes darkened. 'Rest for a bit,' he said slowly, tone frosty. 'I'll go and get you something to eat. In the meantime, if you like, there's a bathroom through that door where you can clean yourself up.' He pointed to the darkened room beyond. I squinted in the direction of his pointing finger, but when I turned back again, Sebastian was gone.

Groaning a little more loudly now that I was alone, I forced myself upright and hobbled into the bathroom, switching on more lights as I went. In the corner there was a small bathtub and shower combination. Beside that was a tiny basin, a toilet, and what I assumed was a bidet. There was nothing remarkable about this room either, but I was so desperately pleased by the thought of a long, warm shower that it might as well have been an ornate Roman bath house.

I ditched my dress and tossed it into the corner, shimmying out of my underwear and glancing at myself in the mirror in front of me.

Wow. I look like shit.

I touched the slight hollow of my cheeks, brushed my fingers across my pale, bruised skin, and stared down at ribs that were starting to protrude. It was no wonder my dress had started to feel a little baggy.

I grabbed my breasts and cupped them.

Ick. Certainly less than a handful now, and they were never a decent handful, anyway.

Dropping my hands to the cabinet below the mirror, I searched for the necessities—soap, toothpaste, toothbrush. I should have known better. Vampires always naturally looked fabulous, so I supposed that human toiletries were the least of their concerns.

I stepped directly into the tub instead, and looked down. Relief flooded through me, as I picked up the ancient bar of soap, which must have been resting there since the previous owners. It was crusty and a little dry but, still, it was soap. Putting the plug into the drain and dropping the crusty soap into the base of the tub, I turned the tap on full and let the hot water flow. A small thrill rose within me at the sight of bubbles slowly forming, and the thought of being clean again almost made me forget about all the pain I'd endured.

Almost.

I sat down in the warm water, shivering with pleasure, and revelling in the feel of it against my skin, as it slowly dissolved its way through eight days of dirt, grime, and neglect. I scrubbed every inch of my skin until there was nothing left but the pinkish tinge of warm, clean flesh and a faint smell of lavender. After this first bath, I went back for seconds and thirds, draining out the dirty tub and refilling it over and over.

'Do you feel better?'

I screamed, my surprised motion sending water splashing in a tidal wave over the edge of the tub. Sebastian seemed to love appearing out of nowhere.

My throat was hoarse, but I still yelled, 'Get the hell out of here!'

Sebastian's face was impassive. 'You left the door open.'

I pulled my knees up to my chest and wrapped my arms around myself in a futile attempt to cover my naked skin. 'Get out!'

Sebastian studied me a moment longer, his eyes tracing over what I could only imagine was the beetroot red of my features, flustered with anger and embarrassment. 'I bought you some other necessities.' He placed a toothbrush and toothpaste on the counter. 'I thought you might appreciate the gesture.'

'Are you deaf? Get out!'

An unknown emotion flitted across his face. 'You're different to how I thought you'd be,' Sebastian murmured, backing up towards the door. As he gripped the handle between slender fingers, a sardonic smile touched the edges of his lips. 'I should have known. Logistics aside, you were always going to be different if you came back.'

'Oh my God!' I squealed, splashing him with another torrential wave of water. 'Get your ass on the other side of that door!'

'I'm going.' Sebastian walked off and shut the door quietly behind him. I stared at it for several seconds, scared he was going to make another surprise re-appearance.

He didn't.

I reached up to the sink and grabbed the toothpaste and toothbrush. Once I was finished brushing, I turned and let the water out of the tub. I was starting to feel better but my throat still burned with a powerful thirst. I needed to eat something before my body started to consume itself.

I climbed slowly out of the tub, grabbing the towel hanging over a hook at the back of the door. The towel smelled musty and in need of a wash, but who was I to complain? I quickly dried myself off, considering my options.

I turned and glanced down at the dirty dress that lay in a crumpled heap in the corner. I never wanted to wear that again—there were too many bad memories associated with it—but I didn't exactly have an alternative.

Taking a deep breath to calm my nerves, I opened the door just a crack. 'Um, Sebastian,' I said tentatively, 'are you there?'

In an instant, his face was an inch from mine. I jumped back, clutching at the towel. 'Did you need some help?' he said, glancing briefly at my half-naked form, his lips only hinting at a smile.

'Um, I actually need something to wear.'

'You're not a nudist at heart then, I take it?'

'Are you trying to be funny?'

'Wishful thinking, I suppose.' This time he smiled wide.

I shut the door in his face, resting my forehead against the timber. 'Please, just get me something decent to wear.'

'Define 'decent'?'

'Not naked.'

He tapped on the door less than a minute later. 'I have something.'

I leant back and opened the door again.

'What about this?' Sebastian said, ramming a coat hanger through the gap. From it hung a nurse's outfit, complete with suspenders, crotch-less panties, and other questionable paraphernalia. He jiggled it around on the hanger. 'This should look pretty good on you.'

I whipped the door open and pushed past him in frustration.

'Or you could just wear that,' Sebastian said, gesturing to my towel.

I ignored him and started leafing through the sparse wardrobe. All the clothing was far too big for me and most of the female outfits that I found seemed to be sex industry rejects. I ended up settling for a white, long-sleeved shirt, baggy enough to pass as a dress.

Tucking the towel securely around me, I slipped my arms through the sleeves and started buttoning up the shirt. Once I got to the bottom, I ripped my towel off and dropped it to the floor. The shirt came midway down my thighs—it would do for now. I rolled up the sleeves and undid the top two buttons, maintaining modesty . Then I grabbed a belt hanging on the back of the wardrobe door and tied it securely around my waist.

At the back of the cupboard I spotted a pair of knee-high boots, threaded with a complicated jumble of laces that would've stumped even Houdini himself. I turned around, holding them up in front of me. 'Is Nicholas a cross-dresser?'

I asked, trying to imagine the blonde vampire prancing around in the shiny black vinyl.

Sebastian choked on a laugh. 'I don't think so. It's more likely that the outfits are here for his partners.'

I flipped the boots over to check their size. They were too big for me but wearing them would be better than running around in bare feet. I was already cold, and bra-less to boot: I could live with wearing 'hooker heels' until I found something more suitable.

Oh, not good.

I dropped the boots as another heaving stomach cramp sent me whimpering to my knees. Sebastian rushed to my side and scooped me up off the floor, lifting me gently over to the bed. 'I need blood,' I said, as he propped a pillow underneath my head. 'Please tell me you have blood.'

'I'm curious about that,' Sebastian said as he grabbed a tetra pack off the bedside table and popped in a bendy straw. 'You're not eighteen, are you?'

I shook my head, the aroma of blood weaving through the stale air of the bedroom faster than I would have thought possible. I reached out for the pack with shaking hands, my canines slipping forward in anticipation.

He held back.

I looked up at him and frowned. 'I need that blood, Sebastian.'

'I can see that,' Sebastian said, holding the tetra pack just out of reach. 'That is why I am curious. I can smell your humanity mixed in with the base scent of your vampiric form, but there's also something else behind that which confuses me.'

I licked my lips, my stomach growling uncontrollably. 'Do you think we can have this conversation later?'

'There's no time like the present.'

I swiped a hand at the tetra pack but missed. 'I won't have a future if I don't get some of that blood soon.'

'Why is that I wonder?'

'I honestly don't know.'

Sebastian looked at me for the longest time, scrutinising my pained features, nose flaring as he took a subtle breath in. I could see he was trying to figure me out, sorting one by one through the various discrepancies in my scent that had once so snagged William's attentions. I didn't know why, but I had a feeling he already knew more about me than I cared for him to.

The way that Sebastian's eyes moved over me, seemingly remembering my features ... I'd seen that look on his face a hundred times before, though from where or when I couldn't say. 'Here,' he murmured, finally passing me the tetra pack.

I snatched it off him. My lips closed on the straw, and I sucked the sweet tasting liquid down. The warmth was satisfaction enough but the taste ... indescribable fulfilment danced across my tongue. Each mouthful gently caressed my coarse, dry throat, quenching the roaring flames that threatened to erupt inside. As I drank, Sebastian's eyes lit up with curiosity.

I sighed at him in appreciation. Heat licked at my appendages, the new blood coursing through my veins gradually restoring vitality to me. As I sucked, the tetra pack slowly grew empty, and my stomach began to feel bloated and sloshy but in a good way.

Sebastian's gaze raked over my body, curious and hesitant.

'What are you looking at?' I said, pulling myself upright on the bed.

'You.'

'Why?'

'Because you shouldn't exist.'

I frowned. 'Well, neither should you … Vampire.'

His head cocked to the side, an eyebrow raised. 'Meaning?'

'Don't judge me. Vampires are supposed to be fictitious.'

'You know that's not what I meant.'

'Do I?'

Sebastian looked confused. 'Don't you remember anything? Don't you know who I am and what happened before?'

It was my turn to look baffled. 'Are you talking about the weird out-of-body-dream-experience we had together in that field?'

His face hardened. 'No, I'm talking about the past.'

'Oh, right. You're talking about my previous dreams?'

'No, I am not.'

I sighed. 'Look, this is whack. As far as I'm concerned, I dreamt you up, you shouldn't even be real. Yet here you are, standing right next to me. How about you give me an explanation for that first and then maybe we'll both know what the hell you're talking about, because I can't figure out how one minute you were in my head and the next you were pulling me out of the IMI.'

Sebastian shook his head. 'It seems we both have questions.' He reached out and drew one finger across my cheek.

I jerked away, still unsure. He took the now empty tetra pack from my hands instead, placing it on the bedside table. 'Do you feel better now?'

'Much.' I was quiet for a second. 'Who are you?'

'I'm Sebastian Marcellus, though I believe we have already been introduced.'

'That's not what I meant.'

He looked into my eyes, searching for something. 'You really don't remember anything?'

'I really don't understand what you mean by that. What should I remember?'

Sebastian's eyes dimmed, the hopeful gleam in them that was so bright moments before slowly ebbing away. His lips grew tight, and his shoulders were slumped as he blew out a breath of frustration. 'Come on, I'll take you home now.'

Home? No, E. You can never go home now.

Tears stung my eyes. 'I can't go home, Sebastian,' I said, shaking my head, trying to shake off the unwanted emotions. 'It's not safe for them or for me. Plus, they'll just drag me straight back to the IMI again, anyway.'

'It's not what you—'

I jumped as the door to the bedroom was unexpectedly flung open and the three other vampires from my dream entered, one-by-one.

'I see you're making yourself comfortable in my home, Sebastian,' said the blonde one named Nicholas.

Sebastian smirked. 'Are we calling this a home? It's more like a shoe-box.'

Nicholas snorted. 'Some of us don't need to over-compensate.'

Caleb and Eric laughed. I felt nervous as hell with them here. I was still weak, no underwear in sight, surrounded by four vampires all pretending not to notice me.

'We're leaving now,' Sebastian abruptly stated, his eyes suddenly drawn to Caleb the Goth. He was focused right back on me, lips parted and body now completely rigid.

'You need to be careful,' Eric urged, his long, dark hair whispering against the sides of his face. 'The Alpha isn't dead, and I have a feeling he hasn't given up on searching for this one, either. He was very determined to get past Nicholas and Caleb.'

Caleb took several steps forward, an action mirrored by Sebastian. 'Can you really blame him?' Goth boy said, licking his lips and eyeing my neck. 'She smells absolutely … delicious.'

Sebastian growled. 'Stay away from her, Caleb. I won't warn you again.'

Caleb's canines grew as he smiled wide. 'Surely you can smell it, too, Sebastian. Her blood is pure—untainted.' He took another side-step towards me and Sebastian growled more loudly, baring fangs as sharp as Caleb's own.

'Sebastian, can you imagine what it would be like to taste her? What it would be like to feel her blood across your tongue? Surely you can sympathise with me,'

'Caleb, knock it off,' Nicholas said, grabbing his companion by the shoulders. 'Your letting your youth drive you. Try to control your bloodlust.'

Caleb hissed, shrugging Nicholas off. 'Bloodlust is a part of my nature.'

'Which I will bleed out of you if you harm one hair on her head,' Sebastian snarled.

Caleb's black eyes focused back on me, steely and determined. 'It might be worth it for a few minutes with her.'

Sebastian's eyes narrowed. 'Just try it.'

I watched the silent standoff. Caleb's eyes never left me, his body tense and posture poised, ready to attack. Caleb's fingers twitched at his sides, nostrils flaring as he vigorously drew in my scent.

Sebastian moved closer, stepping into Caleb's line of sight and breaking his hungry gaze. The muscles in his back flexed, and he looked poised to grab Caleb if he was stupid enough to attack.

Even I would have been hesitant fighting Sebastian. He exuded raw power, his narrow gaze all that would be required to halt most predators dead in their tracks. Caleb was no exception.

'Whatever,' Caleb said finally, breaking his stance, 'I'm out of here.'

'Caleb?' Sebastian asked, relaxing. 'If I catch you trailing us, I'll make sure that Lucius doesn't pay you.'

'Up yours, Sebastian,' he said, flashing the finger as he left the room.

Eric shook his head. 'I swear, these younger vampires are just like infants sometimes.'

'I can still hear you!' Caleb's voice echoed back from down the passage, punctuated by the sound of a door slamming shut.

Eric rolled his eyes, looking back at Nicholas who was now grinning. 'That was the point.'

Sebastian held his hand out to me, face expressionless. 'We have to go.'

Somehow I sensed that slipping my hand into Sebastian's would be too easy, that trusting him would come naturally. The problem was that I rarely trusted anyone. I still had reservations about the way he'd treated me tonight, still unsure where this path was leading.

'It's okay. I won't hurt you, Elena.'

'That's not really my concern, I—'

'Hey, are you going to wear these?' Nicholas said, retrieving the black boots from the floor.

'I don't know yet. I don't know what I'm doing.'

'You're going to freeze if you don't put some more clothing on than that.' He eyed me from top to toe. 'Although … I do like you in just my shirt.' Nicholas took a step towards me, blue eyes continuing to drink in my form, and his lips curved into a sleazy smile. 'I don't suppose that you and I …?' His eyebrows began to wiggle mockingly, a suggestive dance I wanted no part in.

Sebastian leapt in front of me, a hiss escaping his lips. 'Back off.'

Nicholas held his hands up in mock surrender, surprise briefly flirting with his features as he studied Sebastian's expression. 'No harm intended. I was simply admiring her beauty.'

'She is stunning,' Eric agreed.

'Seems a shame to cover her up,' Nicholas continued, heading to his wardrobe and fishing inside. He pulled out a long, black jacket, holding it out to me. 'This should help keep you warm. It's probably too big for you, but at least you'll be comfortable while you're travelling.'

I slipped off the bed, hesitantly edging my way around Sebastian and quickly snatching the coat from Nicholas's outstretched fingers. He was right; it was too big, but was definitely warm.

'I can see you're not in love with the boots, but you should probably consider wearing them, as well.'

I nodded, quickly taking them from Nicholas and grimacing as I examined them from both sides, trying to work out the tricky lacing. 'Hopefully I don't need to get them off in a hurry.'

He smiled, a cheeky grin crossing his features. 'I would be more than happy to assist you.'

Sebastian's hand whipped out and grabbed Nicholas's wrist. 'I told you to back off.'

A puzzled look passed between both Nicholas and Eric, and together they moved backwards. Sebastian spun around to look at me. 'Let me help you.'

'I can do it.'

'Today?'

I looked at the shoes in my hand. 'It's debatable.'

'Sit down.'

'You're so pleasant. How can I refuse?' I muttered.

Sebastian grunted and pushed me onto the edge of the bed. He slipped one of my feet into a boot, then the other. A few seconds later my legs and feet were fully strapped up under the shiny, black vinyl, laces quickly tied and ready.

'Wow. That was pretty quick.'

'An expression I've never heard from a woman,' Nicholas said, smirking.

Sebastian gave him a contemptuous glare.

I stood, wobbling a little in my boot heels and steadying myself before Sebastian could intervene. 'Um, thanks for the clothes, Nicholas.'

'My pleasure.'

'Elena, we need to get going,' Sebastian said gruffly. 'We have a lot of ground to cover tonight, and I want to try and be home again before the sun comes up.'

'Yeah, about that,' I said, edging my way back to the door. 'Besides not knowing you at all and having zero intentions of going anywhere with you, I can't go home. And especially if you and I aren't on the same page about where home is.'

He tracked my movements, flitting over to the doorway and blocking my exit. 'Going somewhere?'

I nodded. 'I appreciate your help and all, even though tonight has been a major freak fest, but I think I want to go at it alone now.'

'It's not an option, Elena.'

I thought about making my way over to the balcony door, but then what was I going to do? Jump? I was unsure if my new abilities extended to defying gravity.

Sebastian cupped a hand against my cheek, his skin warmer than my own heated flesh, but familiar and strangely … desired. 'Don't run, there's no point. I'll find you.'

I shoved his hand away. 'Then where are you taking me?'

'Home.'

'I can't go home. I've said that already and … wait, how the hell do you know where I live?'

The corner of his mouth lifted ever so slightly into a lopsided smile. 'I wasn't referring to whatever home you come from, Elena.'

I frowned. 'Then where are you referring to?'

'Your new home.'

CHAPTER TWELVE: INDECISION

'My new what?' I screeched, running through Nicholas's spartan living room to catch up with Sebastian. He'd already reached the front door.

'Your new home.'

'Yeah, I heard you. I just don't know what made you think I would agree to go anywhere with you.' I stopped in my tracks. 'I don't even know you, Sebastian.'

Sebastian paused at the door and turned around, his unusual grey-green eyes settling upon me with great intensity. 'You *do* know me, Elena.'

I shook my head. 'No, I don't *know* you. You, Sebastian, are a walking, talking figment of my imagination. How can I not be freaked out just by looking at you?'

Three long strides and he was practically standing on top of me, his essence seemingly reaching towards me through the air between us and filling me with a slow burning ache. Sebastian reached out and took my hand, placing it on the centre of his chest. The heat emanating from his supposedly dead body still surprised me. 'You do know me, Elena. You've dreamt of me, as I have of you, because we are connected. We always have been. You may not remember me, but I remember you. I've always remembered you.'

I tried pulling my hand back but he held tight. 'Trust in

what you feel. Trust that I won't hurt you or see harm befall you. Can you do that?'

'I don't know …'

'Are you afraid of me?'

'No. At least, I don't think I am. I'm confused.'

Sebastian smiled, his fingers gently holding my hand. 'Of course you are.'

'But how is it possible that we're now sharing the same reality? Humans rarely have prophetic thoughts, and neither do vampires, as far as I know … yet I didn't just dream about you, I saw you. I touched you.'

'I've lived long enough to know that sometimes events just happen for a reason, Elena. And sometimes everything turns out exactly like it should, even if it takes centuries to occur.'

I slid my hand down Sebastian's chest, momentarily distracted by the smoothness of his skin, and then took a step back. 'That doesn't explain anything. What do you mean centuries past? You make it sound like our meeting was somehow predestined.'

His lips twitched. 'Perhaps it was.'

My eyes narrowed. 'I may not feel threatened or scared of you, but I get the feeling you're lying to me.'

Sebastian sighed. 'All I can say with any degree of certainty is that I know you, and you know me. Think on it … take a chance with me and see what happens.' He stepped closer to me again. 'Surely you can feel the heat between us?'

I ducked around him, heading for the door. Again, he beat me to the doorway and blocked my path. 'Look, Sebastian, I don't know what to think and feel. All I know is that I want to get out of here.'

'You're concerned.'

I scoffed. 'You think?'

I sat down on the arm of the couch behind me. There was no point trying to escape Sebastian; he was too fast. I scrubbed a hand through my still damp hair, closing my eyes and pinching the bridge of my nose. I fought hard against hysterical laugher that had been threatening to bubble up from inside me for days now.

'You know what? I'm starting to think this could all be part of some crazy experiment that the IMI's conducting. I'm probably still in a coma from when I lashed out at Chester in the lab a week ago. None of this is real. It's probably an elaborate delusion Chester planted in my mind as a way to get information out of me.' I finally laughed. 'It certainly explains you.'

Sebastian knelt down in front of me, grabbing my hands and placing them on either side of his face. His skin was so smooth, so perfect. 'This is real, Elena. You can feel me, feel that here you and I are together. You're not at the IMI anymore—you're safe. And I won't let anything happen to you.'

Yeah, heard that before.

I snorted. 'I'm not so sure. This shouldn't be possible, plus you're way too good-looking to be real, even for a vampire.'

Sebastian bowed his head momentarily and laughed. 'You're not so bad yourself now that you're all clean.'

I grinned without humour. 'If you're real, then why are you here? Why did you come for me?'

'To find you. To see if you really did exist.'

I thought about that for a moment. 'Was there ever doubt?'

'Plenty.' Sebastian let go of my hands and rose to his full height, abs rippling as they moved past my eyes. He really was phenomenal to look at, and I wasn't just referring to his physique. His face was almost perfectly symmetrical, nose straight and cheekbones set so high that a fourteen-year-old runway model would be envious. Every angle and masculine plane, right down to that of his squared-off chin, was sculpted in perfect detail.

'Who sent you?'

'You don't believe I did this on my own?' His eyebrow rose ever so slightly, daring me to question him.

'No. If you're real, and Nicholas, Eric, and Caleb are real, then so are the other people from my dreams.'

Sebastian smiled. 'He is looking forward to meeting you, Elena.'

'You mean Lucius?'

'Do you know of him?' Sebastian carefully asked.

'Yes and no. I've only seen him twice, but I've heard you mention his name a few times now.'

Sebastian nodded, crossing his arms in front of his chest, biceps bulging. 'When did you see him?'

'The same time I saw you.'

'Could you touch him?'

I nodded. 'The first time I dreamed of him, Lucius was sitting alone in a stone holding cell. He looked ferocious yet oddly sad at the same time. And then, when he noticed I was there with him, he jumped me. I felt him biting into me seconds before I woke up screaming.'

'He bit you?' Sebastian asked in surprise, brows furrowing. 'That must have been how he got a lock on you.'

'But I woke up.'

'It was still long enough for him to touch your mind.'

I frowned. 'Hey, wait—a vampire with psychic abilities?'

Sebastian nodded, before casting his gaze to the other side of the room. 'You two can come out now. I know you're both listening to the conversation, anyway.'

Nicholas and Eric both popped their heads around the corner.

'You're still here?' Nicholas said innocently, as he leaned into the room.

Sebastian rolled his eyes. 'A fact which did not escape you.'

'You'd better leave soon,' Eric quietly said as he lowered himself onto one of the chairs opposite me. 'That Alpha is bound to find our trail sooner or later.'

'And I'd really prefer if he didn't come sniffing around my apartment,' Nicholas interjected.

'Just kill him,' I said, flashing Eric a steely glance. 'His death would be better for everyone concerned.'

Eric's eyes widened briefly. 'I was under the impression that you might have preferred that we didn't. It seemed to us that you actually enjoyed his company.'

I paled, thinking of his kiss, the taste of his blood, and my total loss of control. 'He's a vânător. Why would I possibly enjoy his company?'

Eric suddenly looked uncomfortable, glancing to his friends for support.

'I think what Eric is suggesting,' Nicholas replied, 'is that we might somehow offend you by killing him, given the passion of the kiss you shared.'

I swallowed. They didn't need to know that I was half-Vânător.

'Yeah, about that,' Sebastian said, lowering himself down onto the arm of the chair next to me, 'why were you so receptive to his advances?'

I looked away.

Sebastian's fingers intertwined with mine. 'Elena?'

I shrugged his hand away and stood up. I had to change the subject, and fast. 'You haven't yet told me you're connection to Lucius and how this all relates to me.'

Sebastian sighed. 'It's not my story to tell, Elena. But I can promise you that it is worth the journey if you'll just trust me long enough to come.'

'I don't know. He *did* bite me.'

'Elena,' Sebastian said gently, my name rolling across his tongue like a delicate caress. 'You can trust me. Lucius will not harm you.'

I stared into his eyes, watching those strange depths swirl in that unusual procession of emerald green mixed with liquid tendrils of grey. I nodded numbly, feeling strangely excited and despondent at the same time, as I really had no other option. 'Okay, but don't you screw me over, Sebastian. You only get one chance.'

Sebastian merely moved his gaze over me, before reaching out and taking my hand in his. 'We should go.'

I nodded. Sebastian stood, leading me towards the front door with my hand still encased in his. He was right about the heat between us—sparks seemed to fly where our skin touched, sending tiny shivers skating up my spine.

'I'll be in touch,' Sebastian threw back at the others.

Both vampires inclined their heads. 'It was interesting meeting you, Elena,' Eric answered.

'Ditto,' Nicholas mused, 'though I do hope we meet again.'

Sebastian ushered me out into the hallway, closing the door hastily behind us. I didn't even get a chance to respond, although I didn't particularly want to meet those vampires again anytime soon.

'How do you want to do this?' Sebastian asked, squeezing my hand.

Nervous energy skittered through me. 'Umm, do what?'

'Our transportation.'

'I'm really well practiced in walking. I can run, too, if the situation calls for it.'

My sarcasm was lost on him. 'Walking is too slow. Every

Alpha in Europe would have found you by the time I get you to Lucius.'

'So, running then.' I looked down at the boots and grimaced. 'Though I'm not too sure how well I'll fare.'

Sebastian scooped me up in his arms and pressed me against his chest. 'How about I do the running instead?'

I smiled wryly. 'In case you haven't worked it out yet, I'm not really a fan of that particular method of transport.'

'Oh, yes?' He raised an eyebrow expectantly, waiting for me to explain.

I rolled my eyes. 'The first time I ended up with a minor concussion. The second time I found out I had a fear of heights. The third time … I was impaled by a tree.'

'Surely not?'

'It's true. I much prefer the human way, especially when there are so many beautiful pieces of machinery that we could drive or ride.' I sighed, imagining the thrum of a Ducati Streetfighter between my legs, still jealous that William had taken one for a test drive just last week. There was a slight pang of guilt as I finally thought of my vampire, while in the company of another, no less. I was still pissed off enough at William, though, and my guilt faded fairly fast.

Hang on a second.

Sebastian laughed as he started making his way down the stairs at a run. 'I agree, but in this case, running is faster, and my bike is currently parked in my garage at home—it's no use to me in Budapest.'

But I barely heard him as I searched my mind, trying to conjure up the page of that Wheels magazine I'd been reading only a week ago. I desperately tried to remember what I thought could be vital information.

Ducati. Now, where'd they manufacture their bikes? Where had William said he'd recently passed through?

I closed my eyes as I stumbled upon the correct magazine page in my memory, concentrating hard in my mind's eyes. I could see the shiny red bike in the centre of the page, the specifications detailed below. The left hand side was scattered with advertisements. Where could it be?

Ducati—that's an Italian made bike. Did he mention passing through Italy?

Thoughts started ticking through my head at speed. I opened my eyes again, feeling the cold wind on my face as Sebastian burst through the door to the ground floor and out into the street. Why would William have been in Italy? Or was I remembering the details wrong?

Sebastian picked up the pace, the speed of his gait pressing me back hard against his chest. I barely acknowledged the movement, caught up in my own head as I trawled through the conversations William and I had shared before he'd decided to split.

William had spoken of change and forgiveness. Who had he been talking about? And was figuring out William's plotted path going to reveal that to me or lead to more dead ends? Was I only thinking of him now because I was in Sebastian's arms, confused and wishing for familiarity?

In the end, I'd never know.

Damn you, William, and your stupid secrets.

'You're frowning,' Sebastian said, stealing a glance. 'Is travelling this way really so bad?'

'I'm not frowning; I'm thinking. There's a difference. And yes to your other question. I much prefer cars. I mean, I can barely hear you in this wind.'

'What are you thinking about?' Sebastian persisted, though he did raise his voice.

'Stuff.' I don't know why, but something told me to keep William to myself. He'd always been an extremely private person, and I imagined that he wouldn't have liked me discussing him with other vampires. Not that I actually knew much about William myself. Most of the things I knew were in direct relation to his persona as a vampire, his current coven—Thomas and Marianne—and some aspects of his childhood that involved his mother. The entirety of the period he spent with his father, and all the time he'd been involved with the Roman Guard, William had kept to himself.

Hmm. There has to be a reason for that.

'Stuff?' Sebastian echoed.

'Yeah, stuff.'

He gave a sharp nod and fell silent.

A few minutes later Sebastian begun to slow down, anyway, finally coming to a standstill on a road crowded with travellers and banked up taxis. The building— obviously Sebastian's intended destination—had automated doors that constantly opened and closed under a constant influx of people. Heat from within escaped into the chilled night air in a hiss but was quickly lost to the noise of honking horns and excited chatter.

Sebastian lowered me to the ground, oblivious to the quizzical looks we were both receiving, mostly from some security guards standing about the place. I suspected the hunting knife, sheathed in leather across his naked back, had a lot to do with that.

'The airport?' I said, suddenly feeling considerably underdressed. If Sebastian felt uncomfortable about his lack of clothing, he made no show of it.

'It's forbidden to leave scented tracks coming and going from our home. That means we'll use normal human transport from now on to help avoid leaving physical footprints.' Sebastian smiled lightly and touched a finger to my nose. 'That also means no more running.'

I shrugged. 'I doubt that I really have a say in the matter anyway.'

Sebastian ignored me, grabbing my hand and leading me quickly through the doors and into the terminal.

'Where are you taking me, anyway?' I said, frowning as I noticed Sebastian pique the interests of people in the crowds we passed. Every woman in the nearby vicinity had turned their head to have a closer look at this shirtless vampire. Not that I blamed them.

'I've already told you—home.'

I marvelled as women from all corners of the terminal started drifting closer, vying to get a closer look at Sebastian. They followed us as we ducked and weaved past security personnel. 'Yeah, I got that part,' I said, looking over my shoulder and frowning heavily. 'Where *is* this home you're talking about?'

One determined woman, creeping at first and now rushing at us from behind, knocked me sideways in an attempt to shove a balled-up piece of paper over Sebastian's shoulder. A listless sigh escaped his lips as he took it from her grasp, simultaneously grabbing me and helping me steady myself. He unfolded the paper, revealing a set of numbers. The pushy woman started talking to him in a foreign language, but Sebastian screwed the paper up again and threw it back over his shoulder.

She was persistent. I'd give her that.

'We're going to Rom—'

'What?' I shouted, as I was shoved backwards again, my fingers slipping from his as the growing crowd of women following Sebastian started to surge around us, pushing me roughly away from him. He spoke again, but I heard nothing except for a roar of giggles and what seemed like a million voices all speaking at once. Some of them actually spoke

English, and I finally managed to piece together what this little stampede was about. It appeared that Sebastian was a magnet for female attention. Even a granny in a wheelchair moving past us practically did a wheelie in chair to get a better look at him.

'Are you famous or something?' I said, knowing that as a vampire he would have no trouble hearing me against the din if he was really listening.

Sebastian tried pushing free of the crowd, expression grim as he reached for me again, finally clasping my hand in his. He did not look happy about all the attention he was attracting and became even more irate when some of them tried holding me back. The crazy women were completely unrelenting, caught up in some sort of weird version of vampiric compulsion.

I felt like I was being dragged reluctantly through a department store during Boxing Day sales, pawed at by needy women desperate to get their hands on my goods. Not that Sebastian was mine.

'What's the deal?' I said, through a mouthful of some blonde's hair that just whipped into my face. 'Did you swallow pheromones for breakfast?'

'No. I just possess certain … qualities.'

'I'll say.'

We pushed on, the crowd groping at us as we struggled to break free. They were groping at me because they were trying to claw me out of the picture, and they reached for Sebastian because, well, who wouldn't want to touch him? I was getting extremely annoyed, though. I didn't like people touching me at the best of times, and some of these women were bordering on the violent. If someone pulled my hair one more time …

Pow.

Sebastian suddenly stopped, the crowd surging around to encircle us. He held up his hand and the crowd instantly quietened down, like a puppeteer pulling on the strings of silence. He looked at each woman in turn, his eyes beginning to darken and his pupils dilating. A language I couldn't comprehend erupted from his mouth, as the women listened with baited breath. He lifted our entwined fingers for all to see, making a show of kissing my knuckles before inclining his head to them in a gentle manner and walking away, toting me behind him.

I looked over my shoulder—all eyes were now riveted on me. For a brief second I felt like I was about to become a victim of a ferocious eye-gouging. I'd never had so many filthy looks in all of my life. Thankfully, the crowd soon began to dissipate and the women drifted away, each staring after Sebastian with longing and adoration, still eyeing me every now and again with extreme distaste. Even the old granny saw fit to roll over my foot with her wheelchair as she pushed off, disappointed. What was up with that?

'Well, that was an experience.' I said, glancing down at my throbbing foot and wondering if it would be politically correct to kick the crap out of the elderly.

Sebastian shrugged. 'You get used to it.'

'Is this a vampire thing or specifically a 'you' thing?' I had never been in a public place with William, Thomas or Marianne, so I was unsure how the general public would react to a vampire's beauty and otherworldly charms.

'It only happens to me.'

'Why?'

'It's difficult to explain.'

'Try me.'

Sebastian nudged me gently on the shoulder. 'You know,

I'm not the only one getting attention. You're quite the showstopper yourself.'

I glanced around the terminal, noticing some of the women that were still trailing hopefully behind us, also seeing the pointed gazes of men who were apparently admiring me from afar. 'It's just the boots,' I said, picking up the pace when I noticed the granny wheeling around for a little more action.

'The boots?' Sebastian murmured, looking down briefly before tugging me around a corner and down towards the Departures Lounge.

I nodded. 'These sort of boots give men the wrong idea.'

He shook his head and laughed, but didn't answer.

Over my shoulder I smiled cheekily at the granny, who was staying on our asses like a pimple you just couldn't squeeze. We'd hit a set of escalators—that'd fix her wagon. She'd never get up them in a million years.

It was right about then that my smile drooped, as I spotted the security guard from earlier also trailing us, hand resting lightly on the handgun at his side. 'Don't tell me your qualities work on *men*, too?' I said to Sebastian as we stepped off the escalator and hurried towards Check-ins and Departures.

'Only if the men are that way inclined.'

I jabbed a thumb over my shoulder. 'What about the one running after us?'

Sebastian quickly assessed the situation and smirked. 'No. That man just wants to shoot us.'

'Oh, that's reassuring.'

He chuckled, ignoring the security guard and quickly tugging me through the security scanners. Which went completely crazy the minute we both walked through them. Every *other* security guard nearby quickly closed in on our position, grim expressions on their faces, guns suddenly in hand and yelling words I couldn't interpret.

Holy crap.

I raised my spare hand in the air, my futile attempt at surrender.

Sebastian grimaced, pulling my arm back down again as the security members began forming a tight circle around us.

'Aren't they supposed to frisk us before shooting us?' I whispered.

Sebastian chuckled lightly. 'Would you really prefer that?'

'Hmm, getting shot or being frisked. What do you think?'

'But you aren't wearing underwear,' he said slyly.

'Well then it should be over quite quickly. There's nowhere to hide anything.'

Sebastian's lips twitched. 'That isn't exactly true.'

'We're about to be shot. Let's focus on that for a minute, okay?'

By now we had drawn a rather large crowd of spectators, intent on getting a closer look at the foreigners who were freaking out security.

'Um, Sebastian,' I said, squeezing his hand tighter. 'I really hope you have a plan.'

He squeezed my hand in return. 'Relax, this happens a lot.'

'Maybe that's because you're shirtless and have a really big weapon strapped to your back.'

Lips curling at the edges and a sparkle of mirth twinkling in the depths of his eyes, Sebastian gave me a heart-stopping grin that could have knocked the socks off just about anyone, including me—if I'd been wearing any. 'Could be.'

I glanced around warily at the guards and scanned the crowds of people, wondering how we were going to get the hell out of this mess without having to hurt someone. Vampire compulsion was strong, but as far as I knew, not strong enough to subdue an entire terminal full of people.

My gaze soon settled on a woman whose eyes were fixed on Sebastian. Unlike the other women in the crowd who were once again trying to claw their way closer to him, this one was studying Sebastian, measuring him up and ...

Uh-oh.

I tugged on Sebastian's hand, pulling him down so I could speak directly into his ear. 'Sebastian, do you see her?' I said, as I discreetly pointed to a woman with short red hair, standing off to the side of the crowd on the left. She was talking hurriedly into her mobile phone, her other hand resting by her side. A subtle blue light flickered across her fingertips; the average person wouldn't have noticed, but I did.

'A Protector,' he murmured.

I flicked him an irritated glare. 'Yeah, a Protector. I thought you said I'd be safe with you? This firing squad and that woman from the IMI over there show me you're not great at keeping your promises, Sebastian.'

He gave me a wry look. 'I promised no harm would befall you, and I meant it. Watch and learn, Baby Vamp. Your faith is about to be restored.'

I gave an indignant snort as the security team disengaged the safeties on their Beretta handguns and started shouting at us in a garble of incomprehensible noise.

A second later, I smelt the full force of Sebastian's intoxicating scent as it descended ravenously upon the surrounding crowd. I saw redhead's eyes immediately go blank, as the flickering light in her hands died.

The entire room went quiet, the mass of huddled humans caught up in a trance. The Protector hung up her phone and sat down woodenly in a chair behind where she'd been standing, pulling a novel from her travel bag and reading furiously. Others followed suit, including the security guards who'd holstered their weapons, about faced and headed back to the scanners.

I watched in amazement as, one-by-one, Sebastian cast his gaze upon each member of the crowd. Each of them broke away and slowly returned to whatever activity they were doing before all the commotion broke out, seeming to forget about us entirely.

As I inhaled Sebastian's scent, and though I believed I'd be somewhat immune to his vampiric compulsion, the feel of it took me completely by surprise. I sunk to my knees, shocked and a little confused. It held a sway over my body that was staggering, stronger even than an Alpha's control, and was powerful enough to cloud judgement. Sebastian could have turned my own mind against me if he'd really wanted to. He wasn't enticing me, yet the ripple of power I felt consumed me utterly, taking the breath from my lips and the movement from my limbs.

I buckled over as another wave of his scent cascaded across my skin, a warm tingle that seeped through my pores, searing me with a familiar fiery heat. 'Sebastian,' I gasped, surprised by the sudden jolt of pleasure that tore through me, 'stop!'

My whole body was afire. Sweat beaded against my skin, and an ache began to build inside of me, throbbing and potent.

'Elena?' Sebastian purred, scooping me up into his arms as a look of puzzlement crossed over his face.

'Stop enticing me, Sebastian,' I gasped.

'I can't, not until we are out of trouble.'

'Please …'

His scent slammed into me all at once, this wave more powerful than the last. The crowd had almost completely dispersed, their normalcy resuming, but it was far too late for me. His compulsion tore through me, shredding the rest of my sanity and exploding within me so intensely that I actually cried out, drawing more curious looks from Sebastian.

He cocked his head to the side and inhaled, his eyes widening in surprise. I was so embarrassed that I wanted to die. I was pretty sure the entire Budapest terminal had just witnessed my very first orgasm.

Sebastian started to laugh, his entire body wracked by spasms of delight. 'Do you need a cigarette or something?'

Kill me now.

'Please stop talking,' I begged, the shame of it unbearable.

Sebastian kept his mouth shut, though his cocky smile was a mile wide. He carried me through the crowds of converging people: they were a heady mass of overcoats, travel paraphernalia, and briefcases. I barely noticed. My face was buried against Sebastian's chest, heat still scorching my flesh, as flagging recent activities drenched me with embarrassment.

'Elena—'

I slapped my hand over his mouth. 'No talking.'

'But you—'

'Don't, Sebastian.'

Slowly, the power of his compulsion began to ebb. My limbs stopped twitching, and I simmered, and then cooled. The further away we got from the earlier crowds, the easier it was to ground myself. When I felt finally free of his spell, I dropped my hand from his mouth, wriggling around in his arms, unrelenting in my desire to be released from him.

'Stay still.'

'Back to telling me what to do again, are we?' I growled, still struggling.

Sebastian gripped me tighter. 'No, I'm simply shielding us.'

I snorted. 'From what?'

'Everyone.'

I looked at the crowds for the first time since the big 'O'. Not a single person was looking at us. Considering Sebastian was half-naked, and I'd just finished riding the pleasure train a-whistlin' through the terminal, it was strange to say the least. 'I don't sense any more compulsion.'

'I'm not using my vampiric qualities right now.'

'What are you using?'

He smiled but didn't answer. Frustrating.

A few minutes later we were approaching an emergency exit door, stationed beside which I assumed was our pilot. He wore a crisp white shirt, which was a stark contrast to his overly-tanned skin and wrinkled features. For a moment he resembled a mannequin, but as he spotted Sebastian and moved over to us, his face broke into a smile.

'*Buona sera,*' our pilot said, dipping at the waist. Overkill, I thought, but the guy was human and Sebastian was clearly not.

'*Buona sera,* Frederico,' Sebastian answered, inclining his head as our assumed pilot opened the door for us and ushered us through.

The man smiled at me momentarily as I walked past, touching two fingers to his pilot's cap and then closing the door behind us. We rushed down a private corridor and straight out onto the tarmac, where a small jet sat gleaming; its engine was already throbbing and ready for take-off. The whole time we walked, he spoke to the pilot in a foreign language—Italian, I think.

'You can put me down now,' I said as we reached the stairs. Sebastian obliged, placing a hand carefully against my back instead, propelling me up the small flight of stairs and into the aircraft. What was our rush?

Frederico pulled up the external stairs and secured the exit door for take-off. He walked to the cockpit, shuffling past us, Sebastian still talking at him in hushed tones. They shook hands. Frederico was smiling as he closed the cockpit door; not at me specifically, but rather at the wad of cash now bundled in his fingers. Now, I wondered where Sebastian had pulled *that* from.

I sat down in one of the many comfy leather chairs, questions swirling through my head like a whirlpool. Besides wanting to know our destination, I also wanted to know more about Sebastian—him and Lucius, the *other* character in my dreams. It was a reasonable request given the amount of faith I was placing in someone I'd considered fictitious until no more than a few hours before.

Sebastian slumped down in the chair directly opposite, quite inelegant for a vampire, who would usually show no sign of weariness. Yet, there it was, written on his tired features. He sat low, slumped down enough that his knees touched mine. The only sign of vibrancy about him was from his eyes, which were forever curious and always swirling with that strange combination of green and grey.

Right now those eyes were focusing on me.

'You have really unusual eyes,' I said without thinking.

'I do not. There is nothing special about green.'

I pulled a face. 'Nothing special? Your eyes move. They swirl, and twist with little ribbons of grey. I've never seen anything like it before.' I paused, thinking about how Susan had always described my own eyes. 'They're organised chaos.'

The skin around Sebastian's eyes tightened ever so slightly. 'My eyes don't move and they don't have grey in them.'

I frowned. 'They *do* have grey, and they're swirling right now.'

I leaned forward in my chair, grabbing at the leather band around his chest and pulling him closer. Our noses almost brushed. 'Look in the mirror if you don't believe me.'

As if on cue, his eyes coalesced into a magnificent green which again soon began to dissipate under growing streaks of grey. His irises seemed to shimmer, almost like they were flecked with silver.

'Cool,' I said.

Sebastian reached across the distance between us, placing a hand on either side of my face, his fingers warm but inviting. My breath came in sharp gasps, his touch feeling too familiar for words.

I considered how close we felt. I had only wanted to look into Sebastian's eyes, but now I wanted more, terrified by a flood of a million confusing memories. As his cool breath brushed across my lips, and those unusual eyes darted across my face searching for permission, I tried to think of a single reason to refuse him.

I could think of only one. *William.*

Before sanity could re-establish its hold, he brushed a feather light kiss across my mouth, singeing my lips. My entire being screamed for more. Sparks seemed to erupt in the distance between us, our twin bodies slowly generating enough heat to power a small country.

Oh my God. What the hell am I doing?

Sebastian pressed closer, his caress turning into a deeper possession. His fingers reached out, grasping for intimacy.

I pulled away from him abruptly. 'Don't do that,' I gasped,

pushing against Sebastian's chest and leaning back into my chair.

Sebastian's expression was neutral, yet his eyes were a picture of rolling thunderclouds, grey and shadowed—tumultuous. 'Why not?'

'I have my reasons.' *William being one of them.*

'Did that not feel good to you? Did it not feel right?'

Kissing always felt good. Mind you, my experience was limited, but so far most encounters had ended well for me. I hesitated. 'You were good.'

Sebastian's nostrils flared as he slowly leaned back into his chair. 'I was not asking for feedback on my technique. I was asking you how it felt.'

'It doesn't matter, because I don't want it happening again.'

Sebastian looked confused. 'I don't understand.'

Neither did I, but there you have it. I wanted to kiss him so badly it hurt, but at the same time I had William to consider and my own trust issues to sort through. They made me wary of him, of something in front of me that seemed too good to be true. And that was exactly how Sebastian appeared to be.

'Sorry,' I muttered, though I wasn't exactly sure why I was apologising.

Sebastian shook his head, a grim smile touching his lips. 'There's someone else.'

It wasn't really a question, so I didn't bother answering. William and I weren't exactly exclusive but he was still important to me, and I owed him my life. He wouldn't have appreciated me getting friendly with another vampire like this so soon after our last encounter, if ever.

I looked out the small windows as our aircraft started backing up across the tarmac. Out of the corner of my eye, I could see Sebastian's grim expression change, his face becoming a mask of neutrality once more. He slowly breathed out, his eyes the only part of him that gave away his true feelings: they were grey, depressing depths that chilled. 'I thought so,' he muttered, eyes still tracing my face.

I frowned. 'What do you mean you thought so?'

His gaze wandered, no answer forthcoming.

'Sebastian?'

'Are you hungry or thirsty?' he said frostily.

I swept my tongue over my lips, feeling their slightly cracked edges. I was definitely thirsty, as it had been a while since I'd drunk anything. I'd just been too preoccupied since the rescue to notice. Shit, now I was bloody hungry, too.

Sensing my thoughts, he opened the console between his seat and the next, retrieved a bottle of water and handed it to me. I snatched it greedily from his outstretched hand, quickly cracking the seal and downing the cool liquid. It was icy against the parched skin of my throat but welcome nevertheless. Now all I needed was a buffet of food and I'd be fine … and possibly some more blood, too.

Wow, I'm never gonna get used to that.

Sebastian watched me as I drank, undoubtedly trying to figure out exactly what I was. His eyes, forever fixed on my face, showed me the depth of his curiosity. They held the same intense inquisitiveness that William had shown when we'd first met, making me wonder if Sebastian and Lucius would understand my half-breed nature, or even accept it.

Instincts. That was what I was going to go with—my instincts. My life might have been totally screwed up right now, but I could still rely on that inner voice, that part of me that knew Sebastian's was the right path; even though I had no idea why. I wished he'd give me some clue to our final destination though, as I hated travelling blind.

Maybe it was time to at least get some directions.

I placed the bottle of water in the cup holder set into the arm of the chair beside me and looked up at Sebastian. 'I think you and I need to talk.'

CHAPTER THIRTEEN: REGRETS

William drew to a stop, as a familiar wind brushed across his face and back like jagged, icy fingers. He glanced into the darkness, scanning through the surrounding trees of the forest, expecting to see an enemy at his back. There was nothing but the sound of his own breathing, the incessant breeze, and an eerie feeling that he was about to be accosted by someone.

William cursed as the feeling intensified, chilling tendrils encircled him, holding him still. This had happened before, at first starting out as a whisper in his mind and then growing into a full-blown physical apparition. There was nowhere to run, nowhere to hide. The being would find him again, just like it'd found him the night of that rave, the night he'd first met Elena.

Elena …

He had been so stupid. How could he have left Elena alone like that? She was definitely going to be furious with him. He'd promised her that he would always protect her, and then fled with his proverbial tail between his legs at the first sign of trouble, leaving her helpless and undoubtedly in the grip of her first vampiric change. He'd be surprised if Elena ever wanted to see him again.

William's tongue glazed his lips, as he remembered the taste of her blood. It had been incredible—everything he'd imagined it would be and more. Tasting her had not only satisfied the Vampire within but, surprisingly, had fulfilled his sexual urges, too. Her blood was like an unquenchable liquid fire and feeding from her had quickly pushed him over the edge of sanity. Her blood had transported him to a place of pleasure so intense that he'd not realised what he'd been doing until it was too late.

William shook his head.

Damn my weakness!

And then Elena had fed from him.

William shuddered again at the thought. It wasn't supposed to happen that way—they were never supposed to exchange blood. Araqiel had warned him to keep his distance, and now he had perverted the course of Fate to pursue his selfish indulgences. William just hoped that his irrational acts had not brought about enough of a substantial change in her to attract unwanted attention, both from the IMI or other vampires. Yet, his uncontrollable thirst had given him few options: it was either leave her or kill her.

That was why this wind followed William. He could taste the displeasure, the disappointment. It stroked at his skin, its gentle kiss promising a visitation. All William could do was let the wind come to him and face the consequences of his actions.

'I feel you, Araqiel,' William whispered to the wind. 'Just say what it is that you came here to say and then go.'

The breeze ceased. The usual sounds of the animals and insects of the forest were falling quiet, even the mindless, little creatures sensing the imminent arrival. The leaves stopped their rustling; the long grass stopped its swaying.

Silence reigned.

William spun around as he heard the flapping of wings, loud and somehow majestic. On a low hanging tree branch before him sat a being he had encountered only once before. It had whispered in the wind to him of a girl that needed protecting. It had told William to call it Araqiel.

It had told him it was an angel.

The white wings kind of gave it away.

Araqiel spread his feathered limbs, wings as pale as snow glowing as the moonlight seemed to stroke them. They were huge, larger than the angel himself, soft.

Araqiel shook his wings, perhaps to dispel the chill in the air or to intimidate, the feathers rustling lightly as the breeze tickled their length. Slowly, they curled inwards, tucked up behind the angel's back and then disappeared.

His long, white-blonde hair—now prominent without the feathered backdrop—glowed like a brightly burning halo. He had it tied back in a neat, low-slung ponytail, strands breaking free and framing his delicate features. Araqiel's eyes were ringed in a silver that accentuated their sapphire depths, and his skin glowed, just like his hair.

Unsurprisingly, Araqiel was attired in white.

He took a few steps backward, uneasy and fearful in the presence of this pure being. The angel was his opposite, William being a seed of the underworld, or spawn of evil, as some might say.

Araqiel shook his head, pulling one leg up onto the branch and resting his arm across his knee. Perfectly poised and perfectly balanced, he was the very picture of serenity— except for a look of disappointment that now marred his beatific features. 'I've been watching you, William,' the angel said, 'and I'm not happy with what I'm seeing.'

William took a moment to gather his thoughts. What could he say to the being that had entrusted him with the duty of protecting Elena? That he'd failed? If Araqiel had the power of omniscience, had seen all that had passed, then he'd know that William could offer him no explanation.

'You have not done as I asked, William,' Araqiel slowly said, carefully enunciating each word.

He cast his glance away from the judgment he saw in the angel's sapphire depths. 'I've failed her.'

'You should not have fallen in love with her. You weren't to get involved. *That* is where you went wrong.'

'How could I *not* love her?'

Araqiel cocked his head to one side, seeming to consider the question carefully before answering. 'She is not yours to love, vampire. I explained this to you—she was made solely for another. Your only job was to protect Elena and take her to the place she belonged. This is why I chose you, because of your strong connection to those others.'

William gritted his teeth. 'I tried, but you asked the impossible of me. That one is wrong for her … I just couldn't. You don't know him like I do, can't see that he will never love her in the way I do.'

'That is not your decision to make.'

William's anger was simmering just below the surface. 'It's Elena's choice who she loves. What if she chooses me?'

Araqiel gave William a look, all patience and understanding, which only further aggravated him. 'She will not choose you.'

'Why not?'

The angel smiled. 'You need to remember what your role is in all this, William. Her purpose is of great consequence to all. Her true destiny can only begin once she has found the others. You must put aside your own feelings and do what is best for Elena, for mankind.'

'I won't give Elena to him.'

Much to William's surprise, Araqiel laughed. Like

chirping birds on an early spring morning, the sound was more wonderful than anything he had ever heard, yet the angel's mirth was infuriating. 'Thanks to your blunder, fate has stepped in directly and led her straight to him.'

'What?' William roared.

'Be calm,' Araqiel said, holding up a hand. 'It is best.'

William's whole body quivered with rage. 'Then why are *you* here?'

'Elena still has need of your protection.' The angel looked off into the distance as if wanting to avoid William's gaze. 'Events have begun to unfold that have only resulted because of your interference in her life. These events hold dire consequences for her welfare. You must protect her when he cannot; it is your responsibility to fix what has been broken. Elena has suffered much more than is necessary because of you, William.'

He scoffed and turned away, not wanting to hear it. William had beaten himself up enough over his choice's regarding Elena, and the last thing he needed was to be reminded of his failings.

'Do not turn your back on me, William,' Araqiel said, coalescing before William in a haze of blazing white and feathered limbs. 'There is no place you can go that I will not find you.'

William sidestepped Araqiel and kept walking, only to find him appear once again, inches from his face, eyes serene. William blew out a breath of resignation. 'Okay. What do you want me to do?'

'You must track the Alpha Roshan. When you find him you will have your answers.'

'And Elena?'

Araqiel placed a comforting hand on his shoulder. His gentle touch flooded William's form with a deep sense of peace and calm. 'Elena will make her choice. You need to remember that it will not be a choice that pleases you.'

'So why should I even bother? Staying away from her would be better for everyone involved.'

Araqiel shook his head. 'If she dies, it would be very bad. She must choose her death to change fate.'

William stiffened in Araqiel's grasp. 'Are you saying that Elena's future is undecided? That she can still choose her path and the people she finds on it?'

A momentary flicker of indecision flitted across the angel's face. 'I cannot interfere with free will.'

'So there is the possibility that she could still choose *me*?'

Araqiel glanced serenely at William for the longest time, his sapphire eyes burning a path to his very core. William knew the angel could not lie, that it was not in his nature.

'The possibility is there, William, but it will not happen. The ties that bind them are too strong for you to break. Your kind will never understand the Greater Truth.'

'You're right, I don't. Why him? He's a no one.'

Araqiel smiled to himself, apparently enjoying a private joke. 'Religious history says otherwise.'

'What?'

There was very little in the world that William hadn't read or didn't understand. This whole situation threw him, and it was so unlike him to be tongue-tied. Of all the people Elena could be tied to, why Sebastian? It made no sense; the man was scum.

Araqiel waved the question away. 'Will you help Elena or will you not?'

William considered the question. Walking away would be easier—easier for Elena, easier for him to forget about her. But he could no sooner forget Elena than he could walk to his true death before the rising sun; nor could he turn his back and let Sebastian claim her for his own. Araqiel had admitted that there was a possibility Elena could change her fate. William just needed to ride that hope.

'I will do as you ask. I will hunt Roshan,' William said with renewed hope, looking back into the angel's eyes, 'but once I have finished with him, I *will* go to Elena and explain.'

Araqiel sighed. 'It is not wise to pursue that course of action.'

William held up a hand to cut him off. 'If there is even the slightest chance that Elena can forgive what I've done to her and love me in return, I will take it. And if not, I will work hard to convince Elena that, ultimately, I am the right choice for her.'

Araqiel shook his head, watching as William collected a backpack full of belongings from underneath a nearby tree and walked away. He turned, giving the angel a quick, mocking salute, and then took off through the underbrush of the forest, disappearing from sight.

Araqiel slowly turned, feeling the burning warmth of the underworld at his back. 'Samael, I see you've left Purgatory to drop in on our private conversation,' Araqiel said calmly, watching as the mighty horned demon darted out from behind a nearby tree.

'You interfere, angel. What would *Daddy* say?'

'What do you want? Does the council know you're abusing the ley-lines to wander back and forth from Earth?'

'Does the council know the extent of your interference, I wonder?' Samael pressed a finger to its whiskered jaw in mock contemplation. Samael's form was an odd mix—a human body with the head of a goat, chocolate brown skin glistening with sweat. Blood red eyes stared back at Araqiel from probing, scheming depths.

'I do not interfere. I merely advise.'

Samael laughed, his nostrils flaring as hot breath escaped them in a whistle of mad delight. His chortling was high-pitched, animalistic. 'Then your team has an unfair advantage. Maybe I should stick around for a while, start messing around with some of your players.'

'Humans cannot be involved.'

'Does that include The Protectors?'

'Yes.'

'Pity I don't play by the rules then.'

'Samael ...'

'Araqiel?' Samael echoed, teasing. 'It's not just the Vampires you are trying to manipulate, is it?'

'I do not know of what you speak.'

Samael snorted. 'There are whispers in the wind that you have meddled yourself, implanting thoughts and dreams in the girl's mind that show an altered version of her current course.'

Araqiel spread his wings in one majestic motion, fanning them wide, and raising to his full height. His eyes gleamed down at the low creature crouching before him, the radiance from within him blinding. 'Can you prove this, Samael?'

The demon snorted. 'If she dreams again, I will see it.'

'Then, so be it.'

Samael laughed, grabbing up at the blackness of night and enfolding himself in its inky depths, as he slithered back behind the trees. 'I'll be watching you, Angel. Leave the girl alone. Leave the Vampires alone. Or there will be consequences.'

CHAPTER FOURTEEN: QUESTIONS

Glancing out the tiny window, I watched as the tarmac disappeared, the lights of Budapest glittering across the horizon like thousands of tiny, earthbound stars. It was a beautiful sight to behold and was a welcome distraction from my contemplating how to broach some sticky topics with the supposed man of my dreams.

'What did you want to talk about?' Sebastian said, tucking a stray lock of hair behind one of his ears.

I looked back at him. 'You talk and I'll tell you when to stop. I want to know everything. I want to know who you are, why you came for me, why you're protecting me, and who Lucius is … 'cos you gotta admit, this whole scenario is pretty surreal.' I stopped as my stomach suddenly gurgled loudly.

Sebastian looked down, a curious smile twisting his lips. 'You're still hungry, even after the blood?' He was probing, but there was no point lying. He might have more food, and right now I could have eaten not just a cake but the whole damn bakery.

'Yes. I'm hungry.'

'Let me get you something.' He stood up and slinked off down the aisle behind me. 'Do you prefer it warmed or chilled?'

Food is food.

I shrugged. 'I don't care.' I swivelled around in my chair, watching as Sebastian moved to a set of mahogany-panelled cabinets at the rear of the aircraft. He opened the first door, behind which were shelves loaded with glasses, plates, and cutlery. The second door had shelves stacked high with tetra packs of Synth Blood. He grabbed one, read the label and then put it back, finally settling on another one from the next shelf down.

Oh, blood.

'Um, Sebastian,' I said quietly, getting out of my chair to meet him at the back of the plane, 'you got any real food?'

He looked me up and down as I approached. 'I just assumed after Nicholas's house and your stomach's cramps that blood would be your craving.'

'I'm still human.'

He placed the tetra pack back on the shelf and turned away from me. 'Are you?'

I could feel the frown forming on my face. 'Surely you can sense I'm a born vampire. That means human until eighteen.'

Sebastian turned around slowly, a packet of potato chips in hand. 'You don't act like a human. You don't even smell entirely human. Born vampire or not, I shouldn't be able to scent our blood within you.'

I shrugged. There really wasn't anything to add unless I wanted to blurt out that I was half-Vânător. No, thank you.

'The strange part is that there is another element in your blood that stands distant from the other—foreign, yet familiar. You aren't what you seem at all, Elena, and you're definitely different from what I thought you'd be.'

'It's not good to have expectations, you know. Eventually you end up disappointed.'

'That's rather cynical.'

'Yet, ironically, true.'

Sebastian didn't disagree. His wry expression indicated he may have been humouring me, which was probably a good thing.

'So, what are you?' he said quietly.

Straight and to the point, so I had to give him points for that. 'Possibly delusional.'

'Delusional?'

I nodded and tried to snatch the packet of potato chips from his fingers. No good. He was holding out on me. 'Only crazy people live out real life fantasies with the people inside their head,' I said, sighing.

'I'm real, you're real. How many times do I have to tell you that?'

I snorted, attempting to claim the chips again. 'Yeah, we'll see.'

He shook his head, packet of chips just out of my reach. 'Tell me what you are, first. I need to know, I need to understand. Your blood is—'

'Yeah, yeah—delicious, mouth-watering, blah, blah, blah.'

Sebastian's eyes widened. 'So you've heard all this before? I guess I can understand why if you've been entertaining other vampires.'

I shrugged. I was real good at shrugging.

'May I ask how *his* blood ended up inside of you?'

I stiffened. 'What are you talking about?'

'Elena,' Sebastian said, whispering my name. 'I can smell another vampire's blood in your scent. Dare I say that it's probably the reason why you crave blood for one so young?'

I looked away. 'What do you want me to say to that?'

'The truth.'

I was doing that damn shrugging thing again. 'I was hungry.'

Sebastian smirked. 'As hungry as when you bit that Alpha?'

I nodded.

'But does that explain the Vânător in your system? I think not.'

Ah, shit, I just can't cop a freaking break. What's all the fascination with my blood? Get a hobby.

'Elena?' Sebastian murmured, lips perfectly sculpted to whisper the sound of my name. Why couldn't I make my voice purr like that?

'Stop it,' I said, changing tact and turning on him with an angry stare.

Confused by the sudden change, Sebastian paused. 'Stop what?'

'Stop saying my name like that.'

'Well, how would you like me to say your name?' He took a step forward, closing the distance between us. I moved backwards, pressing myself against the smooth wall of the aeroplane. But Sebastian moved forward again, completely undeterred. 'I imagine you've heard your name spoken by my tongue many times before.'

How was it possible for that sentence to sound so thick with implication, both dirty and sexy all at the same time?

I almost snorted, annoyed that the fulfilling conversation I'd wanted had disintegrated, turning into an interrogation of *my* life. I shook my head. I could see myself getting all kinds of distracted around a guy like Sebastian—that was already happening. I was too busy focusing on the lilt of his accent and the sweet smell of his breath to keep my thoughts in order. There was also the stubborn lock of silky, brown hair that had fallen loose and swung down in front of his eyes again. I just wanted to reach out and stroke it.

Sebastian touched me first, his fingers brushing my

cheek in a movement that was startlingly fast. I should have pushed him away, tried to maintain some sense of clarity so I could seek out the answers I needed. But how was I supposed to do that when he was touching me?

Food, that was how.

The packet of chips was drawing closer.

Sebastian's fingers trailed back up my neck and touched the loose strands of soft hair that framed my face. He leaned forward, nose skimming flesh, lips brushing a feather light caress across my collarbone and throat.

What is he doing?

Sebastian inhaled, closing his eyes and seemingly savouring my aroma. I expected his eyes to be black when he opened them again. Instead, he dropped my hair and snaked his arms around the small of my back, edging his lips closer to mine. His sweet breath blew in a sensual torment across my mouth.

Yoink! I snatched the bag of chips from his hand and darted away, feeling pretty damn smug.

Sebastian's eyes flicked open, the grey depths swirling with amusement. 'Clever,' he murmured.

'Hungry,' I corrected, ripping open the packet of chips and stuffing delicious morsels of salty goodness into my face.

The smile Sebastian wore dropped from his face as a quiet buzz sounded from behind him. He fished around in his back pocket, pulling out a little silver cell phone. 'Hold that thought.'

I shoved more chips into my mouth. 'No problem.'

Sebastian didn't leave me for a second, as he flipped open the phone and held it up to his ear. 'Yes?' He straightened up. 'Yes. She's right here with me.' He was silent for a few seconds, eyes sweeping over my body. 'She's beautiful—flawless even—but she does come with a few surprises, and one that definitely shouldn't be there.' Sebastian watched my response carefully, but I of course gave him nothing. I simply stared straight back at him, keeping my face devoid of emotion and instead choosing to focus on the food. I did wonder, though, whether the surprising scent he referred to was my Vânător DNA or William's blood.

Sebastian nodded to the speaker, even though they couldn't see him. 'Yes, the very same. I would never have believed it if I hadn't have smelt it myself.' He paused, looking directly at me. 'No, he's gone for now.'

Who? Who the hell is he talking about?

'I'm not sure to what extent,' he continued, 'but there's no other scent like hers, at least not one that I've ever smelt before.' Sebastian looked out the window and then glanced back at me again. 'We're still in the air. I expect we'll arrive in about an hour.' He paused, appearing to listen for a moment. 'Caleb could not be trusted. Nicholas and Eric I left in Budapest. The job was done, and I no longer needed their services.' He paused again. 'No, she was in Bucharest.' The conversation quickly changed to Sebastian's native tongue, his lips moving faster than thought, agitation now darkening his previously impish expression.

But only seconds passed before Sebastian's patience ebbed, the conversation reaching a crescendo of unintelligible garble, and he terminated the call. Tucking the cell back into the pocket of his leather pants, Sebastian took a deep breath and then focused his attention back on me. 'Sorry about that,' he said, leaning forward again and placing his hands back on either side my face. 'Where were we?'

'Eating,' I said, putting my hand on his chest, his skin warm enough to burn. He looked down at where my hand was resting, a crooked and somewhat mischievous grin touching his features.

'Pity.'

I kept him at bay, though, as I had questions that really needed answering. 'Why don't you tell me who you were talking to about me, and where we're going?'

Sebastian grabbed my hand, holding it against his chest as he determinedly pressed himself closer, despite my protests. 'There are more important things to discuss.'

'I disagree.'

Frustration crept across Sebastian's features. 'Everything else can wait.'

'Yeah, I need to know the answer to my questions.'

Sebastian shook his head, his lips drawing into a tight line. 'Kiss me, and everything will become clear.'

I blinked at him, actually speechless for several seconds. Then I burst out laughing. 'That's a really shitty line. Does that actually work on other girls?'

Sebastian groaned, finally releasing me and taking a step back. 'I can see you are going to make things difficult.'

I eased off on the laughter, occasionally snickering as I looked up into his tumultuous eyes. I was surprised to see a mixture of frustration and surprise there. 'Never been turned down before, huh?'

Sebastian banged his fist against the mahogany cabinet. 'This has nothing to do with that.'

'Then, what's your problem?'

He reached for me, his fingers encircling my wrist like steel. 'I want you to see what our minds and souls have seen together—what your dreams have been trying to tell you.'

I chortled. 'Do you really believe in all that fate and destiny crap?'

'Don't you?'

I shook my head, all traces of humour gone. 'I've endured and witnessed enough injustice to make me want to seek out my own destiny, not rely on some unspoken word from above.'

'Destiny or not, Elena, kissing me will give you the answers you seek. Whether you believe this or not, the truth is right here. It would be so easy.'

'If I kiss you?'

'Yes.'

I shook free of Sebastian's grip, grabbed another couple of packets of chips from the cupboard and sauntered off down the aisle. 'You really need to work on your routine.'

He sighed, that universal sound of defeat. 'Apparently so.'

Half an hour later, I'd polished off several bags of chips and managed to plough my way through just as many bags of peanuts. A home-cooked meal was sorely in order to help get me back into shape, but right then I was just happy to be eating again.

'Where is the bathroom?' I asked, licking my fingers clean.

'At the back of the aircraft, behind the cupboards,' Sebastian answered, his voice tight, gaze on me unwavering.

'Thanks.'

I headed down the aisle, found the toilet door and yanked it open, ducking inside the confined space. The bathroom was the very definition of 'compact', housing the standard airline toilet and basin and leaving me no room to even scratch.

Next to the little mirror mounted above the basin, I found a small bag containing a disposable toothbrush, toothpaste, a shoe shiner, and a mini-sewing kit. There was also a comb, and funnily enough, a shower cap. Maybe flushing the toilet on this plane got the place a little messy?

I ripped the plastic packaging off the toothbrush and gave my teeth another good going over. Potato chips stuck in-between teeth was not a good look and I was a little paranoid about my breath since Sebastian had last commented about it. While I was there, I also ran the small, plastic comb through my hair a few times. By the time I looked back into the mirror, I almost looked and felt human again.

'Are you okay in there?' Sebastian asked, lightly tapping on the outside of the door.

I whimpered. I hadn't even done my business yet and there was no way I could go with him standing right outside the door. 'I'm fine.'

I unlatched the door and opened it again. Sebastian was standing almost on top of the door, his face a few inches from mine and looking concerned. Stupid, really.

It's not like I'm gonna fall in the toilet and flush myself out of the plane.

'What took you so long?'

'There's a blockage.'

Sebastian glanced over my shoulder, looking first at the toilet and then at the basin, frowning. I wasn't about to explain that the blockage was me.

I edged my way around him and headed back to my seat. Sebastian followed closely behind. I couldn't hear him walk across the carpet, but I knew he was there. The scent of fresh-sawed pine, fallen rain, and leather filled the air.

Sebastian sat back down in front of me again, stretching his legs out and resting them somewhere underneath my chair. 'Tell me,' Sebastian said, as I adjusted Nicholas's coat and tried to maintain some dignity, 'since you want questions answered, answer me this—how long have you been hanging around your vampire?'

'My vampire?' I said, continuing to adjust the coat and avoiding eye contact.

'Yes, *your* vampire, the one who you've exchanged blood with. What is it about him that you favour?'

'I'm not discussing that with you, Sebastian,' I said, defiantly folding my arms. Obviously, he could sense William's blood within me, but how did he know that William had tasted mine in return? 'It's personal and irrelevant, and since you still haven't even told me where we're going yet, I'm thinking twice about telling you everything you want to hear.'

'You didn't answer any of my questions. What makes you think I should answer any of yours?'

'Are you implying I'm being difficult?' I chided, sitting forward in the chair, anger rising. 'Do you even realise how much faith I've put in you, living in the hope that you're not shipping me off to some Vampire buffet or another testing facility? If anything, I've been nothing but compliant—the least you can do is answer a few of *my* questions.'

'Just tell me his name.'

I shook my head at Sebastian. 'Stop it. I told you, I won't discuss him with you.'

'Why are you protecting him?'

'I'm not, it's just none of your business.'

'Look,' Sebastian said, suddenly almost reasonable, 'just answer *some* of my questions, and I'll answer yours.'

'No.'

His lips twitched. 'Stubborn, aren't we?'

'Pointlessly persistent, aren't we?' I mimicked sarcastically.

Sebastian paused. 'Perhaps I have a solution then,' he said, pulling himself upright in his chair.

'And that would be?'

'Playing hypotheticals.'

I frowned. 'What?'

Sebastian held up a finger to silence me. That irritated me so much I thought about breaking it off—a pointless exercise, but ultimately would have been satisfying. 'I'll go first, just to show you how it's done. Now, let's say *hypothetically* that there was this girl who was trapped in a chimney. She was starving, weary, and under attack, not just from the people she thought were her allies, but from an Alpha that appeared to have a dangerous addiction to this girl, an addiction that somehow enticed the girl to respond to his whims.'

'Hypothetically?' I said with a derisive snort.

Sebastian smiled. 'Humour me.'

I gestured for him to continue, unsure how he believed this game could be beneficial to him.

'So this girl suddenly finds herself about to be rescued by the most ridiculously handsome vampire in the entire world.' Sebastian winked at me, the first real sign of levity he'd shown me since we'd met outside our dreams.

My eyes narrowed at that comment, lips quickly pursing to spite the smile persistently tugging at its corners.

'I'll continue ...' Sebastian said, now grinning at me from ear to ear. 'This vampire is unbelievably and unequivocally the best-looking man she has *ever* laid eyes on. So gorgeous, in fact, that the very smell of his scent makes her fall to the floor and writhe around in pleasure and—'

'Sebastian,' I warned, my frown making a sudden reappearance.

He held his hands up in a show of surrender. 'Now, suppose for a second that she has questions along with this extremely handsome pleasure-giver. Wouldn't it be fair if each party answered a couple of the other's questions until they both were ... satisfied?'

I rolled my eyes and flicked Sebastian an irritated glare. 'She just wants to know where she is going.'

He inclined his head. 'So the girl asks the impossibly handsome stranger where she is going and he tells her— Rome.'

'Rome?' Was it just a coincidence that William might have recently passed through Italy?

Sebastian held that finger up again. This time I lunged for it, but he was already up and pacing the centre aisle, a wicked smile twisting his features. 'She learns that she is going to Rome, and going to come face to face with the *other* man of her dreams, but the why is still somewhat of a mystery to her. So her handsome stranger decides that if she answers some of his questions, then he will happily answer hers. But first he wants to hear the one thing she won't tell him. He wants to hear her speak the name of the vampire she's protecting.'

Not going to happen.

'His name is Prince Charming.'

Sebastian nodded, seemingly unperturbed by my response. Either that or he'd finally realised pursuing William's name was a lost cause. 'And have she and Prince Charming been the object of one another's affections for long?'

'Not exactly.'

'And in this period of 'not exactly', have the two of them ever been,' he fought hard not to screw up his face, 'intimate?'

'That's two questions,' I hissed between clenched teeth, 'and I'm fairly certain the girl you're referring to will, hypothetically, kick the strangely handsome man in the nuts if he asks her questions with those implications again.'

Sebastian stopped pacing and sat down again, his hands clenched into fists at his sides. 'By all means, but now it would be her turn to ask.'

'She wants to know why she is going to Rome, who Lucius is, and how he knew where to look for her?'

'That's three questions, but your handsome host will do his best. She is going to Rome because that is where Lucius's coven resides. Lucius is the coven leader and the oldest of Vampires. Lucius found the girl because she is special in a way that is unlike any other being on earth. She has a power that has caught the attention of another powerful being, just like her, and because she claims to still be human, this is very, very unusual.'

'What kind of power?'

'She has not been very forthcoming, so guessing must be applied. Telekinesis, perhaps? Possibly even psychic senses?'

Hmph.

'Am I close?'

Ignoring him, I said, 'So, this other powerful being would be Lucius then?'

He nodded.

'Why does he want to meet me?'

'Hope springs eternal.'

'What?'

'It's not really for the handsome stranger to say.'

'Will he hurt me?'

'Never.'

'So what's your role in all this? Why are we just meeting now, Sebastian?'

He frowned. 'I thought we were speaking hypothetically.'

I huffed in frustration. 'Yeah well, hypothetical this.' I flipped him off, irritated that simple, legitimate questions were so easily brushed away. Would it really kill him to answer me?

'That's the second time you've done that tonight. I'm beginning to think you don't like me.'

I grumbled some matching profanity under my breath, wondering if it was even worth pursuing this conversation any further. Besides, how could I have an opinion of Sebastian when I didn't even know him? Dreams didn't count, especially since the walking, talking version was so far away from what I'd imagined.

'Games aside,' Sebastian said, looking at the fingers now curled in my lap, 'may I ask what you were doing with the IMI in the first place?'

I flexed my stiff fingers out in front of me, stifling a yawn as I stretched. 'Long story.'

'Only if you want it to be.'

'Why do you want to know?'

Sebastian shrugged. 'I suppose I'm curious as to how you have lived for the last, what, sixteen or seventeen years? And I'm even more curious how you wound up as a captive at all, given what we believe you're capable of.'

'It wasn't supposed to be like that,' I said, glancing out the window glumly. 'The IMI was supposed to be a safe haven for me.'

Sebastian licked his lips, following the motion with agitated fingers. 'The Protectors have never been what they appeared to be. You shouldn't have put your safety in their hands. Like I said to you in Budapest, once our alliance finally crumbles, the IMI will hunt each of us until extinction— they will do exactly the same to the Vânătors.'

'That's a bit of a broad stereotype. They aren't all bad like that, Sebastian.'

'Name one who isn't?'

'My brother, Lucas.'

Sebastian sat forward in his chair and gripped at the arms with his fingers, eyes widening in shock. 'You have a brother?'

'Yes.'

He shook his head, mouth gaping open. 'But how can that be? You just said he is a Protector. Vampires can't be Protectors.'

'We aren't related by blood—I'm adopted. My parents are both Protectors, as is their biological son, Lucas.'

'Oh,' Sebastian said, leaning back in his chair again. 'I guess that explains it.'

'He's still my brother. Blood or not, Lucas always will be.'

'But he helped send you to that place in Bucharest,' Sebastian said, with barely concealed contempt. 'How can you defend someone like that?'

'You don't know him, Sebastian. He didn't send me there; my parents did. And I agreed to go.'

'Excuse me?'

'You heard me. I went there of my own accord, never thinking that the situation could go downhill so quickly.'

'I don't understand why you would willingly put yourself at the mercy of spell-wielding humans motivated by revenge.'

'Because I was protecting the only family I've ever known from becoming victims of a horde of savage vânători.'

'So, then why were you making nice with that Alpha?'

I cringed.

His hands were clasping mine before I could even respond. 'Help me to understand, Elena.'

I looked down at our intertwined digits, wondering if I should just shove him away. There was a list of reasons supporting such a move, but I was weary and tired of fighting.

Sebastian made me feel like I didn't have to fight, and I genuinely felt safe in his presence. Perhaps it was because, in some way or another, he had always been with me.

'A couple of months back, my family and I intercepted what we thought were two stray vânătors. We tracked them to a shipping yard nearby that we'd been tipped off they would be arriving at via cargo ship.'

'Where?'

'Brisbane.'

'As in, Australia?'

'Yes, exactly.' Sebastian stayed silent, and I slowly went on. 'I killed them all—my first major kills using the skills taught to me by The Protectors. A few days later, when we were back in my hometown of Cairns, I encountered some vampires at a party. They were the first vamps I'd ever met. They made good with our local faction of the IMI and explained that their group had been hunting the same pack we'd been after for a couple of years now. That's what had eventually led them from London to Australia.'

'They were the first vampires you had ever encountered?' Sebastian asked, looking mildly surprised.

'And the last, until you and your friends came along. I've led a somewhat sheltered life when it comes to my own kind.'

'What were their names?'

'That's irrelevant to the story.'

Sebastian huffed in frustration. 'Carry on.'

'Well, these vampires had some interesting information. They'd found out that an Alpha had also hit the shores of Australia on the very same cargo ship. At this stage, the Alpha and his blossoming pack had already moved onto two other towns up the coast from Brisbane. By the time my parents had verified the information, women were already going missing.'

'The pack was originally from London, you say?'

I nodded. 'Does that mean anything significant to you?'

He shook his head, eyes suddenly alight. 'Just sorting through my mental debris. Please, continue.'

'John was the Alpha's name,' I said, waiting for a hint of recognition from Sebastian. He gave me no sign. 'I first met him when we were pursuing a lead given to us by those vampires, when we heading back down the coast to Mackay. It was that night that John had his first taste of me.' I swallowed at the memory and looked back across at Sebastian, watching his expression carefully. 'After that, he made it his own personal mission to hunt and capture me.'

'Did he?' Sebastian said quietly, his fingers tightening around my knuckles.

'Yes. A few days after leaving Mackay and returning to Cairns, John sent one of his pack mates to bring me back to their den.' I shuddered at the memory, at all the pain. 'I put up a pretty good fight. I even ended up killing the creature sent after me, but in the end there was just one more waiting to take its place.' I shook my hands free of Sebastian's. Whether he meant to or not, he was starting to hurt me.

'Then what happened?'

I hesitated, sensing rather than seeing his anger. It seemed almost as if Sebastian cared which seemed strange considering our paths had only just truly crossed. 'I spent the next two days alternating between being stuck in a steel cell and undergoing John's perverse methods of torture. He believed that the secret to self-healing was locked away somewhere inside my blood, and if he couldn't find the answers by consuming my blood, then I'd be the perfect cross-breed mate to help breed him a new pack.'

'Is what he thought true?' Sebastian said, voice barely above a whisper.

I shrugged, glancing down at his tense hands, every muscle in his arms straining, veins bulging. 'I doubt it. The breeding part might have worked but drinking my blood sure didn't appear to have any effect on him.'

'Did you …?'

'No. He did not get that chance.'

Sebastian's nostrils flared. 'And why is that?'

'He used me as bait to lure in the vampires who had been hunting him. The plan was to kill them all, but what he didn't count on was their having The Protectors on their side.' I paused and glanced back at Sebastian, who was staring angrily at the floor. His eyes were grey, but the tendrils twisted and turned with ill-concealed ire, and I saw silver flashing in those depths.

'What happened?'

'John died and the rest of his newly-formed pack was eradicated, along with every remaining trace of evidence that they had ever existed.'

Sebastian's eyes again found mine, his brows furrowing in confusion. 'So, if you killed the Alpha, who is this other one hunting you now?'

'Roshan. You see, while I was in captivity, John sent word to the other Alphas. He told them about my unique blood and the possibilities he believe it held for advancing their species. I knew then that if I stayed in Cairns I would be continuously hunted. The best thing I could do for Lucas and my family was to get out.'

'You have suffered,' Sebastian said flatly.

'It wasn't all bad. At least I figured out that the Alphas were the only ones who could continue breeding other vânătors.'

'Elena, some of us have known that for centuries.'

I felt my mouth drop. 'What? Then why have they not been eradicated before now?'

'For the sake of our kind,' Sebastian said quietly. 'You know how powerful The Protectors have become, Elena. If we had destroyed the Vânătors when we first discovered the truth, The Protectors would not have hesitated in dissolving the alliance.'

'But what about all those people who have died over the years at their hands!'

'That fact pains me as much as it does you.'

I sneered at him. 'You've let innocent people die. What kind of person are you?'

Sebastian leant forward in his chair, again gripping their arms, as he levelled his gaze with mine. 'I am the kind of person that understands that to save many, sometimes we must sacrifice a few.'

'So, because you're all too scared to face The Protectors in battle, you would rather cower behind that *excuse* than do something about them?' I glared at him. 'I don't think I want to meet Lucius if he shares the same ideals you do. I would rather fight than stand back and let others suffer because I was too scared to face up to my mistakes. It was the Vampires that created the need for The Protectors, that caused them to band together in the first place, and it was the Vampires who created the Vânătors, too.'

Sebastian shook his head, his eyes wistful. 'There's so much about the world that you don't understand, Elena. I wish I could show you all I have seen and done as I've walked this earth. If you could, you would see that sometimes fighting is not always the best solution. Sometimes events need to unfold and be seen from every angle before we can truly take stock of a situation.'

'There's no excuse for it, Sebastian. You've had the cure for centuries, and yet you've continued to let the situation fester.'

He winced. 'Have you never let someone suffer because you knew in the end that one person's life could change the fate of many if you yielded to such pressure?'

I was about to shake my head, but then I remembered Kate, the human that John had used to blackmail me when I'd been trapped in that cell. He'd thought I'd be able to tell him how I became part-Vânător if her life had been on the line instead of my own. Regrettably, I'd weighed up the cost of her life against the countless others that would be affected by revealing my secrets to John, and consequently, she'd died because I'd refused to say anything.

'Elena?' Sebastian prompted.

I turned away from him—Sebastian was right. But what was that one life in comparison to a century's worth of countless preventable deaths? 'I don't want to talk about this anymore.'

'Alright then,' Sebastian said, leaning back in his chair, its leather surface creaking. He sat silent for a couple of minutes. 'What else would you like to talk about?'

I didn't look back as I spoke. I was still too shocked by Sebastian's revelation. Holding back and waiting for events to unfold simply did not make any sense to me. 'Well, since you're taking me to a vampire I know absolutely nothing about, someone who apparently deals in the fate of human lives and decides who lives and who dies—why don't you tell me something about him?'

'Like what?'

'Tell me how Lucius knew how to find me.'

'A psychic link—through your dreams, I imagine.'

I snorted. 'How's that even possible?'

'All things are possible. Lucius is so powerful that he thinks and feels things that no one else can. He sensed you out there, felt your power speak to him, and so ordered us to find you and bring you back to the safety of our coven.'

'But why? Is there something about me that he thinks he can use or manipulate? Because, I gotta tell you, so far I'm not a real fan of your methods. And I'm not the sort of girl you can manipulate.'

Sebastian shook his head. 'Lucius just wants to know you.'

'Why?'

'It's not for me to say.'

'Well, what *can* you say?' I replied, goading him.

Sebastian moved to the edge of his seat, placing a hand on the arm rests on either side of me and locking my legs between his. He looked cranky, not even slightly amused by my taunts.

'What are you doing?' I said, my hand flattening against Sebastian's chest, his skin warm and yielding under my touch.

He leaned closer still, our lips only inches apart. 'I'm only going to say this once, and I want you to listen to me because I hate repeating myself.'

'Do you have to get this close to me?' I frowned as Sebastian ignore me, his eyes drowning pools of tumultuous grey that seemed to draw me further into their depths. Teamed with his scent, that suffused the overly small cabin space between us, and the mingled heat of our breath, I was fighting a losing battle of wills.

'Neither I nor Lucius intend you any harm. We are bringing you to Rome so that you can finally be in a place that will feel like home to you, a place where you will be accepted no matter who or what you are. It does not matter that you are half-Vânător, Elena—it only matters to us that you are happy and safe. How many other people in your life can you say want the same?'

I sat stock-still. How had he at guessed my werewolf nature? Even William hadn't noticed until his own up-close-and-personal investigation.

'Don't look so surprised. Secrets are hard to hide from me, Elena. Your very essence swims through me; I usually work these things out quite quickly. I also know that you have recently tasted vampire blood and that an exchange has been made.' Sebastian pressed his forehead against mine and closed his eyes. 'I know you. Some details may be sketchy, and some things may have changed, but most aspects of your soul are eternal.'

'What?'

This guy's talking gibberish.

'I know you,' Sebastian repeated.

'You know *of* me,' I corrected. 'Just because you've used your abilities to apparently map out my DNA, doesn't mean that you know *me*.'

He leant forward a fraction further, his sweet breath whispering across my lips. 'Let me know you then …'

I snaked a hand out between his lips and mine. 'Don't try and kiss me, Sebastian.'

'A kiss reveals everything.'

I sucked in a breath. 'Sometimes, ignorance is bliss.'

Sebastian pulled back, releasing me, his eyes ferocious. 'That is almost never true. Turn a blind eye if you wish but the mind always unconsciously seeks answers. Eventually, you'll want them, Elena. Eventually, you will have to kiss me.'

My eyes narrowed, and my nose twitched. 'You're not normal, are you?'

'I am Vampire.'

'Yeah, a real weird one, though. I'm going to keep my eye on you.'

He smiled, but didn't answer.

At that moment we were thankfully distracted by the plane slowly beginning to dip. As the pressure in the cabin started to drop, I blew my nose, trying to unblock my ears. I turned and looked out the window, but saw nothing but darkness. We were still too high up to see anything of consequence, anyway.

I grabbed at the two halves of my unbuckled belt. After mashing them together for a while, and then realising I'd mistakenly picked up mismatched halves, I shrugged and twisted the two lengths into a knot. For now, that would just have to do.

'Can I ask you something?' Sebastian said quietly, his eyes always on mine.

'You're going to anyway.'

Sebastian nodded, quiet for only a moment. 'Why didn't you tell me that you were half-Vânător?'

'Apparently, I didn't have to.'

'I know that. I knew what you were from the first second I first inhaled your scent, but I was wondering why you thought you had to hide it from me.'

'People always judge what they don't understand, Sebastian. And given that I'm a giant question mark, spreading the word to others that I'm a half-breed invites trouble, particularly when others might be afraid of what I'm capable of.'

'And what can you do that should make others so fearful of you?'

I shrugged. 'Okay, maybe it's not what I can do, so much as what I could be capable of.'

Sebastian looked at me blankly.

I rolled my eyes. 'I'm half-Vânător, Sebastian—you do the math. Everyone's ruled over by someone.'

Understanding suddenly dawned. 'You're talking about the Alpha's authority over you, aren't you? I thought that was why you kept leaping into its arms, even though I could see from the look on your face that wasn't what you wanted.'

I nodded. 'When an Alpha command's me, I'm entirely helpless, entirely under their sway.'

'So you must obey without hesitation?'

'Do you see why I sent myself packing off to the Institute of Magical Intervention now? I knew it was the one place the Alphas couldn't easily get to me, a place they couldn't come looking for me.'

'Elena,' Sebastian murmured, 'this is not the life you should have led.'

I shrugged, perplexed. 'What other life is there?'

'The one you should have had, the one you would have been born into. I'm sorry I didn't get the chance to intervene in your upbringing years ago, because things would have been quite different.'

I was frowning again. 'You know, you really are an expert at talking in circles.'

We lapsed into silence, unsure what to say next. Sebastian was right, though—ignorance did leave burning questions in the mind; however, I was not going to kiss him for the answers. This entire situation was too weird.

I looked out the window instead, watching the clouds part and disperse into small puffs of translucence as we descended. I could see the lights of a bustling city below now. 'We're here,' I breathed, feeling strangely unsettled.

'Yes, we are,' Sebastian murmured. 'Welcome to Rome.'

CHAPTER FIFTEEN: FAILURE

Roshan began to slow as he spied the lights of his home city twinkling on the horizon. It had been months since he'd first left, and Roshan was sorely missing his pack and the comforts of his den.

He'd spent the last few hours being chased by two of those damned vampires that had rescued Elena. He'd run, heading straight for Austria, the icy waters of the Danube under his paws before their taste for the hunt had faded. Roshan's hunger had not—he was a werewolf. The hunt was not over until a kill had been made or the trail ended.

Roshan had sensed more than seen their retreat. He realised that their goal had been only to chase him away, not to kill, although there was no doubt they would have tried had the opportunity had arisen. No, their intent had been to keep Elena free of him. Big mistake.

Roshan had doubled back, following their scent trails as they'd headed towards Hungary. As it turned out, they'd been smarter than he thought, and he found himself led to an abandoned factory in the middle of Budapest, their scent trails fading as he'd tried to retrace his steps. He'd even circled back to Bucharest, all the way back to the coal factory, but the wash of a sudden, and somewhat inconvenient, rainstorm had all but smeared the scents beyond recognition.

Roshan was pissed off—there was no other way to describe his current mood. He had been so close to claiming Elena for himself, had tasted her sweetness in his mouth. He had wanted more of her and not just her blood. Elena was a dangerous addiction, with each encounter another smooth hit giving him just enough of a taste for him to crave for more. But, just like in Cairns, he'd let her slip through his fingers again; he now had no other choice but to head back to Paris and tell the rest of his pack that he had failed … yet again.

He'd spent the last month in Bucharest, watching the IMI headquarters in the hopes that Elena would once again stray outside. But as each night passed, absent of her presence, Roshan had begun to fear that he'd lost her indefinitely. It wasn't until one day, when he'd seen an entourage of cars leaving the IMI's underground parking garage, that his interest had once again been piqued.

More out of curiosity than anything, Roshan had followed the cars as they had headed off to the outer suburbs, finally stopping outside an abandoned coal factory. It was then that he'd scented her, all sweetness and purity, her smell drifting across the cold night air like a shot of electricity wired directly into his system. He remembered whimpering at the time, and he hadn't whimpered in centuries, not since he was a pup.

Just as quickly as the scent had provoked his passion, it was gone. He'd searched the area for days for its like but all he'd smelt were Protectors. Roshan could tell their particular scent from a mile off. They'd never smelt like regular humans—there was a strange kind of tang to their aroma, almost as if their blood was tainted with battery acid.

Roshan had considered storming the factory but security

was high, and although he wouldn't admit it, Roshan was honestly a little afraid of The Protector's magic. With an entire pack he could have gone on the offensive, but since he'd been alone Roshan had instead been patient and waited for his enemies to slip up.

The rest, as they say, was history.

Roshan supposed now that he was far away, just entering the outskirts of Paris, that he could try to forget Elena. She was but one female, and would hardly put a dent in his insatiable sexual appetite. Finding a few, random females to mate with would be easy given the extremely masculine physique of the new body he wore; those he found would soon bare him an entire litter of new pups, expanding the power of his pack ever further.

The thought of mating was appealing, if not for the fact that Elena was all Roshan could now think about. Now that he'd felt her in his arms and tasted her lips, he wanted more. He feared he could no longer be satisfied with mere human sex—Roshan wanted Elena, the first female of his breed. He could forgive the vampiric part of her nature; that aspect actually somehow made her blood all the more appealing.

Roshan had been surprised when the vampires had rescued her. He just wished he had some idea of who had been responsible for snatching her away. If he could uncover their leader's identity, then perhaps he would be reunited with her once more.

Roshan threw his head back and howled out into the night, alerting the pack to his presence. Rather than hanging his head in shame, he was going to chalk up the last two months of failure to experience. Being home, he could take all the time that he needed to formulate a decent plan to get Elena back. Time, as usual, was on his side.

Paris—how he loved this city. He loved the culture,

the landscape, and most of all, the never-ending flow of tourism, which kept him well fed.

Roshan smiled and licked his lips. It was time to begin the hunt once more.

CHAPTER SIXTEEN: VALLE SANTA

The aircraft's engine slowed, the dim whirring that steadily thrummed through the cabin dwindling to nothing. Frederico, the pilot, and his co-pilot emerged from behind the thick mahogany cockpit door. The co-pilot was in his early fifties with thinning, grey hair, and sported a tiny moustache that seemed to hover above his pencil-thin lips.

'Paulo, Frederico,' Sebastian said, acknowledging them with a pleasant nod.

'*È sempre un piacere, Signor Marcellus*,' Paulo answered.

Frederico elbowed the older pilot in the ribs. 'Please let us know if we can be of any further assistance,' he finished in English, his accent extremely thick and almost as difficult to understand as Paulo's. Still, I appreciated the gesture.

Sebastian smiled and nodded again, gesturing for them to open the door so we could leave. Frederico crisply obeyed, spinning the locking mechanism in the centre of the hatch and lowering the staircase down onto the tarmac. He and Paulo exited first, but as Sebastian and I followed we found them waiting at the bottom of the stairs for us.

I watched as a shiny, black town car careened across the tarmac, slowing as it approached the aircraft. I felt my heart leap—I was actually here in Rome. I was going to meet Lucius, and I had no idea how to feel about that other than shit-scared. In my dreams he'd instilled a deep fear into the heart of me. Now I was going to face him, and I was having a tough time believing that I'd be capable of handling myself.

I looked down. Sebastian was at my side, holding my hand. This time I didn't jerk my hand away. I felt oddly comforted by the fact that he was with me. 'Don't be afraid,' he said, fingers looped through mine.

'I'm not,' I lied.

'Your rapidly beating heart says otherwise. Do you need me to distract you?'

'Distract me how?'

He smiled.

I scowled at him. 'Umm, no.'

Sebastian led the way, holding my hand and making sure I didn't nose dive into the tarmac. My knees were almost knocking together in fear, which was ridiculous considering the odds I'd overcome in the past.

I slid over the cool leather seat of the waiting car, Sebastian settling in next to me. I tried to fasten my seatbelt with my shaking fingers, but all I managed to do was knock my knuckles a couple of times on the buckle.

What the hell is wrong with me?

Sebastian took over when he saw me struggling, clicking the seatbelt into place with one easy flick of his wrist. He smiled, grasping my hand again and leaving me little choice to resist.

Through the open partition the mystery driver started the car, engine purring. I was so nervous that I hadn't even taken note of the make and model, which was so completely unlike me.

The driver, with a squeal of tires, sped away from the terminal area, taking what looked to be private strips and back roads to get to the main highway. We passed cars packed like sardines in the long-term parking structure, and then crowds of people dodging the blaring horns of incoming taxis. Some people were weaving dangerously between what looked to be shuttle buses, some in a hurry to catch the city-bound train.

We zipped under a broad skybridge that connected the terminals. I saw people in business suits wandering the area with briefcases, heavily armed for business. There were also plenty of tourists about, dressed in outfits that belied the cooler weather. Their smiles were plastered with the panicked expression of the unseasoned traveller, as they shuffled uncertainly through the teeming crowds.

Taking a busier byway, we ducked and weaved around slower cars and scooters. I could now see the city approaching through my window, eyes glued to the scenery whirling past. 'Where are we going?' I asked Sebastian.

'We are going to the villa.'

'The where?'

'Lucius lives in a villa in Valle Santa. It's about a fifteen minute drive from Rome. You are the first person in over four hundred years to learn its location. Not even the two hundred members of our coven know exactly where Lucius resides. We usually conduct meetings in Rome or receive guests through our visitor's entrance.'

'Visitor's entrance?'

'It's an entry point in the city that is connected to the villa via underground tunnels. Of course, there's a thick steel door that bars entry, unless Lucius permits it.'

'Why all the security? Didn't you say he was the leader of the Vampires?'

Sebastian shrugged. 'When you are as old as Lucius is, you get a little cautious and gather a few enemies over time.'

'How old is Lucius?'

'Decrepit.'

I laughed, appreciating Sebastian's levity, although my pulse still beat erratically under my skin. He squeezed my hand reassuringly, as if sensing my nerves. 'Tell me … why am I the first one to be allowed to know the location of his residence?'

The look he gave me was almost sincere. 'Because you are one of us.'

'I don't understand.'

He squeezed my hand again, eyes gently a-swirl. 'It's not what you are but who you are.'

'What do you mean?'

Sebastian pointed out the window. 'We haven't got too far to go now,' he answered.

I looked back out the window again, sighing in frustration. Vampires could apparently be as secretive as the IMI. I went twelve years before I found out I was born a vampire, then a further four before I discovered I was a half-breed. The IMI didn't believe in sharing, but I sure hoped Lucius was different.

The lights of the city receded, appearing as a glowing halo of light in the distant night sky. We were still passing through the houses and streets of suburbia with the bustling fury of a busy city left behind. The further we drove the more countryside we saw. Vineyards, farms and pine forests dotted the landscape, with the occasional villa breaking up the dullness of endless pastures.

'Can you see over there?' Sebastian said, leaning towards me and pointing out of my window. 'Just through that clearing of trees. Can you see the pale pink house?'

I followed his gaze. Once the mass of pine trees had thinned, I caught a glimpse of a pale-pink rendered fence. The fence was covered in trailing vines and elegantly illuminated by multiple exterior fluorescents placed around its perimeter. Beyond that I could see the building Sebastian had been talking about, which was also heavily illuminated against the darkness. I wouldn't have called the villa a house—it was at least ten times, nay, twenty times the size of an average home, quietly tucked back amongst the surrounding pines and spruces. 'That's not just a house,' I stated, awed by the size of the property.

'It's a villa. Lucius has lived here all of his life, as far as I know.'

'And how long would that be?'

'A very, very, very long time.'

The driver took a short left-hand turn, the car exiting the bitumen road and following a cobblestone driveway. This driveway led directly through wrought iron gates that were set into the washed pink walls surrounding the villa. The walls in question were made of stone and rendered with rough strokes. Where the render had crumbled away over the years, bits of stonework poked through; hanging vines had taken advantage of the decay, clinging desperately to the mortar and spreading languidly over its surface. Tiny scarlet flowers comprised most of the perimeter, following the stone wall as it disappeared back into the trees and around to the rear of the villa.

If she'd been with me, Kayla would have gone crazy with delight.

The car pulled into the circular cobblestone driveway, stopping in front of two giant timber and wrought iron doors that marked the entry to the residence. The weathered doors were thrown back against the interior wall, allowing views from the front and all the way to the back of the villa. Through these doors, I could see a beautiful lush garden surrounded by pines, flowers, and hedges. A luxuriant marble fountain flowed exuberantly past the entry, leading the eye through to a lap pool and inviting garden below.

I unbuckled my seatbelt and climbed out of the backseat, slowly drinking in the sight laid out before me. Sebastian was already beside me, watching me as I surveyed the two-story building in awe. The whole structure seemed to sprawl out across the estate, wrapping in a U-shape around the rear courtyard.

The ground floor was exposed due to continuous glass windowing. Each large window was trimmed with a white window box, the same red flowers dangling from each. The roof matched the external rendering and was covered in terracotta tiles that had seen better days. The second floor had French doors leading off of every room and onto small Juliet balconies jutting out overhead. More potted plants in terracotta urns decorated each of the balconies, matching the lower level.

'It's beautiful, isn't it?' Sebastian said, waving a hand around.

I shook my head. 'No, it's more than beautiful. It's breathtaking.'

'There are no bags to take, Mr. Marcellus?' the driver asked pleasantly.

We spun around to face him. I'd completely forgotten the driver had been standing there. 'No, you can go. Thank you, Marco,' Sebastian said politely, stepping forward and handing him a wad of cash. I was starting to wonder where Sebastian kept all that money. He wasn't wearing a shirt and the leather of his pants was tight—real tight.

Another mystery.

Marco tilted his hat in thanks, got back into the car, and drove off down the driveway without further delay.

'Come on,' Sebastian said, pulling me towards the front

door. 'Let's get you to your room so you can get cleaned up properly and change into something more comfortable.'

'My room?' I said, raising an eyebrow.

'Lucius wants you to feel comfortable here.'

'And you're assuming that I'm staying?'

He nodded. 'Once you meet Lucius, you won't be going anywhere.'

'Don't threaten me.'

Sebastian paused, his lips tightening. 'I wouldn't … I'm sorry. I simply meant that you will not *want* to leave once you're acquainted.'

I frowned. 'You're so sure about that, aren't you? Don't get me wrong, I am curious about all this,' I said, waving my hand around at the property, 'but if I don't want to stay there's nothing you can do to keep me here.'

'Why would we force you?'

I blinked. 'Huh?' That was not the answer I'd been expecting. I guess I'd gotten too used to being held against my will, although in truth, Sebastian had never once forced me to do anything. I'd been the one to follow him here, after all.

'Elena, if you don't want to stay after you meet Lucius then you are free to go.'

Out of the corner of my eye, I saw movement. I looked up at one of the balconies, as a curtain shifted and fell back into place. Someone was watching us. 'Forgive me if I don't have much faith in what people tell me, Sebastian. Every time I put my trust in people, they somehow let me down.'

He reached out and touched my cheek, but I jerked away out of habit. Hurt flickered across his features, and he dropped his hand. 'I'm not one of those people, Elena, and neither is Lucius.'

I looked back up at the curtained door above, as sceptical as ever. 'We'll see.'

My jaw dropped in shock, although I quickly closed it. I was determined not to be too taken in by the experience. I was supposedly well-trained, highly skilled and taught to always be wary of my surroundings. I was in unknown territory, in the house of the Master Vampire. Caution should have been my middle name.

Sebastian switched on the overhead lighting.

'This is my room?' I said, glancing nervously over my shoulder and through the door. Another vampire could sneak up on me and I'd never know it.

'Yes.'

'It's nice.'

Nice didn't even begin to describe it, though—my room was entirely out of this world. The walls were covered in smooth plaster and rich, painted terracotta. The architraves, framework, and fretwork were gilded in gold. A faded, hand-painted mural depicting the countryside adorned one wall, with gilded balcony doors that were spread wide revealing the real thing in the background. Slabs of terracotta rested underfoot, undoubtedly cold to the touch. My bed was positioned against the longest wall and opposite the mural, for optimal viewing. A flowing gold canopy hung from above, with soft folds of fabric that splayed out on either side of the pillows.

In the corner was an antique dressing armoire that was also gilded, matching the rest of the room. A softly upholstered chaise lounge reclined next to it, with a side table and a reading lamp beside that, along with a small collection of books. In the other corner, free of walls and out in the open, was a roll-top Roman bathtub and a small pedestal basin.

'It's a big room,' I said, backing up against the mural wall, wanting something solid and safe at my back.

Sebastian nodded. 'You'll find all the rooms are like this one.'

'I don't think I'll be exploring.'

He studied my expression. I wasn't sure what expression Sebastian saw on my face, but he took a step towards me. I'm not usually skittish, but something about this place made me feel quite uneasy, and I found myself sliding an arm's length down the wall and away from him.

Perhaps it wasn't the place itself that made me uneasy, but more the presence I could feel inside. I'd been here just ten minutes and had noted at least ten bedrooms on this level alone. That meant a lot of vampires, yet I'd seen exactly zero. So why were they steering clear of me?

Sebastian stepped back, hurt again showing in his eyes. 'I might leave you alone to get cleaned up,' he said, his voice husky, despite being several feet away from me.

I shivered.

'In the armoire there are some clothes that should fit you, including undergarments and shoes. If you need to use a toilet, just let me know—there's one out in the hall. As you can imagine, we don't have much use for them ourselves and merely have the one bathroom for the convenience of the staff.'

I nodded. I wasn't sure why, because although I could hear the words, I wasn't really listening.

'I'll be right outside if you need me.' Sebastian turned to leave, his movements slow, deliberate.

'Wait.'

'Yes, Baby Vamp?'

When did I acquire a nickname? 'Don't leave.'

His head tilted to the side, curiosity lighting his features. 'I smell fear on you.'

'It's caution. There's a difference.'

'You wish me to stay and watch you change?' A smile threatened to lift the edges of Sebastian's lips, though he was more than careful enough to try and conceal it from me. He'd turned away, but I'd already seen his face. I was growing annoyed by all the incessant come-ons.

I took a bolstering breath, ignoring the innuendo and stepping away from the wall. I reached for Sebastian's turned shoulder, but as my hand found his skin, he turned and my fingers touched his chest instead. I quickly dropped my hand, as that familiar feeling of heat building deep within. I just wanted to get this whole damn thing over with so I could wake up—my denial was still deep-set and riding me hard.

'Elena?'

'I'm not here for the hospitality. Take me to Lucius.'

Sebastian's eyes widened fractionally. 'Now?'

'There's no time like the present.'

He shook his head, not in defeat but apparent amusement. 'Well, that was unexpected.'

'I'd rather be unpredictable than boring.'

'Indeed.'

I let his hand reach for mine. In truth, his touch felt good—I was beyond denying it. Sebastian's fingers skimmed the jacket Nicholas had given me, finally finding my hand, our fingers lacing and palms pressing together. We fit—it felt strange to have noticed that.

Sebastian reached the door first, looking over his shoulder and smiling. The warmth of his honesty made sure he was hiding nothing, yet I strongly believed he hadn't been too forthcoming either. It didn't make him a liar but it did make me cautious of his intentions, and in that regard we were similar. I was betting we could be around each other for a week and still know just as much about each other as we did now. Was my self-preservation kicking in again? Or was it my lack of emotion, the disconnected part of me that needed no one else for comfort? Was I only seeing what I wanted to see?

I shook my head, dispelling those thoughts. Focus was what I needed. Holding Sebastian's hand and being in his presence made me feel safe, but I was not about to be fooled. Everyone had their own agenda.

Shit. I really am in trouble.

'The villa is set on roughly two acres,' Sebastian said, pointing out a nearby window. He was giving me the grand tour, even though I hadn't asked for it. 'There are ten bedrooms in total, as well as numerous entertainment rooms, an indoor swimming pool, living areas, and the great hall where we are headed to now.'

We were walking the upstairs passageway that wrapped around the U-shaped villa. To my left, I could see evenly spaced doors up and down the corridor—the bedrooms. On the right was a balcony view. From over the side, I could see down onto the lower level: the swimming pool, the fountain, and the indoor-outdoor garden. There wasn't much internal wall at the rear of the villa. That area had been left open so that the garden blended in with the living spaces.

There was no furniture in the large passage of the upstairs landing, just those ten evenly spaced doors. Each door was decorated with ornate carvings and wrought iron window insets—they weren't big on privacy here. One door in particular stood out to me, different from the rest. Small, faded pictures had been drawn on the door that looked like they'd been drawn by a child. They only reached as high as the doorknob.

I stopped, studying the drawings. My fingers traced over the small images of lions and funny, little stick figure men decorated with swords, shields, and capes. In the centre of the door was one word—'Lucius'—written in a messy scrawl.

My fingers came away covered in dust. I rubbed the grit down the front of Nicholas's jacket, leaving dirty, brown streaks. Looking down at the door knob, I realised it had not been touched in many years. There was as much dust there as was built up around the wrought iron window in the centre of the door.

Sebastian, seemingly unaware of the distraction, did not notice as I stood on my tippy toes so I could peek inside the room. Judging from its position in the corridor and the front of the house, it had to have been the same room I had seen the curtains moving in earlier. Obviously *someone* still came in here.

Sebastian had walked off a fair distance ahead of me. He was still gesturing and running through the other amenities the villa had to offer, not even realising that I'd stopped. I touched my fingers tentatively to the dirty brass knob and gave it a turn. It made a funny sort of noise as it resisted my grip, a cross between a squeak and groan. I blew at the dust from within the wrought iron window and tried to see through the cobwebs.

'No!' Sebastian screamed, wrenching my hand away from the door. I felt something crunch in my wrist as he flicked my hand sideways, and I found myself falling backwards onto the hard terracotta floor behind me.

I bit my tongue, my teeth drawing blood. Closing my eyes and holding back the tears, I sat, waiting for the pain to subside. Sebastian had broken my wrist! I clutched it to my chest protectively and waited for the bones to re-knit, to become whole.

Sebastian gently re-closed the door like it was made of the frailest glass, precious and easily breakable. He released the door knob carefully, his hands held out in front of him like he was afraid the whole thing would collapse—it didn't. He glanced back at me, eyes neutral, face calm. I had expected to see anger or fear on his face, but I saw nothing.

Sebastian dropped to his knees beside me, reaching out and taking my hand in his, delicately turning my arm around to assess the damage. 'Where does it hurt?' he asked, skimming the skin of my wrist with his fingers.

'It doesn't hurt anymore.'

His grey-green eyes snapped up at me. 'I'm so sorry. Sometimes I forget my own strength, because I usually only play rough with the undead.'

'It's okay. I've had worse.'

Oh, you better believe it.

Sebastian stood up and helped pull me to my feet. 'I shouldn't have reacted that way,' he said quietly. 'I assumed you could self-heal, but I could have seriously hurt you if I was wrong.'

'I doubt that, Sebastian. You'd need a steamroller to kill me, and even then I'm sure if you blew in my ear you'd be able to reinflate me again.'

He smiled begrudgingly. Wow, I must have been feeling a little calmer because I'd just made a little joke.

Yay, good for me.

I looked back at the door, tilting my chin in its direction. 'What gives, anyway? I mean, I get why you don't want me snooping but why the overreaction? Why stop me from going into that room?'

Sebastian glanced back at the door, his face darkening. 'It's forbidden to enter that room.'

'Why? It doesn't look like anyone's been in there for years.' Though I believed I knew better.

'It's a private place. Misery and pain reside in there. You don't need to see it.'

Great, make me more curious, why don't you?

'It looks like a child's bedroom. Was it Lucius's when he was young, before he became a vampire?'

Sebastian shrugged. He was trying for nonchalance but his manner was at odds with the haunted look I could now see in his eyes. It nearly made me reach out and touch him. Nearly. 'No. It was not Lucius's bedroom.'

'Then whose? You said he's lived in this house his entire life. Did he have a family when he was human; shit, if he was ever human?'

Sebastian took my hand again, leading me away from the door. 'It's not for me to say.'

'I feel a story coming on here,' I said, allowing him to guide me, mostly because I couldn't think of an excuse not to.

'Well, it's not a story that you will be hearing from me.'

Frustrated, I chewed on my bottom lip in quiet contemplation. I wanted to ask him a flood of questions, but I had a feeling he'd avoid them all, even if he knew the answers. 'Come on. They are all waiting for you in the great hall.'

Well, that explained the lack of a vampire presence. They'd all gathered to eat me instead.

Lovely.

Sebastian guided me along to the staircase we had ascended earlier. It was set in the centre of the villa, constructed mostly of wrought iron and the same rendered plaster and stone that the walls were crafted from. As we reached the bottom, a short, tubby lady with greying hair suddenly appeared. She was wearing a traditional black and white maid's outfit and carrying a feather duster in her hand. A prop for the expensive house, perhaps?

Tucked into the back of her white apron, wrapped tightly across the folds of the woman's rotund stomach, was a dirty rag that she wiped her hands with. No, definitely not a prop—this woman was the real deal.

It would suck *to work for vampires.*

I snickered, amused by my own pun. Thankfully, no one paid me any attention.

'*Buona sera, Signor Marcellus. Come stai?*' she said, smiling. She definitely wasn't talking to me because I didn't speak that mumbo jumbo. But, then again, if I *had* worked here I probably would have addressed the guy with fangs first, too.

'*Ciao,* Maria. I am well.' Sebastian pulled me forward, showing me off like a prize-winning poodle. 'This is Elena.'

Maria held out a pudgy hand for me to take. It was warm, just as I expected it to be, a positive reassurance that the vampires here didn't eat every human in sight. '*Ciao,* Maria,' I said, echoing Sebastian. That was about as far as my basic Italian stretched.

She smiled warmly. '*Lei parla Italiano?*'

'Lei what?'

'Never mind,' Maria answered, accent thick. 'Signor Marcellus teach you how to speak our language.' She elbowed Sebastian in the ribs. 'And other things, eh?'

'Hey?'

Sebastian gave her a stern look when she started to giggle. 'Don't mind Maria,' he said, shaking his head. 'Her English is not so good.'

Maria looked aghast. 'My English perfect!'

I nodded politely. I didn't want to get in the middle of it. Besides, I didn't really care whether I could speak Italian or not. If things went bad tonight, the only words I would be shouting were *'adios amigos!'*

Oh, wait, that's Spanish. Or Mexican?

Sebastian tugged on my hand again, that familiar jolt of electricity dancing between us. As it happened, our eyes locked for an instant.

I was the first to look away. I watched Maria as she began dusting the framed artwork hanging on the walls, which must have been a good distraction for her. Maybe I should have mentioned the door upstairs? That could have really used a going over.

Sebastian continued the tour but this time was silent. I kept my eyes busy, focusing on my surroundings, trying to ignore whatever lay between us. My eyes passed over the bubbling fountain; the sound of splashing water was soothing, calming.

I looked down into the catchment as we passed and saw goldfish swimming in the bottom. Around the fountain sat a couple of plush outdoor chairs facing the well-lit garden and swimming pool. One small side table was piled high with a stack of *Home and Garden* magazines, and I found myself smirking at the thought of designer vampires.

Maria had started singing. It was off-key, and I didn't know if I felt comforted or irritated by it.

From beyond the gurgling of water and the sounds of the night came voices from behind a nearby door. Through

Maria's rendition of 'Everybody Loves Somebody', I heard my name mentioned. There was no hissing or immediate groan of displeasure after, so I took that as a good sign. When Susan and George had said my name, there was always a grunt that followed. That was the usual effect I had on people.

I approached the door first, Sebastian a step behind. Light from the room beyond filtered underneath the well-worn timber, giving the door an eerie glow. In the short stretch of light that bathed my feet, I could see the elongated shadows of those beyond. Their outlines shifted at first, stopping as my fingers touched the splintered wood. Energy pulsed from beyond the doorway—it called to me, jumping out and into my flesh, coursing through my veins.

Sebastian rapped three times on the hard timber surface. My heart flip-flopped inside my chest and I suddenly felt sick. Sweat dotted my forehead and upper lip, my hand instinctively curling to my stomach. My heart beat set a frantic pace, a stark reminder of my humanity.

Sebastian squeezed my hand, concern pooling in his swirling gaze. 'Are you okay?'

I shook my head. 'No. I think I'm going to be sick, actually.'

I took a couple of shallow breaths, trying to calm my racing heart and frantic nerves—nothing worked. All I could think about was that this might be the last time that I ever breathed oxygen.

'It's the connection, you're not used to it.'

'What?'

Sebastian ignored me and knocked on the door again, though I was sure they would have heard it the first time.

'Come in, Elena.'

Great. Just great.

'Are you ready?' Sebastian tentatively asked, gripping the handle between steady fingers.

I grimaced. 'Hell, no.'

CHAPTER SEVENTEEN: LUCIUS

The heavy wooden doors swung inwards. There was nothing that special about an opening door, unless of course the people beyond scared the crap out of you. I looked beyond and four faces looked back at me, exact replicas of those I'd seen in my dreams, uh … dream reality, uh …

Whatever.

They watched me with open curiosity as I forced myself forward into the room. My feet were dragging on the shiny parquetry floor, weighed down by imaginary lead. Every step took effort but I eventually made it past the threshold.

Bully for me.

A power emanated from the men that was almost tangible, like an electrical current rippling through the air, and the tiny hairs on my arms stood on end. Even the rest of my body hair knew the jig was up—I was helpless against vampires of this calibre.

Energy practically blistered across my skin. It became harder to breathe, the heat oppressive against my pores, almost cloying. My body trembled and my heart leapt into top gear.

A solitary figure stood in the corner of the room, back turned as he glanced out the window and into the garden. So calm, so still—the source of my unease.

Lucius.

He was dressed immaculately in dark pants and a blue pinstriped shirt. His hair was tidily combed and small ringlets dusted the back of his neck. His posture was stiff, hands shoved into the pockets of his pants, eyes forward but always watching. That kind of intensity was alarming yet also somehow compelling.

I forced another step forward, feet still dragging. I was barely even aware of Sebastian's presence at my back. The crackle of the energy beating at my skin seemed to wrap me up like a cocoon, shielding me from outside influence. The further I stepped into the room, the more Lucius's powers seemed to gnaw at me.

'Elena,' Sebastian said, moving from my shadow to pull me close to his side. 'I would like you to meet my family.'

At his touch, I jumped about a mile in the air.

Jittery much?

Sebastian frowned at me, one hand out to steady me.

Yeah, I'd be frowning too if I could see myself. Get a grip, Elena.

A vampire appeared inches from my face, surprise jolting through me again. This time I swore, all class. 'Could you not do that?'

'I apologise,' he said, voice as creamy as butter. 'It's an ingrained habit to move so fast.' Fast wasn't quite the word; even the wind caused by his movements took a few seconds to catch up.

I studied him, mostly staring at the hand outstretched towards me. I knew this vampire wanted me to shake, to return his greeting, yet I couldn't seem to lift my hand. I was suddenly cautious, like a part of me was preparing for the worst.

He dropped the proffered hand, seemingly un-offended. I wished I still had my knife. I wasn't planning on gutting him but it would have made me feel better having it as protection.

'I'm Tiberius,' he said smoothly, taking a step back as if he sensed my unease. I appreciated it, anyway.

Tiberius had curly dark hair that ran down to his shoulders, and he stared at me with large, green eyes. He was probably thirty-five to forty at the most, but how long he had been that way? I had no idea. He was as smartly dressed as Lucius and charisma emanated from him in waves, a pulsing stream of compulsion that was seemingly designed to calm my nerves. But the only thing that would calm me was to stop all these pleasantries and just get down to business.

I cleared my throat. 'I'm Elena.'

'A pleasure to meet you, Elena, I hope you're—'

'Are you going to eat me?' I interrupted. My voice was shaking, but hopefully, no one else noticed.

Tiberius blinked a couple of times and then slowly started to laugh. I was surprised at how human his reaction was but still felt uneasy— his hearty, open-mouthed laughter showed too many shiny, white teeth that were pointed in my direction.

Sebastian squeezed my fingers, not as amused. 'What did I tell you several times already?'

'I can't take your word for it. I need to hear it from them.'

'Elena—'

'Really, we have no plans to harm you in any way,' Tiberius interrupted, his laughter slowly dying off.

I looked into Tiberius's eyes. As far as I could tell, he seemed legit. I guess if he had wanted to kill me he'd have done it already.

I looked to the other vampires, wary. They looked curious to see me but there was no hunger in their gaze. So what the hell did they want from me?

Tiberius's gaze quickly washed over me, briefly stopping at my and Sebastian's entwined fingers. I wasn't sure why I was still holding his hand but probably because I somehow sensed he would never hurt me—it was weird to sense that in a person, yet to hardly know them. And dream snogging didn't count as interaction.

'I see you're making friends, Sebastian,' Tiberius said, his voice tight. He made a point of looking at our hands again.

'Father,' Sebastian said, tightening his grip on me. 'I was merely providing support.'

Father?

'Don't do me any favours,' I said, dropping his hand. 'I manage just fine on my own.'

Tiberius's lips twitched, and he looked back at me. 'I'd like to introduce you to everyone, if I may.'

It wasn't posed as a question, so I simply followed him—slowly, cautiously. I always had one eye on Lucius, though, the stiff figure standing imposingly in the corner.

'As I've said before, I am Tiberius—Tiberius Marcellus—and I am Sebastian's father.'

'I caught that.'

He ignored my sarcasm. Maybe Tiberius sensed that was how I muddled my way through uncomfortable situations. 'These are my brothers, my friends: Marcus, Maximus, and Decimus.' He pointed to each of them in turn.

My eyes were still on the lone figure in the corner.

'In the corner by the window is our father and creator—Lucius.'

Lucius still made no effort to turn around.

'Perhaps we can offer you a seat?' Tiberius suggested politely, gesturing to a small two seater sofa in front of several armchairs. The furniture looked strange sitting in the centre of such a large room. 'We have much to discuss, as I'm sure you can imagine.'

I shook my head, taking several steps backwards and leaning up against a wall. At least that was one angle of approach I had covered. 'I'd much rather stand, thank you.'

Tiberius inclined his head. 'As you wish.'

He took a seat, as did the other three vampires. Sebastian wandered over to the love seat, lowering himself against the cushioning and throwing his legs over the arm. Everyone looked relaxed except for me and the elder vampire in the corner.

'Elena,' Tiberius started, 'that's an interesting name that you have.'

'Not especially.'

'Who chose it for you?'

It seemed like a stupid question, so I frowned. 'My parents.'

'Who are your parents?'

I looked to Sebastian for guidance. He simply shrugged, so the ball was obviously in my court.

'My parents are Protectors.'

'That's not possible.'

'I'm adopted.'

'And they named you Elena?'

Sheesh, kind of belabouring the point here.

'I was named after my birth mother.'

A brief flicker of emotion crossed Tiberius's face. I might not have noticed it if it wasn't for the sudden downturn of his lips. 'Where is your mother now?'

My eyes narrowed as the others leaned forward, awaiting my answer. 'Why do you want to know?'

'Curiosity.'

'She's dead,' I answered flatly.

'How did that happen?'

'Look, what's with all the questions?'

'We're trying to understand you, Elena.'

'Liar. You want something from me, so why don't you tell me why I'm here?' I looked at Lucius as I spoke. His back stiffened ever so slightly, almost as if my words had blown a gentle breeze down his spine.

'Tell her,' one of the other vampires muttered. 'Tell her so she understands.'

'Tell me what?'

Sweat trickled down my back where I was touching the wall. The rest of me was bitterly cold.

'We knew your mother.'

'How?'

'She was a welcome guest here.'

'She was human?'

'Indeed.'

I screwed my face up. 'You fed from her?'

'No.' The word was resounding, definite.

'When did she die?' Decimus asked, his voice soft and understanding.

I hesitated. 'She died before giving birth to me.'

Tiberius showed no reaction to my comment, but Lucius half-turned, lips pressed into a hard line. The skin around the corners of his eyes wrinkled slightly as he narrowed them in what I perceived to be confusion. He cleared his throat as if to speak but then suddenly changed his mind, crossing his arms tightly and staring off into the garden again. Perhaps he'd picked up on the fact that I said she'd died before giving birth to me. I'd thrown up twice when George had first told me I'd clawed my way out of her womb.

Tiberius continued. 'And your father ... do you know anything about him?'

'He's a vampire.'

'How can you be sure?'

I looked Tiberius square in the eyes. 'I think we both know I'm not entirely human.' They would have smelt it the minute I set foot in the door, so there was no point denying the obvious. I wondered if they sensed the Vânător in me as easily as Sebastian had.

'Do you know who he is?'

'Okay, this is going to sound really rude, but I can't help it. I'm just going to come right out and say it anyway. Just because I know your name, and you know mine, that doesn't mean that we're friends now. I'm not going to keep answering your questions when I have no idea who any of you are or why I'm here.'

I pointed at Lucius's back. 'And you … you're kind of freaking me out just standing there in the corner like some weird-ass statue. Someone needs to start talking soon or I'm out of here.'

Sebastian started to laugh. 'She's great. Have you ever met someone so wonderfully blunt?'

My finger turned on Sebastian. 'Don't mock me. I'm surrounded by six vampires in a house in the middle of nowhere, trying to figure out what the hell is going on. You need to shut up if you aren't going to help the situation, because as far as I'm concerned, you're equally as weird as he is.' I pointed to Lucius again.

'You're the one who dreamed about us,' Sebastian taunted.

'I'm probably still dreaming.'

'You're not.'

'Says you.'

'Sebastian,' Tiberius warned. 'Don't push her. You don't know what she's capable of.'

Sebastian was still amused. 'I have a fair idea.'

Tiberius shook his head. 'Forgive my son, Elena, as he often forgets his manners.'

'You're apologising to me? I'm the one being rude and I'm real sorry about that, but I'm totally confused. Please, just tell me what I'm doing here, how you found me, and what the hell you want with me.'

My hands were balled into fists at my sides, and all my fear had evaporated. I wasn't exactly angry, but I was getting extremely irritated by all the personal questions. It would be nice to get a straight answer for once.

'You are here because—'

'Pardon me, but no, not you,' I said, shaking my head at Tiberius. 'I want Lucius to turn around and talk to me. I want to know why Sebastian was sent after me.'

The energy levels in the room surged once more and breathing suddenly became difficult. Great—I'd pissed off the Master Vampire.

Well, at least I was consistent.

I held my ground, knees slightly bent, and hands ready for combat. I doubted I'd have much of a chance to protect myself if Lucius truly wanted to kill me, but I'd kick myself in the afterlife if I hadn't at least tried.

I concentrated on the air, taking shallow breaths, conserving the moist hint of life in my lungs. I tried to slow my heart, pretending that the sudden flare of heat was my imagination and not a direct result of Lucius's growing temper.

He turned slowly, perfectly sculpted features finally illuminated by the overhead lighting. My breathing ceased altogether; fingers were twitching and my heart slowed to a stop. I wasn't scared—at least, I didn't think I was. I was simply caught in the moment, a heartbeat in time.

'Do not fear me, Elena,' Lucius murmured, approaching me slowly.

Time started moving again. 'Is that what you tell everyone before you kill them?'

Smooth. Just keep on reminding him about your mortality.

'Elena, I would never hurt you.'

'I've heard that before.'

'It pains me to think you are familiar with any form of treachery.'

I shrugged, feigning a nonchalance I didn't feel. 'It's—'

'Human?' Lucius finished for me.

'Yes.'

He nodded, a sad smile touching his lips. 'I am not human anymore.'

'Everyone lies.'

'Such cynicism.'

'No, it's just the truth.'

Lucius took another few steps closer but remained far enough away that I wouldn't hit panic stations. I was not in the mood for another vampire pushing my personal boundaries. Regardless, the world around me was shrinking; Lucius kept getting bigger, though his imposing figure completely filling my vision. His were eyes so intense that I couldn't look away.

'Don't think with your head,' Lucius said, drawing closer yet. 'Listen to your heart and feel the truth in my words.'

I gasped, as in a flurry of moving flesh he was suddenly right in front of me. So much for considered movements and boundaries.

'Can you feel that?' Lucius said to me. 'Can you feel the tether of energy between us growing?'

I could feel it alright, and I was surprised my hair wasn't standing on end. 'What are you doing to me?' I took a gasping breath, sliding along the wall, and feeling for the door.

'It's normal, Elena. Don't be afraid—embrace it, and everything will become clear.'

'Embrace what? What the hell is it? Your compulsion? Turn it off, I can't breathe properly.'

Lucius was suddenly touching me, cold hands gripping my shoulders. Slowly, they slid down my arm, groping for my hands. I jerked, and instinctively reaching for a knife that wasn't there.

Damn it!

As Lucius's fingers gripped mine and as our skin touched, I screamed. I felt my eyes rolling back in my head, pain spreading throughout my body like wildfire. Someone had split my skull open, put their hand inside of me and squeezed. Thousands and thousands of images flitted through my mind, and in my mind's eye I saw things that weren't possible, that made no sense. They mingled with my own memories of the past, filling a void inside that I never knew I'd had.

A life flashed before my eyes. It was not my own, or at least, I didn't think it belonged to me. Maria was chasing me around the fountain as a toddler, trying to dress me for a special occasion. Suddenly, I was crying as I fell off my push bike, only to be rewarded by Lucius who presented me with an ice-cream cone. Next, he was teaching me how to swim. After that, I was witnessing my first steps and every growing moment in-between. I even saw myself as I was now, Lucius wrinkling his brows at me in frustration as he showed me how to drive. In this vision, I was bunny-hopping down the cobblestone driveway of the villa in an expensive Bentley Continental GTC.

One after another these images came to me, none of them

true, yet all of them seemingly substantial. I was fighting them, holding onto my own thoughts and memories as hard as I could. I may not have had the best of childhoods but it was still mine.

Lucius touched my face, pressing his forehead against mine, and as he did the pain dulled and the images disappeared. His fingers gripped me tightly, eyes finding mine as I slowly refocused on the present. I saw everything through his gaze, sorting truth from the assortment of lies.

I choked back a sob, breath catching in my throat as Lucius's thumbs stroked my wrists. He kept his forehead pressed against mine, eyes open, laid fully bare for me to see. Tears trickled down my cheeks but not from pain, from recognition.

Lucius was my father.

I watched, still in a daze, as one-by-one the other vampires left the room. Sebastian lingered the longest, finally closing the heavy wooden doors behind him as he left. The only ones remaining in the great hall were Lucius and I, but I was no longer afraid. I was curious, excited, angry, confused—every emotion but scared.

'Do you want to sit down?' Lucius said, gesturing to the loveseat Sebastian had just vacated.

I shook my head, keeping my back to the wall. I needed something solid, something real to hold onto.

Lucius smiled, finally letting my hands go and moving away. Relief swamped me, the air growing thin and my skin cooling. I could breathe again, tears moistening my trembling lips.

Lucius sat down on a nearby armchair, facing me. 'You do not trust me,' he stated, as if reading my mind.

'I don't know you.'

'Do you understand what just happened?'

I shook my head. 'Not really.'

'Yet you know who I am?'

I nodded this time, but couldn't quite bring myself to say the words out loud. 'What did you just do to me?' My head was still throbbing.

'I did nothing. It is normal for a vampiric father and their child to strengthen bonds in such a manner.'

'But what did you do? My head still hurts.'

'I forced you to see the life we would have had together if things had been different. That invisible cord that kept us bound together since birth was finally pulled taut and our two existences slammed together. We are forever bound now, you and I. I apologise if I hurt you, but we had a lot of catching up to do.'

'What does this bond *mean* exactly?'

'I will always have a sense of you. I will know if you are alive and well, or in pain.'

'Does that work both ways?'

'Yes, it does.' Lucius suddenly sighed, eyes filled with sadness. 'So much time we have missed out on, you and I. It pains me to think that I would never have found you, never even known of your existence if you hadn't started using your gifts.'

'My gifts?'

'You think as the Master of all Vampires I cannot sense what resides within you?'

'I don't really want to think about what you can or cannot sense within me.'

He smiled, a genuine smile. It made his whole face seem

gentler somehow. 'I know you are half-Vânător, Elena. I can take a guess at how that happened but the logistics are pointless. You exist, and that is all that is important to me.'

Lucius must have seen the look of disbelief on my face because he hurried on. 'I am also aware that a blood exchange has occurred and that you have partially awakened to some of your Vampiric traits. I set no judgement on this mishap. The blood awakened your bond, helping me to find you.'

'How *did* you find me?' I didn't want to talk about the exchange anymore, I didn't want to discuss William, and I didn't want Lucius uncovering my latest ability. Telekinesis might be a useful skill to keep hidden for the future.

Lucius took a deep, shuddering breath. 'I honestly don't know. I just felt your presence one night, saw you in a waking dream, and locked onto your life-force. You also came to me one other time. I never saw you, but I felt your presence. You called to me, and this is why I sent Sebastian to you.'

He was talking about my dreams.

Great. I'm not crazy, just freaking weird.

'Why send Sebastian?'

'He sensed you, too. Sebastian swore that the two of you had a connection.'

I tried not to look too curious. 'A connection?'

He shook his head. 'I do not understand it myself. There should be no ties between the two of you.' Lucius almost seemed angry as he went on. 'I am forced yet again to reconsider Sebastian's makings. He has been impossible to decipher.'

Random. But, still, I thought it best not to mention that I had been dreaming about Sebastian long before William. 'So the bond between *us* is normal?'

'Yes, but usually only once you become Vampire. I have

no idea how you projected your power over such great distances while still technically human.' His eyes bore into mine. 'Do you have an idea how you did it?'

I shrugged. 'I thought I was dreaming.'

Lucius sat forward in his chair. 'Dreaming? You slept as you came to us?'

'Well, the first time I was unconscious, but yeah.'

Lucius sniffed, angry and amused all at the same time. Lucius looked up, eyes surveying the ceiling. 'You're interfering,' he muttered, but not to me—Lucius seemed to be talking to himself or perhaps some invisible entity. 'Why bring us together, I wonder? What do you have to gain?'

'Are you talking to me?' I said, tapping my chest.

Lucius looked back at me, head cocked to the side. 'I speak to no one in particular, though apparently someone is always listening.' He was definitely smiling up at the ceiling.

'Okay.'

I wasn't quite sure where to go from there. I talked to myself too from time to time, but I usually didn't verbalise in front of company. They'd have thought I was a crazy person if I had. I decided a change of subject would be good. 'So, if I were a full vampire, would you have tapped the bond then?'

'Of course. I had always hoped that you existed, but I never really knew for sure until I felt your power reach out to me.'

My eyes narrowed. 'How could you not know I existed? You made my mother pregnant, so you'd have known that the second you slept with her.'

'It is true,' Lucius said quietly. 'I knew a child would result from our union.'

'So what happened? Why was my mother alone when she died?'

'She found out what I was.'

Tired of standing, I sunk down to the floor; I still kept the wall up against my back, though. 'My mother didn't know you were a vampire.'

'No, she did not.'

'She ran.' I didn't pose it as a question; it was kind of a foregone conclusion, as I knew my mother had ended up on Corsica—no family, no past, with only the clothes on her back. Lucius's face showed regret, showed sadness, so even after all these years he must have mourned her absence.

Lucius sighed wistfully. 'Your mother was a breath of fresh air in my otherwise damnable existence. I miss her every day. Finding out now that she is dead, even after all this time, saddens me all over again. She'd awakened the humanity that lay caged inside of me, a humanity that I thought dead for the longest time. If I can say one thing about your mother, it was that she made me want to be a better person, to change the direction my eternal life was heading in. Your mother made me want to find ways to remember that I was once a man, with morals, hopes, dreams, and above all else ... a soul.'

'You don't think you have a soul?'

He shook his head. 'I gave up my right to one a long time ago.'

'By becoming a vampire?' I snorted. 'I don't think so. Just because you're labelled a vampire, doesn't mean you are evil.'

'I did not say I was evil. I said I have no soul.'

'How couldn't you?'

'I don't know if I could stand to see the look on your face if you knew what I had condemned you to. And I say *you* because you are my daughter—your fate is aligned with mine. You will become an immortal, a member of the damned. If you really knew what ran through my blood and through your blood, what I passed down to you, you would despise me.'

'We don't know each other well enough yet for me to feel such strong emotions.'

'Whatever emotion you do feel for me, I don't wish to be tainted by the truths of my past.'

'I can't imagine feeling anything.'

Lucius looked perplexed. 'But I am your father.'

'Just words, Lucius. I don't know you and you don't know me. I'm having trouble digesting the whole father-daughter thing, and it's already been a rough couple of months. You need to give me time.'

Lucius gave me a short, sharp nod. Although he seemed to understand, he still looked hurt. His eyes drooped.

'So tell me about the soul thing,' I said, changing the subject. I didn't expect Lucius to answer, especially since I had just brushed him neatly aside, but awkward silences just weren't my thing. 'Why don't you think you have one?'

'I don't think, I know. I made a deal with Lucifer.'

'Whoa. As in *Lucifer* … the *Devil*?'

'Yes.'

I started to laugh, but stopped abruptly when I saw the look of deadly seriousness on his face. 'You're not shitting me, are you?'

'No.'

I sobered. 'Why would you make a deal with the Devil? I don't want to rub your face in it or anything, but that seems really freaking stupid. Granted, I've never met the Devil before, but even the movies make those bargains seem like a really bad idea.'

He grimaced. 'In hindsight, it was.'

'Why would you do it? What did you stand to gain?'

Lucius's face hardened. 'Revenge.'

'Revenge? What could possibly have happened to make you exchange your mortal soul to become a vampire?'

'… my pregnant wife and son were murdered.'

'Oh.'

I bit down hard on my tongue. I really didn't have anything else to add. I hadn't meant to say anything so hurtful.

I pulled my legs up to my chest and wrapped my arms around my knees, resting my chin on them I wondered what you could say to someone who had lost everything.

'Selena and Lucius were taken from me just before the first millennia, around 5 BC,' Lucius continued, though I hadn't expected him to; I almost stopped him. He didn't owe me any explanations, but there was a look on his face that gave me pause.

'I was a General with the Roman army, serving under the emperor Augustus. My position also allowed a place among the Senate, whose meetings took me regularly away from my family. One weekend, I travelled to Rome for such a meeting. I was gone for a few days, never thinking that my family would be in any kind of danger.'

Lucius looked down at the ground, hands clenched in his lap. 'Thieves came to the villa. They ransacked the entire house and stole multiple ancient items of great value. As I returned, I saw the destruction. I called out to my wife, for Lucius. I kept pushing forward through the silence of the empty rooms, hoping and praying for their safety.' He closed his eyes, took a deep breath, and opened them again. 'I found Selena first. She was lying naked on our son's bed, streaked in blood, with her throat slashed. She had been brutalized by many men, scored both inside and out with knives. Even after all my time on the battlefield, I had never seen such depravity.'

I almost reached out to him then—almost. What stopped me was the fact that we were still mostly strangers, and if the situation was reversed, his comfort would have felt foreign and awkward. Nothing I could say could have eased his pain, anyway.

'And then I saw Lucius,' he whispered shakily. 'He was floating face down in the bath tub, skin like ice, lips blue. He was dead, and there was absolutely nothing I could do about it. The pain of that knowledge was excruciating. I felt like I would never be able to breathe again ... I just wanted it all to end.' Lucius looked up at me then. Trails of blood were streaked down his cheeks, staining the collar of his navy shirt. I had never seen a vampire cry before, and it wasn't pretty; then again, neither was his story.

He wiped at his face with the sleeves of his shirt. 'I took the knife from its sheath at my belt,' Lucius continued, determined to finish. 'I stabbed myself in the heart, hopeful that ending my life would kill off the pain of my loss. All I wanted was to be with my family again in the afterlife.' His voice had lowered to a whisper.

Jesus.

'I remember waiting to die, waiting to see the face of my wife and child again, hoping that the pain would disappear and give me peace.' Lucius shook his head. 'It didn't.' His eyes settled on me, expectant.

'Why are you telling me this?'

'You asked why I had no soul.' His breath was a little ragged, the words tearing with emotion.

'I did but I never expected you to tell me why. I wouldn't have. I would have told you to mind your own business.'

'You are my daughter. I do not want there to be secrets between us.'

'That's your choice.'

Lucius smiled at me sadly, mopping up the last of the blood on his face. 'Indeed, it is.'

I worried my bottom lip, chewing at the fragile skin as I thought about the paths that we choose in life. Would my birth as a vampire never occurred if Lucius had accepted the death of his family? Would I have been able to accept such death if it had been Lucas who had died? I didn't think so. I would want revenge, too. That was something we had in common but, again, I kept my mouth shut.

'Speak what is on your mind,' Lucius said to me, eyes rimmed in red.

'It's invasive. You've already told me more than I imagined.'

He smiled just a little. 'I gave you the answers that you seek. Does this not please you?'

'I don't think 'please' is quite the right word.'

'You wish to know why I traded my soul.'

I shook my head. 'No, I get it, believe me. What happened to you …' I took a deep, shuddering breath, unsure how to finish. I hoped the sympathy and understanding I felt was amply reflected in my eyes and not misread as pity. 'I guess I want to know how it happened. To make a deal with the Devil I'm assuming you went to hell. Why? From your story, you seemed like a decent enough man.'

'I was a suicide,' he stated. 'Despite a brief stay in purgatory, it automatically gifted me with a one way ticket to hell.'

'Purgatory?'

'A realm of judgement. A council of four decides your fate. Two are demons—spawn of Lucifer. Two are angels—children of God. Rules are followed, a vote is made.'

'God's real, too? Shit. And shiny, golden angels?'

I was swearing a lot today. Lots of surprises, though, so I had a good excuse.

'Vampires and werewolves exist. What makes you think the existence of angels and demons would be any less real?'

'I don't know. I've never considered the possibility.'

My lower lip was starting to hurt from where my teeth were painfully gripping at the flesh. Other thoughts were starting to worry me.

'What is wrong?'

Jeez, he's intuitive.

'Nothing.'

'I sense the lie. You still wish to ask me something.'

What *didn't* I want to ask him? 'You said I would despise you. Why would you say that? What has your revenge cost me?'

'The afterlife.'

'I'll be immortal.'

Lucius gave me a patient look. 'When you do finally die, Elena, heaven lies not in wait for you.'

'I won't commit suicide.'

Lucius flinched. I'd obviously touched a raw nerve.

Crap. 'I'm sorry. I didn't mean it like that.'

'You have nothing to apologise for. I'm the one who seeks forgiveness for what I have done. Because of me, you and every other vampire, born or turned from my blood, will be judged unfavourably and sent straight to hell.'

'I don't believe that. There has to be a way to change that outcome.'

Lucius shook his head, features grim. 'You are the spawn of Satan.'

I frowned. 'Ease up. No need for name calling.'

'It is simply the truth.'

'And I asked for it, did I?'

'In a manner of speaking.'

Silence fell. I stretched out my legs on the floor in front of me, crossing one over the other, and began picking at my fingernails. I couldn't raise my eyes to his; right now, I was feeling all kinds of screwed up.

A long time ago I had accepted that I had no mother. I even came to accept that my father probably didn't want me. At twelve, I digested the news I was going to become a blood sucker one day, and at sixteen, I learnt I was half-Vânător. Now I *knew* someone had to be shitting on me because I'd just been told I was going to hell, too? I was eternally damned.

How's that for unfair?

'Tell me something,' I said, still picking at my cuticles, 'was it worth it? Did revenge satisfy you?' I thought there'd be bitterness in my voice, but more than anything, I just felt sorry for him.

'I can never get back what I have lost.' There was a wistful edge to Lucius's voice that made me look up. His eyes were filled with blood again. 'Revenge was swift, but so was my bloodlust. Lucifer bargained for my soul to make me a monster, and I quickly found that the more of the thieves and their families I hunted down and killed, the more of my lingering humanity was lost. Lucifer had known this would happen, had known that I would become a plague of death, drinking the blood of innocents and tainting all that was good on this Earth.'

'And now?'

'Now my disease has spread, through no fault but my own. I created more of my kind to help me murder those who'd killed my family. I called them my 'thralls'. Some were obedient, some were not. I had never thought that they could replicate the process of exchanging blood themselves, that they could mate with humans, that they could have their own vampiric offspring. My grief and rage had ruined everything.'

'So now you try to police what you started?'

He sighed. 'I try, but vampirism is an epidemic, which has lead to the creation of the Vânãtors. I do not know when it will end.'

'It won't.'

Lucius's eyes searched my face. 'You seem so sure.'

'Why wouldn't you want to be a vampire? Speed, agility, strength, immortality—the only downside is having to drink all the damned blood, but Synth Blood seems to satisfy those needs now. If you pay attention to tabloids and television, vampirism looks trendy.'

Lucius snorted with disgust. 'People are fools.'

'There are no exceptions to that,' I said, looking him dead in the eyes.

'And what of the afterlife? Does vampirism compensate for spending an eternity in hell?'

It was my turn to sigh. 'No, it doesn't, not by a long shot.'

'You are calmer about this than I'd imagined.'

'Do you want me to be bitter and violent? Do you want me to blame you?'

'Of course not.'

'It would be easy to blame you for all my misfortune, you know, but I can't. I can understand your reasons, even relate to them.'

'But now that you know the fate that awaits you ...' His voice trailed off.

'You're referring to an eternity in hell?'

'Yes.'

'I'll have to cross that bridge when I get to it.'

'It's an inescapable fate, Elena. No bridge will help you cross it.'

I scoffed. 'Fate is a ridiculous notion.'

'Do not be so sure. The powers that be are a force to be reckoned with. I may be the Master of all Vampires, but even I do not choose my fate.'

I shook my head. 'But you did choose your fate, if that's what you want to call it. Every decision you have made has led you to this point. I fully intend to be the one that dictates the course along which my life runs.' I laughed nervously. 'So far, I haven't done a really good job of it, but since you seem to believe that we're royally screwed anyway, I might as well enjoy the ride.'

'So cavalier, my daughter?'

I shook my head again. 'No, not cavalier. I'm simply making the best of a bad situation. Wallowing will get me nowhere.'

'I wish that were true.'

I shrugged, wondering if I believed my own words. 'Got any better ideas?'

CHAPTER EIGHTEEN: BEGINNINGS

stared up at the intricately carved and gilded ceiling, familiarising myself with its every shape and pattern. Though the plasterwork was cracked in many places, and had broken and crumbled away completely in others, it was still beautiful. I'd been staring at it for several hours now, my hands clasped loosely behind my head, folded legs resting on silken sheets. Lucius had insisted I rest in 'my bedroom', but I was too anxious to close my eyes.

I kept thinking, worrying, that the door would open and one of the other vampires of the household would 'visit' me against Lucius's wishes. So far I'd been left alone but that didn't mean I felt safe sleeping there. I was tired, though, and the mattress was so soft beneath me. There was also the temptation of falling asleep in silken sheets.

Not succumbing was *difficult*.

The house, sorry, villa was so quiet it was eerie. I'd run through every pun in my head about the dead and silence, but not one had brought a smile to my face. It was just too weird to imagine I was the only one with a beating heart in a house full of people. It also didn't help that the puns were accurate—they were *all* dead.

I hadn't really thought about looking for my father before. Lucius had made it very clear that he wanted me as a part of his life, and I couldn't say that it didn't make me curious, particularly after that little rolling film that supposedly strengthened the bond between us. But I didn't know Lucius. We'd only just met, and it was hard to toss aside the need for caution force-fed to me by The Protectors. So the jury was still out on whether I would stay here and get to know him.

I rolled over in the comfy bed and looked past the glass doors, and out onto the small Juliet balcony. The curtains were pulled back, secured with fringed, gold tassels that hooked over some small brass screws up in the wall. I should have closed them. As it was, by watching the French doors my back was now to the bedroom door. Could I rely on just my hearing, hoping that no one would sneak up on me? Merely wishful thinking.

I rolled onto my back again and hoped that the chilly autumn breeze would keep me awake.

Danger does not cease simply because we desire it.

My old teacher from the IMI was so very right about *that*.

I yawned loudly, my eyes slowly shutting. My head began to nod. A second later I jolted awake, my eyes springing open again to check both doors. Satisfied, I looked back up at the ceiling, watching as the intricate patterns started to blur together, the details smudging, my vision eventually going black.

I don't remember what happened next, but when my eyes flew open again the room was filled with dappled sunlight. The rays of the noon day sun danced across the floor as light delicately pierced through the pine leaves of the enormous trees outside.

Crap. I fell asleep!

I sat bolt upright in bed, my eyes lingering over every inch of the room, praying there'd been no unwanted guests. The armoire I'd dragged in front of the bedroom door was still secure, despite the supposed futility of that action against a house full of vampires. Still, I felt stupid and vulnerable—how could I have let myself fall asleep?

Through the balcony door I could see the leaves of the trees lolling gently from side to side in the afternoon breeze. The sky was set in a magnificent blue with wispy white clouds high above that clumped together unevenly, drifting leisurely across the landscape. Everything about this place screamed fairy tale, but my instincts screamed: *Watch your back.*

I kicked back the covers—someone had pulled them up to my chin. I shuddered at the creepiness of being tucked in by some unknown vampire. I may have instinctively rugged up against the chill in my sleep, a more preferable thought, as I earnestly studied my makeshift barricade and scrambled to my feet. The terracotta was cold underfoot, and so was I thanks to the open doors. I still wore the jacket and dress shirt from Nicholas's, though my hooker-heels had also been mysteriously removed.

Definitely creepy.

My stomach started to gurgle. Inconvenient, but not overly surprising considering I'd consumed very little in the past two weeks. And, given that it had almost been dawn when Lucius and I had parted ways the night before, I'd bypassed the idea of a meal in lieu of solace. Hopefully now I'd find food here somewhere.

I padded quickly over to the armoire, and with little effort, dragged it back to its original location. I threw it open, looking for something fresher to wear, and saw that when Sebastian had said it was fully stocked he hadn't been kidding. I leafed quickly through the clothes, settling on the trusty combination of a pair of jeans, t-shirt and jacket. The t-shirt and jacket were a good fit but the jeans were a little big.

Whatever.

I slipped on some silver sandals I'd found in the bottom drawer before heading over to the basin in the corner of the room. It felt good to splash my face a bit and gargle a little water for my dry throat. My hair was nothing short of disastrous but I didn't really care. I was too hungry, too tired, and too weirded out to sweat the small stuff.

I wiped my hands dry on a small towel and headed for the door. Before opening, I pressed my ear against the timber and listened. Then I stood on my tippy toes to peer through the wrought iron insert. There was no one in the corridor that I could see or hear.

I slowly turned the door knob, opening the door inch by inch and peering out into the corridor beyond. Still no one.

I stepped out and closed the door behind me, treading cautiously down the passage until I got to the winding staircase. After a moment's hesitation, I headed down, marvelling again at the courtyard that opened up in front of me.

I could hear singing now. The voice sounded pretty bad but at least it was familiar—it belonged to Maria, the human housekeeper. She was holding a broom, sweeping the floor between the entry and the courtyard, and smiling warmly up at me as I descended. 'Ciao, Bella,' she sang, sort of. 'You a sleepyhead today, no?'

'I didn't mean to sleep,' I protested, shutting my mouth when I realised Maria might not understand my apprehension.

She frowned. 'What is wrong to sleep? Is bed not comfortable?'

'No, the bed was too comfortable,' I muttered.

She patted me on the arm. 'You finished in your bedroom now? Can I clean?'

'It's not my bedroom.'

Maria made a funny sort of scoffing sound in her throat. 'Is your bedroom! Signor Lucius, he say this to me, and I make bed especially. So, room is yours, *si?*'

I shrugged. No point arguing with her about it. I was about to ask Maria where I could get some food around here when my stomach did it for me. It rumbled at an embarrassingly loud pitch.

'*Cara mia!*' Maria groaned, throwing her chubby hands in the air. 'They do not feed you here. Come, Bella, I make you food. I am a good cook.'

'It's *Elena,*' I said, following behind her.

'*Scusi?*' she said, spinning around.

'My name is Elena, not Bella.'

Maria started laughing. 'Bella is to mean 'beautiful' in my language. I use this for you for nickname, no?'

I felt myself shrugging again. She patted my cheek warmly and turned, expecting that I would follow. I did.

Maria walked quite quickly past the fountain, past two doors on the right, and then stopped at a small wooden door that must have lead to the kitchen. As she threw back the door, she immediately started shaking her head, I couldn't see what had caused her so much displeasure; I was just happy that there *was* a kitchen.

'House so big,' she muttered under her breath, 'kitchen so small.' Maria muttered a few more things after that, but it was all in Italian.

I pulled out one of the timber stools that sat up against the big oak table in the centre of the room. This seemed to be the only food preparation area. The benches off to the side were cluttered with empty glass bottles that were covered in a film of dust. Between the cluttered worktops were old fashioned whitegoods that looked like they'd seen better days. Tucked into the corner were a small refrigerator and a deep porcelain sink that was set into a side bench. An old pot belly stove sat next to the wall in the other corner, and above the oak table hung copper pots, dangling from various shaped hooks.

Maria took a packet of matches from her apron and lit the little furnace that was under the stove. As flames sprang to life inside, she closed the little door at the front with a *click*. Then Maria rummaged around under the oak table, looking for ingredients while I sat watching.

'You like pizza? *Sì* or no?'

I nodded. I was thinking that I'd eat just about anything at this point, even one of Susan's pot-roasts. Salmonella? Who gives a shit when you're starving?

Maria's head ducked under the table again. A second later she was cursing loudly as she pulled a dead rat out by its tail and tossed it with an expert flick into the trash bin in the corner. I was mildly repulsed, even feeling my lips curl into a grimace. I soon stopped, though, realising I was so hungry I probably would have eaten that rat if Maria wasn't whipping up pizza.

Sick.

After washing her hands thoroughly, Maria started mixing together the dough on the table in front of her, kneading the ingredients together and punishing them with her thick knuckles.

'Where is everybody?' I finally asked, wanting to settle my nerves.

'They is out,' Maria answered. 'The men in this house, they not go out much in the day unless to work. They all night owls. Is how you say, *sì*?'

'Yes, night owls,' I repeated and then paused. 'Wait, did you say they go to work?'

'*Sì*. Must make money to pay me, no?'

I cracked a smile, mostly because I was trying to picture vampires with day jobs.

'Signor Lucius and the others go to Roma for the day. They come back tonight, I say. It is hard work to run such a busy company.'

'Company?'

'Synth Corp.'

'Lucius owns Synth Corp?' I asked, the tone of my voice rising in disbelief.

'*Sì*.'

'Well I'll be damned.' I laughed at that, realising I probably would be. My respect for Lucius had jumped up another notch, from '*you make me nervous and uncomfortable*' to '*maybe you aren't so bad after all*'. If he owned Synth Corp, then he'd been helping not just the medical sectors but was also supplying the neutral bars with their tetra packs of blood. So he had partly made up for being damned by giving bloodthirsty vampires an alternative to snacking on humans. His philanthropy was admirable.

'You know Synth Corp?' Maria asked, still working at the dough.

'You could say that. My family has been regular purchasers of their goods for years.'

'Your family? *This* your family, Bella.' She gestured to the area around her, hands covered in flour. I was assuming she meant the household of vampires and not the kitchen utensils.

I shrugged, not really sure how to answer that, so I decided to change the subject. 'Does everyone in the house work for Synth Corp?'

Maria nodded but then sighed dramatically. 'I remember now. Signor Sebastian does not.'

'What does he do?'

It was her turn to shrug. 'That boy, he is a mystery. No one ever know where he is or what he does with time. He disappear for hours on that crazy moto. One day he go kaput, I tell you!'

I stifled a laugh.

Hard to accomplish since he's already dead.

'I know that they is all dead and gone for many years, but I still say that crazy driving will be end of them!'

So she knows she works for vampires. And continues to work here.

Maria punched at the dough in front of her, flattening it out into a small rounded base. 'I not stupid,' she continued, seeing the shocked expression on my face. 'I know they is creature of the night, but they pay me good so I shut my mouth.'

Must be bloody good.

'You not need to worry,' Maria said, looking at me with her beady brown eyes. 'No one here will bite you. Signor Lucius say you are very special and I am to give you anything you need. So first I feed your noisy body and then you do as you please. I will arrange for you. *Sì* or no?'

'*Sì.*'

'*Brava.* Now what you like on pizza?'

'I don't care as long as there are no cucumbers.'

Maria's brow wrinkled ever so slightly in confusion and then she started throwing bits of ingredients over the dough. When she was done, Maria slid the dough onto a copper tray and then carefully placed it into the pot belly stove, closing the door after.

In as little as twenty minutes, the pizza was done. I scoffed it down so quickly that I could barely taste it. I also ended up burning the roof of my mouth but the pain, as always, was short-lived.

'I make you more?' Maria said, grabbing the empty tray from in front of me.

I shook my head, swallowing the last mouthful of pizza. 'No, thank you.'

She looked at me with pursed lips. 'You very skinny. I make you cake instead? That should fatten you.'

I smiled tightly, aware of my current bony figure. 'No, please, I'm honestly fine now. The pizza was just enough food.'

'*Va bene,*' Maria said, unconvinced, but she didn't push the issue. She threw the copper plate into the sink and began cleaning down the tabletop.

I stood up from the stool and pushed it back under the table. I thanked Maria again for the food and then left her to bustle around in the tiny kitchen. While I was alone, I might as well take the opportunity to have a look around. Upstairs I would leave well enough alone, especially now that I knew why Lucius Junior's room was off limits. And I did not need to see what lurked behind the closed doors of those other upstairs bedrooms.

I had already seen the great hall and kitchen, so I moved to the next door along. I knocked first, mostly out of habit, then pushed through and entered the room. This room had the same overly-generous proportions as my bedroom upstairs. The roof and walls were similarly gilded and adorned with painted murals. In the centre of the room was a pool table, the coloured balls stacked neatly in the confines of the triangle and ready for the next break. Behind me, and off to the side, was a high tech hi-fi system with what looked like a multiple-stack CD player.

For curiosity's sake, I wandered over to the CD player and pressed 'Play'. The first track echoed through the room, a melodic song of love and loss sung by an operatic tenor who pierced the silence with a bittersweet sadness.

I shifted along to the next CD. This time the music sounded almost tribal. My ears were soothed by rhythmic drum beats, the sound of pan flutes and voices chanting. I wasn't a fan.

The next CD came up as *Barbara Streisand in Concert*—also not a fan—but clearly someone else was because the CD after that was also Barbara Streisand.

I skipped to the last CD in the stacker. This was quite obviously heavy metal—electric guitars ripped through incomprehensible riffs, the sound of both deep and screaming voices bellowing unintelligible words through a jungle of noise. I switched it off immediately and then checked my ears for bleeding.

I left the room after that, gently closing the timber door behind me. I could hear Maria's voice from somewhere upstairs. She was singing again, her voice gravelly and strained. I would have done anything to get away from that sound, so I moved past the entryway and down to the other section of the house.

I picked a door at random and knocked. As expected, no one answered, and I walked inside. There was nothing else in the room except for a couple of plush armchairs and a grand piano that was sitting near a large, centralised window. The walls of this room were painted with one long mural, even the ceiling. Careful brushstrokes mapped out brightly coloured vineyards, ripened grapes in the foreground hanging from vines that looked so realistic they were tempting enough to taste. Lush, rolling hills kissed the horizon as the golden glow of the sunlight above spread warmth across the green valleys lying below. The painting was absolutely breathtaking, a sight to behold, and seemingly too intricate to replicate.

I wandered over to the piano, running my fingers lightly over the tops of the ivory keys. I pressed down on one gently, and a bright, vibrant tone echoed around the room. Sliding down onto the bench, I started to randomly push keys. Before I knew it, I was playing *Chopsticks*, the only song I knew how to play. This was mainly because I only needed two fingers to play it. Lame, I know.

A slow clap erupted from the door behind me. I bolted upright, my fingers automatically grasping for a blade I still had not replaced. I had to get on that.

It seemed I had an unexpected audience.

I watched as Sebastian entered the room, a motorbike helmet under one arm, his hands clapping more vigorously now. 'Brilliant, absolutely brilliant. You put Chopin to shame.'

I relaxed, feeling no danger in Sebastian's presence. 'Then Chopin must have been a terrible piano player.'

Sebastian set the helmet on a chair by the door, smiling as he removed his black leather riding gloves and added them to the pile. I noted that Sebastian was also wearing a leather jacket and pants, tight clothing that clearly emphasised every lean muscle.

'You've been out riding,' I stated, staring longingly at the motorbike helmet.

'What gave me away?' he teased, unzipping his jacket and shrugging out of it. Underneath, Sebastian wore a plain white shirt.

'Don't you risk a permanent sunburn riding out in full sunlight like that?'

Sebastian patted the top of the helmet. 'As long as my skin is fully covered, the sun can't hurt me.'

'Where have you been?'

'Missed me, did you?' Sebastian said, flashing me the hint

of a smile, as he dropped his jacket over the back of the chair.

I rolled my eyes. 'Hardly.'

He took a few steps into the room, stopping short of where the sunlight strayed through the open window and across the floor. Sebastian ran a hand through his hair, brushing out the long strands and smoothing them down. It made me think about the rat's nest currently on top of my head—I really should have brushed it out.

'So, what have you been doing besides practicing your magnum opus?' he asked, drawing nearer.

I glanced back at the piano. 'Not much. I'm having a little look around at the place.'

'And?'

'And, nothing. I've only been awake for an hour.'

'So you did finally fall asleep?' A stray lock of hair fell in front of Sebastian's eyes as he looked at me sideways.

I grimaced. 'Regrettably.'

Sebastian gestured to the piano. 'Do you play?' He shook his head. 'Actually, what I should have said was, can you play anything decent?'

I ignored the jibe. 'No. I never had the patience to learn a musical instrument.'

'Perhaps I could teach you,' he said, looking at me with his swirling gaze.

I snorted. 'You?'

'Do you doubt me?'

'I don't know you.'

A small smile touched Sebastian's lips. 'Shut the curtains, Baby Vamp. I'll show you just how talented I can be.'

I looked at him curiously, wondering if Sebastian was still referring to the piano, until he gestured for me to hurry up. I turned back towards the window and pulled the heavy velveteen curtains closed, plunging the room into darkness. 'Oh, damn it,' I murmured. I couldn't see more than a foot in front of my own face.

'Don't let the darkness scare you—embrace it.' I could feel Sebastian's voice as his breath blew across my lips. He must have been standing right in front of me, but I could barely make out his silhouette in the darkness.

'The darkness doesn't scare me. It's what's lurking within this particular bit of dark that does.'

Fingers lightly brushed across my cheek, a heartbeat of warm sensations flooding through me, and then Sebastian was gone. In the next instant I heard the piano bench scraping across the floor, knuckles cracking, and then a cascade of resonant notes were reaching out to me across the haunting dark. The melody's tempo was soft and deliberate, a beautifully played piece with complex key changes. My mood lifted as Sebastian rolled without pausing into a jazz piece, and then into a jaunty old Sinatra song that I enjoyed immensely. And for the climax? He finished by poking fun at my lack of skill, playing my earlier piece of *Chopsticks* more proficient than I had.

Then silence. Almost instantly I could feel Sebastian's cool, sweet breath blowing gently against my skin. How easy it would be to lean forward and touch him.

'You play very well, Sebastian, considering it's darker than night in here,' I said politely.

'Do you want to see what else I can do in the dark?' he murmured, his deft fingers finding me again, trailing across my lips.

I shivered, skin afire. I pulled back, grabbing at the material of the curtain behind me and yanking it to open, to reveal a small sliver of bright afternoon sunlight streaming through the window. Painful? Possibly but potentially life threatening? Not likely.

Sebastian hissed, leaping backwards and into the safety of the shadows again. 'That was an overreaction,' he snarled, landing lithely on his feet.

I checked him out. His skin looked fine, so he was obviously over-reacting. 'I'm not used to being touched without invitation.'

'Is *that* an invitation?'

'No, it's a warning. Don't ever do that again.'

Sebastian shook his head, hair falling neatly in front of his eyes. His lips twisted into a grimace, all humour quickly vanishing from his face. 'Why make things so difficult?'

I frowned and made my way over to the door. How do you answer such an ambiguous question?

Sebastian grabbed my arm as I moved past, pulling me to a halt. 'Tell me something,' he said, breathing across my neck as he talked, 'does the touch of my hand evoke any kind of reaction inside of you?'

'Should it?'

His grip tightened. 'Is there anything familiar about me at all?'

'What are you talking about?'

I turned my head a little bit more, eyes finally meeting his. They were completely grey.

Sebastian released my arm, bowed ever so slightly, and distanced himself from me. He forced a smile. 'Forgive me, then. The rules must have changed.'

'Sebastian, what are—?'

He was gone.

I stepped into the courtyard, eyes combing across the expanse for him. Nope, Sebastian was definitely gone.

Figures.

I spent the rest of the afternoon in the Library, curtains opened as wide as they would go. Sunlight filled the room with warmth, easing some of the remaining tension I still felt at living in a house surrounded by vampires.

While searching for the Library, I'd also discovered a comfortable living area housing the largest collection of DVDs I'd ever seen. There was also a huge, lovely looking LCD television mounted on the wall.

Despite the appeal of a few hours of distracting television viewing, the books in the Library were what had stolen my attention. There were literally thousands and thousands of coloured spines staring down at me from a wall of tall shelves, all packed to the brim. The books that currently piqued my interest were religious texts about the mythology surrounding angels and demons, Heaven and Hell. Ever since Lucius had more or less confirmed their existence for me, I'd been curious about their roles and actions here on Earth.

I was right in the middle of reading about Lucifer's fall from grace and the Archangel Michael's hand in his downfall, when I heard the library door open. I folded the corner of the current page to mark my place.

'Elena,' my new father said, appearing just inside the doorway, 'may I come in?'

'It's your house.'

Lucius's smile was tight, shoulders tense as he slowly strode into the room. I felt safer in my armchair, surrounded by a halo of sunlight. He walked through those beams regardless, the afternoon sun touching his skin in a gentle caress—his skin was pale yet unblemished from the exposure.

I stared at him, my eyes growing wider with every step. He sat down in the armchair opposite me, glancing briefly out the window.

'You're wondering why the sun does not burn me?'

'It crossed my mind.'

Lucius opened his hands wide, spreading them out on either side of him. 'One of my many talents. Lucifer did not wish to give me any out clauses.'

'What do you mean?' I said, eyes narrowed.

'I am immune to death. Sunlight does not char my skin nor silver pierce my flesh. I cannot die.'

'That's pretty major.'

Lucius shrugged. 'Lucifer was covering all his bases when he created me. You were right when you said there would never be an end to vampires or vânâtors. If I exist, then so does the evil that I create.' He looked at the book in my hand. 'Searching for answers?'

I nodded. 'A lot of weird stuff has happened recently, and I guess I was just trying to figure out why.'

'You're referring to our reunion?'

'Not exactly.' I was thinking more along the lines of my telekinetic abilities, weird dreams, and the mystery surrounding my connection with Sebastian.

'Are you still so nervous in my presence?'

'Give me a reason not to be.'

'I am your father.'

'A fact which I'm still getting used to.'

'Take as long as you need, Elena. I want you to feel comfortable here. I would like you to stay and eventually live with me, if you can stand it.' Lucius's gaze hardened, something like self-loathing in his eyes. 'I've waited for what seems like an eternity for your return.' He lowered his gaze, staring at the floor.

I swallowed, my fingers flexing, indenting the spine of the book I held. 'I'll stay.'

He looked up, eyes filling with surprise. 'You will?'

I nodded. My options were few and thus far Lucius had shown he was harmless.

'Then I am glad to hear it. You *will* be safe here, Elena, I can promise you that.' He fished around inside his coat pockets and leant forward in his chair. 'Now that you have decided to stay, I have some gifts for you.' Lucius held out what looked like a gold-coloured credit card. 'This is a Platinum Visa card. There is no limit, so feel free to spend as you please.'

I shook my head, pushing his outstretched hand away. 'I can't take that. It still doesn't seem right.'

With slight effort, he forcefully opened my hand and placed the credit card in the centre of my palm. 'Money is of no object to me, Elena. I have more of it than I know what to do with, and I want you to have all the things that you want or need in this life.'

I was still shaking my head. 'I can't—'

'Take it. If you don't use it, that's up to you, but I still want you to have access to my fortune.' Lucius reached back into his pocket and pulled out a small black cell phone, placing it in my other hand. 'Sebastian tells me that you have a brother that you miss terribly. I thought you might like to make contact with him.'

'Just like that?' I said, eyeing both objects suspiciously.

'Just like that. My only request is that you never tell him the exact location of this villa. He may be your brother, but he is still a Protector.'

I found myself nodding again.

'This brother of yours ... what is he like?'

'Lucas?'

'Yes, Lucas. I have seen snippets of your time together in your thoughts, how he has treated you and how much he means to you. Still, I find it difficult to digest that a

Protector would be so supportive and protective of one of our kind.'

I snatched my hand from his and inched further backwards in my chair. 'What do you mean you've *seen* snippets of my thoughts?'

Uncertainty flickered in his eyes. 'Did I not mention that Lucifer endowed me with certain abilities?'

'You didn't specify.'

Lucius sighed and sank back into his chair. 'Sometimes,' he started to say, voice strained, 'sometimes when I touch people I get a sense of their thoughts and feelings. Last night, when I touched you, I saw parts of your life flash before my eyes. I saw—'

'Stop it. Don't do that, don't analyse my thoughts.'

'I did not mean for it to happen but it does help me to understand you better. It showed me that you need my help.' The skin around Lucius's eyes creased, and his brow furrowing ever so slightly. 'I have seen one of my abilities has been passed to you, Elena. You have yet to learn how to control it.'

Lucius, what else have you seen?

'You're telekinetic, as I am.'

'So I have this ability because the Devil gave it to you?'

'And I passed it down to you.'

'That's wonderful,' I muttered sarcastically.

'It's useful,' Lucius corrected. 'With time and a little practice, I can show you how to use your ability without you draining energy.' He paused. 'It would be easier if you were a full vampire but the schedule for your turning has obviously been brought forward to some degree.' His fingers clenched the edges of the armchair. I wondered if his little 'snippets' of my private life had shown him the exchange between William and I, or if Sebastian had shot his mouth off.

'I appreciate the offer,' I answered, not willing to feed his suspicions.

'So you will allow me to train you?'

'Yes. I want to master this thing.'

Lucius nodded in approval. 'Good. We can start later today if you wish.'

'You don't have to go back to work?'

His eyebrow rose fractionally.

'Maria told me you own Synth Corp.' I gave him a genuine smile. 'I'm impressed—a vampire philanthropist.'

Lucius returned my smile. 'It was your mother that motivated me. I wanted a way to coexist without harming the humans. By creating Synth Corp, I've also been able to help a great many people, too.'

'And the neutral bars?'

His smile widened. 'A way to turn a profit from those that benefit from my services.'

'How do you know vampires aren't cheating? They could feed from humans for free.'

He conceded my point with a nod. 'Yes, they could. I imagine that the more defiant still do, but my power reaches far. I can be quite convincing, when I want to be.'

'Then why have you allowed for the continued existence of the Vânătors?' He'd left me the perfect opening to broach the subject. 'Sebastian told me that you've known for centuries that killing all of the Alphas would bring about their kind's eventual destruction. If your power is so great, your word so convincing, why have you not fixed the mess you vampires created?'

Lucius winced, my words obviously striking a chord. 'I'm not sure I can explain it to you.'

'Try, because it angers me to think that many people have died needlessly at their hands. And I'd hate to think that everything I've been through to learn that information was for nothing.'

'I'm sorry for your past pain.'

'Don't apologise, just explain to me why nothing has been done. I admire you but it doesn't explain your neglect.'

Lucius absently scratched at his eyebrow with a long, slim finger. 'After the Vânǎtors were created, I felt a change. There was a rift in Vampiric power, as some of our energies spread to the newer species, a species that *I* had ordered to have killed. I was later grateful for the Roman Guard's failure to hunt them down. A few days after I ordered their execution, I had a dream. It was the first dream I'd had since I was turned.'

He looked at me intently as he continued. 'Vampires do *not* dream. The only reason I could have slept so peacefully that night was so I could receive a vision from another entity.' Lucius looked down at the book I was still holding.

I glanced at the cover, which was an artist's impression of the Archangel Michael standing over Lucifer. Michael's foot was pressed against Lucifer's broken wings as the fallen angel crawled across the ground, the halo of light around his head representing Michael's divinity and good standing with God. Lucifer looked defeated, or so everyone thought.

'You're suggesting that either an angel or a demon implanted suggestions in your mind while you slept?' It was hard not to look a little sceptical, even if the biggest evidence of Lucifer's existence sat directly across from me.

'It is true, though I doubt a demon would have shown me the birth of my own daughter. They care little for such sentimentality. Be it angel or demon, I was warned—I knew that you would be born and that the Vânǎtors would play a vital role. There was a reason why you were never to be fully vampiric, I just … I just can't seem to remember why. I simply believe that their demise would have been detrimental to your future. Now, I am glad the Vânătors were not defeated, if for no other reason than the fact you sit across from me now: whole, unharmed, and powerful in ways even I don't yet understand. And, once you had told me last night that you had been receiving dreams of your own, my suspicions about possible otherworldly interference were confirmed. Now my previous qualms about allowing the Vânătors to live have diminished.'

'You honestly believe that angels brought us together?' I started to wonder why I'd been seeing Sebastian in my sleep long before I'd ever envisioned my father. Did angels play a part in that too, and if so, why?

'It's the only explanation, although I have no idea why they are interfering. Their intentions are usually never nefarious. They are created out of a purity of spirit, so to interfere with a demon's pawns suggests a higher purpose, but what?'

I was still looking at the cover of the book, tracing my finger over Michael's angelic face. I couldn't answer my father. I didn't know the first thing about angels or demons. I was still coming to terms with the supernatural oddities I *was* familiar with.

Lucius suddenly rose, body once again tense and eyes distracted. He reached out absently to pat the side of my cheek, not even noticing when I shrunk away from his touch. 'I have to go. I just came home to give you the card and phone.'

'Where are you off to?' I asked.

'I have to go back into Rome. There are problems I must attend to before I can return to train you this afternoon.'

'Problems?'

He waved a hand distractedly, already heading for the door. 'Nothing I can't handle.'

'Before you leave,' I said, standing up, 'can I ask you something about Sebastian?'

Lucius stopped, turned and looked right at me. 'Sebastian?'

I nodded. 'Yeah.' I didn't miss the quick flick of his gaze to the ceiling above before it settled back on me again.

'What do you wish to know?'

'I'm not sure—your opinion of him, I guess? He's a little strange and I get the feeling he and I have … look, you said last night that you've been forced to re-evaluate his makings, that you couldn't decipher who he is. I'm confused by that since he is Tiberius's son, and Tiberius was a thrall of your own making.'

Lucius's fingers twitched. 'Sebastian is an oddity. I've known him for a very long time, and yet I've never been able to identify with him.'

'But you trusted him to find me?'

'Yes, I do trust Sebastian. His loyalty is not in question, but that doesn't mean I know the first thing about him or even understand him.'

I could feel myself frowning. 'What do you mean?'

Lucius looked down at his watch, glanced upwards again and then back at me. 'He's not like the rest of us. Like you, he is different.'

'How? He seems like all the other vampires to me.'

'He's a vampire, but he's also something else.'

I crept closer. 'Something else?'

'Talking about me, Lucius?' Sebastian said, appearing suddenly in the doorway. He walked no further, light from the windows blocking his entrance.

Lucius stiffened, only for a moment, but it was hard to miss. I found it odd that Lucius, the oldest and most powerful vampire in existence, had been taken by surprise by a subordinate. That raised a whole new set of questions that I feared would yet again go unanswered.

'I really do have to go, Elena. We'll talk when I return.' He brushed past Sebastian, barely acknowledging him. 'Call Lucas. I'm sure he would love to know that you are safe and well.'

I looked down at the phone and credit card still in my hand. When I looked back up at the doorway, both Sebastian and Lucius were gone.

I shook my head and set about dialling Lucas's number. Excitement rose within me. It would be the first time in weeks that I could talk to him without having to censor myself. I had so much to tell him, so much I needed him to help clarify.

The phone started ringing, and I waited patiently for Lucas to pick up. There was barely a moment's pause before the call connected and I heard my brother's drowsy voice on the end of the line.

CHAPTER NINETEEN: INTENTIONS

I sighed, the sound of Lucas's voice a joyous relief as it echoed down the line, warming me to the depths of my soul.

He sounded groggy. 'Who's this?'

'Hey, dumbass,' I said, using my pet name for him. There'd be little doubt that it was me calling.

'Dickhead?' he answered sleepily.

The smile on my face was growing wider by the second. 'Yeah, it's me.'

Lucas cleared his throat. 'Where have you been? It's been over a week since I spoke to you, since you were supposed to call. I've been really worried. Mum and Dad won't talk to me, and I started thinking the worst. Where are you? Are you okay?'

I laughed, my first real laughter in weeks. It felt good. 'Lucas, take a breath. Everything's great. You won't believe what's happened.'

'Where are you?'

'I'm in Rome.'

'Rome? What the hell are you doing in Rome?!'

'I'm staying with my father.' The other end of the line went completely silent. 'Lucas?'

'I heard you. I'm just not sure if I heard you correctly.'

'Oh, you heard me right, Lucas. The last week has certainly been … enlightening.'

'You're with your father,' he murmured, voice trailing off. 'Is it just me or does that sound weird?'

'Yeah, it's weird,' I agreed.

'What's he like?'

'Honestly? It's hard to say but there's definitely some sort of connection between us. Mostly, I feel kinda anxious around him. I'm not sure how to act or relate yet.' I paused, thinking through my previous night's conversation with Lucius. 'He's not a bad person as far as I can tell, but he hasn't made a lot of good choices either.'

'You must be related, then,' Lucas chuckled.

I snorted. 'Maybe.'

'How did you find him? And how did you break out of the IMI? Isn't there a bloody Alpha chasing after you?'

I sighed deeply, settling back into the armchair again, certain this was going to be a long phone call. I had to tell Lucas everything that had happened since William's arrival at the IMI: about my new abilities, Chester's stubbornness, Sebastian, the dreams, and everything else up until this point. If anyone could help me make sense of everything, it would be Lucas.

I quickly launched into the story, pent up details and emotions flooding out of me in a rush of relief. I started with the blood exchange, leaving out the finer points of my and William's amorous activities. Lucas was floored when I explained how I'd discovered my new abilities. He asked many questions, getting audibly angry when I explained the IMI's reaction to my revealed super skills, and crossing over to extremely pissed when I explained that this had led to my imprisonment in a chimney stack. The angrier Lucas got, the quieter he became. He listened intently as I detailed my torturous week in captivity and Chester's involvement.

'I'm going to kill them,' he hissed down the phone line as my story wound down.

'Lucas?'

'You heard me, Elena. Nobody tortures my little sister and gets away with it—we killed John for the exact same reasons. What makes anyone else exempt? I swear to God, I'm going to make every last one of those bastards suffer for what they did to you.'

'I'm okay, Lucas,' I said gently, floored by his outburst. He'd never spoken ill of the IMI before. 'You know better than anyone that I can look after myself.'

'It's not good enough,' Lucas growled. 'We're supposed to be the protectors of humanity, not crackpot scientists trying to play God in some secret laboratory, experimenting on innocent people.'

'I agree.'

'Then why aren't you angry!'

I took a deep breath. 'Lucas, I *am* angry.'

'You don't sound it.'

'That's because right now I'm more worried about you. Lucas, you aren't acting like your usual self. I know you want to protect me, but you've never openly spoken out against the IMI before. Something else must be worrying you.'

Lucas laughed bitterly. 'You got that right. This situation is so messed up.'

My smile had long since vanished, replaced with a writhing feeling of unease in the pit of stomach. 'Tell me what's happened.'

'I found out the truth. I found out the real reason Mum and Dad let you go off to Bucharest.'

I sighed, pinching the bridge of my nose. 'I know, Lucas. The IMI wanted me there so they could monitor me and experiment on me. Chester even told me that if there were any issues with my turning, they were going to kill me.'

'And yet you stayed there!' Lucas retorted angrily. 'If it hadn't have been for your new father's minions rescuing you, you'd still be there and trapped as a play toy for an Alpha.'

'I really tried escaping, Lucas, and did everything I could. I thought I was choosing the lesser of two evils, and I had no idea that things with William would go so badly or that Chester would try forcing the Alpha on me. If I had known, I would have—'

'I'm sorry,' Lucas interrupted. 'I'm not angry at you, I'm angry at everyone I ever trusted.'

'I'm safe now, I think.'

Lucas scoffed. 'It's not over though, is it?'

I frowned. 'What do you mean?'

He spoke as if the answer was obvious. 'The serum.'

'The serum? What are you talking about?'

Lucas's laugh sounded hollow and humourless. 'So Chester told you that you were an experiment, told you that he would kill you on your eighteenth if your turning didn't go as planned, right? But Chester failed to mention that he was going to use your blood to manufacture a *weapon*?'

'What?' I shrieked.

'I found the dossier just over a week ago in Dad's belongings. It outlines your entire life's progress up to this point, your development, and the future plans to cut you up and harvest your insides like some sort of animal. I've known for a week now. I've been trying to contact you, trying to find a way to get to you.' Lucas stopped, his breathing the only noise on the line. 'I was so relieved when Marianne told me that William was coming for you.'

I swallowed, closing my eyes and feeling the lump in my throat. The unease in my stomach was growing.

'I can't believe William just left you there,' Lucas murmured. 'I thought if anyone would help get you out of there, it would be him. I thought everything would be alright, but then you just disappeared. Mum and Dad pretended it wasn't happening, they wouldn't answer my questions, and they wouldn't tell me if you were safe.'

I swallowed that lump down, straining to speak. 'Do you know what the serum does?'

'I wish I knew,' he murmured. 'All the letters said was that they were going to harvest your blood to make some sort of weapon against the Vânătors and Vampires.'

'What could they possibly derive from my blood that would be of any use?' I racked my brain for answers. All that kept circling around in my mind was Stephanie's comments about using my 'special' blood to manufacture cures for disease. That didn't sound bad to me at all, unless the disease they were considering for a cure was vampirism?

What are you playing at, Chester?

'I don't know, Elena. I wish I'd had the time to read more, but Dad busted me before I could and then clammed up so tight that he hasn't spoken to me since.'

'So he definitely knows something,' I concluded.

'We can't trust them anymore, Elena. I'm sorry I didn't see this sooner because we could have stopped you from going to headquarters. This is all my fault.'

'Lucas, how can this be your fault?'

'I knew something was wrong, I could feel it. I knew that things would change being apart from you.'

'Things were always going to change, Lucas. You're a human and a Protector; I was born of the Vampires. Separation is inevitable for us.'

'I hear what you're saying, but your immortality is not what I'm referring to.'

'Well, what do you mean?'

Lucas huffed in frustration and settled into a sigh. 'It doesn't matter. It's too difficult to explain, and I'm not even sure I could, E, but something is different with *me*.'

'How so?'

I imagined Lucas shaking his head from side to side, blonde hair teasing his skin. 'Don't worry—it's stupid. I'm probably just coming down with something like you said.'

My frown deepened. 'Lucas, I said that over a month ago.'

'Yeah, well …'

'Lucas—'

'Let it go. When I know what's wrong with me, I'll tell you. I want to know more about Lucius and this Sebastian guy you mentioned.'

I was reluctant to let the matter drop, but something in Lucas's voice made me reconsider pursuing the subject. 'There's not much to say. I barely know them.' I left out the part about my long standing dreams of Sebastian. It would just make me look crazy.

'Do you feel safe?'

'It's hard to say. I'm nervous, because I've always been surrounded by Protectors, and now I'm surrounded by vampires. I feel accepted but I also feel vulnerable. Both Lucius and Sebastian have assured me that no one here will feed from me but there's always that thought in the back of my mind, you know?'

'Apparently everyone has an agenda,' Lucas said bitterly.

'I'm keeping my eyes open, so don't worry.'

'I'd feel better if I was there with you.'

'You want to come to Rome?'

There was a small silence. 'I think so. It couldn't hurt to have a Protector on your side—an honest one, anyway.'

'I'd like that.'

'But?' Lucas must have heard the hesitation in my voice.

'But I'm not sure it won't make matters worse. At the moment no one knows where I am, including that Alpha. If you go missing they'll know it was to find me, and Susan and George won't stop until you're home again. They'd start a war to find you. And if they finally found you with vampires ...'

'I get your point. I don't like it, but I get it.'

'We'll still keep in touch via phone.'

'And what am I supposed to do in the meantime? When will it ever be safe to see each other again?'

I shook my head, the unease in my stomach turning to sorrow. 'I don't know, Lucas. The only thing I can suggest in the meantime is that you sniff out more information.'

'You want me to stay here and spy on Mum and Dad?'

I grimaced. When he put it like that, it didn't sound so great. 'They have strong ties to Bucharest. Susan and George are personal friends of Chester's. If something was going down, they'd be the ones likely to find out first. If their future plans involve harvesting this serum from *my* blood, you can bet they'll have a hand in it.'

'And how do you suggest I do this without raising their suspicion? They know I've seen the documents, Elena, and they know how close we are. They aren't going to believe everything is A-Ok.'

'They'd expect moodiness, even resentment. But I know how much they love you, how important you are to them, Lucas. They would rather you were there, hating them but with the opportunity for them to still turn your mind against me.'

'That won't happen,' Lucas said flatly.

'I know but it will also give you an opportunity to throw yourself into training, to perfect your craft. You've finished your Year Twelve exams, right?'

'Yes.'

'Good. Now you can concentrate on learning everything they know, training with The Protectors until you're better than they are.'

'But, Elena, I don't think I could stand pretending to be friends with those people, people who knew you were eventually going to be chopped up into little pieces.'

I shook my head and closed my eyes. 'Thanks for the mental image.'

'Sorry.'

'Look, I trained with them for sixteen years. No one at the IMI was ever my friend—I was under no illusions about that. I knew you were my only ally. Lucas, I know you can do this. It will only be for a few months at most, at least until we have some answers. As soon as you find what we're seeking, if you want to still meet with me we'll work something out, maybe move to Mexico.'

'Why Mexico?'

'People do it in the movies and nobody there will know us.'

'Ahh.'

'In the meantime, I think I need to talk to Lucius. He's the most powerful vampire in existence and it stands to reason that he might be able to find out what the IMI is up to.'

Lucas coughed. 'Didn't you just finish telling me that he knew all about the Vânătors and did nothing? What makes you think Lucius will give a shit about this?'

I shrugged, even though I was aware Lucas couldn't see the gesture. 'We need all the help we can get. We don't know what this serum can do nor what it might have already done. If Lucius can help then I'll make him see reason. I'll even pull the daughter card if I have to.'

'Just don't do anything stupid, like going back to the IMI by yourself.'

'I don't do stupid shit all the time, you know.'

Lucas laughed, and this time it was warm and genuine. I really missed him. 'That's debatable.'

I rolled my eyes, chuckling. 'If I make a stupid plan then I promise I'll take backup.'

'Sebastian?'

My skin prickled at the mere mention of his name. 'Probably.'

'What's he like? You haven't really talked about him.'

'What do you want me to say?'

Lucas sniffed. 'I'm just asking.'

'And I'm just saying that I don't have an answer.'

'Elena, what's going on? You're getting defensive for no reason, so I get the feeling there's something here you're not telling me.'

'It's nothing, Lucas, honest. Sebastian's just the son of one of Lucius's thralls.'

'And he lives at the house with you and your Dad?'

'It's a pretty big house, Lucas. We won't bump into each other very often, if that's what you're worried about.'

'But you want to bump into him?'

Maybe.

'Look, I better go and start working on Lucius if we're going to sort something out of all of this.'

Lucas sighed, dropping the subject as I knew he would. 'You better call me more regularly now. I want to know you're okay. You wouldn't understand, because it's a big brother thing.'

I laughed. 'I will. Remember, bro, act normal. No one can suspect that you've turned into a double agent.'

'Easier said than done.'

I sighed. 'I miss you, Lucas.'

'Yeah, yeah,' he said, all nonchalance, 'I miss you, too.'

I grinned. 'Try not to cry about it though, okay?'

'I'm totally hanging up now.'

I laughed as the line went dead. I closed the cell phone and held it close to my chest. I had missed him beyond reason, and hated that Susan and George had betrayed his trust and faith in the IMI.

I tucked the phone in my pocket and pushed myself up from the chair, a little doubt starting to weigh me down. I hoped that I was doing the right thing by asking Lucas to stay in Cairns.

'Ugh!' I grumbled, bumping into Sebastian as I headed for the library door.

Sebastian steadied me, his fingers lightly gripping my shoulders. 'Careful now.'

I shook him off. 'Do you have to appear out of nowhere like that?'

'Moving slowly is a waste of time.'

'Did you want something?' I asked impatiently.

Sebastian gestured to the book I still had clasped in my hand. I looked down at it, curious as to why I had not put it down. 'That's pretty heavy reading,' he commented.

I frowned, confused. 'You're asking me about the book?'

He shrugged. 'I suppose I'm curious why you're reading about angels and demons.'

I finally threw the book onto one of the side tables, glancing at it one last time before scooting past Sebastian and out of the library. He caught up to me in the courtyard, not exactly a challenge for a vampire. 'Where are you going?'

'I'm going to ask Maria to call me a taxi. I can't speak Italian, and I really need to get into Rome.'

'Why?'

'Something has come up. I want to meet up with Lucius now.'

Sebastian stilled me with a single hand on my arm. 'Lucius left only a short while ago. What could be so important?'

I looked down at the hand encircling my arm. Even through the layers of fabric, I felt warmth, familiarity. 'Let me go.'

He shook his head, agitated. 'At least let me help you.'

I retrieved the mobile phone Lucius had given me and held it out for Sebastian to take. He ignored my outstretched hand and headed for the front door instead, but not before grabbing his bike helmet, leather jacket, and riding gloves from the music room. 'How are you with motorbikes?'

'What?'

'Are you going to freak out if we ride on a motorbike together?'

'*You're* going to take me into Rome?'

'It's quicker and cheaper than a taxi.' Sebastian slipped on the jacket and gloves, tucked the helmet under his arm and ventured out through the front doors, sticking to the shadows. 'Are you coming?' he yelled back to me.

I started after Sebastian, my feet moving hesitantly at first, and then suddenly breaking into a sprint to keep up with him. Several different emotions were coursing through my system. The first was fear; the second, anxiety; and the third, excitement. The thought of strapping myself to a motorbike and feeling the cool metal of that chassis throbbing beneath me made me smile. I hadn't ridden a motorbike since my last lesson back in June. So much had happened, and I hadn't gotten a chance to ride since.

I really missed it.

Sebastian rounded the corner of the villa, walking me down a small cobblestone drive and to a massive four-car garage. He leaned down and pulled up the roller door to reveal the contents within.

Hold the freaking phone.

I had never seen so many beautiful pieces of machinery in all my life. Towards the back there was a jet-ski mounted on a trailer, but in front there were at least four different motorcycles. Next to these were a new Bentley Continental GTC, a Mercedes Benz coupe, and—heaven help me!—a Lamborghini.

'Are you okay?' Sebastian said, looking puzzled by the expression of awe on my face.

I nodded slowly, wondering if there was a puddle of drool by my feet. 'I think I just died and went to heaven,' I said, my fingers brushing across the shiny, red finish of the Lamborghini.

'You're into cars?' Sebastian said, cocking an eyebrow in surprise.

I opened the door to the Lamborghini and floated down into the driver's seat, feeling the rightness of the crisp leather steering wheel under my fingers, and inhaling the scent of engine grease, leather, and freshly-vacuumed upholstery. 'While other little girls played with dolls, I was in my room pouring over any piece of literature involving vehicles with two or more wheels. I've always been fascinated.'

Sebastian's surprise soon turned into a smile of mutual understanding. 'I know exactly what you mean. I've watched the birth of machinery, the progression of man's knowledge extending to the creation of planes, trains and automobiles. I never get tired of seeing what marvellous machines they'll invent next.'

I returned Sebastian's smile, imagining what it would be like to walk leisurely through time, enjoying its pleasures without worry as he had undoubtedly done. 'Do all these belong to Lucius?' I said, reluctantly climbing out of the seat and closing the door behind me.

Sebastian shook his head. 'The Bentley belongs to my father. The Lamborghini is Marcus's, and the Mercedes belongs to Maximus.'

'And the bikes?' I said, turning to look at the four very different models.

Sebastian pointed each out individually. 'The Harley Softail is your father's, though he doesn't ride often. He mostly prefers to use the town car or head into Rome via the tunnels. The two Ducati's at the back belong to Decimus—he's a bike enthusiast like me.' Sebastian paused and put his hand on the last remaining bike. 'And this one—'

'Is the latest model BMW K,' I said, running my fingers over the midnight-blue finish. I looked up with a genuine smile on my face. 'It's a beauty, Sebastian.'

'Thank you. I used to have a Kawasaki Ninja, but I ran into a vânător.'

'And?'

He frowned. 'I ran into a vânător. I killed him on impact, but the weight of the creature mangled the bike.'

I found myself laughing. 'I didn't think you meant literally.'

Sebastian seemed to see the humour as well, because he stopped frowning and started to smile again.

While I fingered his motorbike and checked out the two Ducati's, Sebastian walked over to a set of steel shelves, grabbing a spare helmet and leather riding jacket. He tossed them over to me. 'You *should* be wearing full leathers,' he stated, looking me up and down critically. 'Perhaps we should take my father's car instead? Or use the tunnels. I could carry you.'

I looked at the Bentley, and then longingly back at Sebastian's BMW. What's a little gravel rash amongst self-healers? Besides, what were the odds of Sebastian running into another vânător, in Rome, in broad daylight?

I swung my leg over the back of the bike and sat down. There was no way I was taking the tunnels or cruising like Miss Daisy in the back of the Bentley when I could ride this baby. The only option I'd be persuaded to try involved him handing me the keys to the Lamborghini.

Sebastian didn't, so I slammed the visor down on the helmet and slipped on the jacket. He mirrored my actions, but not before eyeing my legs with wandering eyes a second before his visor came down.

Ordinarily it would have bugged me to have been perved on, but now I wasn't so sure. I was surprised that I liked the idea of Sebastian admiring me. What surprised me even more was that, behind the visor, I was shamelessly admiring him back.

Sebastian climbed onto the bike, reaching back once he was settled to grab my thighs and slide me forward until I was sitting against his back. Our bodies melded comfortably, my arms wrapping around his waist. Once he was satisfied that I was settled, Sebastian walked the bike backwards, turned it around, and started the engine. Before I knew it we were roaring down the cobblestone driveway, out through the wrought iron gates, and down the side roads of Valle Santa.

I urged Sebastian to go faster, pressing myself in and hugging him tighter, clamping my thighs against his. I'd never been allowed to go above eighty kilometres per hour back in Cairns.

Colours blurred as I glanced over his shoulder and saw that the speedo had topped one-fifty. Since he was a vampire, I was reassured because he would have perfect co-ordination and one hundred percent control, but I now also understood Maria's fears—riding with Sebastian was incredible, but it was also dangerous. A human being was not built for this kind of speed.

The trip was over far too soon. The city of Rome seemed to spring up out of nowhere, and we were soon ducking and weaving through line-after-line of urban traffic. As the city careened past, I took my time observing the structures, the people, the restaurants, the bars and the businesses. Despite the congestion, the city of Rome and its people appeared to be in no particular hurry.

We careened down a few side streets and into a semi-commercial district, pulling to a stop outside an extremely large, glass-panelled building. It took up about a quarter of a block and was surrounded by other architecturally similar structures. A sign on top of the building read 'Synth Corp—Serving Your Needs'.

How very apt, considering their clientele.

Sebastian pulled the bike into the shadows of a side alley and switched off the engine. He pulled off his helmet, running fingers through his long, dark hair and then turning to face me. 'Are you okay?' he said.

I also removed my helmet, adjusting my hair. Not that it really helped. Then I turned to him and grinned, all teeth. 'Sebastian, that was the most fun I've had in months.'

His face softened, eyes swirling. 'I'm glad you enjoyed yourself.'

I looked away, staring up at the building instead. 'So this is Synth Corp.'

'Yes.'

I swung myself off the bike, careful to avoid burning myself on the exhaust system. I placed my helmet on the seat, averting my eyes from his intense gaze. 'Exactly what is it that you do with your time, Sebastian? Do you work here, too?'

'No, I'm in Acquisitions.'

I frowned, but I could feel the edges of my lips twitching. 'Trading, selling or stealing?'

'Neither.'

'Well, what is it that you acquire then?'

He slid off the bike and leaned down to whisper in my ear. 'Naughty vampires.'

'So you're like a bounty hunter?'

'I'm a tracker.'

Apparently, that was supposed to explain everything.

'So, Lucius is the Law, and you're what? Like the Sheriff or something?'

Sebastian shrugged. 'Or something.'

'You're not very forthcoming are you?'

'Why do you care about what I do?' he muttered, brushing past me and heading down the alley, and then back towards the front entrance. I followed closely behind. 'You've made it quite clear that you'd prefer I stayed away from you.'

'I never said that.'

'But you don't like it when I touch you.'

'Quite the opposite actually,' I whispered under my breath.

Sebastian's back stiffened, but he kept walking. I wondered if he'd heard me.

Shit.

'What is it that you want from me, Elena?'

'I'm just trying to make conversation, Sebastian.'

I grabbed the back of his jacket and pulled on it to slow

him down. Sebastian stopped, his back still to me. I circled around him, coming to stand directly in front. He looked down at me, eyes filled with grey and lips set in a grim line. He sure was moody today.

'Why are you trying to make menial conversation?'

'To get to know you better.'

'To what purpose?'

I tugged on his jacket again, a little annoyed. 'I'm trying to make an effort here. I can see that you're more in tune with the universe or whatever than I am, and that you think I should have unravelled the mystery of our dreamscape connection already, but I have to do this my way. With everything that's happened, with everything that still might happen, I need to cling to what I know and understand.' I threw my hands up in the air. 'For Christ's sake, I just found out angels and demons exist and that I'm the spawn of Satan, doomed to an eternity in hell. I just thought asking you about your day job would be simpler.'

Sebastian grimaced. 'Please do not take the Lord's name in vain.'

I was about to say 'bite me' but then stopped. I stared at him, open-mouthed, unsure of what to say for the longest time, before starting to laugh. 'Are you kidding?'

Sebastian growled.

'Oh, that's just priceless—a religious vampire.' I laughed harder, and even harder still as Sebastian's irritation grew.

I ran after him as he pushed past me. 'Okay, sorry, I know that was rude. You're entitled to your beliefs, I just thought …' I started sniggering again and Sebastian scowled. I grabbed his arm. 'Sorry, I did it again. It's just a little hard to swallow. Let me rewind for a sec, go back and we'll start fresh. I'm just asking you questions because I want to get to know you, Sebastian. I've agreed to Lucius's request to stay at the villa, and because of that, I thought we could be friends.'

It was Sebastian's turn to laugh, but there was nothing humorous in it. 'Sure. We can be friends ... can't wait.' He shot me a discontented look. 'Maybe we can paint each other's toenails later?'

I rolled my eyes and followed after him. Sebastian stuck to the shadows, making his way quickly to the front door, holding it open for me. He bowed low, his expression was mocking as I darted inside.

I was in a spacious lobby, a small reception desk and a set of steel stairs to the left marking the entrance. 'Wait here,' Sebastian said. He loped up the stairs, walked through another door at the top and then slammed it shut behind him. I climbed the stairs, anyway. It was in my nature to be curious, and it seemed doubtful that I'd be in any real danger.

The door opened into a small office. The glass window panes were all blacked out, but the lamps and overhead halogens more than made up for the lack of sunlight. The room contained a group of chairs and a coffee table, with some out-dated magazines spread across its surface. Directly at the front of the office was another small reception counter. This one came with a petite blonde who was already rising from her chair to greet Sebastian.

She launched herself into his arms, running her fuchsia-stained lips over the skin of his neck, eventually reaching his lips. The blonde kissed Sebastian hungrily, nibbling at his seemingly unresponsive lips until he could pry her away.

Sebastian set her down gently, speaking to her in Italian and rubbing his hand across her back. When his eyes met mine, I turned away. It was weird seeing my walking fantasy in the arms of someone else. I wasn't sure how I felt, but I didn't want to let him see any unrestrained emotion on my part.

The woman giggled under her breath. I looked up as she kissed him again and then went back to her desk. I didn't speak Italian, and I wasn't sexually experienced, but I had a pretty good idea what she was telling him with her eyes.

'This is Graziella,' Sebastian murmured, introducing the blonde. 'She's a turned vampire and also a friend.'

Friend, my ass.

I wanted to say 'please to meet you', but I couldn't. She irritated me and I had no idea why.

When I looked back at Graziella, I noticed that she was now eyeing me with genuine interest. She wasn't weighing me up as other females do, judging my choice in clothing, my hair colour, or figure. She seemed to be eyeing me like a vampire—a hungry one at that. As I watched, her eyes began to darken, the sharp hint of fangs framing her lips. 'I think she's thirsty,' I said to Sebastian.

Sebastian turned back to look at Graziella, saying something in Italian before snapping his fingers to get her attention. He spoke sternly, and she instantly settled down, averting her gaze and pulling out a tetra pack of blood from her desk drawer—easy to get when you worked for the manufacturer.

'Sorry about that,' Sebastian said, taking me by the arm and leading me through one of the office doors. 'She's only seventy-five, and your blood is still a little too tempting for her. It's why I asked you to stay—' He stopped in his tracks.

I looked over his shoulder. I could see Lucius, his teeth firmly planted in the side of a man's neck. Blood oozed slowly from the wound, flowing ever faster, as Lucius tore his teeth through flesh and bit through the veins.

Angry, I shoved Sebastian out of the way and ran full pelt

towards him. I grabbed Lucius around the waist and tackled him to the ground with all the force of a professional footballer.

'Elena, no!' Sebastian yelled.

He was too late. Lucius and I fell to the floor in a tangled mess of arms, legs and blood. The helpless stranger staggered and dropped, using the wall behind to brace himself.

I pulled my fist back and punched Lucius as hard as I could in the face, snapping his head back and rattling teeth inside his mouth. Before Sebastian could intervene, I darted in front of the stranger. I was going to protect this innocent at all costs. 'Are you all right?' I said to the man, taking a step to the left as Sebastian crept closer.

'I will be,' the stranger said, rising slowly to his feet behind me.

'Put pressure on the wound. I need you alive if I'm going to try and get you out of here.'

The smell of his blood was making my mouth water and my fangs began to throb. No matter what happened though, I would not bite him. I refused to be like my father.

'You're making a huge mistake, Elena,' Sebastian growled, taking another step closer.

I shook my head. 'No, I'm helping an innocent man.'

'He's not innocent,' Lucius muttered, rising to his feet and glaring at me. 'He's a killer.'

'We all are in some way.'

'You don't understand, Elena,' he continued. 'This man is a danger to society. He's been slaughtering people for two millennia.'

My resolve faltered. The stranger took another step towards me, his breath cold on the back of my neck. He smelt like hot bitumen after the rain. 'I don't believe you.'

'Tell that to the barman he murdered in Paris recently,' Sebastian spat out.

I turned slowly, feeling the stranger at my back, his lips so close to my ear. 'It's true,' he whispered, his hands grabbing me and drawing me uncomfortably close, 'I hate neutral bars and I hate nosey barman. I ripped out his throat and enjoyed every minute of it.'

I started to struggle against him, kicking at his instep and raising my elbow to slam into his ribs. Yet he held me tighter, easily restraining me like a helpless infant. 'And now, young lady, I will enjoy tasting you, too. I thank you for the distraction and the chance to heal.'

'No!' Sebastian and Lucius screamed simultaneously, leaping forward to grab at me, as the stranger slammed my body back against the wall and plunged his teeth deep into my neck. In an instant, Sebastian and Lucius were right on top of him, their teeth buried deep in the flesh of this vampire who dared attacked me. They pulled him off me and slammed him to the ground.

My fingers trembled as I touched the exposed vein of my neck. Warm fluid caressed my flesh, trailing down my neck and pooling in the hollow right above my collarbone. My skin tingled as self-healing kicked in, but my bottom lip still quivered in fear.

How could I have been so stupid?

'You've been holding out on us, Lucius,' the stranger said, laughing as he looked at me with black, heartless eyes. 'You never said that you had a daughter. Especially one that's so tasty, so delicious. It looks like I might have finally found something you value more than yourself.' Mr Psycho smiled at me, fangs dripping.

I held his gaze, memorising that face, remembering it so I could kill him if we ever crossed paths again. Tumultuous black curls that grazed his shoulders and gazing eyes as blue as the sea were forever burned into my memory.

The stranger must have found a hidden reserve of energy, cashing in on my father's distraction—Lucius was too busy looking at me, fear in his wide eyes. The stranger wrenched free of them, thrusting out powerfully with both hands and feet. He sent Lucius and Sebastian sprawling across the floor and was gone before either could react.

The door behind me opened and slammed shut, the breeze from the stranger's hurried exit blowing papers across the room and hair into my eyes. A second later Sebastian tore through the same door and disappeared from sight, hot on his heels.

'What just happened?' I said, turning slowly to meet my father's angry gaze. We were both making such *great* first impressions.

'What just happened,' Lucius said slowly, 'was that you just met Julius, one of my original thralls. And now, thanks to you, he has gotten away.' He shook his head and lowered himself into a chair. 'That man has been the bane of my existence for the last two thousand years. He won't conform to any sort of rules, he won't stop feeding from humans, and now Julius knows I have a weakness.'

'A weakness?' I asked feebly, looking down at the carpet.

'You. He knows of my history, what I did to avenge my family. He was one of the first and understands that family means everything to me.'

'I'm sorry. I didn't realise. I just saw him, he looked human and I thought—'

'You thought I was attacking him.'

I nodded.

'Why do you still doubt me so?'

'I told you this last night and this afternoon—we still don't know each other.'

'Julius is dangerous. Your continuing doubts might cost more lives.'

My nostrils flared. 'I said I was sorry, and I meant it. If he's a killer like you say, then letting him slip away is entirely on me but I won't apologise for defending what I thought was a helpless human. How did he even know that I was your daughter, anyway?'

'Your blood is my blood. Once he tasted me inside of you, he knew.'

Sebastian burst back in through the door, blood still smeared across his lips. 'He's fast, Lucius, I'll give him that. I can still track him.'

Lucius shook his head. 'We'll send Eric and Nicholas.'

Sebastian frowned, wiping the blood from his lips. 'But I can track him, I'm better than anyone else you have. That's why we caught him in the first place.'

Lucius raised a hand to silence him. 'I want *you* here to protect Elena. Julius knows she is mine and will come back for her. I cannot always be around to shield her.'

A meaningful look passed between them.

'I'll call them now,' Sebastian said, sighing as he pulled out his cell phone and began dialling.

'I don't need a babysitter.'

This time Lucius waved his hand at me. 'Why are you here, anyway?' There was no longer anger in his tone but I could definitely sense his irritation. 'I told you I'd be home in a few hours.'

'I have something important I want to discuss with you.' I looked at Sebastian again, who was launching into a heated discussion with Eric over the phone. Suddenly the prospect of hypothetical serums and devious Protectors seemed to pale in comparison to a murderous ancient vampire. 'But, if you need to concentrate on hunting Julius, then we can talk later.'

Lucius raised a brow at me. 'Elena, the damage is done—he is gone. Tell me what it is that you came here for.'

'Okay. Well, Lucas has made me aware of something that I think needs to be addressed.' I paused, thinking of the lengths to which Chester would go to achieve his goals, regardless of how insane they were. 'I think we might have a serious problem.'

Sebastian finished his conversation and snapped the phone shut, popping it back into the rear pocket of his leather pants. 'It's done.'

Lucius inclined his head, quickly training his gaze back upon me. 'What sort of problem?'

'I haven't got full disclosure yet, but since The Protector's hatred of vampires and vânători runs deep, it could be the kind of problem you might be able to help resolve.'

Sebastian and Lucius exchanged glances. 'I'm listening,' Lucius said, leaning forward in his chair, eyes narrowing.

'It looks like The Protectors have their own agenda.'

'They always do. But what sort of agenda?'

'The kind that involves creating some sort of new weapon to use against our kind.'

Sebastian scoffed. 'So what's new? They've been planning to take us down for centuries.'

I nodded, finally understanding his animosity. 'Yes, but in the past they did not have my blood or the knowledge of what I was fully capable of. Now, they do.'

'Elena, what are you saying?' Lucius said, his gaze filled with an intensity that hadn't been there previously.

'I'm saying that I think we need to kick some serious ass and find out what this serum is before the shit really hits the fan.'

CHAPTER TWENTY: PLANS

L ucas landed hard on his back, his breath bursting out of him with one vicious blow. He was left clutching at his chest and wondering how Peter had got the better of him … again.

'Lucas,' Peter said from above him, 'you're not concentrating hard enough today.'

Lucas was well aware of that fact. His mind was clouded, actions shaky. He'd been thinking about Elena all day. She was due to call him soon and he was distracted, constantly looking over at the backpack that housed his cell phone. It being wedged between his mother's legs, who sat watching him proudly from the grandstand, was the worrying part. Hopefully, Susan wouldn't be tempted to answer it if it rang.

Susan and George were unaware of his and Elena's regular phone calls. He'd started taking being a double agent seriously, buying himself a pre-paid mobile phone in case his parents decided to check the log sheets on his usual itemised phone bills. He couldn't risk letting the IMI know where Elena was, and he didn't want to be questioned either.

Keeping this secret would be difficult.

Ever since he'd uncovered the secret dossier on Elena, Susan and George had been watching him like a pair of hawks, probing deeply into his extracurricular activities. They were also monitoring his most recent growth spurt, drawing blood from him weekly for testing, and regularly measuring his relative muscle growth. Lucas wondered if he was Elena's replacement and secretly worried that this was somehow related to his recent awareness of a change within himself. He really didn't want to think that the IMI had a special reason to be interested in him.

'Lucas! Are you even listening to me today?' Peter said, leaning down and slapping him on the side of the face.

Lucas growled, quickly seeing red. Rolling to the side, he flipped his leg up and inwards, clipping Peter on the side of his head. The kick wasn't enough to cause serious injury but it was enough to get the man out of his face.

'Sneaky,' Peter said, rubbing at the throbbing flesh of his temple. 'That move reminds me of something your sister would have done.'

'Is that a bad thing?'

Peter shook his head. 'Elena was always cocky, but she could fight when she wanted to.'

'I need to be better than her.'

Peter raised a quizzical eyebrow. 'And why is that?'

'I'll always be *just* human, so I need whatever advantages I can get. I can't outrun the supernatural—I probably couldn't even beat them in a fight if it came down to that—but if I can outsmart them, even for a second, it'll be enough time to use my magic to kill.'

Peter merely nodded, mild surprise still etched on his features. 'Lucas, I'm impressed. You've never seemed this dedicated to your training before.'

'Like I said, I just want to be all I can be.'

Peter flicked him on the ear. 'Then maybe you should start by paying attention.'

'Is he not concentrating?' George asked, walking stealthily up behind the two of them. His hand tightly clasped the back of Lucas's neck, fingers roughly massaging the firm flesh there. It was a show of authority and Lucas knew it.

'Something on your mind?' George persisted, turning Lucas around to look at him.

'Give him a break, George,' Peter said. 'I showed him some new moves today— it's likely he's just getting confused.'

'Is that right?'

Lucas shook free of his grip. 'Hah. I could pin you to the mat in a heartbeat, Dad.'

George actually looked amused. 'Is that a challenge?'

'I'm game if you are.'

Peter placed a hand on both of their chests. 'Slow down, you two. Lucas, you know that you're not ready for that yet; and George, your blood pressure is still too high to be messing around with such childish antics.'

'Another time perhaps,' George said, eyes narrowing at Lucas.

Lucas rolled his eyes. 'Whatever, Dad. Proving myself to you is pointless.'

'And what is that supposed to mean?'

Lucas shook his head. 'In your eyes, I'll never be a Protector.'

Peter started to look uncomfortable, glancing away from the two men.

'That's ridiculous, Lucas. Your mother and I think very highly of you.'

Lucas shrugged, determined to push the point as far as he could. 'If you thought highly of me, if you trusted me enough to believe I would make a good Protector, then you would have explained to me what was in the dossier I found. God knows, I've asked you enough.'

Peter gasped. George pointed a finger at Lucas's chest. '*We* will discuss this later.'

'It would be about time,' Lucas grumbled.

'Oh, it won't be a conversation you'll like, Lucas,' George barked, heading over to the grandstand to join Susan. He sat down, whispering something in his wife's ear. Susan's face instantly crumpled with displeasure.

Yep, I'm Elena's replacement.

'Are we still training?' Peter murmured, his face pale as he looked to George for confirmation.

George's head bobbed once in acknowledgement.

Peter scratched nervously at the scar across his eye. 'Where were we?' he said, avoiding all eye contact with Lucas.

Lucas's smile was strained. 'I was about to kick you in the head.'

Peter instantly braced for the attack. Instead, Lucas dropped to the floor, sweeping his legs low and taking Peter out at the ankles. Peter crashed to the ground, legs up in the air, surprise etched on his features. The air hissed from his throat, and his eyes bulged as his head hit the mat. Lucas showed no mercy, rolling forward and punching Peter hard in the solar plexus, leaving him gasping.

Peter held up a hand for mercy, still struggling for air. Lucas felt smug but it was a hollow victory. He'd only won because Peter had been distracted.

'I'm too old for this shit,' Peter said, rolling onto his side and clutching at his chest.

Lucas helped Peter slowly back to his feet. 'I didn't hurt you, did I?'

Peter looked at him with searing brown eyes, sweat running in rivulets down his forehead. 'No. You didn't hurt me, but now that you are changing—'

'Peter …' George warned. He must have been listening closely to have heard all the way across the training room.

'Changing?' Lucas asked, ignoring his father as George stood up and strode back towards them.

Peter was looking flustered. That was so out of character for him that Lucas became twice as suspicious about the true intent behind his words. 'I just meant that I've noticed that you're bulking up lately,' Peter continued hurriedly. 'If you keep putting on so much muscle, you might actually start bruising me.'

George approached, his face now an emotionless canvas. He slapped a hand on Lucas's shoulder. 'Lucas *has* been working out.'

Peter nodded. 'Yes, I was just commenting on that fact.'

Lucas frowned, looking down at his arms. He'd only been going to the gym for two weeks, almost since Elena's last call, but hadn't really noticed a change. 'I can't see what you're talking about. I just started doing weights in the hopes that I wouldn't look like a rake for the rest of my life.'

Peter patted the shoulder that George currently wasn't commandeering. 'Well, whatever you're doing, keep it up. Your stamina has also improved.' He patted Lucas again and then he and George walked off. Just like that, they left the room, Susan following hot on their heels.

'Well that was weird,' Lucas muttered, staring after them. He wasn't sure if they wanted to avoid further discussion or that they'd simply decided that was enough practice for one day. Either way, he'd try not to worry about it.

Lucas pulled the training mats to the side of the room, stacking them up in a neat pile. He disrobed, wiped the sweat from his brow and quickly fished into his backpack for his joggers. After lacing up, he threw the backpack over his shoulder and high-tailed it out of the training room.

He ran into Karina at the junction.

'Hi, Lucas,' she said, voice as sweet as dripping honey. 'Where are you going?'

He took a minute to admire the silky look of the raven black hair she sported; it hugged her face like a warm blanket. It took even longer for him to glance away from her vivid green eyes and the ample cleavage that seemed to have sprung up from nowhere in the past few months. 'Umm, what?'

'Where are you going?' Karina repeated, pulling her spell book up to cover her chest.

How is it that girls always know when you're perving on them?

Lucas, figuring he was busted, stared at the tiny freckle next to her lips instead. 'I'm going to the gym.'

She glanced at him quizzically. 'You're really into this bulking up idea, aren't you?'

Lucas shrugged. 'I look like a broomstick.'

Her eyes quickly moved over the length of his body, surveying his frame twice before meeting his eyes. 'You've gained weight.'

Lucas raised an eyebrow, looking himself over for the second time that day. 'I have?'

Karina nodded. 'Not much, but it's there.'

The spell book lowered just a fraction. Lucas got a slight glimpse of hot pink bra. 'Well, good luck.' She left him at the junction, while he stood there, poking a finger at his meat-deprived ribs. 'By the way,' Karina yelled over her shoulder, 'I really like your new haircut.'

Lucas ran a hand over the buzz cut he'd spontaneously decided upon the night before. He only had a quarter inch of hair covering his entire head now, a far cry from his usual blonde, flowing locks. He wondered what Marianne and Elena would have thought about his new look.

Lucas shrugged, following a long passage out of the junction until he'd reached the entry room. He ascended a ladder, opening and then closing the trapdoor behind him, all the while making sure to mutter the Revatarus spell as he left to make sure the entryway was still cloaked in invisibility.

Watching the trapdoor as it disappeared, he left the old drive-in kitchenette with its littering of mail-out brochures and graffiti, and quickly paced his way through the abandoned facility and out into broad daylight.

Lucas took a deep breath—he was finally alone. Who would have thought playing James Bond would be so tiresome?

Lucas stood in front of the bedroom mirror. He'd taken the sweaty t-shirt from the gym off, removed his shorts and shoes, and now stood naked, studying his reflection. Karina had been right—he *had* gained weight.

He pinched the skin next to his hip, gripping more than just bone. He noticed that his stomach was more defined now, his usually twig-like arms slowly developing newly-defined muscle. His shoulders, too, seemed broader. It looked like the gym might be paying off but doing weights did not explain the difference he felt inside.

Lucas jumped as his mobile began to ring, the awesome starting riff to ACDC's *Highway to Hell* filling the air. He quickly slid on a pair of boxer shorts and fished around in his backpack for his phone. 'Hello?' Lucas said, pressing it to his ear.

'It's me, dumbass.'

That was a foregone conclusion since Elena was the only

one who had the new phone's number. 'Took you long enough to call. I've been waiting for three hours now.'

'So sue me.'

Lucas shook his head. 'What's been happening?'

Elena made a disgusted sort of snort on the other end of the line. 'Nothing much. Lucius seems to think I'm in danger, so I'm kind of under house arrest. I tell you, if Maria wasn't such a good cook I'd split from this joint tonight.'

'And the house arrest is necessary because of that Julius guy?'

'Him, the Alphas, The Protectors—name your particular poison.'

'Aren't you popular,' Lucas joked.

'Ha-ha. Honestly, I'd prefer it if I could just come home, rewind the clock, and pretend everything was how it used to be.'

'But that was all a lie.'

'True, but at least then I still felt like I had some control.'

Lucas was actually relieved that Elena had finally found a safe haven. He hadn't met Lucius, hadn't met Sebastian yet either, but from what Elena said they could be trusted. It was better than the alternatives. 'Has Lucius helped you train up your telekinetic ability yet?'

'He's been pretty great actually. We're still a little awkward around each other but I guess these things take time. He's shown me how to handle the gift without passing out, which is awesome. I've been practicing every day, mostly on Sebastian.' Elena giggled, way out of character for her.

'You just giggled!' Lucas remarked. 'Is there something going on with you and Sebastian?'

'What?!' Elena shrieked. 'No, we're just friends!'

'Last time I heard you laugh like that was when you and William first got together.'

'Mind your business, Lucas.'

Lucas grinned. There was definitely *something* going on there, but he decided to keep his mouth shut for now. 'What else have you been up to?'

'Not much, other than watching a lot of MTV. Tell me about you—what's the news in Cairns?'

'Somebody died of boredom yesterday.'

Elena laughed. 'They did not.'

'They really did. It was all over the news. But, as for The Protectors, not much to report there.'

'Have you learnt anything new?' Elena asked.

'No, it's business as usual here. Mum and Dad are choosing to ignore that I saw the dossier, and I brought up the topic of the serum again today in front of Peter. His reaction told me that he *definitely* knows about it. Dad's reaction told me that I was definitely *not* supposed to know about it.'

'I can't imagine it's something they want to advertise.'

'Have you learnt anything at all from your end?' Lucas asked, reaching up to run a hand over his head. It felt so strange to have so little hair.

Elena sighed. 'As far as I know, Lucius has put his feelers out, but according to him so far everything's quiet.'

'What do you think that means?'

Elena snorted. 'Lucius either has shitty contacts or The Protectors are good at covering their tracks.'

'I'm going to go with the latter. We had no idea that Mum and Dad could be involved in such an elaborate plot. I'd say The Protectors are good at being sneaky.' Lucas could hear the bitter edge to his voice, hating that there was any cause for bitterness at all.

I should be able to trust my parents.

'I'm sorry, Lucas.'

He frowned, tucking an arm under his head and leaning back against his pillow. 'What are you sorry for?'

'Everything. Ever since I was born I've been attracting trouble. Maybe if I wasn't around—'

'Shut up, E. You're being stupid.'

'Well, I'm going to fix it.'

Lucas felt his frown deepening. 'How?'

'I don't want to tell you. Knowing you, you'll flip out.'

'What are you up to?' Lucas could feel pressure building behind his eyes. He closed them, blocking out the lights of his bedroom. Maybe he didn't want to know? His adopted sister was especially skilled at biting off more than she could chew.

'Sebastian's coming with me.'

He opened his eyes again. 'Coming with you where?'

'To IMI headquarters.'

Lucas sat upright, fingers tightly gripping the phone. 'Why the hell are you going back there? It's way too dangerous.'

'You're doing your bit; I'm doing mine. I need to figure out exactly what Chester has planned for my blood.'

'You're not listening to me,' Lucas chided, 'it's too dangerous.'

'With Sebastian coming I'll be a lot safer, though.'

Lucas groaned. This all seemed far too familiar. 'Elena, you *always* get caught.'

'I do not!'

'You do. And does Lucius approve of this plan?'

'I haven't told him and I'm not planning to. Lucius may be my father, but he doesn't own me.'

'Well then, Sebastian must be an idiot to be letting you go.'

'He doesn't own me either.'

Lucas groaned louder still. 'There is no way William

would have let you walk into harm's way like this.' He regretted the words the moment he spoke them.

The line went silent. 'I thought I'd asked you not to bring him up anymore?'

Lucas knew that Elena's usual solution to any emotional problem was to just ignore it. He wasn't convinced that would help in the long run. William had tried to do the right thing by leaving and avoiding temptation, yet what he'd really done was piss Elena off more, leaving her at the mercy of the people planning to kill her. The poor guy just couldn't win.

'He was my friend, too, you know,' Lucas murmured. 'I get what he did to you was shitty, but William didn't mean to hurt you.'

'Drop it, Lucas.'

'William could help you now. I could get word to Marianne and—'

'I said, drop it. He left. End of story, nothing more to say.'

'You're an idiot. At least tell me that you have a proper plan for going back?'

Elena scoffed, and Lucas almost smiled. He could picture her rolling her eyes. 'I don't need a plan. I'll just make it up as I go along.'

'That's just about the dumbest thing that's ever come out of your mouth.'

'I'll be okay, Lucas,' Elena said, sounding as if she was trying to reassure herself more than anything.

Lucas shook his head, biting his tongue rather than insulting her intelligence further. This plan could only end badly. 'When are you leaving?'

'Soon.'

CHAPTER TWENTY-ONE: ALLIES

Roshan rolled over and yawned. The mattress he lay on smelt of mould and fur, and was damp from the years it had spent in the darkened basement he called home. The thought of replacing it had never occurred to the creature.

He stretched his paws out in front of him, feeling the crackling of joints and the pull of muscle as he did. Licking drool from his snout and scratching his ear with a hind leg, he then began to stretch all over again.

He sensed the approaching night outside. When the sun finally started to fade, his pack would be free to roam the city without consequence.

Roshan's limbs began to twitch as he felt the start of the change. Fur shed from his skin in clumps, his dark grey flesh suddenly suffused with the pink of humanity. His bones and connective tissue cracked and crunched, louder than before—shrinking, breaking, and healing. Muscles grew, lengthened and recovered, stretching over the newly-formed skeletal structure that comprised his chosen human form. His arms morphed and stretched, now showing fingers instead of claws, his wriggling toes speaking more of feet than paws. Running his fingers down his body, Roshan felt the well-defined proportions of a body chosen long ago designed purely to entice the female form.

Of course, Roshan had taken many human forms over

the years, but this skin suit was his major drawcard. Every time he wore it there was an easy meal willing and waiting, and it was a simple matter to extend his pack through the many, inevitable sexual encounters. Roshan also knew that this was the body that Elena had seen and responded to. Though he had felt her resistance, he had also smelt her underlying desire.

Yes, this human form would keep for a while.

His human eyes now finding focus in the dark, Roshan turned and looked over the sixty other wolves tangled in a bunch on the floor surrounding him. His pack would be lost without his command, helpless to hide in a world that would not accept their existence. He was their father, their mother, their sibling, and their leader. Ultimately, it was Roshan's decisions that ensured the pack's safety and continued existence.

John had let his London pack down, growing too cocky and underestimating the Vampires' power. Roshan would not make the same mistake, would do what it took to ensure pack safety, to extend their life.

Roshan let his gaze slip away from the sleeping wolves, focusing on the concrete ceiling above and, once again, debating his recent decisions. Had he done the right thing? Was making a deal with a vampire really going to help him find Elena?

It had never been done before. Vampires and vânătors did not co-operate, did not bargain, yet Roshan had agreed to pay a price to have Elena. Her life was infinitely valuable. Roshan also hoped that John had been right, that her blood could enable their race to regenerate. If not, the deal he had made with the vampire was for naught—a vampire that had dared to stray into his pack's territory without invitation, a bloodsucker calling himself Julius.

Clawing, drinking blood, and killing were instinctual reactions when he came face-to-face with a vampire. Their blood was much sweeter than human blood, and was somehow more satisfying, as they were harder to hunt and catch. Before last night Roshan had never even paused to consider a lowly vampire's intentions.

'Do not harm me, little wolf, or you will be sorry,' Julius had said, stepping free of the moonlight yet sticking to the shadows. 'I come only to offer you a temporary accord. It seems we both have something in common. I think I might be able to help you with something you want, in exchange for your help.'

Roshan sneered, his lips pulling back to reveal a mass of jagged teeth. 'You dare to step foot near my den and lecture *me*? I could rip you to pieces for that and would enjoy every second of it.'

Julius laughed, tight lips absent of any true mirth. 'I have no doubt. But from what I hear, you seek a certain girl, a girl born of both vampire and vânător. Would that be correct?'

Roshan straightened, limbs his stiffening. 'How could you have know about this? Our races do not run in the same circles.'

'I do not travel in circles, little wolf. I simply make it my business to know things that may be of benefit to me.'

'What is it that you do know?' Roshan asked, his suspicion surrounding him like an impenetrable fog.

'I know that you are searching for her. Word is that you have members of your pack roaming throughout Europe, attempting to hunt her down.'

'You're trying my patience, vampire. I suggest you get to your point.'

'My name is Julius, little wolf. And I know where she is.'

Roshan stepped forward, drawing up to his full height and towering over Julius. 'Tell me where.'

Julius actually had the nerve to shake his head. 'I don't think so. Until you fulfil your end of my bargain, I cannot give you what you desire.'

Roshan growled, the sound low and ominous in his throat. His skin slowly began to change to mottled grey, tufts of soft, downy fur slowly beginning to form on his feet and hands. 'What's your proposition?'

'That we join forces.'

Roshan spat on the ground at Julius's feet. 'You are food, not my ally.'

Julius laughed. 'And once you were nothing more than an obedient lapdog to my kind, but what does that have to do with us getting what we both want now?'

'You dare mock me?' Roshan said, stalking closer as the members of his pack reared up behind him, all ready to defend their Alpha if necessary.

'First, listen to what I have to say, little wolf,' Julius began, 'then if you don't like my deal, we can each go our separate ways.'

Roshan had no intention of letting Julius walk away—he was very hungry. 'What is it that you propose?'

An evil glint sparkled up in Julius's eyes. 'In exchange for the girl's location, I want you and as many members of your combined packs as possible to help me bring down the Master Vampire.'

Roshan scoffed. 'Are you speaking of the legendary leader of the Vampires? Isn't he supposed to be a myth? No wolf has ever seen him, no wolf really ever talks about him. No wolf even knows if he truly exists.'

Julius gave Roshan a cynical grin. 'Trust me. He is very real, and he is the reason that your pack is being hunted into oblivion. He is also the reason I am now relegated to the shadows.' Julius sneered, blue eyes rising up to stare into Roshan's. 'We are at the top of the food chain, yet are forced to hide to protect the fragile minds of the very creatures that provide us our nourishment. Humans should fear *us*, not the other way around.'

'I agree,' Roshan said, but cautiously, 'yet what do you have to gain from the Master Vampire's death?'

'Lucius cannot die,' Julius answered, smiling at the look of surprise on Roshan's features. 'He is the direct creation of Satan himself. Lucius will die when Satan is done with him and not before. Until then, he is forced to continue this life.'

Roshan's pupils glowed like tiny stars. 'Then I do not understand your plan.'

'I want him to suffer, as he has made me suffer. I want all that is important to him to feel pain and die horribly. I want …' He stopped talking, looking back at Roshan. 'I want to avenge my wife.'

'How do I know that you actually know where Elena is?'

'I don't suppose you would take my word for it?'

Roshan growled. 'No.'

Julius shrugged, black curls brushing against his collar. He held a hand up in front of Roshan, concentrating on extending one fingernail until it slowly changed into a long, black talon.

'What are you doing?' Roshan bellowed as Julius's nail drew dangerously close.

'I am giving you proof.'

Julius neatly flicked the sharp talon across his own wrist. Blood oozed from the wound, winding a path down his forearm like a slippery, red snake. The wolves became more alert, the smell of blood dampening their protective instincts, distracting them from their anger. Roshan himself was finding it hard to stay focused.

'Smell her blood in my veins,' Julius said, holding his wrist out to Roshan. 'I have tasted her myself and now understand why it is that you seek her.'

Roshan grabbed the Vampire's wrist, curling his fingers over the blue veins there, massaging out more of the freely flowing blood. He lifted the vampire's arm to his nose, scenting at that which lay hidden beneath.

Elena.

In one swift movement his fangs were out and instinct took over. Julius's blood-streaked arm was soon pressed to Roshan's mouth, tongue darting out and lapping at his blood with even strokes. His teeth grazed the cold flesh, ready for a deeper feed.

'Do you believe me now?' Julius said, hand lightly on top of Roshan's shoulder, pushing him away.

Roshan held on tight, pulling the vampire to him. 'I want more.'

Julius laughed, fingers now digging painfully into Roshan's taut muscles. 'And you shall, little wolf, when you have Elena to yourself.'

Roshan released him, taking a step back and resisting the urge to rub his bruised shoulder. The wound on Julius's wrist was already healing. 'How do I know that you will stand by this deal?' He licked the blood on his lips, feeling a little of Elena's essence travel through him, tempting him.

Julius shook his head, expression serious. 'I suppose you don't, but what other options are there? I'm giving you a chance to hunt and kill vampires *and* find Elena.'

Roshan took a step forward again, pressing his chest against Julius, showing dominance. 'I can hunt and kill vampires any time that I want, bloodsucker. I can find Elena, too. I don't need you.'

Julius didn't back down. 'Maybe so, but you'll never get to Elena without my help.'

'When I find her, she *will* come to me.'

Julius snorted. 'You have to find her first, which I can assure you will not be easy.'

'I'll take my chances.'

Julius's blue eyes slowly leeched of colour, drawing black. His nostrils flared, his lips forming a tight line over fangs that threatened to pierce through his skin. 'Then good luck to you,' Julius muttered stiffly. 'While the Vampires grow strong and The Protectors brew potions that bring about your destruction, enjoy the time you waste in this basement. Elena might cross your path again, but you and I both know that won't happen.'

Julius turned to leave but Roshan grabbed his wrist. 'Wait.'

'Yes?' Julius tried to hide his smile.

'You really know where Elena is?'

'Of course. I make it my business to know these things.'

'Then we have a deal.'

'We do?'

'I will actively begin hunting these vampires of which you speak, but within a month I expect to know Elena's location.'

Now Julius was grinning. 'Kill enough vampires and you will have upheld your end of the bargain. And I *will* tell you where Elena is.'

He broke free of Roshan's hold. 'I'll be in touch, little wolf. If we're going to start a war, it might as well be over the deaths of the right kind of vampires.'

Before Roshan could respond, and with a whisper of wind, the vampire was gone. Start a war? What had the crazy vampire meant by that?

Coming back to the present, Roshan shook off his nervousness and rolled into a sitting position. Around him the pack began to stir, night embracing the land and daylight surrendering to the darkness. He could smell the pack's collective hunger in the air, a longing to stretch their legs and hunt in the city waiting beyond that was almost palpable.

His agreement with Julius played through his head again. Had Roshan done right by his pack? After all, Elena was *his* prize, not the pack's. But in saying that, if her blood was as potent as he'd hoped, her capture would benefit them all.

A few wolves whimpered as they awoke. Roshan leaned over the side of the mattress and stroked the neck and ears of the closest one. This wolf was relatively young, probably less than a year old. It pawed wildly at the air and then rolled over so that Roshan could rub down its stomach.

Roshan smiled.

The pack started to shift into their human forms as they awoke. Vânǎtors naturally slept in their wolf form, but to blend in with the modern world night time brought about their conversion. It was much easier to hunt humans if you took on their forms. Tonight, though, they would start hunting vampires instead—gamey meat, yet sweeter blood.

Roshan gave the young wolf one last pat before turning away. His ears caught the sound of a warning growl. He jumped to his feet, straining for that sound again, certain it had come from one of his wolves in the chamber above.

Roshan tilted his head back, sniffing at the air, scanning it for traces of vampire. He could smell nothing but the damp and rot of the basement. He scented the warmth of his pack's flesh and the hint of sweat on their fur. He smelt cement dust under foot and the strange tang of metal.

His nostrils flared as he caught a whiff of human, laced

with the smell of corrosion, smouldering iron, and metal filings. He'd smelt a Protector.

The wolves gathered around Roshan as he strode through the group, opening the vault door and stalking slowly up the stairs. The scent got stronger with every step, the sound of a rapidly beating heart cutting through the shuffling sound of his pack behind.

Roshan slowly opened the door to the factory above, senses on full alert, cautiously scanning the area. He could definitely only hear one heartbeat, so there had to be but a single Protector.

Good.

Roshan's guttural warning growl echoed throughout the empty factory. He heard the heartbeat pick up the pace, could feel the press of magic constricting the air in the space around him. Breathing was as unpleasant as the stench of the Protector's essence saturating the air around them and smelt somehow familiar.

Roshan quickly shifted back to his wolf form, the rest of his pack following suit. They were strong and fast in human form, but as wolves they had teeth and claws—he wasn't taking any chances with this one. The Protectors were far more powerful than the Vampires gave them credit for, and this magic user was drawing ever nearer.

Roshan started to wonder if Julius had somehow sent the intruder, had betrayed him by leading The Protectors to his den.

If so, they will all die for this.

'Wait!' a voice yelled, the sound echoing across the wide expanse of the abandoned factory. 'I mean you no harm. I've come here to make you an offer.'

An offer?

Roshan stalked forward, still searching for the voice

amongst the rusted machinery, dust-collecting benches, and darkened corners of the expanse. Baring his teeth and snarling at the slightest of movements in his left peripheral vision, he directed the rest of the pack to follow suit and fan out around him. The Protector's heart leapt, skipping and stuttering in fear. This pleased Roshan no end, as it gave him an edge.

'Please,' the man said, stepping hesitantly from the shadows, holding his shaking hands above his head. 'You can see I am unarmed. I promise I won't do anything. I just came here to talk.'

Just talking seemed unlikely. Roshan snorted, flicking his ears back and forth and listening for outside movement, or any other sound that might indicate a sneak attack. The air was still absent of other intruders.

The man slowly lowered his hands, though wisely kept them visible. His fingers still shook, but he was already lifting his chin and pulling his shoulders taut, attempting to exude a calm and control he obviously didn't feel. Roshan was not fooled though; the man's shallow breaths and treacherous heartbeat belying his attempt at composure. 'Please shift to human form so we may talk. I promise it will be worth your while.'

Aren't I popular this week?

Roshan straightened up, his spine lengthening as his body flowed back into a more human shape. He didn't take orders from a human, but it would make it easier to communicate.

'Last time I saw you, little man, you had me caged in a chimney,' Roshan muttered, his tongue reshaping itself. He still had a faint lump on the top of his head from the botched escape to prove it.

'And I apologise for that,' The Protector said, hastily wiping the sleeve of his shirt across the beads of perspiration forming on his forehead. He lowered his arm almost immediately, the swift and unexpected action drawing a chorus of barks and growls from the more protective members of the pack. 'But I, uh, had no choice in the matter,' he continued somewhat hesitantly. 'You were about to steal something that belonged to me.'

'Elena is mine!' Roshan roared.

The man held his hands up, placating. 'It appears she belongs to neither of us now. The Vampires have her.' He practically spat out the word 'vampire' and had uttered with disgust. Roshan was a little taken aback at this. Weren't the Vampires and Protectors aligned together against his kind?

His patience was wearing thin, though. Between the visit from Julius the night before and this member of the IMI now standing in his den, he was pissed off. 'What do you want?'

'My name is Chester, I'm a Protector with the IMI and—'

'I don't care *who* or *what* you are. What are you doing in my den?'

Chester took a tentative step forward, his hands still held out in front of him. Brave, considering Roshan was about to kill him. A lone Protector and his magic could do nothing to slow down an entire pack of werewolves. 'Like I said, I have an offer that I would like to make you.'

'What could you possibly have to offer me? You just said yourself that Elena is with the Vampires.'

Chester reached slowly towards his pocket, setting off yet another procession of angry howls. Roshan's pack snarled and snapped at him, and his fingers stilled, waiting for permission. 'May I?'

'Try anything treacherous and my kindred will take much joy from killing you.'

Shaking, Chester pulled a small, glass vial out of his pocket and held it out in front of him for Roshan to see.

'What is that?' Roshan said, staring at the luminescent liquid.

Chester's lips quirked as he looked proudly at the small vial he held between his fingers. 'It's the answer to all of your problems, vânător, and a chance to finally even up the playing field with our now *mutual* enemy.'

Roshan's eyes narrowed, his whole body rippling with unease. His skin was crawling with doubt, and yet somehow he found his clawed fingers reaching out for this unknown possibility. Despite reservations and shady deals between mutual enemies, he knew this opportunity was going to be interesting. What was he getting his pack into now?

CHAPTER TWENTY-TWO: PREPWORK

Pain teased at the edges of my mind like fingers digging into already bruised flesh. Dull throbbing made my eyelids heavy, blood rushing in my veins and pounding through my head, making me quite nauseous. But I continued regardless, concentrating as hard as I could, and at the same time trying to relax my mind as Lucius had instructed.

'Good, Elena.' That was all Lucius had said—that was all he ever said. It seemed I could really do no wrong lately.

'Higher!' Sebastian shouted.

'Shut up!' I yelled. It was hard to concentrate and talk at the same time.

'Take him higher, Elena,' Lucius whispered next to me. His voice was soothing and encouraging. I tried to ignore the pain, wiping a hand across my sweaty brow and heaping all my concentration on the courtyard chairs I was balancing in mid-air.

Sebastian hovered above me, sitting up proudly on the highest chair, smirking like a four-year-old atop his sandcastle. The object of the exercise—besides not booting Sebastian's taunting butt from the chair and sending him face-first into the fountain—was to be able to fully manipulate my new gift. Lifting and moving an object with the mind was one thing, but being able to do several tasks at once was where true power could be found, or so Lucius kept telling me.

'Higher, Elena!' Sebastian pressed.

'I'll give you higher,' I muttered, concentrating on the throbbing centre in my brain, calming myself and feeding it thoughts of the chair lifting higher, so high I hoped Sebastian's head would take out the ceiling.

He was really starting to bug me lately. It wasn't totally his fault, though. Sebastian had been helpful, present for all my training, and had even showed me a few new moves. The problem was clearly me, because the more I was around him, the more I seemed to like him—and not just in the 'I want to be friends' way I'd advocated no more than a month before.

'You can do it,' he said again, legs dangling over the side of the chair. 'Take me higher.'

'I said, shut up!'

I was yelling again. I'd been doing that a lot lately, too. It seemed wrong to be so mad at someone simply for being attractive. Problem was that I didn't know how to stop, because Sebastian made me anxious—he made my knees quake and my head feel giddy. Not a great combination when I was supposed to be involved with someone else, namely my fly-by-night vampire William Granville.

Lucius's breath was a sudden cool comfort on my neck. 'He's trying to break your concentration. You need to block all outside distractions and focus on raising Sebastian's chair higher than the others.'

'He's heavy.'

'He's not heavy. Your mind believes that to be true but it's not. This gift knows no limit set by weight alone. Elena, you can lift and move whatever you desire if you truly believe you can.'

'Then why does it hurt?'

'Because you're flexing a part of your brain that hasn't

been active until now. If you exercise it enough, telekinesis will become second-nature to you.'

I wanted to believe him. What he said made sense but my head felt like it was going to explode. I was just about seeing stars. I sniffed—was my nose bleeding? A quick wipe with the back of my hand confirmed it.

I discreetly licked off the blood before anyone noticed.

Yum.

As my concentration wavered, the chairs were suddenly dropping back to the courtyard floor and crashing against the terracotta, several bouncing off and into the swimming pool. Sebastian's weight broke the legs of his chair on impact and crushed it underneath him, breaking several floor tiles in the process. My head instantly felt better.

'A little warning would have been good,' Sebastian mumbled, looking up at me from the floor. Those amazing eyes seemed to swallow me whole. What would happen if I let them?

I turned away. 'I didn't do it on purpose.'

'You're getting better,' Lucius said, tentatively touching me on the shoulder.

I wiggled out of his grasp. Even after three weeks at the villa, I wasn't quite ready for that physical affection. I could see that it bothered him that I was so reluctant to tighten our bond, so lately I was trying to reach out to him with words instead. 'Thanks for your help, Lucius. I don't know if I could have learnt as much as I have so quickly without you.'

He bowed his head, the same way he always had when I thanked him. 'I must teach you what I can. I will be leaving soon, and I need to know you can protect yourself, if necessary.'

'Leaving?'

Sebastian flashed me a look. I didn't know him well

enough yet to know what it meant, but I think it meant: *Elena, tread with caution.* I'd told Lucas a week ago that I was looking for ways to get back to Bucharest and find out what The Protectors were up to. If Lucius was leaving I would finally have that chance. Perhaps Sebastian thought I had a crappy poker face and would give away my intentions?

Lucius nodded. 'There have been some... disturbances in Paris. Some vampires have gone missing, too many to be a coincidence.'

'Vânâtors?' I offered.

'Possibly. Whatever the reason, it's a little too close to home. I need to find out what's going on.'

'Do you want me to come with you?'

Both Sebastian and Lucius were taken aback. 'Why would you think that?'

'You said you were training me so I could protect myself. I'm assuming you want me to put some of these new found skills to the test?'

'No. I'm training you because it's your birth right and because I don't want you to be helpless against other vampires when I leave.'

'You mean Julius?'

Sebastian was at my side. His arm brushed mine as he knelt down, surveying the damaged floor with a critical eye. While I forced myself not to touch my tingling flesh, he grimaced, already standing and backing away from the damage. I seemed to be the last thing on his mind.

Sebastian looked over his shoulder. 'I can think of scarier vampires right now,' he murmured, fingers brushing mine as he turned and headed for the stairs.

Marcus appeared out of nowhere, dropping to his knees near the rubble of terracotta. 'What happened?' he shrieked.

I frowned at him. Marcus was being a little melodramatic

over a few broken tiles and one bent-out-of-shape chair. When I looked back at the stairs, Sebastian was gone. He'd been acting strange, too. Why be afraid of Marcus? The guy was a little weird but not exactly dangerous.

Lucius sighed, touching a hand to the vampire's shoulder. 'We were training, Marcus. It was an accident. Elena's still learning to control her gift.'

'Training!' he shrieked again, voice cracking. 'That is why we have two acres of garden! The courtyard is not a training ring. These tiles were imported! I handpicked them in Turkey!' Marcus touched the tiles tentatively, running his fingers over the smooth surface.

'It's not so bad,' Lucius reassured.

'It's a disaster.'

'Can't we just glue them back down?' I said, kneeling beside him and starting to arrange the pieces back together. 'It would be like a mosaic.'

Marcus scoffed, tossing his long dark hair over his shoulder. His almond eyes narrowed to slits, already shifting to black to mirror his mood. 'Glue them back together!' he snorted. 'Do you have any idea how expensive these tiles were?'

'You could buy some more,' I offered, aware of the opulent surroundings and the wealth these vampires had accumulated over the centuries. What were a few more imported tiles?

'They were handmade, one-of-a-kind!'

'Okay, calm down. They're just floor tiles, Marcus.'

Marcus took a calming breath and then flicked his wrist at me. 'Lucius, get your daughter away from me right now before I kill her.'

'Seriously?' I said, wide-eyed and surprised. Lucius hurriedly dragged me back to my feet.

'Seriously,' Marcus replied.

'Over floor tiles?'

Lucius cupped a hand over my mouth, dragging me out of reach before Marcus had a total meltdown. We were in the library with the door closed in a heartbeat. Lucius was laughing. 'You seem to rub Marcus the wrong way, and I find that fascinating. He generally gets on very well with women.'

I settled into the armchair by the window, my surprise turning to disbelief. 'He doesn't come across as a ladies' man.'

Lucius coughed, covering his smile with a hand. 'No, I suppose he doesn't.'

'Marcus is a little strange. Did you know he flipped his lid yesterday because I accidentally spilt some peanut butter on the sofa cushion? Does he have OCD?'

'He will get over it.'

'I hope so. He freaks me out.'

Lucius laughed all the harder, a sound that was warm and full. 'He scares Sebastian, too.'

A smile touched my lips. 'Yeah, I noticed that.'

Lucius was about to reach for me again—I could sense it—but stilled his hand in mid-air, smoothing it through his curls instead. 'I should probably head back to Synth Corp.'

'Now? You've only been home for an hour.'

'I like that you call this place home.'

Whatever. Slip of the tongue.

'You work a lot.'

'Vampires are insatiable and the world needs more blood. I do need to get back though, so will you be alright if I leave you here?'

'Sebastian's around here somewhere. I'm sure if Marcus decides to slice me open with a jagged piece of terrazzo, he'll be the first to know.'

That earned me another smile. 'I'll come back later and we can practice some more.'

We were at that strange moment again that seemed to occur at the end of all our conversations—the uncomfortable pause. I wasn't scared of him anymore, not even anxious, but now I was finding myself stuck in territory somewhere between familiarity and awkwardness. 'Okay, see you later then.'

Lucius nodded, moving out of the room gracefully.

I turned my attention to my book on the side table. It was a permanent fixture; Maria had given up trying to put it away. Sometimes I read through the book of mythology, other times I just sat and looked at the cover, staring at the angels and demons. Yet it was never Lucifer's twisted form that caught my attention. It was the angel above him that I always saw—strong, powerful, and inhumanly beautiful.

Michael.

It was strange how that name resonated with me.

'Hey.'

I looked up from the cover of the book. Green eyes, with twisting tendrils of grey, looked back at me. 'Sebastian,' I murmured, placing the book onto the side table. 'What do you want?'

'The coast is clear. Marcus left for Rome, cursing your name and screaming that he would not rest until the floor is fixed.'

'He's kind of intense.'

Sebastian covered his rising smile with a hand. 'Marcus is …' He paused and seemed to change his mind mid-sentence. 'Yes, he's intense.'

He flopped down into the armchair opposite, still managing to make the movement look graceful. Sebastian pointed to the book. 'You reading that old thing again?'

'I like it. It's informative.'

'I notice that you mostly just look at it.'

I shrugged. 'The cover is evocative. I guess I like the symbolism of good triumphing over evil, or something like that.'

Sebastian shook his head. 'You don't seem to look at the cover in contemplation. You're studying it—memorising it.'

I started to frown. 'Are you secretly spying on me?'

'No, I'm just observant.'

'So am I.'

'I don't think you're as observant as you think you are.' Sebastian's swirling gaze found mine. 'There's probably a few things right under your nose that you keep on missing.'

'Such as?'

Sebastian didn't answer, just kept on staring at me with that intense gaze, as if expecting me to know the answer. And maybe I did. Maybe I just didn't really want to know. I kept my eyes locked on his, determined not to be the first to look away. I usually was, cowering from the heat that leapt through my veins at my body's response to his. Now I was trying to control that reaction so I could manipulate the intimacy that flared between us and find a way to ignore it.

'Why do your eyes keep swirling and changing colour?'

'What?'

I'd caught him off-guard.

Good. 'Your eyes only move when you're around me.'

'Is that so? I suspect it's a trick of the light.'

I scoffed. 'What a crock of shit.'

'Elena,' he chided. Sebastian liked my foul language about as much as Lucius and the others did.

'I asked your father,' I continued. 'He said you had green eyes. Lucius said the same thing, that your eyes have only started changing since I arrived on the scene.'

'Are you so certain it's you?' The sincerity in his voice made me falter. I'd never considered that there could be other options.

Damn, maybe I am being conceited.

Sebastian picked at the material on the arm of the chair, his smile fading. 'Perhaps you bring something out in me,' he murmured, eyes downcast.

'Like what?'

'Something unexplainable.'

'Nothing's unexplainable.'

Sebastian shook his head, pushed up from the chair and stepped towards me. He tapped a finger on the book, his eyes suddenly meeting mine. They were no longer grey, no longer green. Now they were pure silver, just as I had seen in the dreams of my past. 'Some things *are* unexplainable,' Sebastian said, his hot breath caressing my face. 'Some things you just have to feel to understand.' He looked away then, quickly turning and striding out of the room.

I stood to follow him, looking down at the book as I passed. The face of the angel Michael stared back at me, eyes bright and rimmed with silver.

I gasped. Previously, I had never been able to see the angel's eyes in the picture. Michael had always been looking down at Lucifer, studying his prey.

I looked back at the door. Sebastian was already disappearing behind the fountain in the courtyard. Had he done something to change the cover of my favourite book?

I quickly glanced down at the picture again, shaking my head in confusion as I saw that Michael now appeared in his original pose—looking down, eyes hidden. Had I imagined the change? Was Sebastian messing with my sanity, making me hallucinate, or was this *his* ability? Could he create illusions, the very reason I'd been seeing his face everywhere?

One thing was certain: Sebastian was an oddity, a mystery just begging to be solved. Did my dreams of him mean that I was the one who was supposed to crack that mystery, or were they the very reason I should stay clear?

What the hell did Sebastian have to do with me?

CHAPTER TWENTY-THREE: RIDING

zipped my new leather riding jacket up higher, blocking out the cold of the icy December wind. I slipped on gloves to cover my fingers and steadied my feet on the cobblestone ground, straddling Sebastian's motorcycle. Today was riding lesson number five, not that I was complaining. Machinery and I got along well, and Sebastian seemed to be the proverbial grease in the wheels. He shared my love of all things fuel-injected and turbo-charged, which meant I paid attention when he ground out orders for clutch control and smoother gear release. He was determined that I'd perfect the basics before taking to the open road with *his* motorbike.

Fair's fair, I supposed.

Today was also the day I'd be headed back to Bucharest. Was I crazy? Probably. Lucas certainly thought I was an idiot for even thinking about it, but what other choices did I have? The Protectors had my blood, Chester was crazy, and I was the only one who knew the internal layout of the IMI. At least, those were the reasons I kept using to justify said stupidity.

Sebastian slapped the side of my helmet. He mouthed at me to focus, pointing out the three day old scratch on his exhaust where I'd taken an unsealed back road a little too fast for the 'basics'.

I nodded, understanding that another scratch meant

bye-bye to the trip. I was lucky he was even humouring me, because if Lucius learned of my plans, he'd kill Sebastian and then … well, I really didn't have a clue what he'd do to me, but I wasn't keen on finding out. Lucius had enough of his own problems to deal with. That Julius guy was totally creepy.

I shuddered, picturing the letter that had arrived at the villa two days before. It had been addressed to me personally. No postage stamp, hand delivered—again, totally creepy and thoroughly frightening.

Elena,
To taste you was a surprise; to learn of your existence,
a reward. I should like for us to meet again, you and I.
I would like to see your final breath leave your lips and
your eyes go blank as my hands take your life from you.
But, alas, I am certain that anticipation will make that
act sweeter—so for now, I watch from afar, learning your
weaknesses, discovering truths.
One day I will come for you. One day your fear and
your death will feed the revenge I have long since craved.
Wait for me, Elena. I wish to make this last.

Julius.

'Are you okay?' Sebastian said, flipping my visor up.

I jumped, caught in a world of mounting fear. 'I'm fine.'

'Really? Because I'm foreseeing further damage to my motorbike,' he said dryly, touching his boot to the exhaust.

I went to snap the visor down again but he caught my hand in his, bringing it up to his chest as he took a step nearer. 'I'm fine,' I reiterated.

'You're thinking about that note, aren't you?'

'The note, The Protectors, Lucas … it's all the same.'

'We don't have to go to Bucharest. We can let Lucius handle it, like he said he would.'

I shook my head. 'He's distracted by Julius and the dead vampires. The Protectors are probably the least of his concerns.'

'Don't be so sure.'

'And if I told him I was going to Bucharest to find out what this serum was … do you think he'd want to help then?'

Sebastian's lips twitched. I couldn't see his eyes because they were hidden behind shades, but he obviously found my suggestion amusing. 'No. I think Lucius would chain you to the villa at the mere mention of you putting yourself in harm's way. He's grown very fond of you.'

I tore my hand away from Sebastian's. 'You know, I managed just fine on my own before I came here.'

'Yes,' Sebastian said, and with a widening smile, nodded his head. 'It must have been wonderful being held prisoner in a coal factory and hunted by an amorous Alpha. Simply smashing.'

'Don't be a dick. I meant before that. I never said I wasn't grateful for being rescued.'

'You never said 'thank you' either.'

I growled. 'Has anyone ever told you how annoying you are?'

Sebastian chuckled. 'Not lately, although I'm sure you'll be colourful with your descriptions.'

'You're not just annoying,' I said, leaning back on the bike and crossing my arms in front of my chest, 'but you're also—'

'Charming? Sexy? Intelligent?'

All of the above.

'No. You're a, a …'

Jesus, I don't even have an answer. He's practically perfect.
'Just shut up.'

'Is that the best you have?'

'For now.'

Sebastian laughed. What a dick. 'I better watch myself. Your witty comebacks are damaging.'

I gave him a wry look. 'It seems to me that nothing bothers you.'

'Ah, now if only that were true.' He frowned slightly. After a moment's reflection Sebastian tried to smile again, but I could see the grin was forced.

'What's getting you down, Sebastian?'

'Do you really want to know?' The smile vanished. Behind his shades, I knew he was looking directly at me.

I nodded, finding myself surprisingly eager to know. Sebastian was still an enigma. After one month at the villa together with him constantly guarding me, I still knew so little about him. No matter how many questions I asked, Sebastian never really seemed to have an answer. To top it off, when he did answer, it was generally cryptic and impossible to decipher. Yesterday, I'd asked Sebastian for a decoder so I could speak his language. His answer had been along the lines of me needing a good snogging and then all answers would be translated.

Okay. So Sebastian didn't say 'snogging', but he'd pointed out once or twice before that a kiss would clear everything up. But how could I let him kiss me when he confused me so? Correct me if I'm wrong, but wouldn't intimacy complicate the situation further? And William … what the hell was I going to do about that?

I should just ignore both men completely and go back to being the chastity-belt-wearing, anti-man-loving girl I was beforehand. Easy.

Not.

Sebastian slid his shades down the bridge of his nose. Dark eyebrows accentuated the slight slant of his eyes, swirling depths that always mesmerised and confused. 'You really want to know what gets me down?'

'Sure.'

He gripped me by the shoulders and gave me a slight shake. The intensity of his eyes penetrated mine. I felt Sebastian's frustration spilling, his fingers gripping me tighter but not hurting. 'What gets me down is you.'

'Me?' I would have pointed to my own chest, but he was standing too close. His leg brushed mine, his arms holding us locked together so I couldn't move mine away.

'Yes, you.'

'But why?' My voice was a hoarse whisper, and that really pissed me off. Sebastian shouldn't be having such an effect on me. I *wouldn't* allow him to have this effect on me.

I straightened up. 'So, tell me why I upset you?' I said, voice normal again.

Good for me.

Sebastian stepped as far into my personal space as possible, his legs touched mine. If the bike hadn't been wedged between my legs, it would have been likely that our bodies would have intertwined instead.

My breath caught in my throat, and a small gasp escaped my lips as his head lowered towards mine. Was he going to kiss me? Was I going to let him?

Sebastian broke the spell and stepped back, slapping the side of my helmet, and pointing at the exhaust again. 'That's why you get me down. You damage my property.'

Confused, I frowned. I wasn't sure what had almost just happened. One minute I thought we were having a moment; the next, we were talking about the stupid exhaust pipe again. 'It's just a scratch,' I managed to say, rearranging my features to hide the hint of disappointment that I felt.

Jeez.

'Just a scratch,' he echoed, 'a scratch that could have been avoided if you had been paying attention.'

So much for his earlier concern.

He slapped my helmet again harder, throwing me off balance. My head was knocked to the side, but I snapped back up quickly, planting my feet on the ground and gripping onto the bike to stop myself from falling by squeezing my thighs together. Any ordinary human would have crashed to the ground, possibly crushed under the weight of the bike, but my superior strength gave me the upper hand. It still didn't stop me from snarling back at Sebastian. 'Why the hell did you do that?'

He struck out like a hissing snake and snapped my visor back in place. 'I think you know the answer. If I'm going to risk my neck by taking you back to Bucharest, I want to make sure that you're alert and ready for anything.'

His voice was muffled with the visor down, so I flipped it back up and planted my hands on my hips. 'I have been training with The Protectors for over four years, you know. I can handle myself.'

Sebastian tilted his head to the side, no doubt surveying me carefully behind the darkened lenses of his glasses. 'Four years is not so long.'

'It is when you train almost every day.'

'Well, take a little advice from someone who is much older than you—you're not ready.'

'I could take you, Sebastian.'

'You could?'

Sebastian feigned a blow to my right side and then punched out with his left. I caught his fist in mid-flight, starting to smile. That was right before he kicked my feet out from under me and then pushed the bike over. I tumbled to the ground, the bike wedged between my legs.

I yelped in frustration. My leg was trapped under the falling motorcycle's heavy bulk, and my hands scraped on the cobblestone driveway as I attempted to brace myself.

'You've scratched my bike again,' Sebastian said, kneeling and shaking his head at me.

'You pushed me, you idiot!'

Sebastian rose, easily hoisting the bike off of me. 'Which would not have happened had you been planting your feet and held your frame,' he pointed out. 'It's just more proof that you're not ready for tonight.'

'What's happening tonight?' Marcus enquired, eyebrow rising as he stepped through the double doors and onto the cobblestone driveway. Judging by the stiffness of Sebastian's shoulders, Marcus had taken him by surprise, too. Good. It was nice to know I wasn't the only one freaked out by vampires sneaking up on me.

'Nothing,' I lied, pulling myself to my feet and dusting my jacket off. My new gloves had scuff marks on them.

Just great.

I glared at Sebastian, hoping I'd get an opportunity sometime in the future to kick his ass off the back of a motorcycle, too. It didn't seem likely, so I focused my attention back on Marcus. He still seemed quite pissed off at me. He hadn't been able to get replacement tiles for the courtyard, as the original artisan had died about eight-five years ago. So apparently the whole courtyard was going to have to be re-done. I'd offered to help, but Marcus pretty much told me where I could jam that idea.

He shook his head at me. 'I can taste a lie. Did you know that, Elena?'

'No, you can't,' I drawled. 'That would be like saying you can hear colours.'

Marcus's eyes narrowed and his cheeks went red. I was starting to recognise that look, and realised that I'd developed quite a particular talent for pissing him off. 'What were you talking about?' he repeated, voice low and controlled, but drenched in an anger begging to be unleashed.

I shrugged. 'The million different ways why Sebastian is an idiot.'

Sebastian glanced at me over his shades, lips pressed into a tight line. Okay, so apparently now wasn't a good time for jokes. Marcus seemed to agree because he took three steps towards me and gripped my chin, forcing me to meet his eyes. The almond-coloured depths swirled, darkening as the colour seeped away. The smell of freshly cut grass tickled my nose, creeping up my nostrils and slithering down the back of my throat.

I swallowed, tasting the bitterness of my lies, feeling a growing urgency to reveal the truth about my plans to head to Bucharest, to reveal what I'd been trying to keep a secret from everyone for over two weeks. And as Marcus's fingernails dug into my skin, pulling my face closer to his, I knew that he was trying to compel me.

I started to squirm in his grip, closing my eyes to fight him. 'Get off me, Marcus.'

'Tell me what you're doing tonight.'

The need was so strong now that I felt my mouth slowly open to spill all my plans. Then I felt Sebastian's hand touch me. Even with gloves on, I felt the power of his own compulsion soothing me, calming me and …

Oh, boy.

That fire that seemed to steadily burn in the pit of my

stomach whenever Sebastian was around suddenly roared to life, just as if someone had thrown gasoline onto those flames. My toes started to curl up inside my boots. The surface of my body ached so fiercely that I almost turned to ask Sebastian to finish what he'd started in the Budapest airport.

Almost.

'We're doing a movie marathon on the LCD TV tonight,' I blurted, jerking my head away from Marcus's bruised fingers and Sebastian's smouldering heat. I felt breathless, unsteady on my feet. My knees really didn't want to cooperate.

Marcus looked confused but let me step away. 'A movie marathon?' He looked at Sebastian. 'Is this true?'

Sebastian shrugged but didn't answer. Typical.

'I thought you had plans with Graziella tonight?' Marcus asked.

I pulled a face. Sebastian seemed to have plans with Graziella nearly *every* night. Or at least, that was what I assumed every time he went into the city and didn't come back for hours at a time.

Jealous? Me?

'I don't see how my plans should concern you, Marcus,' Sebastian said calmly.

'If you are planning on leaving this one alone while the rest of us leave to hunt Julius,' Marcus said, pointing at me, 'then it does affect me—because it will affect Lucius.'

'Elena will not be left unattended under any circumstances.'

'Not even for a bathroom break?' They both looked at me sternly. 'Okay, jeez, lighten up.'

'I'm not certain you understand the gravity of the situation,' Marcus said, looking solely at me. 'You have sparked both Julius's curiosity and the IMI's interest.'

'Believe me, I get it,' I said, 'which is why I'm planning on watching movies.'

'Something in your words makes me doubt you.'

'How's that my problem?'

Sebastian pinched my arm, hard.

Marcus eyed me with a vicious glare before spinning on the spot and heading back inside. 'Lucius wishes to see you both in the courtyard at six.'

'Aye-aye, Captain,' I muttered under my breath as he disappeared inside. I turned and looked at Sebastian, who was already looking back at me. His gaze made me a little uncomfortable.

I jabbed a thumb over my shoulder. 'Is he always so uptight?'

'Only around you, it seems.'

'Lucius said the same thing.'

'Perhaps it's true then.'

'Whatever. You can't please everyone.'

I snapped the visor on my helmet down and reached out to take the motorbike from Sebastian. I swung my leg over and started the engine. It thrummed to life almost immediately, vibrating beneath me, reminiscent of the unsated need I still had burning inside.

I focused on the bike instead, adjusting the mirrors, and re-gripping the throttle, the engine revving louder at the touch of my hand.

I cringed as I looked down at the new scratches on the side of the chassis. I was a little depressed for the bike—it had looked so shiny and new until I'd started practising on it. This last set of scratches was all on Sebastian's head, though.

'You want me to ride with you today?' Sebastian said, gesturing to the seat.

'Worried I'll trash your bike completely?'

He slowly smiled. 'It's a bit late for that.'

I snorted, the sound lost under the helmet. 'I think I'll manage.'

I'll show him.

I focused on the cobblestone driveway, flicking the bike into gear and easing off the clutch. As I gave it some gas, the bike shot forward and I was almost at the gates before I realised I had to slow down. Ever since the note from Julius had arrived, Lucius had insisted that I stay within the confines of the villa—literally. I should never have shown it to him.

I slowed the bike to a virtual stop as I reached the gates. Placing my feet down, I spun the bike around with the ease, and took off back towards the house again. When I neared the fountain, I leaned in low to the ground as I turned, my knee splaying out for balance. I looped the fountain twice, heading up and down the driveway a few more times before screeching to a stop in front of Sebastian. Grinning, I switched off the engine.

'You're doing well,' he said, helping me lift off my helmet, 'but bike riding skills aren't going to get you out of trouble if—'

'Yeah, I get it, Sebastian. You think I'm helpless.'

'I didn't say that.'

'But you were going to.'

Sebastian didn't seem to have an answer to that. Even if they weren't his exact words, I could almost read his mind.

'I don't think you're helpless, I just worry.'

'Why? Have you suddenly warmed to the idea of you and I being friends?'

Sebastian shook his head. 'We could never be just friends, Elena. I think you know that.'

'Do I?' I was just dying to hear his explanation.

'Being friends with you would mean that I have no desire to pursue a relationship. That would be a lie.'

'So would the relationship. I already have someone, and you have *Graziella*,' I snapped out sarcastically, 'and that Spanish chick from the sports store in Rome, the blonde at the coffee shop up the road, the brunette that you—'

'Okay, I get it,' Sebastian said bitterly. 'You think I'm a player.'

I dismounted the bike carefully and rested it on the kickstand. 'Aren't you?'

He shook his head. 'Far from it. If only you knew, Elena.'

'So tell me.'

'And ruin all the mystery?'

'So, if we're not friends, then what are we?'

'Another mystery to solve, I expect.'

I screwed up my face and unzipped my jacket, removing the gloves, too. 'You really are a dick.'

That made him laugh. 'Maybe I am, but all the mystery has stirred your curiosity. Eventually, you'll come to me for answers.'

'I'm not going to kiss you, Sebastian.'

He shrugged, turning to head for the house. 'We'll see.'

A single paving stone, hidden at the edge of the courtyard's water feature, was the key to accessing the villa's underground tunnels. I was yet to investigate these but the vampires of the villa came and went so irregularly that I had yet to catch them using it.

Tiberius was demonstrating to me how to access the tunnels and holding chambers below. He tapped the paving stone with his foot, a succession of grinding and whirring sounds soon following. Then the fountain began to slide slowly across, water sloshing up the sides of the tiles and little wet droplets raining across the floor.

I bent over and peered into the dark hole beneath the fountain, noting a small set of stairs that seemed to wind down around a central column. Tiberius, Lucius and the other vampires had already started their descent. I hung back, wondering how a whole month had gone by without me noticing a secret chamber, of all places, under the damned fountain. If I'd looked closer at the steel grate set into the floor right next to it then perhaps I would have seen that the Romanesque holding cell from my earlier visions and dreams was hidden beneath. I'd just thought it was a drain.

The tunnels under the villa were similar to the visitor's entrances located back home at the IMI. They allowed a Protector to see who was seeking entrance without fear of retribution if their entry was denied. Tiberius had explained that these lower tunnels ran to various locations all over the city, which was essential for vampires avoiding the sun. The only people who knew the true location of the villa were Lucius, his thralls, Sebastian, and now me—but Julius was a problem. He knew where we lived.

If I were him—an apparent vampire criminal mastermind—I would have taken out an ad in the Yellow Pages and posted our address. If Lucius was as unpopular as he made out, giving up the location of the villa would really have caused havoc.

As I descended the stairs behind Sebastian, I trod carefully, my human eyes unable to see as well as his in the dark. Sebastian must have sensed this because he took my hand, carefully guiding me down each step.

At the bottom of the stairs I noticed a little bit of light penetrating through a hole in the wall, kind of like a tiny laser beam. I pressed my eye up against it, peering into the room beyond. I could see the wooden table from my dreams and the grate that let light in from up above. The maps I'd seen in my dreams were still sprawled across the surface of the table.

'Look after her while we're gone, Sebastian,' Lucius said gruffly.

I pulled back from the wall, temporary blinded by the light. All I could see was the back of Sebastian's head. He was standing in front of me, almost shielding me from my father's touch, which was a good plan. We couldn't risk him using his abilities and seeing flashes of anything we had planned.

'I always watch over her,' Sebastian answered. There was a weird sort of undercurrent to his words that made me shiver. Sebastian must have noticed because he gently squeezed my hand.

'Will you be okay, Elena?' Lucius asked me from somewhere in the darkness in front.

'I can look after myself.'

'Is it not alright that I am concerned for you?' He sounded a little hurt.

'Concerned is fine, but everyone seems to be belabouring that point today.' It was my turn to squeeze Sebastian's hand. I felt him stiffen.

Point taken? Maybe.

'We'll only be gone for a few days,' Tiberius added. 'I'm sure Elena will be fine.'

I heard an exasperated sigh coming from the rear.

'What is it, Marcus?' Lucius said.

'I forgot to set up the digital TV to record *Project Runway*.'

Project Runway?

I leaned forward and pressed my smiling lips against Sebastian's ear. 'Is he serious?'

Sebastian's vibrating body told me all I needed to know—Marcus was serious, and Sebastian thought it was as amusing as I did. Big, bad vampire was going to miss his favourite TV show.

'What's wrong with *Project Runway*?' Marcus grumbled.

'Nothing,' I sniggered, grabbing Sebastian's shoulders for support and burying my face against his back, 'nothing at all.'

'She's mocking me, Lucius,' Marcus hissed.

'She's not mocking you, Marcus. Let's just leave now. We have important matters to attend to.'

Marcus's growling made me want to laugh all the harder. Sebastian was shaking so much that I wondered who was going to break down first. Thankfully, the vampires left without any more attempted conversation. I heard their footsteps walking down the passage, then a door opening and closing with a thud, then the sound of the locks engaging.

'Something is seriously wrong with that one,' I said, laughing out loud now.

'He can still hear you,' Sebastian warned, though his voice was laced with amusement. He touched my hands—which were still resting on his shoulders—and pulled my arms so that they wrapped around him, pressing my chest against his back. I felt Sebastian tilt his head to the side, the softness of his cheek brushing against my lips. For a split second I seriously considered taking things further.

But I pulled back. 'Come on. We have to get going, too.'

Sebastian sighed, releasing my hands. What was it with him and trying to jump me in dark places, anyway? I was going to have to start carrying a torch.

When we reached the top of the stairs, Sebastian clicked closed the fountain entry. Water sloshed against the floor as it rolled back, dampening the top of my boots.

'I just have to get my stuff.'

I jogged across the tiled courtyard and towards the staircase that led to the second floor. I was going to need my backpack if we were leaving for Bucharest. I'd had it stashed under my bed for days, prepped and ready for the long trip ahead.

Lightning quick, Sebastian appeared in front of me, my pack slung over his shoulder.

'Did you just get that now?' I said, taking it from him.

'It wasn't hard.'

'So you just went into my room uninvited and went through my things?'

'It was quicker than waiting for you.'

I shook my head at Sebastian. 'What if there was something I didn't want you to see?'

'If you're referring to the feminine hygiene products on your nightstand, then we can safely assume I've seen items like that before.'

I could feel myself turning red—not from embarrassment, but from anger. 'I wasn't actually, but thank you for this awkward moment.' I pushed past him and headed for the door.

'I apologise if I've embarrassed you, Elena.'

Ignoring his apology, I said, 'How long will it take us to get to Bucharest?' I couldn't hear him behind me, but somehow I knew he was there.

'If we took the jet we could be there in just over an hour.'

'Lucius will know where we went if he checks the account. Plus, if we take the jet I wouldn't get a chance to ride your bike.'

'The jet would be safer, Elena. We could avoid any roaming vânătors along the way.'

'I haven't killed anything in ages,' I moaned. I turned when I realised Sebastian wasn't behind me anymore, and he wasn't laughing with me. 'Ah shit. It was a joke, Sebastian.'

'It didn't seem like it,' he replied blandly, appearing once again at my side.

I shrugged, watching his face from the corner of my eye. 'I thought you were a badass vampire? Don't sweat the small stuff. If we encounter any vânătors, it'll give me a chance to practice some of my new skills.' I rubbed my hands together. 'Plus, I'm starving and haven't hunted in ages.' I could see that I'd shocked him again. 'Jesus, Sebastian. What am I going to do with you?'

'Is it at all possible for you to avoid blasphemy?'

'Probably not.'

Sebastian pushed past me, scooping up his bike helmet from where he'd left it earlier by the side of the house. He didn't need his shades now that it was getting dark, and so tucked them inside his jacket. 'I think we should stop in Budapest and formulate a plan before we head to Bucharest. We can stay at Nicholas's place. The Alpha didn't track us to his apartment, and Nicholas is currently away helping to find Julius, so we'll be left alone.'

I raised an eyebrow at him. 'Alone?'

He deliberately met my gaze. 'Scared?'

I blew him a raspberry. 'Of you? Never.'

'Do you want the first ride?'

My brow lowered into a frown. 'What?'

'The bike,' Sebastian said, 'Do you want to ride the *bike* first.' What did he think I was thinking of riding? Him?

I answered by slipping on my gloves and zipping up my jacket. 'Of course I want to ride the *bike* first.'

'Fine, but once we hit the border of Slovenia, I'm taking over. The Vânătors and The Protectors know that Italy is our country—they don't bother us too much here—but outside of the border, I can't be so sure.'

'You sound like Lucius. Roshan's probably stopped looking for me by now.'

Sebastian eyed me dubiously. 'I very much doubt that. If the roles were reversed, I would keep searching for you forever.'

'Why?'

He stiffened, eyes clouding over for an instant. But just as quickly Sebastian changed mood, like the flick of a switch. He looked me up and down slowly, grinning, a teasing look on his face that I'd never quite seen before. And yet that look didn't quite reach his eyes. 'You're a nice piece of ass.'

'Say what?'

'You're a nice piece of—'

I punched him hard on the arm. Those words just felt wrong coming out of his mouth. Being crass just didn't suit him, and was possibly an attempt at deflection. Still, he deserved the punch.

Sebastian shrugged, turning his back to me and sliding his helmet into place. He moved to the back of the bike and secured our belongings, and if he was bothered by my reaction he didn't say.

There was nowhere else for the conversation to go so I gave up trying for the moment. I slipped my helmet on, kicking a leg over the seat of the bike. Sebastian slid onto the seat behind me, pulling me close. Wrapping his arms around my waist, he waited for me to start the bike, as silent as the dead.

At the end of the driveway the wrought iron gates opened like an invitation, the bike now thrumming underneath me in anticipation. As I edged forward, Sebastian's feet left the ground and his thighs clamped around me. We were off—no backing out now.

'Are you ready for this?' I could hear Sebastian's voice through one of the tiny speakers located inside my helmet. His voice sounded hollow, full of static. The sound was so unexpected that I even jumped a little, the bike wobbling.

'Are *you* ready?' I mocked, not sure I could legitimately answer without being called a liar.

'I was born ready, Baby Vamp.'

'Good to know. Make sure you tell me where to go.'

'Let's start with the end of the driveway and go from there.'

'Was that sarcasm?'

'I wouldn't dream of it.'

The iron gates of the villa soon disappeared in the darkness of my side mirrors. I shivered, my skin crawling with anticipation and a healthy dose of fear. I was actually scared to go back to Bucharest. Despite my bravado, I was so fearful of being trapped by Chester again that I almost turned the bike around, serum be damned. The only reason I stayed true to my course was Lucas. The thought of him back home in Cairns, snooping for information from his own parents, while I sat in the lap of luxury doing nothing at all, made me feel ill.

'What are you thinking,' Sebastian asked.

I changed gear and picked up speed, as I crossed from a side road and onto one of the busier streets that lead into the city. 'Choices.'

'Choices?'

'I think this might not have been one of my most brilliant ideas.'

'It's not too late to turn around.'

'I can't. I need to know what the IMI are up to.'

'Why? Let someone else worry about it.'

I squeezed the throttle under my fingers. 'I can't. Call me crazy, but I spent sixteen years with these people. I want to believe that this serum might have been worth all their lies and deceit.'

'You said that Lucas found documents suggesting it was a weapon *against* vampires. How can that be a good thing?'

'What if the weapon is simply a cure?'

'What?'

'What if my blood and the qualities they've managed to harness cure vampirism—as in, it makes vampires human again.'

'Why would they do that? A weapon suggests destruction.'

'The beliefs of The Protectors are supposedly built on protecting the sanctity of human life, Sebastian. Three hundred years ago they delved into the magic arts to protect the people of their villages, not to gain power. By finding a way to cure vampirism they could kill two birds with one stone. Technically, we vampires will die, but our humanity will once again be set free.'

Sebastian scoffed. 'You say The Protectors value the sanctity of human life, yet look at what they put you through. They had every intention of killing you, or worse still, leaving you in the torturous clutches of the Vânătors.' He tapped my thigh 'Turn right up here and then cut a left onto the freeway.'

I followed his directions carefully. 'I'm one person.'

'What are you saying, Elena?'

I guided the bike onto the freeway with ease, merging with the heavy flow of traffic. 'Stephanie, one of the scientists, asked me if I would have donated my blood willingly if it had been for a good cause. I thought she might have meant curing cancer or something like that, but what if she meant curing us? In either case, isn't my life worth less than everyone else's?'

'No,' Sebastian answered quickly. 'Your death would be …'

'I'm glad to hear in a roundabout way that you would miss me, Sebastian, but you get my point. If the IMI has developed a cure then I can understand Chester's methods.'

'Even if they include killing you?'

'I'm not saying I like the idea, but if what I say is true, I can understand the importance.'

'You don't want to be a vampire?'

I thought about that question carefully. Running faster than cars, being exceedingly strong, looking gorgeous and living forever certainly had its appeal, but being one of the Damned had its downside. 'I don't want to be a vampire if it means I have to go to hell.'

'You won't necessarily go to hell,' Sebastian said.

'Oh? Do the spawn of the Devil have a different vacation spot I don't know about?'

'You go to Purgatory first,' Sebastian continued, ignoring me. 'Then you're brought before a council of equal standing and judged.'

'What? How do you even know that?' The bike rocked from side to side as I turned my head around to look at him.

Whoa, not a smart move.

I focused on steadying the bike, Sebastian's arms and legs clamping down around me. 'Watch the road,' he barked.

'I *am*. Sorry.'

'Get off at the next exit and follow the signs pointing to the road to Florence.'

'Sebastian, how do you know about Purgatory and judgement and whatever?'

'Please just drive, Elena.'

'I want to know, Sebastian. I get why Lucius knows—he's been there. What's your excuse?'

'And I want life to be simple but it never is.' He sounded almost wistful.

'Just tell me about Purgatory.'

Sebastian laughed, taking me by surprise. 'Maybe I've just read the same books that you have.'

'A likely story.'

His laughter was short-lived. Sebastian was still learning how stubborn I could be.

'I shouldn't have said anything,' he whispered.

'Ahh, so you do know something?'

He muttered something in Italian, and then said, 'I'm done talking now.'

Four hours later I pulled the bike over for re-fuelling, just outside of a picturesque town called Padova, forty kilometres west of the water-logged city of Venice. Sebastian still hadn't spoken other than to give me directions. We'd passed Florence by, driven through Bologna, and both remained conspicuously silent.

It was just after ten now, and I felt cold, miserable, and a little awkward. My legs felt bowed and my fingers were stiff. I was scared of getting to Bucharest and now Sebastian was ignoring me, so it was turning into a fabulous night. But it was soon to get even better, as I watched the forty-something year old female gas attendant suggestively stroke the petrol bowser and proposition Sebastian in Italian. I was seriously going to have to learn at least some of the language.

Approximately an hour and a half later, I pulled the bike

over again. We'd reached Gorizia. It was a small town at the foot of the Julian Alps, which bordered Slovenia and the twin town of Nova Gorica.

I was feeling pretty pleased with myself. I thought I'd handled the motorbike well; we'd covered the six hundred odd kilometre distance in good time.

I killed the motor and lowered my booted feet to the ground, stretching my leather clad legs out in front of me and marvelling at how stiff they had gotten in such a short amount of time. A good stretch and a groan passing my lips, however, seemed to ease the numbness in my fingers and toes.

Sebastian slid backwards off the seat, making it easier for me to climb off the bike. I didn't fancy trying to swing my leg over his head, and to be honest, I wasn't sure if I could. I was flexible, but I wasn't a double-jointed gymnast.

'You did well,' Sebastian said, holding the bike while I dismounted, 'but now it's time for me to show you what this beautiful piece of machinery can really do.' His voice was stiff, almost mechanical. I would have said it was the microphone interference, but after four hours of the silent treatment, I wasn't so sure.

'Do I need to be strapped down to the bike for this?' It was a poor attempt at humour on my part.

He swung his long leg over the bike and took up my previous position at the front. 'No, you just need to hang on.'

'Why do we need to move so fast? Is there something wrong with keeping to the speed limit?'

Sebastian pointed to the darkness ahead. I couldn't see anything except the brightly lit border crossing where three guards monitored the comings and goings of people crossing. Was he planning on crossing illegally?

'I can see two vânătors prowling beyond the border, about five clicks over that way.'

'Do you know if they sense us?'

He shook his helmeted head. 'Not yet.'

'This motorbike isn't fast enough to outrun them, is it?'

'No.'

'Okay, no biggie. They're just regular vânătors, right?'

'Yes.' Sebastian's tone was even but cool, and questioning.

I slid onto the seat behind him, pulling myself closer to his back. 'So we'll kill them if it becomes an issue.'

He stiffened. 'That's not part of the plan, Elena.'

I scoffed. 'Will you stop treating me like glass? We knew riding might be dangerous—'

'And yet you still insisted on doing it,' Sebastian interrupted.

'So sue me. I wanted to ride the motorbike.'

'It was a stupid idea. I can't believe I let you talk me into it.'

I rolled my eyes to myself. 'We're six hours in now, might as well keep going.'

Sebastian grunted and started up the bike, gunning the throttle. He did have a valid point. Travelling by air would have been safer, not to mention quicker. I blamed the irrationality of my decision entirely on the allure of the BMW.

Oh well.

I held on tight. Sebastian was surprisingly warm, so I snuggled closer.

We took off so quickly that gravel spurted up from the rear tyre like a hailstorm, raising clouds of dust and leaving a smudge of black rubber behind as we fishtailed off.

So much for being inconspicuous.

I hung on for dear life, watching the blur of lights as the border whizzed past. I heard the momentary sound of frantic yelling and then splintering timber as we smashed through the boom gates. Debris raining down around us.

'Bloody hell!' I shouted as the bike flew across the border and into Nova Gorica. 'Why did we just smash our way through border security?'

'Do you have a passport or any form of ID on you?'

'No.'

'Then evasion was necessary.'

'But those vânătors would have definitely noticed that.'

'It was inevitable.'

I couldn't argue with that. I looked to my left, then my right, expecting some form of pursuit. I imagined police giving chase and helicopters trailing us with spotlights. It seemed fitting given our recent criminal activities. 'I don't see anything.'

Sebastian slowed, ducking and weaving through side streets like he knew the place. 'You won't. Those vânătors won't attack in the open.'

'Maybe they won't attack at all.'

'Perhaps.' He sounded doubtful.

'What about the police?'

'We'll be long gone before they have a chance to set up roadblocks.'

I couldn't argue with that either. We were riding so fast that I doubted whether either Speedy Gonzalez or the Road Runner would have been able to keep up. Lucas would have totally thrown up by now.

The town thinned out. Buildings soon turned into dwellings, dwellings gradually became few and far between, finally leaving empty, desolate patches of highway surrounding us. I could sense that the vânătors were close by now. I didn't know how, but I knew they were there.

'You're right,' I said to Sebastian, 'they're following us.'

Muscles bunched, his back stiffening. 'I know.'

Just like that, the bike screeched to a halt, ramming me

up against Sebastian's back. My helmet hit his, rebounding backwards and barely catching myself before I was thrown sideways by furry flesh.

I screamed, landing on the ground awkwardly. It hurt. 'Sebastian!' I could barely see. I was already reaching up to snatch off the helmet when a clawed paw batted me powerfully sideways.

Concentrate, Elena. You're about to get your ass kicked by a dog!

I felt myself roll several times as I slid down the slope at the side of the road. I landed in a ditch with a *thud* that stole breath, but managed to fumble off my helmet so I could at least see what was attacking me. I gulped at the fresh night air.

The vânător leapt forward without hesitation and swung a clawed paw at my face. I ducked, turning my head and flipping back to my feet. Not bad for being so disorientated. 'Sebastian!'

He didn't answer. I could only assume Sebastian was having trouble of his own, or locked in his own quarrel with the other vânător. I was going to have to figure this out on my own.

I scanned the darkness. The creature had darted away but I knew he was still out there. My skin tingled with that knowledge.

I scrambled up from the ditch, fangs lengthening as I channelled all my energy into my vampiric abilities. My vision sharpened ever so slightly—I could see Sebastian about a hundred meters to the right, locked in combat with the other werewolf. And now I could see my vânător as he slowly began slinking around behind Sebastian's motorbike, his claws tapping against the bitumen, a tactic he'd no doubt used before to conjure fear.

I shuddered. His desired effect? Absolutely.

I rallied my courage. I'd taken on two vânǎtors by myself before and killed two others with my bare hands. I could do it again.

Crouching down low, I poised myself for the imminent attack, spreading my fingers out on the ground, nails digging into parched soil to steady myself. I leant forward, baring my fangs with a hiss.

The vânǎtor poked its muzzle around the edge of the bike. It sniffed at the air, lips pulling back across its yellow fangs, saliva dripping down grey fur and splashing against the ground like droplets of rain. His head loomed larger towards me, black eyes finally meeting mine as the rest of his body swung around to meet me. We were eye-to-eye— his breath was fetid, spreading with a suffocating heat that made me want to dry reach.

I held my ground, held his gaze. I was waiting, daring him to make the first move. The wolf faltered, throwing his head back and beginning to howl.

My hand snapped forward and grabbed its throat, fingers tightening around the jugular; I strangled it in mid-howl. A moment later the wolf's hind legs quivered, and then it was pushing off powerfully from the road and launching itself into the sky, dragging me with it. I went flying up for a heartbeat, the wolf and I intertwined, before my hand slipped and I began tumbling back to the earth. I hit hard, my cheek smashing into the stupid bloody exhaust pipe of Sebastian's beloved motorbike, my ankle twisting and my wrist snapping in two. I did what anyone else would have done—I screamed. Then I swore, moaning in pain, desperately wishing my body would start healing itself.

'Elena!' Sebastian quickly reached my side, gathering me in his arms.

'Where did my wolf go?'

'He must have jumped.'

'The odds were even. There was no reason for it to flee.'

Sebastian pulled back the sleeve of my jacket to assess the damage to my wrist, and then ran his fingers over my cheek. 'Are you okay?'

I scrambled up from his lap. 'I'm fine. Did you at least kill your—'

The smell of blood hit me like a club to the head. Its potency drew me in, and my mouth began watering. My fingers twitched; the aroma made my fangs ache.

I knew the signs—I hungered.

I cut a glance over to the dead vânător on the other side of the road. Its bloodied fur glistened like oil, the colour so dark it was almost black. I could feel myself moving forward, crawling on my hands and knees, as I scuttled across the road like a crab in the sand.

I reached for the dead thing. I should have been repulsed. I should have had second thoughts. I *should* have had a knife and fork.

I licked tentatively at first, gently probing at the ragged flesh and furred edges. Gentle probing soon turned into a frenzied lapping, my tongue shovelling up the still warm blood oozing down its neck. I shuddered with gratification, and even though I could feel Sebastian's eyes on me, I could not look up. As the thirst took me, I became impervious to all judgement.

'Elena, we must go now,' he said. From the corner of my eye I could see the toe of his boot. Sebastian was standing over me, watching.

I shook my head, lips now locked tightly around the vânător's throat.

'If your wolf has jumped, then he will return with company,' Sebastian pressed, voice tight.

I finally pulled back, taking a deep breath and wiping blood from my mouth with the back of my hand. It was funny to think that a few months ago I would have dry-retched at the thought of such an act. Oh, how the mighty had fallen.

'We really need to go.'

I nodded, understanding the implications. Somewhere along the line these wolves were tied to an Alpha, and that Alpha could be Roshan.

Sebastian grabbed his helmet and put it back on, signalling that I should do the same. 'The Police and those vânători will be looking for us all through Slovenia now. We need to get out of this country as soon as possible.'

'Are we going to Croatia then?'

He shook his head. 'I'm taking you back home. Lucius was right, this whole thing was a mistake. You're on everyone's Most Wanted list at the moment. I can always come back on my own and check out their headquarters after, if you're still not willing to put this whole serum thing to rest.'

I gripped his shoulder like my life depended on it and squeezed as hard as I could. 'Sebastian, you can't take me home. I need to know what the IMI are planning and how it'll affect everyone I care about.'

'It doesn't matter, Elena.'

'Of course it matters!' I shouted. 'Everything that has gone wrong in the last few months is my fault. I have to try and fix it, or at least figure it out.'

'The Protectors may or may not be up to anything sinister, but their actions are their own and are no fault of yours.'

I scoffed. 'Funny how I always seem to be involved though, isn't it?'

'You can't change things, Elena. Fate has a funny way of working itself out, even when you're fighting it.'

'I don't believe in fate.'

'But it believes in you,' Sebastian said, reaching forward and brushing a lock of hair away from my cheek. 'Even after everything you've been through, fate still saw fit to guide me to you and bring you back to your family, a family that will always love you and care for you. Isn't that reason enough to put this dangerous plan behind you and head back home where you will be safe?'

I dropped my hand from his shoulder and pushed away. 'I want to go to Bucharest, Sebastian. Staying in the safety of the villa helps no one.'

'It helps Lucius,' Sebastian said gently, giving me some heavy-duty eye contact. 'What do you think would happen to him if he ended up losing you, on top of losing his beloved wife and son?'

I winced. 'I didn't realise that everyone knew.'

Sebastian smiled but there was no warmth behind it. 'I guess I was just as curious as you once. I wanted to know what lay behind the upstairs bedroom door, too.'

I was quiet for a moment. 'I can't be responsible for Lucius's past demons, Sebastian. What happened to him was terrible—the worst thing imaginable—but life goes on. I can't sit back and do nothing when there's a chance I can fix some of the problems I've caused.'

'What problems have *you* caused?'

I could see Sebastian was growing impatient. He'd wrenched his helmet off again and stood there looking at me with his burning grey eyes.

'Julius getting away, attracting the Vânător's attentions … hell, even simply existing so the IMI could use my blood for whatever nefarious intentions they desire. There's a lot,

Sebastian, including dragging you along on this trip. I know you'll get in trouble for allowing me to leave the villa.'

'I don't care about all that.'

'Well, then why are you upset about my choosing to come?'

'I don't want any harm to befall you.' Sebastian shook his head, sighing in defeat as his body slumped against the bike. 'So much could go wrong. If anything happened to you—'

'It won't,' I interrupted, placing my fingers to his lips, and then quickly moved them away again. 'We'll look out for each other.'

Sebastian was shaking his head. 'My life is infinite. You only get one more chance. Becoming a vampire does not make you invincible.'

I frowned. 'One more chance at what?'

His eyes found mine. 'Life.'

'So?'

'So, if you die, that's it. You never come back, we never …'

Sebastian's voice trailed off. He had a faraway look in his eyes that sent a chill down my spine.

'What are you talking about?'

Sebastian's features sharpened, his eyes clouding. 'Just get on the bike, Elena. If you persist on pursuing this endeavour then we best leave before more vânători return.'

'That's it? No explanations.'

'That's it.' He shoved his helmet back on and snapped down the visor.

I guess we were done talking.

CHAPTER TWENTY-FOUR: BORDERS

Passing through Slovenia and into Croatia was much easier than I'd expected. This time I was prepared for Sebastian smashing right through the border. The border patrol really was inefficient—before the guards could react or go postal we were already speeding through falling debris. Spotlights searched, the guards' shouting following us on the wind, and then we were suddenly off again. Sebastian had sped through so fast that my fingers ached where they clenched at his waist. My legs were cramping up and my elbows throbbed from being locked in the one position. I wanted to stop, but knew we couldn't. Vânători were already in pursuit again.

According to Sebastian, there were at least six of them following us. Not good, but at least they were at a distance and not attacking.

'They're still there,' I said after half an hour of tense silence, getting my first real glimpse of fur and fangs from the corner of my eye.

'I know,' Sebastian answered. 'We lingered too long where those last vânători ambushed us. These new ones must have picked up our scent and joined the hunt.'

'Why not attack? It makes no sense for them to hold back.'

'I honestly don't know, but I don't want to stop here when we're so clearly outnumbered. If we can just make it to the next town—'

'Is that what all those lights are up ahead?'

'That's Zagreb, the capital.'

'So you want to stop there?'

'I don't want to stop anywhere, but we don't have much choice,' Sebastian said, leaning forward and tapping on the fuel gauge. 'They'd be less likely to attack us in a populated area.'

'Do what you have to do. Stop somewhere just outside of town to avoid revealing too much to the public if something goes wrong, but close enough so that they'll think twice about attacking. You never know—we might lose them on the highway.'

'I doubt it.'

We rode in silence for another few minutes. I watched the city spring up around us and felt my growing disbelief as our pursuers continued to follow us into the more densely populated area of the city's outskirts. Our one saving grace was that, as a group, we were all moving too quickly for any normal people to get a close look at—we were just vague shapes speeding through the night.

'Look,' I said, tugging on Sebastian's left shoulder, 'there's a service station just up ahead on the left. Can we pull in there?'

'It's too crowded and both exits are bottlenecked. If we need a quick getaway we'll have to find something more accessible. There's a place I know of on the other side of town that we can escape from quickly if need be.'

The petrol station disappeared behind in a blur, much like a mirage glimpsed from a distance. In its place and off in the distance, I saw a brief streak of grey-matted fur, a quick flash of pointed white teeth, and the faint shimmer of black, beady eyes. The creatures' ever-nearing presence sent a shiver down my spine, the fear not helping my ever-growing need to locate a bathroom. It had been hours since I'd last been.

After almost twenty-five minutes of nervously watching the wolves as they stalked along beside us, and as we ducked and weaved through the city traffic, Sebastian told me we were drawing near to the other service station.

I started counting. I needed a distraction from the wolves and to take my mind off my bladder issues. I was starting to regret lapping up all that blood earlier. 'Sebastian,' I said, tugging at him reluctantly. 'How much longer? I desperately have to go to the bathroom.'

'Really?' he said, begrudging. 'It's only been eight hours. Didn't you go before we left?'

'I think that blood went right through me. And the vânătors … well I guess they make me nervous. But seeing how you need to stop for fuel, anyway—'

'Can't you hold it? Those wolves will move on us as soon as we stop and we can't afford to be separated right now.'

I frowned, even though he couldn't see my expression. 'No, I can't hold it, Sebastian. I'm still human, and I can't help it.'

'Elena, I can't fuel the bike and watch over you while you go to the bathroom, too.'

'I get what you mean but, *argh*! I don't want you to watch over me in the bathroom, no matter how good your intentions are.'

'I don't know about this, Elena.'

'There really is little choice. Either I go to the toilet now, or I wet my pants and rust up your bike.'

Sebastian didn't answer as he slowed the bike down, turning off the main road, and pulling up quickly next to the unoccupied fuel pump closest to the pay station. 'This is as close to the toilets as I can get, so make it quick.'

'I'll be right back,' I said, as I lifted my helmet and shimmied off the back of the bike.

'Be careful!' he shouted after me.

I waved Sebastian off, jogging into the small convenience store attached to the service pumps. I scouted the area for that universal symbol indicating there was a toilet here of the more female kind. I found it almost immediately, a fact I was thankful for because I was practically hopping from foot to foot now.

I moved to the rear of the store, gripped the door's handle and twisted. I began to curse loudly when the door didn't budge; it was locked. My frayed nerves and cramping bladder already had me in a bad mood, so I didn't hesitate—I snapped the lock in two and ripped it off. It wasn't that hard, really.

The service attendant looked up at me as I entered the corridor leading to the bathroom, but I was halfway through undoing my fly and too focused on looking for the stalls to give a shit about the breaking and entering.

When I was finished, I quickly flushed, washed my hands and face, and brushed my hair away from my eyes. Gripping at the plastic counter in front of me, I slowly stared at the reflection looking back in the mirror. 'What have I gotten us into?' I said. 'We're in the middle of Croatia with six werewolves hunting us and we're hiding in a bathroom.' I shook my head and slapped the image staring back at me. 'I should have listened to Sebastian.'

I opened the door to leave, staggering back in surprise when I found a man standing directly in my path. 'Sorry,' I gasped, but then caught myself; there was nothing to be sorry about. The man had short blonde hair and generic brown eyes, and was fairly unassuming. But the average human doesn't walk around completely naked and that fact sent alarm bells ringing off inside my head.

A vânător.

To the left of me, out of the corner of my eye I noticed that the back door to the store had been forced open and was barely hanging on its hinges as it leaned awkwardly against the wall. To my right, the door I had entered through had now been closed to prevent any of the public from interfering. I stood very still, not wanting to provoke this wolf in man's clothing. 'What do you want,' I asked quietly.

'You,' he answered, voice hoarse and slightly accented.

'That's not really an option.'

The creature growled. 'I offer no choices. I smelt your blood, and I want it.'

'Who's your Alpha?'

His eyes narrowed in confusion. 'What does that mat—'

'Answer me. Who is your Alpha?' I straightened up, making myself look taller than I felt. I needed to know if Roshan was behind this hunt, and if he was, I needed to know how he'd found me so quickly.

'My Alpha is known as Elias.'

'Does he know about me?'

The vânător's eyes were drawn tight, and it looked angry now. 'You were *my* find and you are *mine* to kill. My Alpha does not need to know who I feed on.'

So this wolf was just in the wrong place at the wrong time. Or maybe that should have been the other way around.

My eyes wandered over the red marks on the vânător's throat. 'Ahh, I recognise you now. You were the wolf who ran away from me earlier tonight.'

He growled angrily. 'I did not run away, I called for reinforcements. You have a member of the Italian coven with you, and I can smell his aged blood.' He shook his head. 'And something else …'

'So you were afraid of the vampire?'

'Cautious but never afraid.'

'Are you afraid of me?'

The vânător laughed. He put effort behind it, giving himself a good thigh slapping. 'You're a human girl. It's you who should be afraid.'

I shrugged. 'Probably.'

I reared back and punched the creature in the face so hard that I cried out as my knuckles connected, smashing into his cheek and splintering bone. His head snapped to the left, connecting with the brick wall behind him with a loud *crack*.

Fear and shock were in his eyes as I slowly licked a drop of his blood from my lips, making a show of savouring its flavour. The creature's body bulged and flowed as it tried to change, but I would not let it, stepping mercilessly into him with a blow that snapped the bridge of his nose and sent him reeling.

He hit the brickwork again, this time with a wet *thud*, and sagged to the floor. The werewolf's eyes rolled backward, blood smearing up against the wall and dripping to the floor. He must have lost consciousness then because his eyes dimmed and went black. Uncertain, I checked for a pulse—there was none. The creature was dead.

I gazed longingly at the pool of redness surrounding his limp form, longing to taste that special flavour, to savour the way it felt as it flowed over my tongue. My body was expecting me to feed, but I couldn't. Sebastian was alone outside with five werewolves.

I grimaced. The encounter had been a little messy considering there were potential witnesses about. I should never have fought him in such a public place. There'd be no way to clean all of it up in time before someone interrupted me. Or was there?

Get rid of the body first.

I grabbed the vânător by his hair and dragged him to the end of the toilet corridor, his body a wet sack in my hands. As I pulled him out the back, avoiding what remained of the door, the winter wind hit me like a slap in the face. I shivered, looking around for somewhere to discard the body. A large industrial-sized dumpster stood to the right of the door—it was going to have to do.

I hoisted the creature in my arms and managed to lift his body high enough to slide half over the edge of the bin. I grabbed his ankles and flipped the rest of him inside. His body landed with a *thump*, a puff of foul smelling trash wafting up to greet me. It wasn't a pleasant experience.

Standing on tippy-toes, I peered over the edge of the rusted metal carcass of the trash bin, my lips twitching but not from amusement. My eyes lingered on the dead thing at the bottom. I would never have imagined in my life that I would be stashing a body in a dumpster—it was funny how things often turned out. What would Lucas say if he saw me now, drinking blood like Diet Coke and disposing of bodies like a serial killer?

I left the lid open. Sunrise was a little way off yet, but when it came the body would disintegrate into nothing but smoke and ash. In the meantime, I hoped that no one would go through the rubbish until morning … unless, of course, the blood led them there?

Shit.

I glanced back inside. Smears of blood lined the floors and walls like something out of a horror film. I briefly wondered if there was something wrong with me now that the sight of blood no longer made me uneasy, and remembered the first time I'd seen a dead body—it had been on a trip to Brisbane, while hunting John. The Alpha's pack had killed a night patrolman at the shipping yards. Back then I couldn't even glance at the body or blood without having to turn away in horror. Had I witnessed so much horror and violence in the last four months that I'd become emotionally detached? Was becoming a freak better than being traumatised?

I shrugged and concentrated my energies on the problem at hand. I reached out and grabbed the water pipes that ran along the corridor's ceiling. After a few moments of grunting and tugging they finally erupted, spewing clean water across the walls and floors, washing away most of the traces of my bloody encounter. Walking back into the toilet cubicle, I kicked in a toilet cistern, sending a tidal wave of water flowing out into the corridor.

Well, that should cover it.

I hope they have insurance.

Wiping my hands on my wet leather pants and feeling pretty satisfied with myself, I quickly circled back around to the front of the building. I watched the darkness in case of another ambush, almost running as I looked for Sebastian.

As I rounded the corner, I relaxed as I spied Sebastian. His manner was alert but casual. He didn't turn to look at me, even though he surely would have heard the commotion in the bathroom from where he was standing. Sebastian was keeping his eyes firmly fixed on the car yard next to the service station.

'Hey, don't worry about me,' I muttered sarcastically, 'I'm totally fine with being accosted by naked men in the bathroom.'

Sebastian seemed to be ignoring me, still pumping gas into the motorbike. Despite the danger, he had still managed to find time to draw a small, admiring crowd of women, one of whom was the cashier from inside the gas station. I wasn't surprised, but I definitely felt annoyed.

'Never mind, I can see you're busy. Carry on.' Sarcasm continued to spew forth from my mouth in an uncontrolled stream, until the group of women parted, and I got a distracting view of supple leather cupping that perfectly-formed backside.

Jesus. It should be illegal to unleash that on the public.

I took a deep breath and mentally slapped myself.

Shit. This is sooo not the time to be admiring Sebastian's arse.

Yeah, he was hotter than hell, but his ever-watchful gaze was still directed towards the car yard and that worried me.

I began to hear a familiar growling mingled with the wind, a sound like distant thunder. I pressed my back against the gas station's dirty brick wall and peered down into the car yard, trepidation now filling my mind.

I could see their huddled forms now, sitting patiently, hunched forward and ready to attack at the least notice. Nestled in-between the parked vehicles, the creatures watched me with a keen interest and shining eyes. Why hadn't they attacked yet? Was it Sebastian's presence that held them back? Did they sense something in his gaze?

I could clearly see as one of them glanced towards the rear of the gas station, undoubtedly expecting his pack mate's return. It wasn't going to happen.

It was amazing that none of the women had yet noticed them, but perhaps they were still distracted by Sebastian's leather-clad rear end; however, even in the darkness the werewolves stood out like sore thumbs—big masses of grey fur and long, pointy teeth.

A handful of unimpressionable men had stopped pumping gas long enough to notice, perhaps realising as I had that there was only a small amount of bitumen and barbed wire fencing separating the creatures from the rest of us.

A couple of old Croatian men, cigarettes dangling from their quivering lips, craned their necks to stare across at the car yard in disbelief. It wouldn't be long now before someone yelled out and the werewolves would leap forward, fangs bared and ready for the kill.

But what can I do?

Use your gift, a voice said, quietly echoing inside my head. I was getting pretty tired of hearing inner voices other than my own, but in this special instance the advice was welcomed.

I studied the wolves carefully, staring each of them down in turn, and wondering just exactly what I could be capable of. Their DNA comprised an intricate part of my genetic predisposition. Could I somehow manipulate that bond? Could I telekinetically touch them or would I need to try something a little more direct?

Lucius, have you trained me well enough?

I felt for the werewolves with my mind, searching for something tangible within our blood bond that could bind them to my will; there was nothing there. I guess my abilities didn't extend to manipulating psychic links, so I was going to have to focus on other possibilities.

Instead, I studied the cars the vânători lay huddled between. Each vehicle was an object—granted, they were large, but still objects. And Lucius had patiently explained to me that an object, of any size, could be manipulated.

Trying to ignore the sudden, panicked cries of the clear-headed gas station patrons, I saw the cluster of cars I was focusing upon began to shake slightly, creaking and vibrating from side to side. I concentrated on wrapping cords of pure energy around each individual vehicle, pulling on those strings like a master of puppets. The effort was almost overwhelming, and I'd already been developing a headache after that bathroom incident.

A small Volkswagen Golf achieved lift-off first, followed by a rapidly rusting Fiat Punto. The wolves jumped up on their paws, whining. I could read the confusion in their eyes.

The cars rose higher off the ground, their chassises jerking uncertainly, my parlour trick now drawing cries of disbelief from the human spectators and howls of uncertainty from the wolves. As one particularly panicked vânător dared to take a few steps towards me, I panicked—big time. The cars all slowly rotated inward, hovered uncertainly for a few seconds, and then smashed together with enough force to make their insides outsides.

As the cars ground roughly against each other, howls rippled through the night air, before abruptly dying off as my wall of metallic death advanced. I watched, mesmerised. Arterial red sprayed outwards, dripping from under the wreckage like squashed pulp from a juicer.

The carnage left me with a heart that beat out of control, my eyes wide and mouth dry.

What have I done?

'What the hell?' Sebastian uttered, suddenly appearing at my side. He surveyed the aftermath of my destruction, wide-eyed. 'Did you just do that?'

His hand found mine and drew me back to myself. 'Yes,' I answered, voice trembling.

Yeah, I did that.

The enthralled women who had just been perving on Sebastian came hurrying over to where we two were standing by the brick wall, directly across from the car yard fence. The male motorists had formed clusters of eager voyeurs several feet from the barbed wire, the sound of grinding bones, screaming and tearing flesh being quite hard to ignore.

There were gasps of shock now ringing out from every member of the gathering crowd as they peered into the yard and surveyed the still moving twisted pile of metal. Parts of mutilated wolf could be seen strewn across the ground and peeking out from in-between bits of crushed automobile. The now deceased pack was silent, but the cars continued to writhe and contract and groan.

I quickly severed my telekinetic ties with the cars. They dropped to the ground in a ball of twisted metal and body parts, a resounding *crash* that elicited more shocked gasps from the onlookers.

'We should go,' I said to Sebastian, tugging on his arm and practically dragging him back to the bike.

He just stared at the metallic mass in stunned silence.

Great. He thinks I'm a monster now, too.

'Sebastian,' I said a little more forcefully this time, 'we need to go … now.'

He nodded slowly and spun on his feet, trailing quickly behind me.

I ran back to the bike and shoved my helmet on, waiting for Sebastian. I slid in behind him as he mounted up. Tyres squealed as the bike lurched forward, taking off in a hiss of burning rubber and smoke. People swivelled and stared at this latest disturbance. Some pulled out their cell phones to take photos of the wolves' massacred remains or to dial emergency services. This was going to be a tough one to explain, and I was glad we wouldn't have to.

I took a second to absorb what I had just done. Yes, I'd killed vânători before, but never with that degree of violence. I'd killed five at once using only the power of my mind and that goddamned disturbed me. It wasn't the ability itself—it was that I had merely thought about crushing their bones and splitting open their flesh, and those thoughts had rapidly become reality.

I leaned my head against Sebastian's shoulder and closed my eyes. I had a splitting headache and my aching conscience wasn't helping. I'd thought of nothing but survival before the incident, and now I wasn't so sure. Did I enjoy this power, the kill? Was I turning into the very things that I hunted, or was I somehow worse?

'Elena, are you alright?' Sebastian murmured through the comlink.

'I'm not sure.'

'Are you tired? Do you feel ill?'

'There's so much wrong with me … it's hard to know where to begin.'

'Well, I'm going to head straight to Nicholas's apartment in Budapest. It's away from the hunting grounds of any of the known packs. Stragglers won't know to look for us there. It'll also give us a good chance to get our bearings and figure out what our next move is.'

'Sure.'

'Elena?'

'What?'

'Whatever it is that you did back there, it'll be okay. We'll figure it out.'

I didn't answer him. Instead, I wrapped my arms tighter around Sebastian and kept my eyes closed. The pounding in my head was quite bad now and talking only made it worse. Besides, silence was a blessing and right now I had a lot to think about.

I came awake to Sebastian's hands gently rubbing my thighs. It was a miracle that I'd managed to fall asleep still holding onto Sebastian and the bike.

'Are you awake now?' he said quietly.

I pulled back groggily, my fingers stiff. I looked around, lifting the bike helmet off and rubbing at sleep-laden eyes.

'We're in Budapest already?'

Sebastian nodded, waiting for me to dismount before he slid off. He removed his helmet, and placed his and mine on the motorcycle's seat. Without asking, Sebastian wrapped his arms around my back and thighs, and hoisted me easily against his chest.

'Sebastian, what are you doing?' I complained.

'You don't look so good.'

'I just have a headache. It's either karmic retribution or the usual side effects from prolonged telekinesis usage.'

'Either way, you're not well. Let me take care of you.'

I was suspicious, but too tired to really argue. 'How?'

'I'm going to jump us both up to Nicholas's balcony and then you can rest.'

'Don't you have a key like everyone else?'

'Nicholas is not expecting us. He's in Paris hunting Julius, remember?'

I nodded, snuggling closer. Sebastian felt so warm and safe, different from any other vampire I'd known before. William was always cold; so were Thomas and the other vampires at the villa. Sebastian was special.

The wind blew hair into my eyes, but the trip was short. Sebastian landed deftly on the balcony rail, balancing us precariously for a few seconds and then dropping down onto the terrazzo floor. He set me down gently and opened the French doors, wandering in to switch the bedside lamps on. 'Wait here,' Sebastian said to me. 'I'm just going back down to grab our helmets and backpacks before some thief decides to run off with them.'

I waved him off, weariness gripping me hard as I slumped down onto the bed. I shimmied off my leather gloves, riding boots and leather jacket, throwing them in a pile on the floor. I glanced at the clock on the bedside table—it was nearing four o'clock in the morning. We'd been on the road for roughly ten hours.

I inched my way up the bed and collapsed against one of the soft pillows.

'Making yourself comfortable?' Sebastian said, dropping our packs onto the floor by the bed and the helmets onto the nightstand. He closed and locked the French doors behind him, and then turned to me.

I rolled away from him. 'I guess so.'

I felt the mattress dip behind me. 'Elena, what's going on? You've been particularly quiet since we left Zagreb.'

'I was asleep.'

'That's not what I meant.'

'It's nothing. I've just got a killer headache and I'm really tired.'

Sebastian touched my shoulder, rolling me back over to look at him. He brushed his fingers through my hair, smoothing it away from my face. I could feel myself frowning. He was usually never this persistent, and ever since we'd argued at Synth Corp, Sebastian had stayed distant. I'd said that friends were all we would ever be and he'd not been happy with that. Now, was I?

He was staring down at me now, eyes intense. They were mostly green at the moment, grey tendrils twisting out from the centre like gnarled branches. 'Talk to me,' he said, touching my hair again, confusing yet comforting.

'I can't. I don't even know what's wrong with me.'

'Are you so sure that the problem is you?'

'You saw what I did tonight. You tell me?'

'Elena …'

Sebastian moved closer, his hand sliding down to cup my face.

'Don't,' I said, turning away. 'You're looking at me like I can do no wrong. I'm not innocent, Sebastian. What I did tonight—'

'Was necessary.'

I rolled back over to look at him, shaking my head. 'Was it?'

'Killing them is the only way, Elena.' Sebastian's voice was gentle, filled with understanding.

'Killing them, yes, but torture?'

An unknown emotion flickered in his eyes. He looked away quickly. 'Are you sorry that you eradicated them all?'

I lay back on the pillow again, staring up at the ceiling. 'I'm sorry they had to die like that, yes, but also …'

'But, what?'

'But I think there is a small part of me that revelled in the violence and enjoyed it.'

'And yet you say you feel remorse, Elena. You're sorry for your actions and I think even sorrier that you feel so much at their deaths.'

'I didn't even flinch when I killed the other one in the bathroom.'

Sebastian nodded. 'I know, I heard, but that was self-defence.'

I could feel the tears welling up in my eyes yet refused to let them flow. 'How can you even look at me right now? I just admitted that a part of me enjoyed the kill.'

'You have also expressed regret. You know the difference between right and wrong, Elena. We wouldn't be on this trip if you didn't have good intentions, although if I'm honest, I'm not sure if we should continue on with you in such a fragile state.'

I laughed, tears finally spilling down my cheeks.

'What is it?' Sebastian said, wiping them away.

'No one has ever called me fragile before.'

'Maybe they just don't know you like I do.'

I frowned slowly. 'You don't know me either, Sebastian. I appreciate you trying to make me feel better, but you really don't know me.'

Sebastian moved away from me then, sliding further down the bed until he was lying on his side, propped up on one elbow. He looked down at me. 'You keep saying that yet you refuse to change things.'

'I've already suggested we be friends, Sebastian.'

'I don't want to be just your friend.'

I felt a tightness in my chest at that, and my breathing quickened. 'There's no other choice.'

He reached over, fingers trailing down my arm, down to my hip. 'There's always a choice.'

I pushed his hand away. 'I have someone, and he wouldn't like sharing.'

Sebastian's nostrils flared, his lips growing tight with anger. 'The vampire who deserted you in Bucharest? You're still waiting for him to return to you?'

'No, not exactly, but we do need to talk before rash and,' and then Sebastian was smoothing his hand across my hip again, 'impulsive decisions are made.'

He leaned forward, obviously taking my intake of breath as an invitation. 'Just one kiss,' Sebastian murmured, his breath cool and sweet on my lips.

I pressed a hand to his chest. 'No.'

He growled, a piece of shoulder-length hair falling and

brushing against the side of my cheek. It tickled and smelt of soap. All I could think about was how that hair would feel against my naked body as I lay underneath him, the smell of his skin mingling with mine as he tasted my flesh.

Shit.

My teeth were already lengthening. My vampiric soul was caught between wanting to lose myself to his charms and slamming him up against a wall, hard.

Before I knew it Sebastian was on top of me, the weight of his body against mine. His arms brushed against mine, torso resting against my rib cage. He kept his face not more than a few inches from my own; it became increasingly difficult not to focus on his lips and the tongue that occasionally swept across it.

I had the sudden urge to wrap my legs around his waist, pull him into me and imprison his lips with my own. I was rapidly losing my control around him, and that scared the shit out of me.

'Sebastian, get off of me. I don't want this.'

He made no effort to move. 'I think you do.'

'No.'

Sebastian looked down at me for the longest time, his eyes a swirling mass of emotion that I couldn't decipher. He dipped forward but I pushed harder against his chest, turning my head away.

'Elena.'

'Get off me, Sebastian, or I'll bite you.' I snapped my fangs at him, hoping he'd get the point.

He did, pushing off the mattress and away from me. Sebastian moved away so he was reclining on his side at the end of the bed, staring speculatively down at my end. 'You know it's a natural reaction, right?'

'What is?'

He pointed to my fangs. 'They reveal themselves at moments of intimacy, anger or danger. I know that you're not threatened or even really angry at me, so ...'

I blushed. 'So you assume the reaction's from attraction.'

'Well, I want you to be attracted to me, Elena.'

'Why, for God's sake? You have every woman on the planet falling at your feet when you walk past. Why the hell do you need me, too?'

'We have history.'

'Why? Because you know I've had a few random dreams about you over the years?'

'Have you ever stopped to question why?'

'Of course I have,' I snapped. 'I think about it all the time.'

'And what have you come up with so far?' Sebastian said, all calmness.

I propped myself up against the headboard. He watched me cautiously, eyes half-hidden under dark lashes. 'Nothing. I don't know why I sometimes see your face in another person's features or why, whenever I close my eyes, you're there. Is that what you want to hear, Sebastian?'

'No,' he said slowly. 'I want you to want to know why.'

'Then tell me, if you have the answer.'

He shook his head, suddenly looking very tired. 'I can't.'

'You can't or you won't?'

'I can't. It's against the rules.'

I smashed my fist against the thick headboard, punching a hole right through the middle of the wood. Sebastian looked up, eyes wide.

'What rules? Why is it whenever you and I finally get to talking it always turns back into riddles? And you want to know why I won't kiss you?' I added angrily. 'It's because of this—what would I be getting myself into with you if I did?'

'Elena, I'm sorry. It's never been this complicated before.'

'Before what? See? This is what I'm talking about. You never say anything that makes a lick of sense.'

He rolled onto all fours and stalked towards me like a cat. I watched warily as he settled down next to me, our arms touching. 'I want you to understand,' Sebastian said slowly. 'I want you to know everything, but I have secrets, and those secrets I must keep. Do you understand?'

'Hell, no.'

'You have secrets, Elena.'

'Not really.'

'Yes, you do. You hide one from me even now.'

I snorted. 'I am not.'

'Your vampire.'

'William is none of your business.'

'William?' he interrupted. 'So, finally, you say his name out loud.'

Uh-oh.

I pushed Sebastian away and rolled to face the wall, effectively turning my back on him. 'I need to sleep now. I'm tired.'

'Too tired for the truth?'

'I won't talk about him, Sebastian. What happens between William and I has nothing to do with anyone, especially you. You have your secrets, so let me have mine.'

'Your secret is a danger to you.'

I glanced back at him, glaring angrily. 'What?'

'He tried to turn you. I can still smell his scent in your blood. You do realise that's a crime in our coven?'

I shook my head, really too tired for all this. 'He did nothing of the sort. The blood that was exchanged between us was due to my fault alone.'

Sebastian looked bewildered. 'How could it possibly be

your fault? *He* bit you. He drew your blood and shared his with you!'

'I wanted him to!' I shouted back. 'We were caught in the moment. I was wrapped in his arms, lips locked and blood flushing under his skin, and then I asked him to cross that line. I wanted him inside me.'

Sebastian recoiled as if I'd just slapped him. His bottom lip trembled ever so slightly, eyes gone wide and unreadable. 'You wanted *him*.' The sound of his voice came out as a choked whisper.

'Yes, I wanted him ... I want him,' I corrected, driving the stake home. 'If things hadn't gone so wrong we'd probably still be together right now. The only problem, and the reason he eventually left, was because he's just too damned moral for his own good.'

'How can that be?' he murmured, his voice choked with emotion. 'You and William.'

'Me and William what?' I demanded.

Sebastian looked away, his whole body going limp. 'He should never have touched you. No one is supposed to touch you.' He stopped. 'He should have known.'

'What should he have known, Sebastian?'

He shook his head, that old stiffness coming back. 'It doesn't matter. Maybe you *should* go to sleep now.'

'No, I want to know.'

'Do you really want to know, Elena? Or do you still think fate is a joke?'

'Both.'

'Go to sleep, Elena. It's been a long day.'

'Don't patronise me.'

'I am tired.'

'Liar.'

Sebastian glared at me, eyes swirling again. 'I *am* tired,' he breathed, looking away again. 'You have no idea how tired I really am.'

'You're a vampire. You don't need to sleep.'

'But I want to. So, shush.'

'Don't shush me,' I chided.

'Then be quiet, please.'

I huffed in frustration. 'You're a total ass. I hope you know that?'

'Consider me informed.'

I glared at him, wishing I could drill a hole between Sebastian's eyes. His lids were now closed, arms folded across his chest, head leaning back against the broken headboard. He was calm, and I was confused and angry.

I rolled over again, hugging myself. There were so many twisted tales kept hidden from me, so much mystery. Most of it stemmed from my own stubborn reluctance to trust Sebastian, but how could I? How could I put my faith in a dream? Why couldn't he just talk to me?

I shouldn't have been surprised. My whole life was a lie. Secrets had always sheltered me, had surrounded my growth and ensured I was plucked like a ripe berry by the hand of the IMI. Perhaps I just didn't want to fall down that rabbit hole again?

I stared at the bathroom door until my eyes began to hurt. I couldn't stop thinking about Sebastian beside me, and I couldn't stop thinking about William, wherever he was.

Wait.

My body stiffened. Sebastian must have sensed it because he shifted next to me on the bed. 'Ask me, Elena.' He seemed to know what was coming next.

'You know William, don't you?'

He didn't even hesitate. 'Yes. I have known William all of his life.'

'And you don't like each other, do you?'

'We were once close, but things changed.'

'And now?'

'Now he covets the one thing I truly want.'

That was enough truth for one night.

I closed my eyes. I must have fallen deeply asleep. I welcomed the silence, the numbing darkness. I touched it and wrapped it around me like a warm blanket.

I dreamed. As always, Sebastian played a starring role.

Tonight, he was watching me, propped up on an elbow in bed beside me, naked and ready. Sebastian's eyes were pure silver. When he kissed me, it was like all our other kisses had been in dreams—welcome, comforting and right. It was only here that I had the courage to reach out and touch his body, his flesh so familiar it was frightening.

Here I could fall into his caress without consequence. Here I let him brush his lips across my skin and whisper in my ear. There was no escape from the truth here. And I wasn't sure if I wanted to escape, even if I could. Fear was for reality alone.

CHAPTER TWENTY-FIVE: RULES

woke to sunlight streaming through French doors, the rays' warmth piercing through layers of clothing and warming me to my core. My eyelids parted, and I drank in the glorious dawn of a new day. My fingers busied themselves rubbing across my stubborn lids, trying to clear the blur from sleep-fatigued eyes.

What time is it?

'You're finally awake,' I heard Sebastian say from somewhere across the room.

I sat up on the mattress and searched, bleary-eyed, for his form. I couldn't see him anywhere. 'Where are you?'

'Down here.'

I crawled along the mattress until I came to the end of the bed. Sebastian was lying on the floor, one leg crossed over the other, both hands behind his head. He was a vision of calm.

'Why are you lying on the floor?' I said, lying on my stomach with my head hanging over the edge of the bed. My insides did a little flip at the sight of him. I vividly recalled how his body looked poised above me, naked and ready. These dreams were going to kill me, I could feel it.

'There's no sun down here,' Sebastian answered, studying my face.

I concentrated particularly hard on ignoring my

memories of last night. Instead I said, 'Why didn't you just leave the room if it's too bright in here?'

'I couldn't risk leaving you alone in a room with an unguarded point of entry. As easy as it had been for us to enter through the French doors, so could someone else.'

'But the vânătors would be sleeping now.'

He looked at me in surprise. 'True, but not all vampires are asleep right now.'

'Since when do I have to worry about vampires?'

He smiled, if only just a little. 'You seem to forget just how tasty the scent of your blood is. That will inevitably attract attention.'

'Are there vampires in the area right now?'

'Don't worry. I'll protect you, Baby Vamp.'

'Sebastian …'

'Only one,' he conceded.

'Anyone we know?'

He gave me a wry look. 'Someone I know rather well.'

'Who?'

'Caleb. It appears that he has been squatting in this apartment in Nicholas's absence.'

'Why?'

Sebastian shrugged—difficult to do while lying down, but he made the action look graceful. 'Why is the sky blue?'

'Wait,' I said frowning. 'Isn't he the one who wanted to feed off me?'

'Yes.'

'Well, that sucks.'

'Don't worry. When Caleb finally returns I will remind him of the rules. He will not harm one hair on your attractive head.'

I rolled onto my back and looked up at the ceiling.

'Sebastian, how come you're not insatiably attracted to the scent of my blood like everyone else?'

'Who said I wasn't?'

'Your eyes don't go black like the others when you're near.'

'I can control myself.'

I looked back over the edge of the mattress, my hair falling down into his face. 'You must be really, really old then,' I said, grinning.

For some reason, Sebastian hated talking about his age. The only reason I knew he was old was because I could remember William once telling me that born vampires over five hundred years were the only ones who could fully suppress their thirst. A turned vampire had to wait a thousand years before his bloodlust subsided.

I was pretty sure Sebastian was a born vampire, given his ties to Tiberius, although he did look a little older than eighteen and that still confused the hell out of me.

Sebastian spat out a piece of my hair that had fallen into his mouth. 'What is it with you and your incessant need to know my age?' His eyes narrowed, and he swiped my hair away from his face with his hands.

I shrugged. 'I was just wondering whether I was talking to the person who invented the wheel?'

'That's very amusing, Elena. But I'm afraid that the wheel was invented long before I was born into this life.' Sebastian tugged playfully on my hair.

'And that would be ...?'

'Google it.' He reached up and pushed my head away to keep my falling curtain of hair out of his eyes. 'Elena, I think we need to talk.' His face had suddenly become so serious that I didn't even complain about the rapid jump in topics.

'What's wrong?'

'It's about last night.'

I screwed my face up. 'We don't need to rehash.'

He waved a hand at me. 'I was referring to the Vânători. I think we need to reconsider heading into Bucharest.'

'Sebastian, I explained why I need to—'

'You're not ready,' he said, quickly silencing me. 'Those wolves that hunted us last night were there by chance. They only continued the hunt because they smelt your intoxicating scent. If we cross into Romania, homeland of vânători everywhere, I can't ensure your protection.'

'They stay out of Bucharest, Sebastian. Chester told me so. There are too many Protectors in the city for their liking.'

'Elena, I still think—'

'I have to, Sebastian.'

His eyes were serious. 'I have a really bad feeling about this.'

I ignored him. 'I think we should stay here until Friday night. From experience, most of The Protectors leave headquarters around six to head home for the weekend. Some stay for dinner in the mess hall but by eight o'clock the only ones remaining are those who stay in residence. How long will it take to get us there by foot?'

'Elena, if I do this with you, we are not going in on foot.'

'Sebastian—'

'No,' he said, answering harshly. 'We'll have to cut through the Carpathian Mountains and I won't risk you like that. If we go, we're flying.'

'If we go? We didn't come all this way just to turn around and head back to the villa.'

'We should never have come in the first place,' Sebastian muttered.

'True, but here we are.' I reached down and touched his arm. 'Everything'll be fine, Sebastian. I can handle it if something goes wrong.'

'Can you handle it?' he said, looking at me sideways.

'I'll push my conscience to the side if I have to.'

'That's what I'm afraid of.'

My hand dropped from his arm. 'Me too.'

We were both quiet for a moment. 'Have you considered that the reckless behaviour you're exhibiting might be because you're half-Vânător?'

'It's crossed my mind.'

'So do you think your decision to go to Bucharest is based on impulses from the part of you that's more beast than not?'

'No. This decision is exactly like the old me.'

'Have you felt different lately?'

I frowned. 'What do you mean?'

'Since the exchange with William, besides the new telekinetic abilities, have you found yourself—shall we say— easily excitable?'

'Huh?'

Sebastian looked right at me, licking his lips. I suddenly became very aware of his body, the silkiness of his hair, the curve of his lips—everything.

'You're half-Vânător, Elena. You must have a bigger sexual appetite now.'

'What?'

He growled, grabbing my wrist and pulling me off the bed, fingernails biting my flesh. We rolled together, and we ended up with me pinned underneath him, our bodies perfectly aligned. Sebastian moved forcefully between my legs, pushing himself hard against me. I gasped for breath.

'Get off me, Sebastian,' I whispered, my breath coming in short, sharp pants. I wanted to kiss him so badly I ached.

'Do you see?' he said quietly, his eyes searching my face.

'See what?'

'You're dangerous. This whole plan is dangerous.'

'I don't understand,' I gasped as Sebastian roughly grabbed my thigh, kneading the firm flesh as he pressed himself closer still.

'This is how you react to me and you say you don't want me. How would you react in a territory filled with Alphas? I've seen how Roshan dominated you. Romania is filled with vânători, Elena. I'd be a fool to drop you in the middle of it.'

I held my breath as he shifted his weight, separating our two sprawled forms.

Sebastian sighed, rolling off me and up onto his knees. He looked sadly down at me. I couldn't move—I felt boneless, unsatisfied and stupid. I knew Sebastian was trying to prove a point but I hated him right now for showing up my weaknesses.

I crawled slowly backwards, heading towards the sunlight. I was safe in the sunlight and away from him I could think straight.

'You're scared of me,' Sebastian murmured.

I could feel my bottom lip trembling. 'I'm not afraid of you, Sebastian.'

'Then why are you running from me?'

'I'm running from myself. I don't like me when I'm around you.'

'You'd react no different to an Alpha.'

'It's not open for discussion,' I said, finding myself again, my resolve strengthening. 'If you don't want to come with me then fine, but I will go, Sebastian, with or without you.'

Eyes widening, now it was Sebastian's turn to be angry. 'You have no idea what you're asking me to do, what will happen if something happens to you.'

'So enlighten me.'

He hissed, punching the drywall next to him. Chunks of plaster rained on the floor. 'This isn't a game!'

'Then teach me the rules!' I yelled back.

'I can't take you to Bucharest.'

'Fine.'

'Fine?'

'Yes, fine,' I repeated. 'I'll just find my own way there.'

Sebastian threw his head back and roared. When he looked back down at me, his eyes flashed with silver. Just like my dreams, just like I'd seen countless times before, they glowed with an unearthly fire that mesmerised. Suddenly, I was crawling on all fours, reaching out to touch him to satisfy some deep, primal urge.

'No, Elena,' he said, scuttling backwards, 'don't ask me to do this.' His anger had evaporated, replaced by a curious fear.

I reached for Sebastian, my hands running over his chest, my eyes entranced by the silver glow in his own. He slumped forward, my eager touch bringing a low whimper from his lips. 'Please. Refusing you is almost impossible but I must.'

'Take me to Bucharest, Sebastian. Protect me from harm and watch over me.'

'I can't,' he said, wrapping his arms around me. 'If you die—'

'I won't. You'll be there to make sure that doesn't happen.'

Sebastian looked down at me, his eyes slowly fading. The silver light ebbed away, replaced by a dull grey that was the colour of storm clouds. Quickly, he stood. 'Alright. Okay, Elena, but we'll need help if we're going to do this.'

'You can't tell Lucius,' I pleaded.

Sebastian shook his head, taking another step back. 'Have a shower and get cleaned up. I'll figure out what to do next.'

I got to my feet, still confused but comforted. 'Thank you, Sebastian.'

I made a beeline for the bathroom, backtracking only

momentarily to scoop up my backpack. I paused at the door, turning to look into the pained expression on Sebastian's face.

'Sebastian?'

'Yes?' he said evenly, his eyes on mine.

'Answer me one question.'

'What is it?'

I took a deep breath. 'Why do I dream about you?'

Sebastian pondered the question. 'Why do you think you have dreams about someone that you've supposedly never met before?'

I shrugged, and then thought about it more seriously. 'I guess we must have met before, somehow.'

'Go on,' he encouraged.

'I didn't make you up. You're obviously real, so we must have some sort of history, although I remember nothing.' I shook my head, trying to dispel my clouded thoughts. 'I remember so much from my childhood, but why can't I remember meeting you? I wouldn't have forgotten that.'

'Time is irrelevant.'

'I don't think I understand.'

'The concept is a lot to consider.'

'And you know exactly what's going on between us, don't you?'

Sebastian took a step forward, body tense. He didn't look angry so perhaps he was practicing restraint. 'It's been a never-ending pattern up until now, Elena.'

'A never-ending pattern,' I repeated. 'Does that mean the rules have changed now?'

He nodded. 'One mistake could change everything—your vampirism already has.'

I was thoughtful for a minute. 'I still don't understand.'

I hated feeling this dumb. I was grasping for an answer

that seemed right in front of me, a solid wall that I could reach out and touch but still seemed unable to penetrate.

I gripped the doorframe for support. 'Sebastian, I—'

'It's okay,' he whispered, hands again relaxing by his sides. 'Just go and have your shower, Elena.' He flashed me a tight smile.

'Yeah,' I mumbled. 'A shower would be good.'

I walked off, closing the bathroom door behind me and leaning back against it. What the hell was wrong with me? I'd just recently turned into a merciless killing machine, and on top of that I was now contemplating a relationship with Sebastian? I needed to get my head back in the game and remember why I came here in the first place.

Dropping my backpack, I proceeded to strip down. I tried to concentrate on the task at hand, which was discovering what the IMI's serum was being developed for. Until I had my answers, Lucas would feel obligated to further worm his way inside of the IMI organisation. It was too much of a burden for him to carry alone, so if I needed to go to Bucharest for anyone, it was for Lucas's sake. The sooner I had my brother back by my side where he belonged, the sooner everything would be better.

I turned the taps and felt the hot caress of water beat down on my back. Jeez, it would be so good to see Lucas again. We'd been separated for far too long now, and his absence felt like I had a hole in the centre of my heart, like a piece of me was missing.

But that was a feeling and I had to get used to it for now. As much as I believed that we would eventually be reunited, the fact remained that my imminent immortality would eventually tear us apart again. Lucas was a human and therefore saddled with finite life. Sooner or later he would grow old and die, but I would still linger on forever.

Unless …

Frowning, I started soaping myself up and washing my hair. I considered the idea my mind was suggesting. It was selfish and undeniably a mortal sin, yet I couldn't help wanting to keep the one person I actually loved and cared for alive and safe.

I could turn Lucas.

Alive. It seemed a funny word. How 'alive' could you say a vampire was? Your heart stops beating and the grace of God leaves you; you find yourself passing into the hands of Lucifer and then must resign yourself to the idea of an afterlife in hell. Could I really do that to Lucas—sweet, honest Lucas?

I shivered at the thought.

He'd be the first Protector to ever become a vampire. The combination of his magical and vampiric abilities would make him virtually unstoppable. But even with the possibility of all that power, Lucas seemed to like vampires and would undoubtedly cause no problems for the race. He had never intentionally sought power, control, or immortality, had just wanted to be re-united with me. He wasn't like Chester, Susan, George, or any of the other Protectors. They were …

My train of thought immediately crashed into a ravine.

Oh my God. How did I not see this before?

Rinsing my hair clean, I quickly switched off the warm water, jumped out of the shower and wrapped myself up in a towel that was hanging on the back of the door. 'Sebastian!' I squealed, as I threw open the bathroom door and ran into the bedroom.

A second later he was by my side, wrapping me protectively in his arms and spinning us around on the spot. He snarled, glaring around the room, and then rushed us back into the bathroom, fangs out. 'What is it? Who's here?'

'No one's here. I just think I might have figured something out, something important.'

Sebastian released me slowly, eyes still darting warily over my features.

I grimaced, looking at his soaked t-shirt. 'Sorry, I didn't mean to wet you,' I said, running a hand across the patch.

'It's fine,' Sebastian said, looking down and placing his hand on mine. 'Tell me what's got you so worked up.'

I pushed him out of the bathroom and down on a patch of shadow at the edge of the bed, and sat down next to him. Sebastian looked me up and down, licking his lips slowly. 'Do you think you could put some clothes on first?'

I looked down at the towel wrapped loosely around my naked form. 'Wow. I totally spaced.'

I dashed back into the bathroom. No more than a few minutes later, I re-emerged in a fresh pair of denim jeans, t-shirt and a warm sweater. My wet hair had been pulled into a ponytail. I strode out of the bathroom and did a little twirl in front of Sebastian. 'Better?'

He swallowed and looked away. 'Even with your clothes, you're still distracting.'

Like he could talk—Sebastian was wearing those black leather pants again with a red t-shirt that seemed to hug his chest like a second skin. 'I'll take that as a compliment.'

'It was intended as such,' he murmured, turning back to look at me and sliding a pair of sunglasses on. I caught a quick glimpse of blackness behind them.

My expression crumpled, unsure what I had done wrong. 'Are you angry with me?'

He shook his head. 'Should I be?'

'But your eyes … ?'

Sebastian adjusted the glasses nervously. 'It's nothing. So let's hear the big news.'

I dropped onto the bed beside him. 'If not angry, you must be thirsty.'

'Elena, it's nothing.'

'Why didn't you feed on that vânător you killed last night?'

'It's irrelevant.'

'Why don't you have a tetra pack then? You know I brought some with me, just in case.'

'It will kill me.'

I rolled my eyes. 'Don't be so dramatic. It's pretty close to the real thing.'

He said something under his breath. It sounded like, 'I wouldn't know.'

'What?'

'It's nothing. I just have rules that I have to follow, and I'm more interested in the epiphany you've yet to divulge, so get on with it.'

'More rules,' I mocked.

'Yes, more rules,' Sebastian snapped.

I shoved him, hard, pissed that I was now more concerned about Sebastian going postal and killing the townsfolk than airing my concerns about The Protectors. 'Starve then. See if I care.'

'Elena, I'll manage.'

'Your voice lies, Sebastian.'

I flicked out my fangs and nipped at the flesh at my wrist, shuddering with delight. I'd forgotten how good I tasted and lazily licked the blood off my lips. I shoved my wrist towards him. 'Just do it.'

Sebastian slowly took my wrist, mesmerised by the red

flow as it reversed and started to ooze back into my wrist again. 'I can't.'

'Do you want me to look away,' I said, a smile touching my lips. His eyebrow rose marginally, but Sebastian didn't answer, merely politely pushed my arm away.

I sighed, tired of this game. 'Well, if you're not going to eat, then fine. But I still need to get some food into me.'

'Do you wish me to go find you something?'

His sincerity made me laugh. 'Thanks, Caveman, but I've got this one covered. Just take me to a cafe or something, and I'll hunt and gather my own food. Then I will tell you all about my latest theory.'

Sebastian stiffened. 'More reckless behaviour, I presume?'

'No, but you probably won't like what I have to say.'

'Elena, just tell me,' Sebastian muttered, reluctantly following me out, taking the lead as we left the apartment.

'Ha! Now who wants answers?' I mocked, jogging down the creaking stairs to keep up. 'Food first, then you can yell at me.' I sucked at my lower lip, amusement quickly fading as I wondered how I should ease into my latest revelation.

Sebastian just grunted as he glanced back over his shoulder at me.

Budapest's weather was like a slap to the face as the rusty door of the apartment building slammed home behind us. I smoothed my hands up and down the sides of my arms, determined to spread warmth into my suddenly chilly limbs. I wished I'd double-layered but there was no way I was jogging back up all those stairs again to grab my coat.

'So who was the first person to turn a human into a vampire. I mean, besides Lucius when he made his twenty thralls?'

Sebastian stilled, though I doubted it was the frosty wind that gave him pause. 'Julius was the first. Why do you ask?'

'Julius?'

He nodded and continued on, glancing both ways before dragging me out into the road. An old 1975 Trabant rounded the approaching corner like a crazy cart on rails. My breath caught in my throat as the disgruntled driver, handlebar moustache a-quivering, spied us and honked in displeasure. He slammed sharply down on the brakes, the powder blue Trabant skidding and squealing to a stop just inches away. Sebastian slapped the hood in annoyance as we passed. We left the Hungarian waving a stiff finger at us.

We quickly walked down the relatively empty adjoining street, keeping close to the sides of the buildings and sticking to the shadows. Strangers that did brave the cold passed us, coats pulled tight around them, shoulders hunched and eyes on the ground. Old newspapers and cigarette packets crowded the well-worn pavement, sticking to the bottom of our shoes like discarded chewing gum. 'So what happened?' I finally asked, falling into step with Sebastian. 'What made Julius turn his first human?'

His suspicious sidelong glance made me sniff, rub my nose, and refocus my gaze back on the pavement at my feet. 'For love.'

'Love, huh?'

Sebastian touched my arm with tentative fingers, an attempt to draw me to a stop as another car roared past. I kept walking, unharmed, yet slightly disturbed that I was this unfocused, finding myself distracted by the weird parallels I was drawing between Julius and myself. Love?

Sebastian's fingers fell away, finding the smooth flesh of his chin and scratching it in agitation. 'Elena, what's really going on?'

'So, Julius was in love ...'

Another sigh escaped Sebastian's lips. 'Julius wanted to turn his wife and make her a part of his new life.'

'Go on.'

'He remembered the ritual involved in his own turning and tried to replicate the process.'

'What went wrong?'

'He wasn't prepared for her bloodlust.'

'Oh, because she wasn't a thrall, she was a turned vampire. I think I understand the rest,' I said, following Sebastian across a small courtyard and into the crowded street beyond. 'His wife went on a killing rampage, didn't she?'

Sebastian nodded. 'Back then we didn't know that turned vampires would eventually learn to suppress their appetites. We assumed that she was just too dangerous to keep around, to control, particularly when Lucius heard of the plague.'

'A plague?'

'Yes. Together, Julius and his wife went on a blood binge. Julius felt that with his immortality, super strength, speed, and only a minor susceptibility to sunlight, that he was unstoppable. He may not have had the same blood lust as his wife but he still enjoyed the kill. Between the two of them, if unchecked, they had the potential to wipe out entire towns.'

'I gather that's when Lucius stepped in?'

'Lucius was no angel himself but he warned them—they needed to control their bloodlust or they risked exposing us all. With no previous ground rules, Julius couldn't understand why they would now hide their nature, as vampires were clearly the top of the food chain. Lucius offered him one chance to fall into line, but Julius rebelled, now completely driven by bloodlust alone.'

'Tell me that Lucius kicked his ass?'

Sebastian grimaced. 'Lucius challenged him, easily besting his former thrall. He won, or at least he thought he had won.

Not having killed one of his own kind before, he slit their throats and left them to die. Julius survived, but his wife was a turned vampire and was vulnerable to a human death.'

'That's kinda sad.'

'They killed a lot of innocent people, Elena.'

'So that's why Julius despises Lucius and wants to kill him.' I coughed. 'And wants to toy with my insides.'

Sebastian nodded. 'Revenge is a powerful motivator, especially when it stems from lost love.'

'Agreed, but I can still understand why he did it.'

'You offer him pity?' Sebastian asked, surprised.

Here we go.

'I'm just saying that I understand his motivations. Julius wanted to be around the person he loved for longer than her mortality allowed.'

Sebastian's brows furrowed. 'Why do I get the distinct feeling that you're working up to some kind of point here?'

I smiled. 'You're perceptive.'

'If you're agreeing with Julius's choice to turn a human, then I can only conclude that you have similar ideas.'

'Now, now,' I quipped, 'don't judge me.'

'Lucas is a human Protector, Elena. He can never be what we are.' Sebastian's voice came out low, a warning.

'Unless he's turned.'

Sebastian stopped in front of a small, shady cafe and gripped me by the shoulders. 'That can't happen. Turned vampires are too unpredictable. Just imagine one with magical powers.'

'I have,'

'Elena—'

I held up my hands in surrender. 'I hear you, Sebastian, believe me. I didn't bring up this whole subject to debate morality and your rules with you.'

He let go of my shoulders, grabbed a chair and pulled it out for me. 'Then why are we discussing turning Lucas into a vampire?'

I sat down, shushing him as I quickly scoped out the vicinity for people eavesdropping. 'Keep it down.'

'No one is listening, Elena.'

I leant forward conspiratorially as Sebastian seated himself across from me. 'Regardless, I think it's highly possible it could happen.'

'Elena, it can't.'

'Will you stop that?' I snapped. 'I'm not talking about turning him. I'm talking about The Protectors, their whole organisation.'

Sebastian frowned, waiting.

I shook my head at him slowly. 'The serum, Sebastian, the serum. At first I thought it could be a cure but what if it's not? What if they're using my blood so they can figure out how to be like me—like you?'

'The Protectors hate us. They initially formed to help fight us off, to fight back. I don't think they want to be us.'

'I think you're wrong. Immortality is definitely a drawcard, as are the other gifts we naturally possess. The only obvious flaws are the thirst and the aversion to sunlight. Otherwise, being a vampire or like a vampire is a very attractive prospect, Sebastian. Even the Vânâtors want my blood, thinking it'll cure their deficiencies. What if The Protector's motivations are exactly the same? What if all they desire is to be more powerful than vampires so that they can finally end what was begun those three hundred years ago? What if this serum that they are developing will give them the gift of immortality and finally match us, strength for strength?'

Sebastian leant back in his chair, dropping his hands into

his lap. He stayed silent for a long moment. 'I really hope you're wrong about this.'

I shrugged. 'Maybe I am? But I know Chester well enough to believe he's up to something sinister. He and his team have been studying the effects of my blood for the last sixteen years. He was absolutely fascinated by my reaction to the Alpha, and even more so when he discovered my telekinetic powers and inhuman strength. I could see the desire on Chester's face every time he looked at me. It wasn't just from curiosity—I think he wanted to be me.'

'How would they be able to develop something as complex as the process of our exchange, the blood and venom transference, and brew it in a test tube for distribution? Any vampire aware of the details of that process would never have given The Protectors such information.' His brows puckered together. 'Did you?'

'After the way they treated me? Why would I give them anything?'

'Does Lucas know anything more?'

I shook my head. 'Not as far as I know. But Lucas would have told me if he learnt something new.'

'Are you sure about that? He is a Protector, and you were just talking about turning him vamp. Maybe Lucas has his own motives for helping you. Maybe he's known of The Protector's intentions for a while and figures staying close to you will eventually lead you down the path of turning him for his protection? Turn one of them, turn all of them? Maybe the serum is a distraction from the actual objective?'

A growl escaped my throat and my jaw tensed, fighting my fangs as my instincts gave way. 'Don't ever implicate my brother in their evil plans again, Sebastian. I trust Lucas more than any other person on this planet, and that includes you. He would never betray me, ever.'

Sebastian shrugged. 'I'm just saying to be aware of every angle.'

'You're wrong about him. Move on.'

He held his hands up in surrender. 'Okay, calm down. What do you want to do?'

I bit back my temper, unclenching my fingers. I slumped back in my seat. 'I don't know. What can we do?'

'Informing Lucius would be a good start.'

'I intend to, Sebastian. But I also intend to get some concrete evidence before bothering him with this.'

'So you're back to putting yourself in harm's way again? What if you're right and the IMI are already running tests, creating mutated vampires?'

'Surely they couldn't have developed anything that complex so quickly. It's only been a month since I was last there. At that time, Stephanie was still grasping for answers to the pathology of my blood.'

'Could you consider the possibility that they never discussed what they were really working on around you? After all, you're the donor. Lying to you is how they get results.'

A waitress from inside the cafe waltzed out to take our orders, interrupting the conversation. She stopped the second she eyed Sebastian, closing the distance between them in a heartbeat and leaning down to talk to him in Hungarian. She flashed him an awful lot of cleavage. If she'd been any closer she'd virtually be sitting in his lap.

I rolled my eyes, groaning. 'Tell her I want pancakes,' I muttered.

Does he have to attract every woman we come across?

I glanced out over the street, watching the traffic streaming past. Amongst the sea of moving pedestrians, there was a brief lull and my eyes settled on a figure that was

standing peculiarly still. His hair was like a flaming torch—
pink, spiked, yet still against the breeze. His gleaming eyes
were mesmerising despite the several meters of bitumen,
crowds and cars that separated us. As blue as the deepest
ocean, his eyes were filled with the absolute certainty of a
predator, watchful and unblinking.

The figure took a step forward. I didn't see it happen,
but I sensed those eyes draw nearer. A smile curved his
predatory lips, exposing elongated canines. The tip of his
tongue brushed lightly across the pointed edges, droplets
of crimson suddenly painting his lips a ruby red. I smelt
his blood, felt his hunger beat towards me like a pulse on
the wind.

My heartbeat slowed, practically thudding to a halt. I
felt an insistent pull at my flesh, sensing invisible hands
clasping at my shoulders and dragging me to my feet. I
rose, walking across the street, moving towards the figure
without thinking. His eyes were magnetic, beautiful, a sea
of beauty that I would drown in.

I pushed through traffic and then the crowds of people,
slowly approaching. I saw my hands were stretched in front
of me like a zombie, battering rams to anyone who got in my
way. I knew it was compulsion that drew me dangerously
closer but I couldn't seem to stop, attracted to the smell of
his blood and the press of his thirst.

Strong arms closed around me, pinning me against a firm
chest. 'Stop, Elena,' his voice whispered in my ear, and I did.
A metaphysical blanket of safety and love seemed to wrap
itself around me, blocking out the mind tricks of the other.

'You're no fun, Sebastian,' Caleb said, suddenly appearing
in front of us both. He hissed as the sun lit upon face,
moving to the shoulder of the road to stand under the shade
of a tree.

I rolled my head back against Sebastian's chest. The skin across his face was starting to blister and turn an ugly shade of red. 'What are you doing?' I said, spinning in his arms. 'You're going to fry!'

'I'm protecting you.' He growled at Caleb, flashing fang. A passing pedestrian shrieked and ran in the other direction.

'Protect me in the shade!'

Caleb was laughing, slapping the top of his thighs with his hands. 'You're too much fun, Sebastian. I would not have harmed her but enjoy seeing you risk harming yourself to keep her safe.'

A rush of wind and the feel of the ground disappearing underfoot told me Sebastian had shifted us away in one swift movement. We now stood under the front stoop of a produce store, sheltered by a sagging tarpaulin now faded like yesterday's news and covered in vast amounts of pigeon waste. Crates of potatoes, onions and a few less than desirable bushels of apples monopolised the standing space, tiny insects already setting up home in the rapidly aging produce.

'I can feel your thirst, Caleb.'

'And I yours.' Caleb's smile widened. 'We could share her.'

'I'm not a Christmas cracker,' I interjected.

Caleb laughed harder. 'Dinner with a sense of humour—I like it.'

Sebastian shook his head, drawing me closer. 'You aren't going to feed off her, Caleb, any more than you'll feed off any other human.' There was an edge of authority to his voice that was difficult to ignore.

Caleb studied Sebastian in absolute stillness, his gaze unwavering. After several deep breaths his stiff posture fell away and his face relaxed. 'I was going to a neutral bar before I ran into your Elena.' His shoulders slumped a little, which made Sebastian seem to calm down, too.

'We need to talk, Caleb.'

'I'm sorry, Sebastian,' Caleb said, cowering. It was such a marked change in demeanour that it left me wondering how much power Sebastian held over the other vampires.

He waved a hand at him. 'I know. We need to talk about something else.'

Caleb looked up, his eyes locking on Sebastian's. 'I sense a favour's about to be asked.'

'Let me take Elena back to Nicholas's apartment and then we can talk.'

'Am I going to like this?'

Sebastian smiled at Caleb. There was nothing pleasant in it. 'I haven't had any complaints yet.'

What the?

CHAPTER TWENTY-SIX: HELPLESSNESS

My foot tapped frantically as I kept glancing between the clock next to Nicholas's bed and the doorway, expecting to see Sebastian walk through at any moment. He'd been gone for over an hour and I was less than pleased. I'd thought Sebastian and Caleb would talk here, in the apartment, where I could listen in.

Apparently not.

It was just after noon. I was still hungry and now Sebastian was keeping more secrets from me. He'd mentioned wanting to enlist help if we'd moved forward with my plan but hadn't mentioned why discussing those plans with Caleb would be for their ears only. I felt useless, left out.

My other leg started bouncing in time with the first one. Great—I was pissed off, nervous and possibly developing a mild case of Parkinson's.

I glanced back at the clock again—only two minutes had passed. There was no point leaving the apartment to find that neutral bar. I could be wandering the street for hours; I could also wind up dead. Sebastian had been particularly insistent on that point.

Instead, I thought about Chester and his minions. Could I be right about their intentions? Would the IMI have backed such a plan, or had I been right the first time? Was there a cure on the horizon?

I looked back at the door again, my feet pounding out an incomprehensible rhythm on the carpet.

What's taking you so long, you bastard?

I gave up and flopped back onto the bed, staring up at the ceiling. I wanted my mind to go blank. I didn't want to think about the whirl of things going round in my head—the serum, Julius, Lucas, Sebastian, or even William. I wanted ...

What do I want?

Six months ago I was living a relatively normal life. I was born with funky genes, yes, but was still just a teenager. Now it felt like I was in the centre of and the cause of so many disputes that I couldn't see my way straight through the tangled web that had been weaved around me. How had everything gone so pear-shaped? Sometimes it was just exhausting being me. When was I ever going to have a normal day?

'We're back.'

I shot forward at the sound of Sebastian's voice. I was about to start in at him for deserting me but stopped when I saw Caleb, standing in the doorway beside him. He was a ghost of his former self—pale, eyes vacant, with lips that were curved into a lazy, fixed smile.

I slid off the bed, waving a hand in front of Caleb's face. His lights were on but there was no one home. 'What's wrong with him?' I asked Sebastian, frowning.

'He's drunk.'

'What? How is that even possible?'

I snapped my fingers. Caleb blinked, but that was it.

'I can't explain it to you,' Sebastian answered cautiously. He was watching me, already moving away as if he sensed the confrontation building up between us. I didn't arc up like I usually would, though. I was mesmerised by the blood

I saw drying on the top of Caleb's shoulder. There were also a couple of stray drops on the skin of his neck.

'What happened?'

'I cannot explain it, Elena.'

'Why? Because you think I won't understand or because you don't have the words.'

'Both.'

I pointed to the blood. 'Did you hurt him?'

'I did not.' Sebastian's eyes told me that he spoke the truth. The smile on Caleb's face confirmed it.

'Whose blood is that?'

'It belongs to Caleb.'

I was frowning, frustrated. 'You really shit me off, Sebastian.'

'I am aware.' His face was blank, neutral.

I worried my lower lip, staring at Sebastian, wondering if he'd eventually grow uncomfortable and for once just explain to me what the hell was going on. I had a feeling we were going to be staring at each other for a while, but eventually Sebastian was the one who looked away. He reached into a plastic bag he'd brought in with him and grabbed a tetra pack of Synth Blood, slapping it against Caleb's chest.

'Drink this,' Sebastian crooned to him, voice hypnotic.

Caleb blinked, shaking his head and looking down at the tetra pack against his chest. He slowly lifted his hands to take it, looking cautiously at Sebastian as if asking permission. 'I feel strange.'

'It'll pass,' Sebastian assured him, shuffling Caleb into the living room and helping him into a chair.

I sat down on the armchair across from Caleb, watching him carefully. 'Caleb, do you know what Sebastian did to you?'

Sebastian gave me a sharp look, obviously not happy with me prying. If he just talked honestly with me, I wouldn't have to ask so many questions. 'Elena, that's enough.'

'Just shut up, Sebastian.'

'Sebastian didn't do anything,' Caleb finally answered, stabbing a straw in and taking a long, greedy sip. As he drank, he seemed to look more, well, normal. As normal as I had ever known him to be, anyway.

'Then what happened to you?' I persisted.

Caleb shrugged. 'I don't remember. What does it matter?'

I turned just in time to see the satisfied look on Sebastian's face. He wasn't smiling exactly, but I felt a certain relief radiating from him. Crazy, top secret Vampiric crap was definitely going on, and I was going to get to the bottom of it.

Caleb looked contented as he drank, his eyes darting watchfully around the room. They didn't contain the same sense of menace I'd felt in the street and now that his thirst was being sated they were a beautiful colour again.

'It's good,' Caleb said, licking his lips. 'I always liked O positive.'

Sebastian shook his head. 'It's the most common blood type. I don't think you're fussy at all, are you, Caleb?'

Caleb shrugged again. 'Blood is blood. It all tastes good to me.' His eyes swivelled to look at me again. 'Although, there is some blood I hunger for more than others.'

Sebastian growled, low and menacing. Caleb laughed, choking on a mouthful of blood. 'Relax. I get it; she's yours.' That drew another growl from Sebastian.

I shook my head. I was getting tired of the theatrics at this point. 'So what's been decided in my absence?' I demanded. 'You were both gone for over an hour. Sebastian, tell me that you talked to Caleb about Bucharest.'

Sebastian's words spilled out, growling all the louder. 'Yes, we discussed it.'

'Great,' I said, clapping my hands together. 'When are we leaving?'

'Well, better to go sooner rather than later,' Caleb answered, tossing his now empty tetra pack in the rubbish bin over in the far corner of the room with uncanny accuracy. 'I have plans for Sunday night.'

'You're not going to tell me I'm crazy for going back?'

Caleb grinned at me. 'Are you kidding? I don't say anything to a woman she doesn't want to hear.' He winked at me, which felt slightly less than comfortable. 'Besides, I'm assuming Sebastian will provide ample compensation for my services.' Caleb glanced at what I could only imagine was the throbbing pulse of my neck. 'If he doesn't,' Caleb said, licking his lips, 'perhaps you and I can come to some sort of special arrangement.'

I didn't think for a second that sex was on his mind. 'I'm not going to open a vein for you, Caleb, whether you come or not. Frankly, I don't care if you do. Sebastian's the one who thought we needed the extra help.'

'And I still do. This is madness, Elena,' Sebastian said.

'Change the record, Sebastian. I'm getting sick of hearing your doubts.'

He threw his arms up and then started to pace the floor, keeping his face turned from me at all times. I didn't need to see it to know what he was thinking.

'So,' I said, turning back to look at the more receptive party. 'We're going to have to sneak in.'

'Sebastian said the place is a hotel.'

I nodded. 'It is but with Protectors everywhere, we'll have to be careful. I'm amendable to flying there like Sebastian requested. He's right because flying will leave fewer trails and it's probably easier to avoid vânători while in the air. Once we're there, though, we do things my way.'

'And how are you planning on bypassing their security network?' Sebastian asked bitterly.

'We sneak in via the air-conditioning system. That was how William found me without getting caught.'

Sebastian rolled his eyes and glanced away again, continuing to pace.

Jealous much?

'William?' Caleb said, looking confused. 'Is he a vampire too?'

'Yeah.'

'Hmm, William,' Caleb said, repeating the name thoughtfully while he scratched at his spiky hair. 'That name's familiar. What's his last name?'

'I'll never tell.'

'Hey, Sebastian? Isn't your br—'

'Shut up, Caleb,' Sebastian interrupted. 'She doesn't like to talk about him, and frankly, neither do I.'

Caleb held his hands up in surrender. 'Whatever. I must be mistaken. Obviously the wrong William.'

'So we go in through the air-conditioning,' Sebastian continued. 'Then what?'

I raised an eyebrow at him before continuing. 'Well, we wait it out until they close the laboratories for the evening. Then, when the areas are clear, we drop in and find out where they are storing the serum or any documentation relating to it. Then we destroy it all.'

'Sounds easy,' Caleb said.

'It does, doesn't it?' I answered, frowning.

It would never be that simple because I'd had enough trouble escaping the first time. And the second time they'd moved me to the factory, a more secure facility. Maybe I was just trying to fool myself into thinking that I was braver than I actually was? Maybe I just needed to prove that this half-breed was as capable of solving a mystery as everyone else was.

Whatever the reason, I was going back to Bucharest.

Am I an idiot?

Absolutely.

Bitingly cold and heavy, the wind gripped and pulled at the skin on my face with its invisible fingers. I glanced sideways, trying to see into the distance ahead. Did the streaming currents of light mean we were nearing our destination?

'Almost there,' Sebastian whispered into my ear.

'I hope so,' I said. 'Where's Caleb? It's hard to see anything at this speed.'

'Right here,' Caleb murmured, somewhere nearby. 'Do you think I'd let my next meal get too far out of my sight?'

I laughed in spite of myself. 'Please, you can stop it now.'

Caleb's answering laugh was all kinds of sinister as it played against the force of the wind, sometimes as loud as if he were right next to my ear, other times soft and barely audible.

A change of topic was a good idea. 'Are there any vânători nearby?'

'Always,' Sebastian answered. He sounded tired.

'Are we in any immediate danger?'

Sebastian looked down at me with eyes as black as the night itself. 'What do you think?'

I was thinking that Sebastian had turned sarcasm into an art form. I was jealous. 'It's my scent, isn't it?'

'Well it isn't my aftershave,' Caleb replied dryly.

Great. Two smart asses.

'I'm going to jump now, Elena,' Sebastian said, changing the subject. 'I'll try to be as gentle as possible landing.'

'Are we there?'

'Yes. The top of the hotel looms close by. I think at this angle our approach up to the air-conditioning ducts will be easiest. Are you ready?'

'I'm ready, boss,' Caleb answered.

Sebastian muttered something unintelligible under his breath. 'I was talking to Elena.'

'Whatever.'

I felt Sebastian tense and then spring upwards, barely breaking stride. Pressure briefly battered the top of my head, flattening my hair and pinning my limbs down like lead weights. Then I was weightless, wind changing direction as we sailed back down. The top of the hotel came into focus and then … we landed.

Sebastian hit the ground with a *thud*, careful but not exactly quiet. I bounced in his arms, bruised by the stiffness of his limbs and the abrupt stop. 'Whoa, steady. Are you okay?' he said, looking me over for damage.

'I'm fine. Put me down.'

Caleb landed beside us, cement cracking under his feet. He looked down and grimaced. 'Whoops. My bad.'

Sebastian rolled his eyes, lowering me to the ground. I stumbled slightly, waiting for all of the blood to rush back to my legs. 'I can't believe I'm back here,' I said, looking across the rooftop. I felt a little foolish for saying it out loud. After all, coming back had been my idea.

'We can leave anytime you want,' Sebastian repeated, touching my shoulder tenderly.

'No. We probably pissed Lucius off enough just coming here. We stirred up the interests of a couple of vânători and you made Caleb bleed. We might as well make it worthwhile.'

'Sebastian made me bleed?' Caleb asked, looking confused. Had he already forgotten everything we'd talked about earlier?

Sebastian's eyes darkened, expression changing. 'Wait. Did you just say that Lucius hasn't approved or financed this little fact-finding mission?'

Sebastian looked away, nostrils flaring.

'Sebastian, please tell me she's joking, because you distinctly failed to mention that rather important fact when you talked me into this.'

Sebastian ignored him, moving over to the air-conditioning vents.

'You could have told me I signed on for a death mission,' Caleb continued. 'If the freaky shit The Protectors are into doesn't get me killed, then Lucius will sure as hell finish me off just for helping you.' He shook his head, sounding scared. 'You both have immunity.' He pointed to me. 'You're his daughter and Sebastian is his head tracker—he won't kill either of you. Nope, he'll just take his aggression out on the pink-haired smart ass who stupidly agreed to be your muscle!'

'Shut up, Caleb,' Sebastian and I said simultaneously.

'Oh, I see you're even finishing each other's sentences now. That's sweet,' he muttered bitterly.

'Look, I'll pay you another ten thousand if you just shut up, Caleb.'

'Dollars?' I shrieked, staring at Sebastian in disbelief.

He winked at me. 'Yes, dollars.'

'You didn't think I'd get into this shit with you for free, did you?' Caleb said, rubbing his hands together. 'Sebastian, you got a deal. Another ten thousand certainly eases my conscience. My mouth is closing as of … now.' He paused for all of two seconds. Then, 'is there more money involved if I get severely injured?'

'Like insurance?' I asked, still dumfounded by the ludicrous amount of money about to be exchanged.

'Yeah.'

Sebastian cocked an eyebrow in irritation.

Caleb sighed, taking the hint. 'Okay, I'm shutting up … now.'

I hurried to Sebastian's side. He was in the middle of lifting the grill work away from the top of the conditioning units. 'How much money are we talking about here?'

Sebastian seemed distracted. 'Does it matter?'

'Fifty,' Caleb said over my shoulder.

I jumped. He hadn't been there a second ago. 'That's a lot of money, Sebastian—too much.'

'Hey!' Caleb moaned, frowning.

'I told you I had a bad feeling about this, Elena. I'll do what I think is necessary to keep you safe.'

'You sound like someone else I know,' I muttered, thinking about William and his stupid campaign for morality. If he'd just taken me away from all this earlier, then maybe, just maybe, things would be different now.

I shook my head and refocused on Sebastian's face. He was frowning down into that dark shaft like the Bogeyman waited at the bottom. 'Is there a problem?'

He pointed down the vent. 'It's a long drop. I think you'll be fine going down, but climbing out again? I'm not sure you'd be able to do it, and given the confined space, I won't be able to carry you either.'

'Okay, so we'll do our business down on the IMI's floors and then I'll crawl back into the vent, head to the lower levels and leave the building right through the front door like all the other tourists.'

'What if someone recognises you?'

'It's a risk we'll have to take.'

Sebastian nodded, but he wasn't pleased. He quickly glanced back at Caleb. 'Wait for a few minutes and then follow us down. I don't want you crashing into Elena at the bottom of the shaft.' He looked pointedly at the cracked concrete of the roof and then back to me again. 'I'll be coming with you.'

I looked down the narrow shaft and shook my head. 'There's not enough room for both of us at once, you said it yourself.'

'If you flatten your body against mine there is.'

Caleb snorted. 'I'll have to remember that line.'

While they were both distracted, I climbed over the lip of the shaft and then let go. Behind me Sebastian could be heard venting his irritation. It didn't last.

I slid down and around an S-bend, which slowed me down enough so that when I crashed into the following ventilation system I didn't fall right through it. I did however land with a rather loud crash, dinting the clear pattern of my footprints into the metal underneath.

So much for a quiet entrance.

I stayed perfect still, listening for sounds of alarm. There was nothing, not even the sound of Sebastian's voice. I moved quickly, shuffling along the vent as I heard the descent of another body behind. Sebastian landed gracefully and without a sound.

He was a damn show off.

Sebastian looked down at the indentations my feet had made and shook his head. 'That's why I wanted us to come down together. I always make less noise.'

I flashed him a fake, little smile. 'Okay, point taken,

expert. Now, tell me what you see, hear and smell, because I'm getting nothing.'

He sniffed, frowning. 'Me too.'

Sebastian turned and began creeping silently through the ventilation shaft behind. His body was bent at half height as he struggled through the maze of small ducts, and the venting around us became smaller the further we travelled, so small that Sebastian eventually had to crawl. Silent, I followed behind him.

Approaching a vent opening, he stopped, turning somewhat awkwardly to face me in our cramped confines. I crawled up beside him, trying to see what Sebastian was looking at. Our shoulders and hips brushed lightly, sending a rather disconcerting flood of impulses through my body. The first impulse was to throw him down and kiss him senseless, and the second just made me blush.

'What's wrong?'

'Nothing.'

'I can hear your heart beating faster, and your skin is nearly glowing.'

'I'm sorry.'

I glanced at him sideways, expecting black eyes and drawn canines. What looked back at me were the swirling depths I'd grown accustomed to.

'Sebastian, you're not thirsty.'

'Should I be?'

'Yes, earlier today you—' I stopped talking. I had flashbacks of Sebastian's earlier struggle, and yet, now everything was okay. His eyes were subdued and his vampirism in check. That could only mean one thing. 'You've fed.'

'What?' Sebastian said, pretending to study the grate

again. I knew I should have been focusing on the task at hand, but this seemed important.

'You fed.'

'I'm not sure I understand what you're getting at, Elena.'

Bullshit.

'Yeah, you do. And I think you know exactly what I'm talking about. You wouldn't feed from me, and you wouldn't feed from Synth Blood, and I know you wouldn't feed from a human. I'm pretty sure I caught you saying something like that last night. So?'

'So what?' Sebastian said, starting to get angry.

'You fed on Caleb, didn't you?'

'Don't be absurd.'

'Admit it. You like the taste of vampire blood.' I couldn't stop myself from sounding smug.

He cupped a hand over my mouth. 'Stop it.'

I shook my head, looking him dead in the eyes. There was no way I was letting this one go. I'd finally found someone who was a bigger freak than me. Vampires aren't cannibals—they didn't even feed on vânători, let alone other members of their own race.

'Elena.'

'Don't *Elena* me,' I mumbled into his hand.

Very slowly he released me. Sebastian sat back against the vent, looking deflated.

'Talk to me. You know I won't quit asking now I know I'm right about this.'

Sebastian's expression was pained. He pointed back down the shaft. 'If I promise to explain when all this is over, will you agree to keep quiet for now?'

He didn't want Caleb to overhear anything. I could understand that. 'Do you promise? No tricks?'

'No tricks. You guessed, so I guess I'll have to finally explain that aspect of myself to you.'

'More of those rules again, huh?'

He nodded. 'The world would be chaos without rules. They apply even to me.'

'Rules are made to be broken, Sebastian.'

He laughed. 'Spoken like a true renegade. I don't think you'd be popular where I come from.'

'And where is that exactly? Oh, and don't think it hasn't escaped my attention that you seem older than a regular born vampire, but you're not exactly a turned one either. I'm not even sure that Tiberius *is* your father.'

His smile grew wider. 'The mystery must be killing you.'

I afforded him a smile in return. 'Don't get me started.'

Sebastian shook his head at me and then pointed to the vent in front of us. 'Let's start by telling me what we're looking at here.'

I glanced down and decided it was time to get back to work. 'It looks like my old room, so that's probably what it is,' I said, unsure as there was no furniture or adornments down there. 'It could just be a spare room, or they might have cleaned my room out after I left. We should keep moving, see if we can find the labs from here.'

'Would you like to go in front?'

I thought about the spectacular view I'd miss out on if I went behind. 'It's not necessary. I'm sure you'll lead us in the right direction.'

Sebastian turned and shuffled forward. 'Suit yourself.'

'Can you sense anything?' I said, crawling happily behind him again.

He kept moving. 'Nothing. It's strange, though—I can hear people talking on the levels several floors down, I can smell human blood—probably tourists—but I'm not picking up a Protector presence. I can smell old scents but nothing new.' I heard him sniff. 'There's some vânători close by, but they aren't near this building as far as I can tell.'

'As far as you can tell?'

'There are a lot of humans in this building, Elena. Their scents, both artificial and real, are abundant and mix up my senses.'

'Maybe that's one of the reasons the IMI put their headquarters at the top of a hotel—misdirection.'

'That makes sense. Even I didn't know where this place was.'

'You never did tell me how you found me.'

'I felt you.' Sebastian stopped in front of another opening and looked down. 'This looks like a lab of some kind.'

I squeezed in beside him again. 'It's Stephanie's lab. She's that blood specialist I told you about.'

'It looks empty.'

I looked more closely, noting the absence of vials, blood testing machines, and other general lab equipment. The only stuff still left in the room was a desk, a telephone, a small cot in the corner and the workbench. Otherwise, the room was empty.

A bad feeling suddenly hit me in the pit of my stomach. Without thinking, I grabbed the vent and pulled it open.

Sebastian grabbed my hands. 'What are you doing?'

'I'm going down. I have a feeling this isn't the only empty room.'

'Elena, you can't—' He choked on his words as I dropped down into the room below. 'There are motion sensors everywhere,' Sebastian finally finished, calling down at me and sounding defeated.

I looked back up at him and grimaced. 'Are you sure?'

He tapped his finger impatiently against the tiny device that sat wedged on the underside of the open vent.

'... I just set that off, didn't I?'

Sebastian looked down at me and nodded. 'Why don't you ever listen?'

I shrugged. 'It's a defect. I'd get used to it if I were you.' I glanced around the bare room. 'How much time do you think we have before someone comes running?'

He dropped down lightly next to me, graceful and sleek. 'That depends on *who* or *what* they are sending.'

'That's reassuring,' I said, glancing around the room.

I walked over to the cupboards where I'd seen Stephanie keeping her documentation. Glancing inside only proved that they were as empty as the lab. 'Maybe she went back home to the U.S.,' I said, sliding the drawers of her desk out to reveal nothing of particular interest. 'I'll need to check the main lab to confirm. Can you hoist me back into the vent?'

'What's the point? They already know we're here.'

'You're right. Sorry about that.' I crossed the room, opening the door and ushering Sebastian into the carpeted corridor beyond. I watched as his eyes traced every detail— elevator, exit points, security cameras—his fingers brushing against the white walls as we walked towards the main laboratory.

'And what are you thinking now?' Sebastian said with a wry grin.

'I'm thinking that I owe you one if I get us into trouble over this.'

'You're leaving that open to wild misinterpretation, Elena.'

'Keep the favour within reason.'

'I'll think on it and get back to you?'

'You do that, Sebastian.'

I stopped in front of the main lab door and touched the access panel. I'd not been permitted entry in the past unless accompanied by Chester or one of his assistants, and the door certainly wasn't opening now.

Time to be subtle.

Stepping back from the door, I kicked out hard, slamming my foot into its timber surface. The door's smooth surface splintered, bursting from its hinges and flying across the laboratory. It landed with a loud *BOOM* against the opposing wall.

'That'll do it,' Sebastian muttered sarcastically as he pushed me back, stepping around me first to inspect the lab.

'They're gone,' I whispered, shaking my head in disbelief. 'This lab is completely empty. It looks like they must have moved the entire facility to another location. That's why you can't smell anything here except humans—it's just a below-average hotel now.'

'I hope you two realise that you tripped some sort of motion detector coming in here,' Caleb whispered gently against my ear. He'd snuck up on me from behind like the little creep that he was.

Great skills, Elena.

I screamed and slapped him. 'Don't scare me like that!'

Caleb's smile was devilish. 'I know. I can hear your heartbeat stuttering.' He closed his eyes and cocked his head to one side, seemingly savouring the experience.

Then Caleb was frowning, his face strangely contorting, inch by inch. His eyes suddenly flew open, expression panicked. 'But I can also hear that we are—'

'In deep trouble,' Sebastian muttered, finishing his sentence.

Caleb's face was whiter than white. 'That's a freaking understatement.'

'Is it The Protectors?'

Sebastian shook his head, glancing up at the air-conditioning and then back towards the door. 'No, not The Protectors. This could be worse.'

'Worse how?' I was pretty sure I knew the answer; I just didn't want to hear it.

'Vânători.'

'Sebastian, you very recently told me there weren't any near the building.'

'There weren't. Five minutes ago.'

I backed up a couple of steps until my back was pressing against the wall. I tilted my head back, drawing in a deep breath and mentally sorting through the various scents suffusing the facility's interior.

Bleach, disinfectant and other cleaning chemicals had recently been used to wipe the labs and rooms clean. Other smells? Apple scented powder that had been sprinkled over the carpet. Above that, the smell of chlorine coming from the swimming pool. I couldn't smell the stink of vânători and I couldn't smell an Alpha.

I let out a sigh of relief. No Alpha—no problem.

I moved away from the wall and started climbing up onto the workbench so I could stand up near the air-conditioning duct. Before I had even hoisted myself halfway off the floor, Sebastian was roughly grabbing me and whisking me away from the vent. 'What are you doing?' I said, as he pressed me close to his chest. 'Shouldn't we at least be trying to get out of here?'

'They're in the vents,' Caleb noted as Sebastian held me closer.

'Okay … my bad. So what are our options?'

'Well, I'm just going to take a minute to kiss my ass goodbye,' Caleb said as he sunk to the floor and pulled his knees up to his chest. 'Might I suggest you both do the same?'

Sebastian growled low in his throat. 'Just stop talking now, Caleb.'

I looked up into Sebastian's panicked expression. 'How many are there? I can't scent them like you can, not unless they've been injured. And I can't smell an Alpha. So, can't we just fight them off? I can just crush the ducts with them inside it.'

Jeez, E, psychotic much?

Sebastian shook his head at me. 'No, there's too many.'

I felt the blood draining from my face. 'Sebastian, exactly how many are there?'

He swallowed and brushed a slow hand through my ponytail. 'Twelve are coming at us through the vents above, with two almost on top of us. There are five more coming up the elevator, and another twenty worming their way through the ducts in the lower flooring.'

'Thirty-seven vânãtors,' I squealed. 'Thirty-seven animals who want to drink our blood?'

'You can see why I'm lavishing all this attention on my ass right now,' Caleb said, as he looked up, body slumped, 'because tonight will be the last time that I'll ever see it again.'

'Shut up and get up, Caleb. We need to protect Elena.'

Caleb groaned loudly, pulling himself back onto his feet. 'I should have stayed in Budapest. What can you really buy with fifty thousand dollars in this day and age, anyway? Inflation sucks.'

Ignoring Caleb's ranting, I cupped Sebastian's face in both of my hands and looked up into his unmoving eyes. 'If we fight, then we fight together.'

He shook his head. 'I can't let you get hurt.'

'And I can't let anything bad happen to either of you because of me.'

Sebastian smiled briefly and glanced up at the vent above. 'Your father is going to kill me for this.'

I pulled his face back down to mine. 'This isn't your fault.'

'Do you think Lucius will care whose fault it is if he loses another child?'

I couldn't really argue with that. 'Let's worry about that when it happens, okay?'

'I won't let it happen.'

'Then don't.'

Sebastian pulled me against him, gently resting his head on top of mine. The whole time I'd known Sebastian, I'd never really understood him, but in that moment I knew that he would truly die for me. I think that said far more than words ever could—his actions alone revealed the true mark of his character.

Then the moment was gone, as a vent above busted open and a vânător slammed down onto the lab table in the middle of the room, taloned nails clinking menacingly against its surface. Another one followed, and then another, and another. The lab suddenly seemed very small as it filled up with crawling, snarling mounds of fur.

Sebastian whirled on his heels, grabbing me by the hand and rushing us out into the passageway at maximum speed, with Caleb in tow.

'What are we going to do?' Caleb said, keeping pace as we neared my old bedroom.

'If we can bottleneck them in this one area, it might make them easier to hold off.'

The vânătors rushed out into the corridor behind us, crashing in a rage against the opposite wall before bounding after us, howling and snarling.

Yeah, okay, hold them off.
Hilarious.

I stopped where I was. There was really no point going any further. 'They're going to get us anyway, Sebastian. It might as well be here and now. There's finally nowhere else left to run.'

I summoned up my Vampiric soul from deep within, letting it rumble furiously towards the surface. It erupted out of me in a noise so loud that the crowd of vânători rushing towards us stopped dead.

'Sssssssssssssssssss-ahhhh.'

I gave myself over completely, leaving my humanity behind and surrendering to that other, unnatural self that pumped furiously within my veins. I felt goodness evaporating from within and the darkness rising up, filling me to the brim, to overflowing.

I was corruption; I was fear.

I was The Damned.

I crouched low, leaning forward, savage instincts firing as I leaned down on perfectly balanced toes and fingers, poised to wreak havoc. My fangs flicked out, and I briefly tasted my lower lip, blood oozing down from my chin. Senses sharpened, as my eagerness to rend and tear flesh grew to almost uncontrollable heights. I'd never felt more dangerous.

Sebastian and Caleb drew up beside me, embracing their Vampiric forms to the full. Their eyes were raven black, devoid of emotion, their skin bordering on the translucent. Veins of blue pulsed beneath the surface, wrapping taut muscle like blue, steel cord. With nails of black that were strong and thick like bone, and dripping canines that matched my own, we hungered as one for the kill.

The wolves surrounding us measured eight in number, but I sensed more coming. The air vibrated with our collective power, the violence of our intent thick and tangible.

I leapt, throwing myself into the impending fray, my blood rising as the wolves howled in response. I collided brutally with the first wolf I saw, fur and toughened flesh cracking like a whip as we fell to the ground, rolling and biting. I vaguely heard the sounds of Sebastian and Caleb behind me, but theirs were not cries of disbelief or caution. No, I heard the sound of flesh tearing, and the sweet smell of blood spurting through the air.

I buried my fangs into my wolf's throat, with several of the others gnawing and tearing at my legs. The pain was intense and I kicked out violently, but was consumed by the fight, focused enough to disregard the terror. I would heal.

Fresh, warm blood emptied into my mouth. Feverish with excitement, I powerfully tore away at the flesh until nothing but arterial red cascaded over my lips, flooding onto the floor around me like the breaking of Hoover Dam. Breathing was difficult through the remains of his torn jugular, but death soon remedied that.

I yanked my left leg out of the fanged grip of another wolf, feeling the flesh of my leg tear away in chunks. I swung it around and kicked a third right in the face, smashing its jaw in two and watching it slump to the floor with satisfaction.

Painfully, I flipped myself back up on my feet, cringing as my legs slowly began to heal. They were bitten and bloodied but when another vânător came charging at me, I whirled around. It buried its teeth deep into my arm before I had a chance to fend it off. Bone crunched, but I punched out hard with my other fist, its snout my favourite target.

Another wolf threw me down to the ground, burying row upon row of pointed fangs deep into my hip. This time I screamed.

'Elena!' Sebastian roared as he snapped the neck of the

wolf he was wrestling and pounded another one so hard that its jaw was left dislocated, swinging by viscera and tendons.

I watched Sebastian as he tried to wade his way towards me through the pack, Caleb fighting behind only as hard as his fifty grand had bought us. As one vânător after another descended upon them from above, I saw Sebastian realise that getting to me was impossible. There had to be at least twenty of them now, all of them snarling for blood.

Our blood.

I heard the *ping* of the elevator as the doors opened, and several more wolves rushed down the passage to join the fray. I tried as hard as I could to shake free of the pack piled on top of me, but there was nothing I could do to free myself at this point without a weapon. We were severely outnumbered and this time everyone would die. And it really would be all my fault.

I was growing weak, my vision darkening. I tried to think while I could, considered telekinesis, but what could it do? There were no objects around to control.

Unless …

From within myself I summoned every ounce of remaining strength that I could muster. I put pain in a little box at the back of my mind and closed it tight, focusing instead on the metaphysical and the power I needed. Drawing on reserves I never knew I had, I tried to believe this would work, that I had the strength inside of me.

Blasting the door to my right off its hinges was easy. I sent it hurtling into the hallway, straight into the side of a vânător that was leaping at Sebastian from behind. The wolf was thrown across the passage, landing with a loud yelp. It hobbled forward briefly before finally collapsing with a whine.

I refocused my energies, hoping that manipulation of

other matter besides solid objects was just as possible. Niggling pain at my temples warned me that this would eventually hurt but I would not be dissuaded.

Moments later, I couldn't help but smile as in my mind's eye a swelling tide of water started forming at the edges of the swimming pool in its room nearby. I could feel the power within me, picture it clearly as it gathered momentum, caressing a path across the top of the water. It gathered around the restrictive edges of the tile work, alive and flowing, wet and totally tangible but controlled only by the power of my mind.

I explored the extent of that manipulative power, watching through the opening to the pool room as the water rose in a monumental wave, stretching and taking on the appearance of arms as it loomed mightily up to the ceiling. I laughed, choking on my own blood as I pushed it, my creation, on with one final command.

The torrent exploded out through the pool room doorway, erupting like liquid flame into the passageway beyond and slamming into the occupants with deadly promise.

Vânǎtors yelped, howling and whining, rolling away as the water surged and swirled around them like a torrential tidal pool. One by one, it scooped us all up in its wake and roughly whisked us down the corridor towards the elevators. Several of the wolves hit first, pain-filled barks and yips cut off by the sudden impact of their kin and the fast flowing torrent eagerly rebounding off the elevator doors. It started to fill the corridor, and we would all be consigned to a watery grave. The fear in the eyes of my foes was nothing short of my own brief courting of that emotion. I'd marked each of these creatures for death.

Focus, E. Stay in control.

The passage filled quicker than I'd thought. I barely

had time to take a breath before the entire contents of the swimming pool enveloped us whole, taking with it what little, precious oxygen there was left.

It took a lot of strength to contain the torrent in one area. I focused particularly hard on shaping the water as if it were a moving, living being, blocking the opened doors with my mind and convincing the water there was no escape. It seemed to listen, moving as one solid object, containing us all within its bulk.

I spun around in the water, bubbles forming as I looked for Sebastian and Caleb, wary of keeping my mouth shut to contain what little air I had left. It was only by sheer force of will alone that I didn't panic. Determination kept me focused, centred.

The vânători had finally released me in the flood, attempting to paddle towards the surface for some air. There was none. I made sure of that, leaving no surface to swim to. That was exactly what I'd created—an inescapable box.

The once clear liquid was now tainted red. A corpse floated past but I barely saw it through the viciously churning water. Paws scrambled in the wetness, seeking safety, seeking air. I maintained control, shielding with everything I had, an uncomfortable burning sensation starting up behind my eyes. Soon it would be a stabbing pain, and eventually it would be too unbearable to endure. I just needed to hold out, outlast each of the foes until one-by-one they'd drowned.

I struggled, desperate for Sebastian, unable to see through the sea of paws and wet grey fur. Some wolves still tried to snap at me when they realised there was no getting out, but I floated away, forming the water around me as a secondary barrier.

A hand reached for me through the murkiness, and I took

it. I was pulled through the obstacle of twitching limbs, vânători fighting for their last remaining breaths of air. A few bubbles escaped my mouth, pain constricting my lungs. My air supply was small but it was too soon to let go.

Sebastian pulled me to his side, smiling. I could see nothing but relief on his face as he motioned to the water around him. I could tell he was proud of me. Sebastian wasn't worried about drowning, though—he was already dead.

Pain searing my insides, another bubble of air escaped my mouth. I looked to Sebastian, worried. My lungs began to spasm uncomfortably, more air spilling out of my control. My head was pounding, imploding.

I was pretty sure this was it for me.

Sebastian pulled me closer, wrapping his arms around me. I felt his lips touch mine and they parted, pressing down hard over and around my own. He breathed out and oxygen flooded through me, inflating my lungs and filling me once again with life. Pulling him closer, I breathed him in, dizzy with the sweet taste of him.

Sebastian pulled back, feeling me sag with relief. He tapped his wrist. 'How much longer?' he mouthed at me.

I pointed to one or two vânători still twitching violently above us. Then I sliced a finger across my throat. He seemed to understand that I wanted them dead, all dead.

Caleb was somersaulting in the water around us, having a jolly good time as he bounced off the invisible walls of the shields I'd erected. I laughed giddily, giggling and letting loose another precious bubble of air.

Sebastian gave me a lopsided grin, motioning with a crook of his finger for me to come to him again. He bundled me close, pressed his lips against mine, intentions not entirely honourable this time. Air had filled up my lungs again, but the subtle, sensual probing of his tongue quickly changed my mood from one of desperation to desire.

And then I lost it. As my concentration died, the mental shields ruptured and water thundered down around us, rushing for every opening and crevice it could find. It spilled down the corridor, and suddenly it was like we were white water rafting. Sebastian and I were torn from our embrace, thrown back against the walls.

I gasped for breath as my head broke the surface, the tidal wave sweeping me roughly along the passage until enough water had washed away for me to finally stand.

Fatigued, coughing and spitting out bloodied water, I stared aghast at the amount of dead bodies littering the passage and dropped to my knees.

'Are you okay?' Sebastian said, kneeling beside me, his wet hair dripping in his eyes.

I wrapped my arms around his neck, holding him close—relieved, exhausted. 'We did it.'

'No, *you* did it,' Sebastian said, returning the embrace.

'Ah, guys?' Caleb murmured, backing up towards us, his feet sloshing on the wet carpet. 'Can we save the congratulating for later? We've got another problem.'

Sebastian went stiff in my arms, lifting his head to stare at the corridor behind me.

'It's not over, is it?' I said, pulling back a little, but too terrified to look or let go. Sebastian didn't answer me. He just kept staring, gripping me tightly as if my life depended on it.

I turned slowly in his arms, desperate for this nightmare to be over. I was tired, scared and at my wit's end. I had no more tricks up my sleeve.

The sodden passage was littered with at least another ten breathing vânătors. I could only conclude that these were the ones who had made use of the lower vents, biding their time until they could silently sneak up on our position.

I recoiled from Sebastian. It wasn't because I didn't like the feel of his arms around me or the fact that we now had an audience—it was through fear of hurting him. Any free will I'd had before was about to be taken from me and it was all because of who was standing directly in the centre of the pack.

Dangerous and determined, his amber eyes focused directly on mine.

Roshan.

'Well,' he said, stepping forward. 'This *is* a pleasant surprise.' He took another step, holding out one human hand toward me. 'Elena, will you now please come to your Alpha?' He was probing, asking, nothing more.

There was no Alpha timbre to his words, so I stayed exactly where I was. My lip was curling, my vampire self repulsed by his presence, the vânător in me rejoicing. Either way, I intended to make the most of the last few minutes of self-control I had left.

'Huh?' Caleb said, turning to look at me in confusion. 'What's going on? This is the second time in a month that I've seen you two in the same room together, him barking out orders that you seem to want to obey.'

'She's special,' Roshan answered. 'She is the best of both worlds—both a vampire and a vânător, with powers beyond our wildest dreams.'

Caleb took a cautious step back, raking me with a look of displeasure. 'You're a half-breed? I didn't know they even existed! How is this even possible?'

Roshan chuckled lightly. 'Oh, it's possible, which is why Elena will soon be coming with me.'

Sebastian rose to his feet, helping me up. He pushed me

behind him, a final act of protection. 'You can't have her, Wolf,' he growled out between clenched teeth. 'You saw what happened to the rest of your pack here tonight. We can finish the rest of you off just as easily.'

Major bluff.

Roshan roughly patted the wolf beside him and stepped towards us. His long, dark hair fanned out around him as he moved—an ebony curtain I longed to run fingers through. 'Elena knows the score. Whether you like it or not, Vampire, she'll be leaving here with me tonight.' Roshan rubbed the ears of another wolf, staring at Sebastian with his piercing eyes. 'It's your choice whether you die by our hand or by hers.'

'What?' Caleb bellowed, glancing at Sebastian for confirmation.

'Little Vampire, Elena is mine to control,' Roshan clarified.

Ahh, shit.

Before Sebastian or Caleb said something that would get them killed, I clenched my teeth and stepped around Sebastian. Refusing Roshan's orders was impossible. I knew that, and after what I'd just done to a room full of vânǎtors, capitulating was better than what I *could* end up doing to Sebastian and Caleb.

Sebastian grabbed my arm, fingers bruising me. 'What are you doing? They can't be trusted.'

'Sebastian, there's no choice.'

'There's always a choice!'

I pried his fingers away from my arm. 'I'm half-Vânǎtor. You know the deal.'

'I can't let you go with him. You know that, Elena.'

'You don't have a choice,' Roshan growled. 'Now relinquish your hold on her before I tell her to kill you both.'

I spun around, glaring at Roshan. 'No you won't! I will

come with you, Roshan, but only if you let Sebastian and Caleb leave here unharmed. You are not to follow them or hunt them down.'

Roshan scoffed at my suggestion. 'Who are you to order me around when you're all clearly outnumbered and easily enslaved?'

I answered by throwing up an invisible barrier before us, the same slippery surface that I'd created in the lab with Beryx. I had no idea how I'd done it then, but now it felt as easy as breathing—picking out particles from the air and forming them into an impenetrable net.

The wall rippled and sparkled, shimmering only an inch away from my outstretched hand. The wolves on the other side pounded against it, but could draw no nearer, not even Roshan. He was yelling at the top of his lungs. His lips were moving, throat contracting, but my mental wall blocked him, blocking out his Alpha sway. I couldn't keep this up, though. I was already far too weak.

'Sebastian,' I said, my eyes shutting slightly under the strain, 'you have to let me go. Roshan isn't going to hurt me. He wants me to strengthen his species. These creatures have taken my blood before. I will recover.'

'No. He doesn't just want your blood, Elena. He wants to bed you!'

I closed my eyes, a slither of pain slicing through me. 'I know, but I can handle it. I have to.'

'Elena, no.'

'Sebastian, this is happening. No point arguing.'

He shook his head stubbornly. 'I would rather die than leave you to the wolves.'

'Pardon the pun,' Caleb said quietly.

We both turned to glare at him.

He grimaced. 'Hey, I'll be quiet.'

I tentatively touched Sebastian's arm. 'I'm not giving you a choice. It's the only way that we can all stay alive.'

'He will feed off you, rape you—'

'I know.'

'How can you do this? To suggest it is madness!'

'Sebastian.'

He took a deep breath, pain filling his eyes. I pressed a finger to his mouth. When he finally stilled, I dropped it.

'How will I find you?' Sebastian asked.

'You're the best tracker Lucius has. You will find me.'

'Elena, we could—'

I stepped away from him and pointed to the vents. 'Go.'

'Elena, I—'

'I said go!'

I let my wall disintegrate, stepping back a few feet and right into the vânātors' midst. The mass of wolves pawed at me, nuzzling me with their noses and pushing me towards Roshan. He was standing in the centre of the group, arms open, expectant.

That aroma of raw earth and sweaty masculinity touched my senses. Roshan wrapped his arms around me and pulled me to him. It felt like coming home, like admitting defeat.

I cringed, as he kissed my forehead, rubbing rough hands up and down my arms. 'I'm glad you made the right decision.' Roshan turned, looking back at Sebastian and Caleb who were watching the exchange with disgust. An evil smile spread across his face. 'Now, kill them both.'

'No!' I screamed, throwing my wall up again. Several wolves had already leapt and smacked into the wall with a *thud*, sliding to the ground.

Roshan laughed. 'My, my. You have learnt some tricks in my absence.' He paused and looked intently at Sebastian. His hands were pressed against my shield, his face distorted by the murky depth and shimmering surface of the barrier. Roshan waved a hand at his wolves. 'Never mind. I can see that hurting the vampire is going to be impossible while you're protecting him. Perhaps I can find other ways to satisfy my needs.'

My eyes never left Sebastian's. I mouthed for him to go, but he wasn't listening or didn't care. My head throbbed and my knees were shaking, on the verge of collapse.

Roshan grabbed my chin, his grip hard enough to break skin. 'Kiss me, Elena.'

'Never.'

I struggled out of his grip. I felt a moment of satisfaction when Roshan's hand dropped and I moved away. That satisfaction was swiftly stolen away, consumed by the scent of his Alpha command as he pushed for my submission.

Please, not again!

Stepping forward, I wrapped my arms around his neck and pressed my lips to his. The kiss was chaste, quick—dispassionate. Every nerve ending rejoiced regardless. The rest of me shut down. From the corner of my eye I saw Sebastian, pounding his fists against my wall, screaming out my name, helpless.

'Go!' I yelled, finally wrenching my lips free.

Sebastian shook his head, pounding again and again until his knuckles bled.

'He's determined, isn't he?' Roshan murmured, leaning down to nuzzle my neck.

'Let them go,' I begged, voice barely above a whisper. 'I won't fight you.'

Roshan cocked an eyebrow. 'You will willingly come back to my den without protest?'

'Yes. I will do as you ask if you just let them leave, unharmed.'

The pain in my head was virtually unbearable now. Any minute I was going to collapse, no longer able to protect anyone. Sebastian and Caleb would be lost to Roshan's bloodlust or the remaining pack would surely tear them apart.

'Alright,' Roshan said, nodding. 'If it would make you happy, then they will be allowed to live.'

I looked back into Sebastian's face, saw his hands were a bloodied mess. There was so much anger there, so much fear, and all of it because of me.

I released the shield and staggered back, relief consuming me.

'Elena,' Sebastian growled, charging forward regardless of the ten furry obstacles in his path.

As one the vânători growled menacingly, awaiting Roshan's command.

'Stop where you are, Vampire,' Roshan hissed. 'Elena and I are leaving now. My pack will be watching you carefully to make sure that you don't follow us. It is her wish that you be let free, so I shall appease her just this once. If you follow us, my pack will be ordered to kill.'

Sebastian strode forward. 'Elena, I can't. You know I—'

'Please just go!' I shouted at him. 'Stop being an idiot. Weigh up the odds.'

'Sebastian,' Caleb said. 'We're outmatched and we're out of water. I think we should do as she says.'

He hissed at Caleb, turning his gaze again to Roshan. 'I *will* come for her.'

Roshan laughed. 'Good luck with that. The world is a mighty big place and I excel at hiding.' Without waiting for a response Roshan spun on his heels, grabbed me by the arm and dragged me towards the elevator. My feet dragged across the wet carpet, splashing water up to my knees, and hindering Roshan's efforts as I looked back over my shoulder.

Caleb was trying to restrain Sebastian. He was not altogether successful in his attempts. Trying to pin a pissed off vampire who is older and stronger than you up against a wall would always have proven problematic. Sebastian was snarling and growling, fists flailing and repeatedly landing punches on a now bloodied and bruised Caleb.

Roshan surged forward, kicking the security door off its hinges, spraying the room with debris. The door crashed through into a bank of cabinets that had probably once housed the security monitors.

I gripped the edge of the doorframe, splinters pressing into my palms and cutting me deeply. I glanced back at Sebastian one last time, meeting eyes heavily mottled with stormy grey, a thunder cloud of tumultuous emotions. I saw hopelessness, desperation and just a hint of defeat.

I looked away, afraid I'd die inside if I continued to watch, afraid of what I'd come to regret.

Laughing, Roshan yanked hard on my hand and ushered me down the wet stairs. He pushed one finger into my back, growling whenever I dared to look back.

The last thing I heard was Sebastian. His roar of frustration was heartbreaking, echoing off the walls and shaking the opaque glass windows in their frames. Heavy glass ruptured, shattered into a million pieces by the powerful torment in his voice. Or perhaps that was the sound of the two of them breaking free. I didn't know, but it was a sound I would never forget as long as I lived. That sound made me more determined than ever to get out of this mess in one piece and make up for all the wrong I had done.

How would I do that?

I didn't have a freaking clue.

EPILOGUE

Caleb watched Sebastian's mounting fury as he strained, hoisted a parked station wagon over his head and threw it across the deserted street. He barely glanced back at the devastation as it crashed through several parked cars, setting off alarms, and the resulting metal debris taking out street signs and traffic lights.

'Whoa,' Caleb said, tentatively touching his shoulder, 'you need to calm down before you take out another city block.'

Sebastian ignored him, shrugging Caleb's hand away and then kicking a lone Harley motorcycle into a nearby residence. Screams could be heard coming from inside, lights quickly coming on as the residents rushed through their house, expecting the worse.

Caleb grimaced. 'Was that really necessary?'

'About as necessary as this,' Sebastian growled, picking up the parked van next to him, spinning it above his head and hurling it into the house across the street.

'Sebastian,' Caleb pleaded, 'you're going to trash this entire neighbourhood if you don't rein in your anger. I know you're upset that Roshan has Elena right now, but breaking apart some nice Victorian-style homes isn't going to make you feel any better.'

'This might,' Sebastian muttered as he pulled a broken traffic light out of the ground. He walked right up to Caleb, swung the metal pole from hand to hand, tested its weight, and then swung it straight at Caleb's head.

Caleb staggered, explosions of colour bloomed violently in his vision. The steel punched across his cheek with a *crunch*, sending him sailing back through the air. He landed on his back on top of a car, crushing the centre of the cabin. As glass shards and metal flew everywhere, he sagged, head swimming with pain.

Thanks to his abilities, Caleb was relatively unharmed but it still hurt like a bitch.

Groaning, Caleb pulled himself from the wreckage, shaking his head to clear his vision and delicately licking the blood from his lips. He watched blearily as Sebastian continued stalking down the street, a wide trail of destruction left in his wake.

Yeah, Sebastian was taking this pretty badly.

Caleb was a young vampire. He'd only known the guy for twenty years, but during that time he'd never seen Sebastian so unhinged, especially not over a chick. Sebastian usually loved them and left them—literally. Now he was destroying public property across country borders. He'd started his rampage in Romania; they were now currently tearing up Hungary. If Caleb hadn't have known any better, he'd have thought Sebastian was in love with her, but no. Sebastian never swooned over women. Elena was Lucius's daughter— that had to be what was driving him to the brink of insanity. And when Lucius found out Elena had been handed over to the Vânători, he was going to kill someone.

Caleb just prayed it wasn't him.

Dusting glass from his shoulders, he took off after his friend, a friend who was about to throw another car, this time into a nearby dry cleaning business.

Shit, Sebastian!

Caleb cringed as the minivan hurtled through the plate glass window with a resounding crash, decimating walls and destroying the roof of the shop on impact. Alarms went off like crazy, and in the distance Caleb could hear the sound of emergency vehicles approaching.

Caleb ran to Sebastian's side and walked with him as he silently fumed. His eyes were black as raven's wings, clawed hands now buried deep in his pockets, and a damn good place for them to be if Caleb was any judge. If only there'd been a way to restrain his feet, too.

'Sebastian,' Caleb said tentatively. 'I'll come with you to meet with Lucius if that's what's bothering you about all of this.'

'Are you sure you don't want more money?' Sebastian sneered at him.

Caleb tried not to consider the offer seriously, but it had crossed his mind. 'She'll be alright, you know.'

Sebastian stopped abruptly and grabbed Caleb by the throat, lifting him off the ground. His talons dug deep, drawing gouts of blood. 'She won't be *alright*,' he hissed. 'I just left her in the hands of the worst kind of predator.'

'She's half-Vânător. He won't hurt her,' Caleb whispered through a constricted throat. It was a good thing vampires didn't really need to breathe or this might have been uncomfortable.

Sebastian threw him a contemptuous glare. 'Roshan wants to mate with her, did you know that?'

'I might have caught an inkling of that.'

Sebastian curled his lips in disgust and dropped Caleb to the ground. 'Just leave me alone.'

'Sebastian, we'll get Elena back. We just need to be united, we'll tell Lucius together and—'

'Don't pretend to be noble, Caleb. It's only the money that's made you stay this far. Just get out of my face.'

Caleb scrambled to his feet again, falling into step beside him. 'Look, I know that you are really upset right now but you need all the help you can get. If you want to find Elena, then you need to be able to count on your friends.'

Sebastian was quiet for the longest time before he spoke again. His shoulders were slumped now, his hair swinging down in front of his eyes, shielding him like a silken executioner's hood. 'How am I going to tell him that I lost his only daughter to a pack of vicious wolves?'

'Who, Lucius? Just tell him exactly what happened. Let's face it—it's not like she really gave us a choice.'

'Leaving the villa was my mistake. She's my responsibility. I failed her and Lucius.'

'Sebastian, what happened tonight was not your fault.'

Sebastian's laughter held no humour. 'You understand nothing of how important she is. I've waited centuries for Elena and now I've let her slip through my fingers.'

Caleb didn't quite know how to answer that, so he shut his mouth. What more *could* be said?

Sebastian stared moodily ahead, picking up the pace. The landscape whirred past as he started to run. He knew that the sooner he found Lucius, the sooner they could begin looking for Elena. Although he'd tried throughout the night to find her, Roshan was smarter than he'd given him credit for. Her scent was covered, mixed in with hundreds of others. They'd undoubtedly jumped far away, leaving no trails to follow.

Sebastian was the best tracker there was. He could find anyone or anything given enough time, but he was livid at himself tonight. Of all the people he had ever wanted to find, he'd wanted to find Elena the most and he hadn't even been able to do that. Sebastian had been around long enough to see what Lucius was capable of and given that he had no soul, spawn of Satan and all, Sebastian was reluctant to cross him … ever.

At least he had found *her* again. Sebastian couldn't have taken another two thousand years without her. Elena was the reason he had given himself over to Vampirism, given away a mortal life for the unending chance of rebirth so he could be with her this final time. But now she was gone again, and it really was all his fault.

Sebastian slowed to a stop as he felt the vibrations from his phone as it rang. He cursed as he saw the name flashing across his LCD screen. Talk about timing. Hesitantly, Sebastian pressed the talk button and held the phone to his ear.

'Sebastian?'

'Yes, Lucius?' he answered warily, now looking over at Caleb who was shifting from foot to foot nervously.

'How is Elena? Can I speak with her, please? She's not answering her phone.'

'She isn't here.'

Lucius was silent for a moment. 'Then where is she, Sebastian?' The tone of his voice made it clear that he was not happy about this turn of events.

'Gone.'

'Sebastian, what is going on? Where is my daughter?'

Sebastian closed his eyes and breathed for courage. 'Roshan, the Alpha vânător has taken her.'

There was a brief moment of silence as Lucius digested those words. It was soon followed by a scream of rage so brutal that Sebastian had to yank the phone away from his ear. Caleb squirmed uncomfortably and shot Sebastian a sympathetic look.

'What?!' Lucius roared. 'How could you let this happen? I placed her in your care, you imbecile, and you were supposed to keep her safe!'

Sebastian bowed his head in shame. 'I know. I've failed you both.'

'I want you in Paris immediately and when you get here you better have an excellent explanation for how this happened. Or, so help me Lucifer, I will see you punished from now until the ends of eternity.'

'I understand.'

Sebastian hung up, sliding the phone slowly back into his pocket. There was nothing Lucius could do to make him feel any worse. Punishment until the end of eternity was exactly what he deserved. Elena may be strong and capable, more so than even most vampires, but she wouldn't be able to resist Roshan if he forced himself upon her.

He internally convulsed at the thought of that wolf touching her in any way, shape or form. It already chaffed his nerves that William had touched her, but to now have a vânător think he could possess her completely—that just made him violently ill.

'It'll work out,' Caleb said, patting him on the shoulder. 'You'll see. We'll join forces and we'll get her back soon.'

'Not before Lucius strings me up and sacrifices me to Satan.'

Caleb frowned, confused. 'Is that really likely to happen?'

'He's done worse.'

'And yet you stay with him?'

'I had no choice.'

'Is he your maker?'

Sebastian shook his head. 'No. I stayed because I knew eventually he could give me something I wanted.'

'And what's that?' Caleb asked, following.

Sebastian flashed him a sideways look. 'Guess.'

As the sun threatened to clip the rear of the mountains in front of him, Sebastian left Caleb behind to ponder, racing through the border and into Switzerland, vowing to himself that when he finally found Elena again he would never let her go.

Ever.

Whether it was Lucifer or God himself who stood between them, Sebastian would not let anything stop him from finally showing her the truth, not even the rules that bound him. Hell, Elena needed to know, needed to understand everything that was at stake.

All Sebastian could say was that he had to get her back, regardless.

And Heaven help *anyone* who got in his way.